LOST IN BLUE

Parker Arding

ISBN-978-1-8382448-2-8
ISBN-978-1-8382448-3-5

CONTENTS

TORN IN BLUE

The story so far... Available now.

Trapped in a loveless marriage and torn between two lovers, Alexandra Clarke-Lawrence's life spirals out of control. Her New Year's resolution to break her addiction to sex lasts forty-eight hours. But that becomes the least of her problems when she's pushed to the limit by two very different men.

Meeting Hayes Barton on a family holiday makes her question everything she thought she knew about love and herself. In unfamiliar territory, her unrequited love for Hayes starts to dissolve who she is. And her ability to protect herself.

When Alex meets up with old acquaintance, Trevor Porter, she has no idea what he's capable of. Or what he will make her capable of. He thinks they are twin flames; the same soul in two bodies. She thinks he's a psychopath. But she can't deny there's something supernatural between them. Does Trevor understand her like no man ever has? Or is he a dangerous criminal who will stop at nothing to get what he wants; her.

With the help of many men along the way, Alex attempts to save her sanity and find true love. Will she succumb to Trevor and his unorthodox courtship? Or will the perfect but elusive Hayes finally reveal his hand?

LOST IN BLUE

Happiness has an expiry date and time is running out – fast. This time the stakes are higher and there's further to fall...

The Clarke-Lawrences are having a family Christmas, and things aren't going to plan. Alex has backed out of leaving her toxic marriage, and Conty has promised to change. She knows she has to stop sleeping with other men. Well, two in particular. And come New Year's Eve, it's crunch time.

Conty's past finally catches up with him. And it's worse than Alex could have imagined. When events take on a life of their own, and it looks like someone is out to get her, Alex panics and falls back into old patterns of thinking... Tall, blonde, blue-eyed, and unavailable.

Does Hayes still have power over Alex's emotions, or is he no competition for the gorgeous but psychopathic Trevor? Old habits die hard, but the new habits live, or rather love, harder. Trevor claims to be her twin flame, and he's talking a big game. The only problem is, he's played sick games before. Can she really trust him?

Hiding secrets of her own, Alex makes rash decisions that will alter the course of her life. All her dreams come true, but at the end of an idyllic holiday sailing around the French Riviera, two worlds collide with catastrophic results.

To all those living happily ever after, never let anything stand in your way; love will always be the answer.

TWIN FLAMES

The New Age concept of twin flames theorises that one soul can split into two people; a divine masculine and feminine, although the distinction doesn't necessarily relate to biological sex.

Twin flames are thought to meet under difficult circumstances where one or both parties are married, there is a large age gap, or they live on opposite sides of the world. Twin flames usually meet for the first time, or reconnect, later in life, after children. Many people experiencing the twin flame phenomenon report not knowing about the concept until they meet in physical form and can't explain the intense connection.

There is consensus that twin flame relationships go through stages, starting with soul activation and ending with a final union. Twin flames are thought to have a pre-birth plan or contract that plays out according to divine timing. The purpose of Twin Flames is spiritual ascension and healing for the individuals, and the world.

Twin flames commonly report having sixth senses, such as telepathy with their divine counterpart and seeing constant synchronicities related to their twin. Many claim they interact with their twin flame on another level of reality.

Like many New Age theories, the existence of twin flames isn't provable, but variations on this theme can be found in many ancient mythologies and religions. For example, Greek mythology commonly depicted people being split in two when they were created. Any system of thought, which includes the concept of a soul, projecting a part of itself into human form, allows for the possibility of twin flames. For example, Abraham-Hicks's extensive body of high-quality literature, states that only a portion of the soul projects into a human body. The further implication of this work is the possibility of multiple twin flames, as the soul, or inner being, can project multiple parts of itself.

There are more complex categorisations of types of twin flames, the stages they go through, the dynamics of such relationships and where they originate from. But essentially, twin flames describe a spiritual bond between two people. This is very different to soul mates, who have different souls. Twin flames share the same soul. And meeting your twin flame is reported to be a life-changing experience.

PROLOGUE

Everyone bursts out laughing.

"What's so funny?" I ask.

"We've all been there, Alex. I'd forgotten how bad those early stages are," Doc says. He's become the unofficial leader of our unofficial, secret Twin Flame Chasers support group, held in the pub, after the official, 'Living with Love Addiction' meeting (LLA).

"I only attempted to write a poem," I continue.

Silence.

"We've all done it at some point or another," Petra says.

"Done what?" I ask.

"Write poetry. What did you think I meant?" Petra says.

"Oh you know, the usual; stalk them in person and online, constantly crying in public, staring at people as they look like them, seeing their face in everyone you look at, seeing their face when you look in the mirror, laughing sarcastically at unbelievable signs and synchronicities no one else can see and you can't explain, spend every second researching twin flames or reading message threads, having to stop and close your eyes as their energy is so intense around you, not wanting to wake up as you've dreamt about them, meditating in the hope of raising your vibration enough to bring them back," I say.

"Don't forget joining every online twin flame support group, booking sessions with multiple twin flame coaches, psychics and astrologers," Kevan adds, laughing. "I must have spent a week's pay on that."

"How is that even possible?" Petra chimes in.

"I went hard, baby," Kevan laughs.

"Too funny. I bet you were too sensible to be fooled by all that," Petra says to Rose.

"Gosh, no, I went there. In the early days, anyway," Rose replies.

"Oh god, I've been booking sessions left and right," I confess.

"Writing bad poetry is par for the course and the lesser of many evils," Doc says.

"It's not that bad," I protest.

"Does it rhyme?" Doc raises an eyebrow.

"Err...," I stop.

Everyone breaks out laughing.

"Get another round in and we'll hear it," Doc says.

Twin Flames

If you're asking if they are, then they're not.
There's no doubt about it, and you're in soul shock.

From heaven, you're dropped in fire to die.
Who you were is destroyed, so say goodbye.

You'll search for answers and find twin flames.
Declare it's pure fiction, but the fact remains.

You are two parts of the same whole.
They are you and you have one soul.

Fight it, scream, and run for your life.
But to no avail, there is no respite.

You'll wish it was just romantic love.
Soul mates, that there are plenty more of.

You try to get back to before you met.
Away from the vibe that's messing with your head.

You hear their thoughts and feel what they feel.
Every second, of every day, only they are real.

I don't believe it, you'll say again and again.
Signs are everywhere and it's not just their name.

Everything is supernatural, they say it's ascension.
You scream for it to go away, but it has no intention.

You'll take mental illness over this crazy deal.
Better to be delusional than this Twin Flame seal.

It's like the best and worst of romantic fiction.

You wonder how you can survive a second without them.

The visceral need, the intensity you dread.
You are one in every thought, step and breath.

By now you know every detail and theory.
Surrender and heal, but you've become too weary.

You thrash around trying to stop the pain.
Cutting cords isn't a thing when you are one and the same.

Nightmares and panic that we're lost in blue.
Trying to find my way home, and back to you.

Finally, you pray to God, please help them to see.
I'm in hell and it's the final union we need.

Silence.

"That's it, I'm finished," I say, putting my phone down. "Okay, you're right, it was bad. I'm still working on it."

The five faces around the table look shell-shocked.

"Well say something," I push.

"So you're praying to God," Doc says.

"Yes. thought I'd give it a go."

Nobody is laughing now.

"Is it working?" Doc asks.

CHAPTER ONE

Have you chosen love yet, baby?

Why is the time always 11:11? Trevor's message glows on my mobile phone. The pregnancy test is hidden underneath.

In my case, it's been less about choosing love and more about transactional sex. Well, it was until I met Hayes and Trevor met me. He's deluded with his crazy theories. How can he get from our sick, sordid history to, 'we are twin flames', whatever that means? It's a miracle we aren't both going to prison after what happened earlier this year. What he's really asking is, have I left my husband?

Now isn't the time to reply. Sitting around the table, set for afternoon tea, in the smart department store, is my family. I thought I was coming here to meet Conty alone. He pre-empted my plan to ask him for a divorce. Walking in on your husband fucking his second, third (or whatever she is) cousin doesn't provide much scope for selective viewing. In retrospect, it was obvious. Marina, Conty's so-called cousin, was a constant presence in our lives from day one. Why didn't I see that coming? I'm shocked. But as I found out the hard way with Hayes, I don't have a monopoly on affairs.

Conty thrives on out-manoeuvring people, and ambushing me with the children for a surprise birthday tea gives him some breathing space. I need some too – Trevor is intense. I'm still processing everything that happened. Ice skating at Somerset House was a revelation. For a while there it felt like love, and I forgot he's a dangerous psychopath who recorded us having sex, or rather playing a sex game, without my knowledge, and then semi-pretended to revenge porn me. Plus everything about us is odd, almost supernatural. Constantly seeing his name last year, before I'd even met him; the repetition of the number one… and I'm beginning to think I imagined what happened by the pool. It's not possible that Hayes could be making love to me, yet I'm in another dimension, for want of a better word, with Trevor. When Trevor texted me after, confirming what I'd felt, I was so freaked out I had a mini-nervous breakdown.

Then there's the recurring dreams and the odd telepathy. He knows what I'm thinking; I don't care what he's thinking. I've never believed in the supernatural, and I'm not going to start now.

Why did I tell Trevor I would leave my husband? Oh yes, that's right. What is it about him and loos? At least the one at Somerset House wasn't derelict, like the one in the park the first time we had sex. I say the first time, but in theory, it could have been the second time. No one remembers who they did at parties decades ago, and everyone knows those hookups don't count. Separating what's happening in my marriage from what's happened and is still happening with Trevor is essential.

The question isn't about *choosing love*, as Trevor puts it, and leaving Conty for him. There's no doubt in my mind – leaving Conty is the right decision, just not for Trevor. Meeting Hayes a year ago woke me up and shone a harsh spotlight on how toxic and abusive this marriage has been. The real question is, can I end my marriage? When Trevor was holding me up against the wall of the loo in Somerset House, in the aftermath of coming all over him, leaving Conty felt a real possibility. Trevor makes everything sound easy, but now that I'm sitting here, opposite my husband and children, back in reality, my resolve is dissolving. No situation is perfect, and they are my family.

Around the table, the children smile and chat incessantly with each other. The four of them look grown up. And that's because... they *are* grown up. Two are in the second half of their teenage years, and the younger two are already in double figures. All are at boarding school full-time. They have their own lives. For a long time, their ages made leaving this marriage unthinkable. Conty would have used them to spite me. The children became a ready-made excuse on the rare occasions someone questioned me as to why I didn't leave him.

But it's not true anymore. They are long past being the glue holding us together, if they ever were. There has never been any question of leaving Conty, no matter what. And there have been a lot of 'whats' that matter.

Our eldest daughter, Elizabeth, gets up. "We're going to look around the Christmas department." The natural ease she conveys floats above the tension.

The other three follow her.

"See you soon," her brother Nick calls.

It's not clear if they are being polite and can sense we need space, or genuinely want to do some Christmas shopping. The latter is most likely. Our relationship has been like this their whole lives. This is normal.

The cheery birthday wishes have dissipated, and alone, Conty and I avoid eye contact. He has his thinking face on, and his squashy features are held tight. I don't know what to worry about first; Conty fucking Marina, Trevor and our sex tape, Hayes and our non-affair, or my phantom pregnancy.

This is new territory for us. Conty and I have never had long, angst-ridden conversations, fighting to tally up emotional or behavioural points in our marriage. Or endlessly trying to square our divergent narratives about the trajectory of our relationship, both clinging to our own unverified data points, that we replay again and again to prove different perspectives.

There's been nothing so normal. Our marriage has been about Conty abusing me, and me trying to survive it. We are two toxic people co-creating. I've gained this insight, at least. I'm part of the problem. Conty is right. As a therapist, I'm not self-aware.

Conty breaks the silence. "What happened at the party doesn't have to be the end."

This is the first time in twenty years he's referred to something he's done that could end our marriage. Even now, it's a red herring. He's not referring to belittling and berating me in front of all the guests; our family, friends, neighbours and business associates. Conty regularly humiliates me in public, and his behaviour at our Christmas party was tame compared to some of his vicious public attacks. These events are so common they go by without comment.

Less regular was Trevor pushing Conty over, so he ended up sprawled on his arse. After what I did – or rather, nearly did – I thought he was striding over to tell Conty about our sex tape. But it transpired that Trevor was defending me. The first and only time I'm aware of that anyone has dared tackle Conty in public. In private, people have sympathised, usually saying they can't believe he did or said X, Y or Z and that they couldn't live like that. People are frightened of Conty – not physically, of course. He's only five foot eight, and round, but he makes a formidable enemy. People are wary of the power and influence he wields, and his ability to find and ruthlessly exploit the cracks in people's armour. These are the key skills of a barrister, and Conty has spent most of his life arguing in courts. I suspect he enjoys humiliating people. He tends to want sex after he's been nasty to me and I've cowered.

"It was a one-off, a tiny error of judgement, and the lines got blurred. That's all," he says.

That's one way to describe it. Is sex with your cousin legal? He's never once in our marriage given me cause to worry about fidelity. He's objectively unattractive, but now I think about it, a lot of women are turned on by money and power.

"Don't throw away twenty years of happiness over a one-off incident. Don't forget you embarrassed and humiliated me at the party." He puffs himself up, warming to his reasoning.

Happiness – really? Our marriage has been more like two decades of emotional abuse. At least he's predictable. The table is already turned in his mind, making me the one who embarrassed and humiliated him. He exudes confidence that may or may not be authentic. He has every reason to think I won't leave him. All these years I've put up with everything he's thrown at me. And he's reading the situation correctly. I'm wavering.

"It was only human. I needed comfort after dealing

with your difficult behaviour. I'll concede it was sought inappropriately. But you can't condemn me for that."

A familiar thought pattern is set in motion. But this time, it's like I'm observing someone else's mind. There's no stopping the chain once the first rationalisation occurs. The thoughts fall like dominos: it wasn't that bad, I'm overreacting, I'm at fault too, it takes two to tango, being late for the party triggered him, he thought I'd been drinking, there's no point in discussing it, next time will be better, he will stop behaving like this soon… The thought chain ends with, *I don't need to divorce him.*

Acceptance brings emotional relief. The children's faces flash through my mind. My brain rearranges itself to smooth the situation over, so I can carry on. One more chance. That wouldn't be so hard. And he's right, I can't condemn him for having sex with Marina, not with my extensive history of fucking other men.

"I turned to my family for comfort. It was a reasonable and rational response under the circumstances."

He'll address the jury next: *I put it to you that fucking Marina, a trusted member of my family, was entirely justified and acceptable, and the defendant must be found not guilty.* As opposed to guilty but pardoned. He could own his shit and say sorry. But he's not sorry. He's blaming me for pushing him into it. And as for Marina, she might look like a plump and homely middle-aged Greek woman, but she's not as benign as she makes out. It's clear how much she dislikes me, and I'm sure she's behind some of Conty's worst behaviour. Yet, he refuses to countenance the prospect.

"We can get past this, Alexandra. It was a one-off mistake," he continues.

What he doesn't know is, he's preaching to the converted. Staying faithful is hardly my strong point. Infidelity hasn't been a deal-breaker before, and it isn't now. I can get past him fucking Marina, but these things are best kept under the radar. The situation doesn't provide any space for self-denial. Staying under these circumstances sends a clear message: I will put up with anything. But haven't I sent that message already by staying for so many years?

The real problem isn't about who is fucking who. It's about the quality of our relationship. The success of a marriage isn't calculated in years; how many couples stay miserably married for decades? A beautiful and wise older friend once told me she wished she'd divorced her abusive and philandering husband decades ago. She'd spent many years angry and unhappy. One day she woke up in her eighties and realised what had happened. The success of a marriage has to be judged on quality. A ten-year marriage of happiness and respect is more successful than a sixty-year marriage of passive disrespect and subtle misery you stop noticing. The swallowed dissatisfaction, that settles into the lines of your face, and makes you a high-definition realist, with a disingenuous mantra; *no marriage is perfect and you've got to work on yourself.*

"Well, say something."

"I agree." My response is automatic and designed to avoid conflict.

His face relaxes.

My energy contracts. I'm crazy to think our marriage can survive. No matter how many men I fuck, there's no way back to where I was before I met Hayes. I'm not the same person I was a year ago.

"It will never happen again," Conty continues.

Hayes embracing me in that Alpine ski resort car park, the day we met, was the closest thing to love at first sight I've experienced. A world of emotion opened up, and for the first time, it wasn't about fucking. Love and sex became possible. And now I've felt it, I can't un-feel it.

"Let's forget about all this nonsense." Conty picks up my hand. His fingers are like uncooked clammy sausages, not quite long enough to wrap around mine.

I push revulsion aside and let him grip me for a few seconds.

Reality kicks in. Trevor's right, and I have to choose love. I can't do this. Settling for anything less isn't possible.

"You don't love me, Conty, and you treat me..."

The sentence dies on my lips. This is a flashpoint, but the progression was gradual. Why did I stay for so many years with a man whose modus operandi is abuse? I don't have self-esteem issues, and I've never been short of men, yet I've refused to stand up for myself, let alone leave.

He picks up where I left off. "That's not true; we've been happy for the last twenty years."

Protesting the fact he doesn't love me would be ridiculous, and he ignores it. The lack of love is a given. But happiness ...

"How can you say that?" No stretch of the imagination could describe our relationship – the constant criticism, disrespect, seething hatred, vicious attacks on my confidence, self-esteem, my behaviour, and every single thing about me – as happiness. What he means is he's been happy I've put up with his behaviour, and I've been happy finding ways to survive. Staying has been a choice I've made, over and over. This loveless, toxic relationship has been my life for so long I've brainwashed myself into blind acceptance.

Trevor woke me up from the stupefied, zombie state I was living in and activated my conscious awareness. He also physically attacked Conty in public. On second thoughts, perhaps I should disregard everything Trevor says. But he's right. Why is he always right? I need to stop thinking about Trevor. And I need to leave Conty.

"I know I've been difficult to live with over the years, but what I did with Marina shocked me, and I don't want to lose you."

'Difficult to live with' is as close as we are going to get to him admitting his behaviour. And it's not me he doesn't want to lose, it's the respectability of marriage. I'm under no illusion about his feelings for me.

"It's not that easy, Conty. I can't carry on as we have been."

Why can't the words translate into action, as they would for a normal person? Why can't I leave him? What's wrong with me? I'm going to stay, and he knows it, more than I know it.

Veering between staying and leaving every few minutes isn't helping. Big life decisions require stable emotions and a believable level of certainty. Playing for time is the only option right now. Once this situation settles down, clarity will come.

"We choose to stay together and keep putting one foot in front of the other, Alexandra."

I take a sip of Champagne and stop. Should I be drinking? Of course, I can drink. It was stupid to buy a pregnancy test. I've just turned forty-seven, and I'm peri-menopausal, not pregnant. I'll throw it away later, out of the house in case Conty sees it.

"Are you listening to me?" he continues.

"Yes, sorry, I was thinking."

"I can change. I don't want things to go back to how they were before either."

The frown is heavy on my face. Does he even know how things were before? You can't fix a problem you don't know about.

"Divorce isn't an option, Alexandra. We both agree. And at your age with four children. Do you honestly believe any man would take you on with all your problems?"

Not that again. He's referring to my scoring highly on tests of high-functioning autism, ADHD and dyspraxia. He loves to use these as tools to excuse his behaviour and reinforce how difficult I am to live with. He married me knowing those things. Besides, we never spend long enough together for them to bother him. They are primarily issues he uses in his case against me, or in his attempts to get me to use them against myself. The irony is that because I don't have normal emotional responses to his behaviour, that, at least in part, has enabled me to stay married to him. And interesting that he assumes I'd want to move on with another man.

"Starting again isn't an option. Let's concentrate on having a wonderful Christmas."

He's not quite on the right track but finds a chink in my

armour. There's never been a divorce in the Clarke-Lawrence family. And that's what I signed up for. Till death do us part. Ironic that loyalty has been my downfall. Clever of him to combine it with an attempt to chip away at my confidence and self-esteem. I've always been able to see how his abuse works in the third person. My training as a therapist allows that insight. I've always thought seeing it protected me from the damaging effects. Now, I'm not so sure. Stockholm syndrome springs to mind.

I smile, but the driving force is resignation. The hope that should be there isn't incipient.

"I knew you'd agree." He smiles back, satisfied with how the conversation has gone.

I'm not sure I do agree, but I'm willing to give this marriage a chance and see where it goes. And as for having a wonderful Christmas...

CHAPTER TWO

The curtains are open, but with dawn not yet breaking outside the window, the splendour of Cedars's Estate, our home, is pitch black. The irrational fear something terrifying might emerge from the darkness stops me from looking out more intently to see if it has snowed overnight. Feeling along the wall, my finger rests on the light switch. The hesitation is an automatic response. Conty hates lights on at night, and provoking him is to be avoided. It takes a few seconds to overcome the trepidation and flick the switch.

My bathroom is warm, and the carpet, although threadbare, is familiar and reassuring beneath my bare feet. I close the door behind me. Should I do it? Just to reassure myself. I tear into the serrated edge and the wrapping splits under my fingers. The insubstantial white plastic stick is heavy in my flimsy grasp. Nothing is in the two tiny clear windows, but it's obvious what will be there. And that will be confirmation of my inability to accept I'm past having children.

I'm not pregnant. I've always had a strong biological urge to become pregnant. This is my subconscious mind mourning the loss of fertility. Indulging in the fantasy I could still get pregnant isn't healthy – my periods have been irregular for ages now, and months without a period is normal. I've also read it could be to do with the amount of physical training I do. Having a low body fat percentage isn't good for balancing hormones.

I refuse to engage in this irrational thinking; accepting I'm finally menopausal is the only way forward. Coming to this conclusion makes me feel better, and the pee I've saved in my bladder goes to waste. I'll get rid of the unused pregnancy test later. For now, I stuff it in the lining of my small suitcase.

Around the edge of the door, Conty's sleeping outline is visible. There's no desire to jump back into bed, slide up behind him, and bury my face in his back. I could put my arm over him and go back to sleep, happy and content I'm with my husband. Forcing myself to behave as if we love each other might help me get over the repulsion. I'll try another time.

I've had sex with a lot of men behind Conty's back, but the only other man I've slept next to during my marriage has been Trevor. And that was an accident. I turned up at his flat for sex, drunk after the rock club, but passed out and slept in his arms all night. The sound of his heartbeat in my ear, our fingers entwined, and... why am I thinking about how that felt? I'm going to have to tell Trevor I'm not leaving Conty at some point. May as well be now.

I pick my phone off the side table and type him a message:

I'm going to make my marriage work. We need to stay away

from each other.

My phone goes back on the bedside table, face down. Trevor's name and reply won't be displayed on the screen. Like anyone with secrets, that's the first thing you set up. My phone has been like this for over a decade.

I head to the kitchen to make a cup of coffee.

The therapist in me is screaming; it will take time and emotional labour to make this marriage work. That and not having sex with other men. Well, two in particular: Trevor Porter and Hayes Barton. Except, I'm not a therapist anymore, after having a two-minute stand with a client's husband. He's now a missing person. I must call Rachel again, to see if he has been found. She hasn't been picking up. I'm the last person she wants to hear from, but I have to try to help.

Hayes still hasn't been in contact. I begin trying to figure out why, yet again. I'm not sure whether the sex we had just before Christmas was make-up or break-up. Either way, I'd have expected him to tell me he'd gone away. How hard would it be to send a message telling me what he's doing? I'm crazy to think he cares. It's a dangerous business, making assumptions about what Hayes should do. Maybe his wife, Annabel, is onto us after my impromptu mini-nervous breakdown at their house late in the summer. Or perhaps he's busy with work. This past year, waiting for contact from him has driven me crazy.

I should have learnt my lesson by now. Hitting the gym will help dissipate some of the nervous anxiety sitting in my stomach. I stretch my hands over my head and bend to the side, flexing my lateral muscles. The coffee machine makes a low hum.

"Don't you ever put clothes on?" Conty sneers, walking through the kitchen door.

He's wearing thick red tartan pyjamas and a racing green dressing gown that reaches his knees. Black velvet slippers on his feet. His frizzy auburn hair sticks out to the sides. I can count the number of times I've seen him in the kitchen, in his pyjamas, on one hand. So this is special.

"Do you possess nightwear?" he continues.

"Funnily enough, I don't. Well, I do have tracksuit bottoms and a t-shirt I call my pyjamas. Sorry, I wasn't expecting to see you down so early," I say, moving back.

He looks past me, trying to ignore that I'm naked in front of him, and stops short of tutting. His cold eyes, uncomfortable for once, dart around, trying to avoid my body. I've taken him by surprise.

The kettle heats on the Aga, and he sets a teacup and saucer next to it. His head hasn't stopped shaking, like he can't comprehend how anyone could walk around their home naked.

I grab my mug out of the coffee machine and take a sip of the creamy latte.

"You do know we own coffee cups, don't you?" he says, not expecting an answer. "Why do you always use the mugs? They're for the staff. How many times do I have to teach you these things?"

His wife is in the kitchen naked, and he's worried about what type of cup I'm using. I'm not sexually attracted to him, but he's my husband, and we need to move past what happened with Marina. Maybe I haven't tried hard enough to get to know his sexual likes and dislikes.

"You know, you're a bit over-dressed in here." I walk towards him.

"I'm perfectly cool, thank you."

I lift my coffee mug and raise my eyebrows. "How naughty of me to use the wrong cup. You can punish me if you like."

"Have you lost your mind?" he splutters. The words barely make it through his quivering lips.

I'm as shocked as he looks that I said that. Trevor is finally rubbing off on me. I've always wondered if Conty was suppressing kinks. I meant he could do what he wanted. There must be another way.

"I'm sorry. I shouldn't have said that. Let me make it up to you." I drop to my knees in front of him and go to undo his dressing gown.

"It's Christmas Eve, Alexandra. That will not be necessary." He backs away. "Mrs Wilksmore will be here soon, and the children could come down at any moment."

"What? The children are teenagers and could sleep for England. Surely there isn't a no-sucking-cock rule on Christmas Eve. And the housekeeper won't be here for—"

"Do you have to use vulgar language?"

I stand up, unsure whether to persist. The thought of giving him a blow job makes me accept defeat.

His face is the same colour as the red kettle now whistling on the Aga. He blusters about, making his tea and avoiding eye contact. He clearly doesn't want to be persuaded.

What's the point in trying? I sit down at the kitchen table. My sexuality has always disgusted him. Even in the early days, he didn't seem keen on anything but perfunctory, occasional sex. It usually lasts ninety seconds, in the missionary position. It's like he's only had sex with me for reproductive reasons. This was not the case with Marina that night. She sounded like he was doing a good job. Madonna-whore complex springs to mind. There's always the possibility he simply doesn't fancy me.

Conty puts down his tea opposite me and switches on the

radio. The early morning talk show is deep in a debate about the cost of living crisis. He heads off to get the papers that will have been delivered. We get three main broadsheets for us, along with a couple of the tabloids, which Conty leaves around the kitchen for the staff. His snobbishness never ceases to amaze me, but he secretly reads the tabloids.

He throws the bundle down between us with a loud thump.

My breath catches in my throat, and my heart thumps in my chest. *Oh no.*

The front page of the trashiest tabloid reports: *TECH BILLIONAIRE ATTACKS PARTY HOST.* There's a photo of Trevor, towering over the male police officers on either side, walking towards a police car. He's smiling like he's walking a red carpet.

I grab the paper as casually as I can manage and open it up to the second page.

Trevor Porter, billionaire founder of Porter Vision Security, is alleged to have assaulted the host of a high society Christmas bash. This follows his recent arrest on suspicion of an undisclosed sex crime. After leaving the party, Trev hot-footed it back to London, where he put on an amorous display with reality TV star Kira Shona, at the Panther Pitch lap dancing club. Trev, a regular on the party circuit, has had a string of high-profile romances, including the actress Fifi Jones and singer Rosanna Parsons. His latest squeeze, Swedish supermodel Victoria Andersson, was spotted leaving his penthouse apartment in the weeks before Christmas. Watch out, Kira.

I don't bother reading the rest of the article, which no doubt describes Trevor's love life in further lurid detail.

How dare he do this. He looked tight with that girl at the Christmas party. And the second photo attached to the article is not in fact Victoria leaving his flat. It's my back, as I walked out of his apartment building towards a black taxi. I'm wearing blue skinny jeans teamed with black high-heeled boots. It was taken the day I found out about Hayes's other girlfriend. I was devastated and went over to apologise to Trev for what I nearly said to the police, and to talk about our sex tape. Although there was no talking, just more fucking.

"I'm thinking of reporting him for assault," Conty says, shaking the broadsheet to its full height and putting it up in front of this face. "Drugs are rife with these entrepreneur types. He was clearly high."

In my haste to shut the newspaper, I knock my mug over. Coffee spills over the table.

Conty shakes his head. "I'm sick and tired of cleaning up after you. You need occupational therapy. Dyspraxia doesn't just go away."

There's no time to stabilise my voice; I need to stop him.

"Yes, good idea, I'll book an appointment immediately after

Christmas."

"Pleased to hear it."

"I'd leave it. We don't need that kind of publicity, do we?" The pitch of my voice, in my head at least, borders on hysterical. "They don't know who he assaulted or they'd have named you in the paper."

"I will be the judge of that. There were enough witnesses," he says.

I jump up and take the tabloids to the back room off the kitchen, away from Conty. Out of sight, out of mind.

My legs feel like they might not support me.

"I'm going to get dressed."

What am I going to do?

CHAPTER THREE

"Alexandra, we need to leave," Conty calls up the stairs. The pacing begins again. His huffing and puffing reaches my bedroom. He's been avoiding me since our encounter in the kitchen this morning. It's not been obvious, but somehow he's always had to be somewhere else – getting ready for the Boxing Day hunt, working with the gamekeeper on shoots, or in meetings with the estate farmer.

It will be safer to talk in the bathroom.

I hold the phone to my ear. "This is serious, Trevor," I whisper, exasperated that he's failing to grasp the predicament we're in. "How long until Victoria denies it's her leaving your flat? And they realise someone else is involved in you attacking Conty? And he's thinking of reporting you to the police for assault."

He laughs. "Like fuck he is. He won't report it. I'll sort it, baby. That crazy bitch has it in for me. She's stirring up trouble. But Vic is sound; she won't complain or explain. She's way above tabloid trash. Today's newspapers are tomorrow's fish and chip paper. No one cares."

"What do you mean? Who has it in for you?" There must be a lot of women who have it in for him, Kira and Victoria for a start.

"She's a ball-breaker that one, fuck knows what's she up to. No one believes tabloid crap."

"Of course, people believe it. And do you have to use misogynist language? Who has it in for you – the journalist? In fact, don't answer that. I don't care. And you know it's not crap, it's true. I'm in the middle of a family Christmas, and I don't need this shit."

"You do care. And I'm not a misogynist, baby; I love women. But yes, I know the journalist, and that piece is a cheap shot. It's hardly true. I'm not a billionaire, yet. And I wasn't arrested, I went to the police station voluntarily. That photo made out I was arrested for attacking Conty. They questioned me about targeting you with revenge porn, not sexual assault. I'm still not sure they believe I didn't rape you, after what you said."

I flush with shame. "I'm sorry, you know I told them the truth, and I've called to withdraw my complaint. But as you know, it's not up to me. The Crown Prosecution Service will decide. I'll call the police again in the New Year to reiterate I don't want to press charges and won't cooperate with any investigation."

"Let's forget about all this and enjoy Christmas. Why don't you come over, and I'll calm you down? We can talk about how you're going to leave, and plan an exit strategy."

"What? Didn't you get my text? I've already told you. What

part of *I'm staying with my husband* do you not get?"

"The part where you stay with a man who bullies and belittles you. You can't just text me to say you're staying with him. We need to discuss everything properly. How about New Year's Eve?"

"*We*? There is no we, Trevor. I'm going to Asia for New Year and then skiing. Not that my plans are any of your business."

"I love you, baby. We can get through this."

I'm stunned. Where did that come from?

Conty calls through the door of my bedroom. "Who are you talking to this late at night and on Christmas Eve? We're going to be late. Again."

"I've got to go."

"I know you love me too, baby. Think about it. The offer is there."

The phone lands on the thick white bath mat with a thud. I pull on my cashmere overcoat and add some soft pink lipstick, then hurry out of my bathroom and down the stairs.

"Sorry, it was a client having a crisis. Christmas is a difficult time of the year."

"Wow, you look wonderful, Mummy," Elizabeth, our eldest daughter, says. Her eyes sparkle with love.

I give her a hug. "Thank you, darling. I love you so much."

Elizabeth looks like me. At sixteen, she's as tall as I am, with long, wavy blonde hair. Our younger daughter, Athena, is more of a mix. She's tall for twelve but with a shock of bright auburn hair. Her luminous green eyes give her an other-world aura. A bit like Ophelia.

Conty rolls his eyes at Elizabeth as she compliments me. He clearly can't believe anyone could say anything positive about me.

"Ready?" I ask.

"We've been waiting for fifteen minutes, and you ask us if we're ready?" Conty says, shaking his head.

"We only just got here, Dad," Theo says.

"It's okay, darling," I reassure Theo. "Why don't—"

"Let's go." Conty cuts me off and waves his arms, as if he can shift everyone out of the door by his gestures alone.

* * *

Midnight Mass at our local village church is a joyous affair. Hymns are sung with vigour and cheer. Everyone knows the words and melodies of Christmas carols, unlike other hymns, which usually require a few loud voices to guide everyone else. And even then, the result is an odd, out-of-time song about incomprehensible events. By the time you've grasped how the hymn is meant to be sung, it's over. Then you're grappling with the next counterintuitive rhythm.

Conty parks on a narrow lane close to the church, and we all get out of the four-by-four. The air is bracing under the deep blue velvet sky, clear and full of twinkling stars. A waxing moon is luminous and bright. The stone arch up to the church is decorated with a large, lush evergreen and holly garland. Red berries sit in little groups among the spiky green leaves. Mistletoe hangs in the middle.

It takes two seconds to dismiss the idea of kissing Conty under it. He's ready to blow a gasket. With a bit of luck, the service might mellow him. It's going to be a long Christmas.

A few Nordmann fir trees growing around the entrance to the churchyard are decorated with strings of white lights and oversized baubles. Glowing stars sit on their tops. A trail of white lanterns hangs on the smaller trees, outlining the narrow winding path up to the huge wooden doors of the church. There's only room for two at a time.

I take Conty's arm to walk up the path.

He stiffens and changes his foot.

We are out of sync.

The odd gait forces me to let go of him and drop back.

His round shoulders, clad in a black cashmere overcoat, bluster up the path in front of me.

"Lord and Lady Clarke-Lawrence, greetings." Father Andrew is standing under the ornate stone doorway leading into the church, welcoming people.

It always jars me when people address us with titles. Conty obtained a life peerage ten years into our marriage, mainly on account of his powerful friends. Barristers belong to the biggest old boy network in the world. Access to every exclusive club and event. Conty wanted to sit in the House of Lords and have access to members. So we became Lord and Lady. I ignore the title, but Conty uses it all the time.

"Hello, Father Andrew." Conty shakes his hand.

I smile and stop to let our four children into the church ahead of me.

The girls go first, and Athena links her arm through Elizabeth's.

Nicholas, our eldest son, waves me in before him. He's about four inches taller than me now, about six feet, film star height. He's eighteen, so I can't imagine he's going to grow anymore.

"Thank you." I walk in.

Theodore, our younger son, follows me, and I turn to take his arm.

He snuggles into me.

Nicholas ruffles his hair.

Our sons are the best of friends, despite the four-year age gap. A new baby would be a different generation to them. Why am I still thinking about this? I'm forty-seven years old and on hormone replacement therapy. In theory, conception is possible as I'm still having intermittent periods, but the odds are low to non-existent. That's why it didn't occur to me to use protection. Although, catching gonorrhoea from Trevor was a stark reminder that preventing pregnancy isn't the only reason to use protection.

I need to stop thinking about pregnancy. I'm not pregnant. And I need to stop thinking about Trevor. He's not the man for me.

The urge to find a seat in a back pew and slink down into hiding is irresistible. James Woodly puts a stop to my plan by waving me over to the space he's saving for us at the front.

I wave back.

He might be one of Conty's closest friends, but James has been a good friend to me too, and has had my back on more than one occasion. We had sex for a year too, which was fun. I ended it after Christmas last year. We came close to getting caught fucking in the back of the car while Conty and the children were inside the house.

James gives me a warm hug.

His wife nods hello.

I'm sure she doesn't know about us, but she takes her lead from Conty, so barely acknowledges me.

Where's Conty? I glance to the back of the church to see

what's holding him up.

He's been waylaid by the elderly contingent he so happily entertains. One of Conty's strengths is he's a prolific networker and knows everything about everybody. I'm the only one he's not interested in.

Tracy, my hairdresser, catches my eye and blows me a kiss.

I wave back and smile, but wince at the memory of my last appointment…

Tracy thought she was cheering me up with the latest gossip. She told me about Hayes's long-term affair, with someone else. People are surprisingly candid at the hairdresser's, and what Tracy doesn't know about village life, you don't need to know. Allegedly Hayes has been seeing someone behind his wife's back for years. And the relationship turned nasty. This doesn't surprise me. Hayes's brand of on/off, hot/cold attention is a head-fuck. And it drove me crazy. Tracy had no idea.

Hayes and I were involved. I say involved, and we did have sex a few times. But if I'm honest, our relationship was more about me being hopelessly and irrationally in love with him. He said he loved me too but was deep in my body at the time, so that didn't count. He talked a big game and convinced me he cared. And I was starved of any kind of care when I met him. The perfect storm.

Conty arrives and positions himself on the other end of the pew, as far away from me as possible. Maybe the kitchen incident is still disturbing him. I'm clutching at straws. This is how he's treated me for years. Already we've slipped back into the patterns of our marriage.

The church begins to quieten as people settle in for the service.

Why didn't Hayes tell me he'd left for the Caribbean and his native New Zealand? No matter how many times the question runs through my mind, there's no satisfactory answer. I only found out when I asked James where he was, at the disastrous Christmas party. Then again, I did end whatever Hayes and I had after we had sex on a dog walk. At that point, I was convinced, Trevor was going to ruin my life. He thought I'd lied to the police and reported him for rape. Then there's the small matter of me smashing Hayes's hand in my bedroom door at a hunt event, after he tried to explain why he'd been so distant. He was trying to help me after I slashed my palm with a bread knife. It descended into a screaming row and … the blood all over the cream carpet in our bedroom after we'd had sex with my hand pissing blood was difficult to explain. The housekeeper thought I'd had my period, so didn't mention the carnage to Conty. Otherwise, she's his little spy and would have told him everything. Hayes left after. What else could he do?

"Now everyone stand; we are starting with 'Once in Royal David's City.'" Father Andrew instructs from the front of the church.

CHAPTER FOUR

Mulled wine is served in warm glasses, and candlelight softens the sombre grey architecture. The church smells like Christmas, the scents of hot spices and incense hang in the air.

Trevor will be sending me messages after our telephone call. He surprises me with all this talk of love. We've been all about sex, although our ice skating trip to Somerset House was a revelation. It felt like we were teenagers on a first date, and there was magic in the air. His blue eyes sparkled as the snow drifted down around us, and... Thank goodness for the loo incident; it's just about sex.

Scott Davidson breaks into my thoughts. "Are you riding out tomorrow, Lady Clarke-Lawrence?" He's the master of the hunt and reminds people at every opportunity.

"Call me Alex," I say for the hundredth time. "No, not this year, Scott, my riding still isn't good enough." He never tires of this charade. I'm hopeless at riding, and against hunting. I can just about quash my feelings of disgust into neutral; live and let live. But chasing a little animal to be torn apart by a pack of dogs doesn't sit well with me. Conty loves hunting, of course.

"I can give you some riding lessons—"

"Not trying to get into her knickers again, are you, Davidson?" Charles smacks Scott so hard on the back he just about avoids spitting out his mulled wine.

"Hello, Charles," I say.

Scott scoffs and shakes his head in disgust, walking off.

"Crushing bore. Re-fill?" Charles doesn't wait for an answer. He takes my glass and heads to the makeshift counter serving mulled wine.

Lucinda comes hot on the heels of her husband and gives me a warm hug, kissing both cheeks. "How is everything? We missed the Christmas party kerfuffle, but everyone was talking about what happened."

She's talking about what Trevor did, no doubt.

"Kerfuffle is one way to put it. I dread to think what people are saying."

"Oh, not much. Only that a guest pushed Conty over and called him a bullying cunt."

"Does anyone know why?" My stomach turns over. I need more wine.

"From what I can gather, Conty was giving you a very loud and public dressing down at the time. Some thought he was defending you, but James went around clarifying it was over bullying on a board they both sit on. He told everyone it was a case of mistaken identity."

Well, that's creative. Thank goodness for James.

"I'm not sure what happened," I say, "but yes, Conty was

talking to me at the time."

"*Talking to you?* Alex, what he does is abuse. Why do you pretend it isn't happening? You have to get out. This is going to kill you. Even Charles has had words with Conty about how he treats you, and you know where the bar is set with him."

A deep breath helps to stop me from frowning. My mind is blank. I've made my bed, and this incident will pass. I glance over at Conty; he's holding court with Father Andrew and has most of the parish council hanging on his every word.

"There you go, darling. I've souped it up with some whiskey. That'll do the trick," Charles says, handing me the glass. "The only thing better than whiskey on the rocks is a hot toddy," he continues. "Am I right, or am I right?"

"Piss off, Charles, we're having a moment here," Lucinda says to her husband.

"Come on, ladies, you know whose side I'm on. I know where my bread is buttered," he protests, attempting to kiss Lucinda.

A laugh makes it out of my mouth despite the vague concern settling over me. "Don't worry, I need to mingle anyway."

This is all too close for comfort. Trevor should never have turned up at that party.

I scan the room, but James is nowhere in sight. He must be outside, sneaking a roll-up. I know his habits inside and out after our year of subterfuge. I head off in the direction of the door.

The cold air in my lungs is a welcome respite from the cloying smell inside. I spot James, leaning against the uneven stone wall.

He calls over, “What are you doing out here? Don’t tell me you want to sneak off for a quickie for old times’ sake.” He blows out a cloud of white smoke.

“Very funny. Do you remember we had sex in your car around this time last year?” The memory floods back.

“How can I forget? Mrs Everton walked past and asked why the windows were steamed up. I had to pretend I was sorting non-existent dogs out.”

His wife would have been in the church… “What we did was wrong,” I blurt out. Guilt is unexpected and novel.

“Bloody hell, since when did you develop a conscience? It was harmless fun. Don’t start getting all holier than thou, and spilling your guts in the name of truth, especially not about Lover Boy.”

“Lover Boy? You mean Trevor?” I ask.

“Of course – who do you think I mean? Please don’t tell me there’s someone else you’re in love with?”

Other than Hayes Barton, no. “It’s not about love, but yes, Trevor and I have been involved,” I say, without hesitation.

“Pull the other one. Come on, don’t forget I was standing

there after he pushed Conty over and asked if you were all right. I saw the way you two looked at each other. I knew I had to get you out of there. You may as well have put a neon sign in a speech bubble above your heads, saying, *love, love, love*."

"Seriously?" I'm not convinced that was the case, as it isn't the case.

"Yes, and you shouldn't have asked about the woman he was with. Jealousy emanated from you. You're not good at hiding your real feelings, Alex. It was obvious to anyone with eyes."

"That's not true. Conty has never suspected anything over the years."

"Yes, because most of the time it's just been sex and meant nothing to you. But when you're feeling it –"

"I wasn't feeling anything."

"You're not good at hiding emotion, Alex. You two are clearly in love."

"Do you think everyone thinks that?"

"No, because I got you out of there. To make sure, I went around telling everybody that the incident was over a board wrangle. I tried to protect Conty, too, by saying it was a mistake. He might be a cantankerous old git, but he's one of my oldest friends. You need to stop seeing Lover Boy, you're in too deep with that one."

"You're wrong. I have no feelings for Trevor. I came out to

say thank you. Lucinda told me you'd smoothed it over."

"You know he's talking about reporting Lover Boy to the police for assault?"

"Yes, he mentioned it after… it was… I was." Words desert me.

"In the paper?" He raises his eyebrows.

"You saw that?" I ask, alarmed.

"You could hardly miss it. The tabloids had a field day."

"Oh fuck." I put my hand over my mouth. "Everyone is going to see it."

"Don't panic, nobody cares, Alex. And nobody will identify it's your back in the picture. But Trevor is clearly an unsavoury character and in trouble with the police. No smoke without fire and all that."

"Trevor didn't do it. I won't go into specifics here, but he didn't sexually assault anyone, James, I can promise you that."

"You need to be careful. He's dangerous. I'll work on Conty. He's averse to scandal. I'm sure he won't report it to the police. He likes to blow off hot air."

"Thank you for helping," I say, embracing him.

"So – you do want a quickie," he laughs, and grabs my arms, spinning me around to push me up against the wall.

I shrug him off, laughing.

"No high jinks without me now," Charles says, coming out

of the church, probably to take something a lot stronger than a roll-up. “I’ve just about had enough. That parish council wouldn’t know goodwill if it got on its knees and—”

“Goodbye, gents, enjoy.” I head back into the church.

James is right. Seeing Trevor has to stop. It’s too dangerous.

CHAPTER FIVE

The message sits open on my mobile phone.

My face is frozen.

Alexandra, Conty deserves a break without tension. You need to put him first for once. You only have yourself to blame. If you weren't such a cold bitch, he wouldn't have done it. You've been warned. Regards.

Regards? What the...? After what Marina did, she dares to blame me, his wife. She's online and can see I've read it. With no intention of replying, I close the app. My phone makes a thud on the covers beside me. She makes out I'm the one causing the tension. And as for her warning me; what's she going to do? Fuck him again? It doesn't surprise me that Conty didn't tell me she was going to be with us in Asia and skiing. Marina being an integral part of our social life is a given. And if there is a holiday she hasn't been on, it was too long ago to remember, or has never happened.

My phone vibrates next to me, and I flick open the messaging app again, dreading a follow-up or her demanding an answer.

Happy Crimbo, Baby.

A picture loads, of a velvet Christmas hat with a white bobble on top. Why is Trevor sending me a Christmas hat? Oh, the hat is over his hard...

I'm not in the mood after Marina's message, but a smile spreads over my face. We need to stop this, but not today. His cock is a welcome distraction from thinking about the prospect of another holiday with Marina.

Nice hat I type back.

He replies instantly with another photo.

The hat is gone and...

Enough of that. No time for wanking now. Better start cooking soon or Christmas lunch won't be on the table until dinner time.

* * *

"I'm not going, Conty." After Marina's nasty message this morning, being civil over two holidays might be too much of a challenge. "The next plate of vegetables is ready to go on the table," I call out.

Theo takes the plate off me.

"Not going isn't an option, Alexandra. The flights were booked months ago. You can't suddenly change your mind. You are going."

"No, I'm not, Conty. I don't want to go to Asia again this year. Last year was bad enough. And I'm not going skiing after, either."

"What do you mean, bad enough? Our hosts were generous to a fault and couldn't have done more for us. Yet you ruined the holiday by attacking me."

He has no idea just how generous... Hayes invited me into his bed for a cuddle, and cue – a year of emotional hell.

"I nearly died falling on a ski slope for fuck's sake. And you —"

"Do you have to use vulgar language? And stop being melodramatic. Why is everything a drama with you? Nothing is ever good enough."

"That is not true, I—"

"I've never been more embarrassed to call you my wife. The whole restaurant witnessed your childish tantrum. You almost upended the table storming out."

"Now who is being melodramatic? I did not storm anywhere." I need to stop talking; arguing isn't going to solve the problem. Smoothing the situation over is the best bet.

"Could you be more selfish? What about the children? They will be looking forward to the trip."

"The children can go with you."

"We're not babies and don't mind Mummy not being there," Nick says, picking up on our conversation. He arrives back from the dining room to get more plates. "Skiing has never been her thing. She can stay here and relax."

Conty picks up the potatoes and huffs off.

A thud reverberates around the kitchen as he slams the serving dish down in the next room.

Not inviting anyone else for Christmas lunch was a mistake. With only six of us, there's no one to defuse the tension. Plus, my cooking isn't up to much. The kitchen has never been my natural habitat, like it is for some women.

Finally, everything is on the table and we sit down.

I start with the sprouts, spooning them onto plates.

"Have you quite finished, Alexandra? The meat should go on first," Conty snipes, brandishing a carving knife.

The children chatter away about their friends and school. Phones or devices have never been allowed at the dining table, so they have learned to talk to each other.

"Come on, Conty, it doesn't matter what goes on first." The mood needs lightening.

"Of course it does. You have no respect for traditions or how things are done. Would you have us eat like dogs?"

"No, of course not... It's just... Look, I'm sorry, let's have a nice lunch."

"Good, that's settled then, you're coming." Conty looks triumphant.

"I didn't say that. I'm not going to Asia or skiing this year."

"Honestly, Dad, we don't mind Mum staying here," Theo

says.

The muscles in Conty's face contort tight around his mouth.

"*Dad? Mum?* Did you get those phrases from your mother? What are those schools teaching you?"

"Come on, Conty, let's enjoy lunch," I say.

He ignores me, and we sit in silence, facing each other at opposite ends of the table.

The children sit two by two on either side between us.

Conty's now red face screws up as he looks around the table, and he blows air out of his nose. I'm guessing he thinks I've humiliated him in front of the children. Is that what I've done?

Watching him, my stomach tenses, and the knots of fear switch off my hunger. Barely concealed anger and distaste contaminate the air. Our truce didn't last long – a week – and he's reverting true to form. I shouldn't expect miracles, and it's a process. Just be reasonable and look for constructive ways to soothe the situation. Reset my emotions. But it's more than finding tolerance and being reasonable. I can't bear to be around him at all. My already strong sense of smell has gone into overdrive, and even at a distance, he repulses me.

"Who decorated this table?" Conty says with a sneer.

Silence. He doesn't wait for an answer.

"It's vulgar and kitsch." He picks up one of the crackers and throws it into the corner of the room.

He watched me arrange the table earlier.

I attempt to defend myself. "The crackers are from Harrods for goodness sake, and filled with luxury goods. Besides, there's nothing wrong with kitsch."

"I think the table looks amazing." Theodore picks up a cracker and offers one end to Athena.

"Well, you would, you're a child," Conty says, like the fact means his opinion doesn't count.

"Hardly a child, Conty," I say.

"The table looks like it's been dressed by a demented toddler." He waves his hand around the room.

Theo and Athena ignore him and pull in an exaggerated tug of war.

Snap.

Athena wins.

"Yay," she says.

"What's in it?" asks Theo.

Athena dives into her lap and picks up a bottle stop. "Wow, that looks like real silver. You have it, Daddy." She hands the present to Conty.

"Piece of tat," he says and flings the gift in the corner with his cracker.

There's no reaction around the table. The children ignore him and act like nothing unusual happened.

I'm never sure if they are being polite or are so used to his modus operandi that it doesn't register with them. At least being at boarding school protects them from the daily misery he peddles.

"Okay, here's the joke. Why was the turkey in the pop group?" says Theo.

"I don't know. Why?" I say.

"Because he was the only one with drumsticks."

They fall about laughing, and the joy is infectious. It doesn't matter that the joke isn't funny. The point is it's Christmas, and we're all together.

Theo puts the red paper crown on.

"I'll tell you what's a joke; this turkey. I can't eat it," Conty huffs. "Dry as a bone wouldn't be an exaggeration. Are you trying to choke me?"

"I'm sorry, perhaps I left it in the oven a smidgen too long." An apology and acknowledgement of his concerns might appease him.

"And to think that Leith cookery course costs thousands." He shakes his head and throws the slices of turkey off his plate. They land in the corner of the room with the expensive cracker and bottle top. "The dogs can eat it later."

Silence reverberates around the room as what he's done sinks in.

Throwing food and presents is a bit far, even for him.

The atmosphere between Conty and me had already taken a downturn, but it's nose-diving now he has realised I'm not going on holiday. Those trips have been miserable for years. If Hayes hadn't been there last year, I could have died falling down a ski slope with jet lag. I'm not going back there. Plus, the prospect of seeing Marina is making me feel sick, let alone the effort it would take to be civil. And then there's Hayes and our non-affair. No, best I stay away.

"Come on, Daddy, turkey is dry meat. Everyone knows you have to add gravy." Elizabeth has the gravy boat and pours a load over her meat.

"So adding salty lumps will help?"

He's back to sarcasm. She was only trying to help.

"I love gravy," Theo says. "Give it to me next."

Conty glares at me from the other end of the table, like I've put the children up to appreciating the meat and being happy.

The fight is gone. There's no desire to retaliate. This stranger is the man I married and share four children with. He watched me give birth to our first child, albeit from the safety of the other side of the room, but he was there. We shared a wedding day. Those special milestones changed us from single to married and from people to parents. Yet we've never been close. The jealousy when his friends like me or praise me emanates from him. I'm not someone he respects or likes, so why should other people? And as for love… Has he ever loved me? I don't understand. What did I do that was so wrong to deserve him treating me like this?

"Right, here we go, the Kings College and Cambridge choir, 'Away in a Manger,'" Nick says, grappling with the sound system. "This is your favourite, isn't it, Dad? I'm hoping to join the choir like you did."

Pride fills me. Whatever the state of our marriage, we've done something right. Our children seem happy. Conty is outnumbered. Everyone else is in high spirits and determined to enjoy Christmas.

Conty glares at him then turns his venomous attention to me.

The smile dies on my lips. My face is set in stone. It's going to be a long lunch.

* * *

We sit around the fire afterwards to exchange presents. It's always annoyed Conty how much I like Christmas. He constantly goes on about how I buy 'unnecessary' gifts and that my parents spoil the children. He would prefer to exchange gifts on Christmas Eve, like the Royals. I've always insisted we do it on Christmas Day, with the majority of Great

Britain. Yet more evidence of my 'vulgar' and 'crass' behaviour.

Nicholas is closest to the tree and hands out presents.

Conty unwraps the gifts from me like he can't quite be bothered. I've brought him a monogrammed dark brown leather travelling case for his cufflinks, and a matching diary. I added hunting socks at the last minute. He needs new ones.

He discards them without a second look. "I thought I'd get you something after Christmas in the sales," he mutters in my direction.

Not even a thank you. He hasn't bought me anything himself for years, so my expectations were low. It's more of the same, but after what happened with Marina, I'd have expected him to make an effort. This doesn't look or feel like a new start.

The children squeal with delight, opening their presents.

A big smile spreads over my face. I'm transported back to when they were toddlers. I'd creep into their bedrooms and cover their beds with brightly wrapped toys. Conty refused to get involved. He was 'horrified' by the 'ghastly' uncontrolled opening of presents on Christmas morning. He made it clear he thought it was 'common' and 'uncultured'. But I'm glad I insisted and gave them those precious childhood memories. Nothing can change that now.

The girls hand me a present.

I rip open the wrapping paper.

"You are not a child, Alexandra. Show some restraint," Conty moans.

A bright red cashmere jumper feels like love in my hands.

"Do you like it?" Athena asks.

I jump up and fling my arms around each of their necks. "It's gorgeous. I love it. Thank you so much, darlings."

Nicolas hands me a little box with a red bow.

"Wow, you didn't need to get me another present."

Conty turns away from us. "Wow, wow," he mimics. "Who uses that term?"

I ignore him and remove the wrapping paper carefully this time, opening the box slowly.

Antique ruby and diamond drop earrings are displayed against the silk cream lining.

"Absolutely stunning. Thank you so much, my babies."

Conty tuts. "*Babies*."

"We thought they'd match the jumper," Theo says.

I'm so grateful I could cry. "That was very thoughtful. I love them both. They are perfect together. I'm going to—"

This is the final straw for Conty, and he cuts me off. "I'm going for a walk. Something is sitting heavy in my gut. I do hope I haven't got food poisoning."

"We'll come with you, Daddy," Elizabeth says, jumping up.

The children head off to get ready.

"You don't have food poisoning, Conty," I say, once they are out of earshot.

"Alexandra, it is not acceptable that you change your mind at the last minute. You are coming to Asia and then on to the skiing holiday. It's not open for discussion."

I'm reaching my limit, and anger threatens to consume me. "Conty, if your little girlfriend didn't blame and threaten me, I might be more willing to go."

"Don't you hiss at me like that, you ghastly snake. You make things up, Alexandra. And if you were referring to Marina in that degrading and insulting statement, there is no question of her blaming or attacking you. She would not lower herself to your shoddy standards, as much as you would like that."

He stands up and pushes his flattened red nose in the air and his round belly out. His small beady eyes look like black stones aimed at me.

"I'm not making things up. She texted me this morning and blamed me for what happened between you two, and warned me."

"Don't be ridiculous," he spits, "you poisonous, lying snake. She would never do such a thing."

"I am not lying, and don't call me names. That's exactly what she did."

"Well, prove it. Give me your phone and show me the

message." He holds out his hand.

Fuck, fuck, fuck. The photo of Trevor's cock is next to it. I should have deleted it.

There's no way he can see my phone. I grip it harder.

"I rest my case." His nose pushes higher in the air, a victory sneer on his lips.

The desire to scream makes me clench my teeth.

"Ready, Daddy? Let's go," Elizabeth calls.

CHAPTER SIX

Breakfast was over long ago, but I don't have the energy to move. Two odd things have happened this week. Firstly, Conty has the power to hurt me again, with his nasty, belittling behaviour. And secondly, my desperate need to sleep with other men, which has consumed me for as long as I can remember, has eased up. The two are connected. I'm no longer using sex to spite Conty or soothe the pain of his hatred. And my feelings are finally in the normal range. Hardening myself to what was unacceptable wasn't emotionally healthy.

My phone vibrates next to me.

Did you have a good Christmas? Looking forward to seeing you skiing. Hopefully, we will get some time alone together. We need to talk.

What? It's been weeks, and he gets in contact like nothing is wrong. I wonder what we need to talk about; my terrible skiing? How he saved me from a serious accident last year? How he strung me along for months... or how I could be pregnant with his baby? All of the above, perhaps?

It's ridiculous at my age, to be imagining I could be pregnant. There's no point in doing a test, that's giving in to irrational thinking.

I'm not going skiing.

Why? I need to talk to you. I'm sorry for the silence, but she had a crisis before Christmas, and I had to deal with it.

Who? His wife or his girlfriend? I imagine half of England has had a crisis over Christmas. He has no idea what he's put me through. What's the point? The cycle repeats; I'm excited to hear from him, we start getting close, he leaves me for dead, and I spend weeks getting over him, withdrawing.

I hold the phone against my chest. What should I write back? *I've missed you so much please don't leave me again. Why are you doing this to me? I can't take anymore.* No, that might be a bit much.

"We're off now, Mummy. See you later," Nicholas calls from the back door.

Everyone is joining the Boxing Day hunt. Except me.

"Be careful, darling, and watch out for Athena," I call back.

"She'll be fine, Mummy, have a lovely morning."

The back door clicks shut.

Phone clutched in hand, I head to my bedroom. The stairs feel insurmountable. I look back down at the flagstones. An unwelcome image of blood flowing out of my head, forming a sticky pool, jars me. I was lucky I didn't kill myself, swaying around and clinging to the bannisters after the Christmas party.

Did I just imagine myself dead on the floor? I'm starting

to scare myself. The things going on in my life are messing with my head. First I start developing a conscience and feeling guilty about what I did with James, and now I'm imagining my death. Must be death of the ego and of the person I once was, the therapist part of my brain reassures me. I've never been into New Age, spiritual shit; thinking is overrated. I prefer action, usually sexual.

I stop outside Conty's bedroom. Nausea washes through me. I stood in the same spot before Christmas, in a whiskey-induced haze, thinking I was going into my room. I close my eyes and swallow hard. I'm not going to let this affect me. The door swings open, hitting the wall.

Frozen to the spot, I stare at the white sheets. The image of Marina with her legs around Conty's back, red toenails glowing in the dark, is branded on my memory. Transposed against the pillow is a fan of black hair. Marina's face is contorted in pleasure with Conty deep inside her.

Flashing red catches my eye. Conty refuses to buy a smartphone and has bought a brand-new Blackberry before they go out of production. I'm against any kind of personal invasions of privacy, but this is a sign from the Universe. Nothing wrong with being selectively spiritual. He probably hasn't set a password yet.

I pick it up.

Charles has sent him a message, but I'm more interested in what Conty wrote first, so I scroll back.

Honestly, Charles, you have no idea. I respect your opinion, but she lives in a dream world. I'm not in any danger of losing her but thank you for the concern. She'd end up on the top floor of some tower block on benefits without me. She's refusing to go to Asia and skiing. She likely has some more cosmetic surgery planned, so needs the secret downtime. I think she's had a facelift. She looked glowing at lunch yesterday and not her usual emaciated self. I'm sure she has a narcissistic personality disorder, as well as anorexia and all the other known issues; dyspraxia, ADHD and autism – you name it. I've had to put up with a lot. You'd think being a therapist she'd be a bit more self-aware. I had to endure the worst cooking I've ever tasted over Christmas, and on a table that looked like it had been dressed by a demented toddler.

A very predictable diatribe from Conty, he parrots this stuff constantly.

Charles's reply is so conciliatory I skip it and scroll back until I find Marina's name. There's no question of him stopping seeing her. Conty made it clear on day one Marina is non-negotiable as she's a relative. She predates our relationship and has been there throughout our whole marriage. She must be around his age or a bit older but is a plain woman from Greece. It didn't occur to me he'd ever fuck her. I believe his claim that it was a one-off, and they'd never had sex before. She would have comforted him after Trevor attacked him at the Christmas party. I, of all people, know how one thing leads to another. But every grown-up knows you have to *want* one thing to lead to another, or it simply doesn't lead to another.

Marina writes, *Morning, My Dearest Constantine, wishing you a very Happy Christmas. I do hope it won't be insufferable with Alexandra, and you will be looked after. Warmest wishes, and love always, your family, Marina.*

He replied, *Thank you, my darling. I will try my best as always. Hope you're having a lovely Christmas with the girls. Why is Demetrius over in the UK? I'm very much looking forward to seeing you on our holiday. I trust it wasn't a problem securing the same apartment so you will be next to us. It's a miracle the Bartons asked us again after Alexandra's performance last year. I gather Annabel wasn't keen, but Hayes talked her around.*

Of course, Hayes did. I'm not sure what he's expecting on the trip; more of the same. I'm not going, anyway. We were lucky we didn't get caught cuddling in his marital bed. The chalet was full of people. Maybe the crisis was Annabel not wanting to invite us on the skiing holiday. Who knows, and I'm not sure why it matters. At least he's back in contact. That shows he cares, a bit.

* * *

Light relief from all this angst is the way forward. I'm getting way too analytical and applying it to my own life is never a good thing.

Stretched out on my bed, my hand slips down into my cream lace knickers. A delicate diamond bracelet sparkles with every flex of my wrist. It was the last offering from the Tiffany Advent Calendar Trevor sent me. He claimed it was a sorry for posting our porn video on a website, which turned out to be a fake website he constructed for my benefit only. And for sending photos to my children's school, of me standing in his office dressed as a slutty secretary. The calendar arrived close to Christmas, so I had to open a lot of doors at once. I felt like I was dripping in jewellery.

Trying to think of nothing or control my thoughts isn't working. What does it matter what I think about? Trevor and his huge cock drive a wave of pleasure through me. Thinking about how aggressive he can be pushes the pleasure up a notch. The way he looks at me. How he moves his hips and stops with his body deep in mine, applying the pressure of his whole body on mine.

Hayes holding me down by my bloodied hand and fucking me hard on the floor in this room.

Gentle morning sex with Trevor, his warmth and love. The way he looks at me and is so sure … An orgasm drives through me in record time, can't be more than ninety seconds. I've always been impatient, sexually.

The relief is fleeting. A long deep sigh; I'm not feeling better.

Bet you can't guess what I'm thinking? I type.

You're thinking about my cock aren't you, you dirty bitch?

At least Trevor tends to reply within minutes, if not seconds, which is more than Hayes ever does. And he's predictable. I know where I stand with him.

No, Trevor, I'm looking at the beautiful Tiffany bracelet that came out of that advent calendar you gave me.

I'm still in shock that he gave me such an extravagant gift. I had to hide it from Conty. But he did sell his IT company for a shed load. And if the web is to be believed, he's a billionaire. Funny he objected to the comment about his net worth in the newspaper article. Reports of him attacking Conty and being taken to the police station for questioning over sex crimes, clearly aren't important. He makes me laugh. But nothing can change the fact that he recorded us without my consent and tried to use it as leverage to get me to see him.

Haha, now I know you're lying, he correctly surmises.

OK, you're right. I was thinking about that photo of your cock, while I was wanking myself off. Bracelet looked pretty on my wrist, though, I reply, not mentioning that Hayes's ripped torso sneaked in there too.

That's more like it. I know you, baby. I'm with my children now, or I'd call you for another round. Did you think about New Year's Eve? Come on, don't go to Asia, stay with me?

Well, I'm free now. What's the harm?

Love to, but no kinks, beating or choking me with your cock again.

I'm never going to forget what he did to me in his office, playing *slutty secretary gets punished.* Holding me down and beating me with his belt over his desk was the least of it. His cock is a lethal weapon. I've never been fucked like that. I didn't even know it was possible. The STD clinic thought I was a victim of domestic violence, the bruises were so bad. I've watched the video he made a couple of times now. And shockingly, he was right. I did end up telling him I loved him. I enjoyed what he did at the time. He's spectacular, but I'm not keen on a repeat performance. For a while, I felt frightened, of him, and I'd never have believed that was possible. There's a lot of impossibles he makes possible.

Spoilsport.

Everything happens so easily with him. I'm meant to be ending it. No one ends relationships at Christmas though, do they? I'll do it, again, after New Year.

I forgot to reply to Hayes but have lost the thread of us, so will leave it for now.

* * *

The children run around picking up last-minute items to go in their hand luggage.

Conty has been ready to go for the last five minutes and is pacing the hall.

The driver takes the last suitcase off me and carries it out into the freezing air, towards the people carrier waiting to take them to the airport.

I turn back and lock eyes with Conty.

It is too late to pretend I haven't seen him.

My stomach clenches and crackly pain radiates out around my abdomen.

He's been behaving like this since Christmas Day. I've never made a stand like this before. He thought I'd change my mind about the holiday if he made it clear how unhappy he was with me staying behind.

The children arrive in the entrance hall. The door is open, and the air in the house is only marginally warmer than the dead of winter.

"Have a happy New Year's Eve, Mummy," Elizabeth says, hugging me.

Athena joins in with the boys, and we huddle together.

Conty turns his nose up. He's always frowned on public

displays of affection. The fact that this isn't public and in our home escapes him.

The children head over to the people carrier. Frozen gravel crunches under their feet, and their breath is visible in front of them.

Athena waves in my direction.

"I love you, darling, have a good break," I call after her.

Conty gives me a final sneer. "Goodbye, Alexandra. Enjoy your downtime."

"I hope the trip goes well."

"I'm sure it will be most tranquil, spending time with my family without your constant drama."

"That's not fair, I—"

He walks over to the car without looking back.

I'm beaten and can hardly speak. What's the point in defending myself? I don't have the energy. No matter the issue, there's no winning. And by winning, I mean getting my point at least considered. Why does he want to hurt me? It's like he thinks I'm made of stone. I'm resigned to nothing changing, ever. Black-and-white thinking is rarely helpful, and even though I'm aware of it, the feeling of hopelessness is unshakeable. I've shown him, again and again, I will put up with whatever he throws at me. And the impetus for change his sleeping with Marina provided, is already fading. We are slipping back to the status quo. I may as well see Trevor. And get back to business as usual.

He slams the car door, and they pull away.

My back is against the closed door like I'm defending the house from attack. Or desperate to keep something from getting out.

He's gone.

My breath reaches the pit of my stomach, and I exhale slowly. I lean my head back and breathe normally. Suppressed exhaustion uncoils and rises to the surface. There's time for much-needed sleep, before heading to London tonight.

CHAPTER SEVEN

Trevor opens the door barefoot. A white towel stretches around his hips; he has no top on. His dark hair is wet, standing up in thick, uneven spikes. He's like an advert for a troupe of male strippers, except bigger – much bigger. He stands around six foot eight, so even in skyscraper heels I could only kiss him if he bent down. I'm unable to take in as much of him as there is.

"Hey," he says.

His face is open and relaxed. An endorphin high from the gym is a familiar feeling. Although, he always acts like he doesn't have a care in the world. And he's had at least twenty years to get past that twenty-something youthful arrogance. Life is easy when you're on the fast track to being a billionaire, are borderline psychopathic, yet somehow manage to connect with everyone you meet. It shouldn't be possible for those traits to coexist. Not to mention, he'd be just about the best-looking man most people have seen. Somehow he manages to combine pretty boy looks with thuggish brutality. Every time I look at him my mind goes into conflict trying to work him out. Best stop trying and focus on what we do best.

Will he object if I drop to my knees right here in the doorway? We're both grown-ups, and we're already having sex.

There's no need for dilly-dallying around.

He walks away to the open-plan kitchen.

I close the door and follow his back.

My gaze moves from the width of his shoulders back down to where the towel lays around his waist. When we met up, around this time last year, he was slightly overweight. A year later he's still solid but has a lot of muscle definition. His abs are visible as he moves.

When he looks like that, it's easy not to ask questions first.

He pours a measure of claret-coloured, thick syrup into the bottom of a sparkling champagne glass. It's Crème de Cassis.

Standing close to him, the smell of fresh sweat is faint in the air.

Any attempt to hide the fact that all I can think about is him holding me down on the floor and fucking me is futile. I know what he's capable of, and that overrides everything else. I'm permanently aroused around him.

He looks up. "Come on, baby, you can at least wait until you've had a drink," he says, taking a bottle of Dom and pushing his fingers around its neck.

The memory of coming with his hand around my neck makes me hold my breath for a few seconds.

There's a loud pop when the cork comes out. It doesn't overflow. He tips the bottle, and the champagne fizzes all over the sweet blackberry liqueur.

I keep looking at him.

"I'm sweaty from the gym, and you don't want to go there."

"Oh, but I do want to go there, and now."

"I know you do. But you're going to have to wait."

He hands me the chilled glass and bends to kiss me full on the lips.

For a second everything fades, and I fade into everything.

Pulling back, we stay looking into each other's eyes.

"Okay, that's enough intimacy for one night," I say, and attempt a laugh.

"Baby, that's enough intimacy for all eternity."

I can't process his comment. "Forget about all eternity, my patience levels are that of a two-year-old."

He laughs. "I know. Tell me about it."

"I do love Kir Royale, though."

"I know that too."

But he doesn't and can't know I love Kir Royale, because I've never told him.

"How do you know?"

"You don't want to know."

"You're right, I don't. I'm not into creepy mind-reading unless it's applied to my sexual needs or the crap you peddle about synchronicities and twin-whatever-they-ares."

"Doesn't matter what you believe, baby. I know you can feel it."

"All I want to feel is your cock deep somewhere in my body. You know I'm a sure bet, right?"

"You can't be anything else but, baby."

"What does that mean?" I ask.

"You figure it out."

He's got some crazy ideas, more suited to teenagers in need of a fairytale love theory to justify their sexual desires. We don't know each other at all. The sum total of our past interaction is a ten-minute stand I don't remember at a party twenty-plus years ago. My guess is we fucked in a cloakroom or bedroom. I'd remember if we went home together. Followed by brunch early last year in a workmans' caff. He suggested we go see his motor shop, and five minutes later we had rough sex in an abandoned loo. I passed out at this flat after going to a rock club about a week later, and he held me all night. Then we played slutty secretary gets punished at his motor repair garage, and that led to... Better not to go there. We did have sex again, the day I found out about Hayes's other girlfriend, but there wasn't much talking. And we went ice skating, and it was magical...

This is not helping.

"Actually, I don't care. Come and fuck me now. You smell so

good."

"You like dirty and sweaty?"

"Is that a trick question?"

"Try and relax. I'm heading to the shower."

"I like clean too, I call after him."

With him looking like that, this is about as much word foreplay as I can stand. Will he think it strange if I strip off and join him in the shower? I've never understood build-up and anticipation. Most of the time, our sex is illicit anyway, and there is a finite amount of time before we get caught, so we have to skip to the main act. But he's right. I need to relax; waiting isn't a problem. We have all night. I can enjoy the drink and snoop around his penthouse apartment.

This pad must be over 8,000 square feet. I'm betting you can't buy a bigger residential space in South London, bar some kind of converted factory. This is a purpose-built block. And he's spent a lot of money on interior design. The whole place smacks of expense. There's a seamless flow from sitting to dining to relaxing space. The style changes from ultra-modern and high technology to a more traditional country feel with dark wood and deep colours. My oldest friend, Gerry and her husband Michael, would love this place. It reminds me of their warehouse set up in Old Street, though that's rawer and more industrial. This place screams sleek and tasteful.

A rapper or hip-hop band I've never heard before starts up, filling the air with a clarity that's top of the range. Invisible speakers must be embedded in the ceiling. A few high-end candles are dotted around with extravagant flower displays. The smell coming off them is woody and fresh.

Outside the window is a large space that follows the length of the interior. It looks like you can walk around the perimeter of the flat. The walkway is sheltered, and lights built into the concrete above, glow in the dark. It starts with light wood decking but turns into smooth grey stone. There are extensive plants in large ornate pots, and there could be a water feature, but I can't quite make it out.

The lights over London twinkle like glitter; the Thames glints in the moonlight. Snow is forecast for later, but now thick, dark grey clouds are gathering. The city skyline merges into the room.

What are other people doing on New Year's Eve? Perhaps going to clubs, house parties, dinner parties, or gathering in Trafalgar Square, or by the river for the fireworks display. We'll be able to watch it later from this high up.

"Like the view?"

Trevor comes up behind me and puts his hands on my shoulders. The smell of sweat is gone, and in its place is what must be a customised scent. I've never smelt anything like it. It's almost floral, but there's a strong undercurrent that reminds me of teenage boys. It's from a lost era of aftershaves attempting to embody masculinity. It suits him.

"Yes, spectacular."

His fingers work into the muscles of my neck.

The downward pressure is too much, and pain radiates out.

"Ow." My neck flexes as I struggle to subdue how much it hurts.

"That hurts?"

"Yes, sorry, I'm tense. I've never liked massage."

He's finding knots that have been there for years.

"Don't you ever relax?"

There's a loud knock on the door.

The unexpected intrusion activates my startle reflex.

He ignores my overreaction and heads over to answer it.

Trevor didn't mention anyone joining us. Don't tell me he's ordered call girls for an old-school orgy or a kinky sex game. He might look like an angel, but I've never met anyone with such diverse sexual tastes. I've only slept with a woman once. Well, that's not quite the extent of it. It was two women at the same time, and in public. Not exactly in public, a fetish club dark room, so semi-private. I'm still not sure if Conty's friend watched. And we've become friends – not friends with benefits, but actual friends.

Two men walk into the flat. One is in chef's whites and carrying a work bag. I vaguely recognise him. He starts setting up in the kitchen. The other man is wearing a black suit and heads over to the bar.

I'm relieved. After the Christmas I've just had, anything more demanding than vanilla straight up is off the menu.

"What do you want for dinner?" Trevor asks, coming back over to me. "The chef is from Mortimer's, so he specialises in seafood but can do anything."

The man sets a box down on the counter.

I squint in his direction. I've seen him on a TV travel show.

"What do you mean, he's from Mortimer's? He's William Mortimer, isn't he?"

"Yes, he is. Well spotted."

William Mortimer comes over and shakes my hand. "Mrs Clarke-Lawrence, it's a pleasure to be cooking for you tonight. What do you fancy?"

"Thank you, er..."

This wasn't what I was expecting. A takeaway, glass of fizz and a fuck on the sofa would have done the trick. Trevor feels unknown all over again. And what I thought I knew was wrong. He's not just a pretty thug with a big bank balance, bigger cock and a penchant for brutal sex games. I'm glad I'm wearing a smart black dress and high heels. I just expected that by now, it would be torn off me and lying on the floor. Wining, dining, and especially talking, isn't required. I'm still disconcerted about our conversation earlier.

"Do what you do best, Morty, and we'll enjoy it."

Trevor saves me from not being able to make a decision.

They shake hands.

Morty pats Trevor on the back like they are old friends.

"Okay, mate," he says and heads back to the kitchen.

"You know William Mortimer?"

"Yes, we went to primary school together, round here."

Trevor picks up my hand.

The next natural question, *So you grew up around here,* doesn't make it out of my mouth.

I look up at him.

He smiles down at me.

The bones of my hand feel fragile in his. The way we fit together confuses me. We feel like a whole. How is that possible? We barely know each other.

"Let's sit down," he says, breaking eye contact.

The whole apartment, at first glance, looks open plan. But there are separate rooms, and he leads me into a formal dining room I hadn't suspected existed.

The floor is honey-coloured wood. A long glass table that must seat around fourteen, has two places set for dinner.

Dominating the room and covering a substantial part of one wall is an abstract painting. A ball of fire swirls around, metamorphosing upward into two flames. They merge into the shape of a couple embracing. Deep red, orange and yellow give the painting a vibrant and energising quality, like it has depth. The canvas is dynamic, as if the flames are moving towards one another. Around the couple, a halo of blue, green and gold spreads out like an aura. The whole wall looks like it's glowing. I've never seen anything like it. It takes me a while to pull my eyes away, but I don't want to encourage his silly ideas, so I say nothing.

Trevor follows my eye-line and smiles, challenging me to comment.

I pretend not to notice him, and look around. The room is darker than the rest of the apartment. Two candles sit low on the table.

The waiter follows us in and pulls my chair back.

"Thank you," I say, but I can barely string two words together.

Trevor pulls out his own chair and sits opposite me, at an angle.

He reaches for a remote control. As he does, his light pink herringbone shirt stretches across his shoulders, outlining his bicep. We should have fucked the second I got through the door, then I could focus a bit more. Wanting him like this is uncomfortable.

"Don't look so pensive," he says.

The waiter puts napkins on our laps and asks, "What would you like to drink?"

"I'll have a French 75, please," Trevor answers, immediately. "You?"

"The same, please." Choosing a drink is beyond me. Get a grip. We will fuck soon, and everything will be okay.

The waiter moves away, leaving us alone. Trevor points the remote control to one side of the room. The dark glass covering an entire wall becomes clear, giving us panoramic views over central London.

I finish the glass of Kir Royale and look out over the rooftops. My eyes dart around, looking for landmarks, something to anchor me.

"You know, you always look wild and desperate, like you might bite or bolt."

"I don't think so," I protest. "Really?" He's probably right, as I do feel wild and a bit desperate a lot of the time. Casual sex has definitely got me through the last few years.

"Yes, and that's why men want to dominate you. We can sense that the only way to calm you down is to fuck you before you run away. You need it, right – the sex? It makes you feel calm."

I'm not sure I agree with his unsolicited analysis, so change the subject. There's a lot we shouldn't talk about. Keep it light.

"Nice apartment," I say.

"Don't change the subject. Talk to me. Really talk to me."

"I don't want to talk to you, really talk to you, whatever that means."

"Okay, you win. Yes, it's a nice apartment. I like modern architecture and minimalist design."

I relax a little.

"It's the complete opposite of Cedars Estate," I say, "with its ancient history and antiques. It's more like a mausoleum than a home." Conty inherited it from his father. Although his family doesn't quite make the ranks of the aristocracy, Cedars has been in the family for over a century.

He lights up the room with his laugh. "There's a lot that should be ancient history, namely your marriage to that ponce."

"Thirty seconds and we're back to deep and meaningful?" He doesn't know how to make small talk either. "You don't throw away twenty-plus years of marriage, Trevor."

"Your relationship has been over for a long time. You know that, right? It was over the minute you first fucked someone else."

"What? So you've never fucked someone else while being married? Who made you judge and jury?"

"I'm not judging you, baby. I'm your partner in crime. And of course, yes, I've been unfaithful. The minute I put my cock in someone who wasn't my wife, I ended the relationship. I just didn't know it."

"Why don't you stop the psychobabble and concentrate on putting your cock in me?"

At least this is the Trevor Porter I know, direct and to the point. He likes playing games, though.

"Burying your head in the sand won't help," he says.

"I'm not burying my head in the sand. I came here for sex."

The waiter appears with our cocktails and a tray of canapés. There's Oscietra caviar and oysters.

"What I mean is, you can't keep pushing the fuck button every time something goes wrong in your life or you feel bad."

He's right, but I don't want to face it, and certainly not tonight.

"You do know that diets always start tomorrow, don't you?"

He laughs. "I've got your back, baby. Hope you like seafood."

Trevor picks up an oyster and slides it into his mouth. It's followed by a gulp of his cocktail.

I love the way he eats with abandon. He loves food. I'm the same. The conversation dies in my mind. I want to press the fuck button, as he puts it, and now. Making more eye contact than necessary, I pick up a blini covered with small, salty black eggs, and slowly ease the whole thing into my mouth.

He doesn't take his eyes off me, and for a second I think I've tipped him over the edge; that he's going to lose control and give me what I need.

"You're so beautiful," he says.

What? That wasn't the desired response. This isn't a seduction. He knows I would have fucked him with the front door still open.

"Thank you." The sexual tension is broken. I'm immediately conscious of my forty-seven-year-old lined face. I lower my gaze. No one would guess he's a similar age. I'd be the oldest mother at the school gate. Potentially being pregnant jars me. I'm too old and menopausal. And it could be his... No, it wouldn't be his. Well, whose would it be? Hayes's? I did fuck Hayes the same week. The word slut springs to mind.

He recognises the flash of anxiety. "What's the matter? You don't like me saying you're beautiful?"

"No, it's not that. I'm flattered." There's no way I'm telling him I could be pregnant, and he could be the father. But it might not be his. I need to stop thinking about being pregnant.

"You're very down to earth and humble for a woman who looks like you do. I've dated enough princesses. I even married a couple of them."

"I'm no princess. You know what a dirty slut I am."

Finally, an opening to steer the conversation onto safer ground.

"That I do know. I love that about you. We get each other on all levels. There's no trying or working hard to understand each other."

"This conversation is going from bad to worse," I say, letting the thought come out of my mouth unfiltered.

"Oh, baby, this is just the beginning."

"I'm not good at emotional intimacy, and I've had enough of this deep and meaningful shit."

"*A little less conversation, a little more action*," he jokes.

I lean over towards him. "Yes, you got it. Let's press the fuck button. How about you lift up my dress, pull my knickers down, and slam my body over the dining table? Then hold me by the hair while you fuck me from behind until I'm begging you to stop because I've come so many times that I can't stand it anymore?"

He laughs. "Trust me, baby, I've already thought about doing that at least twenty times since we walked into this room. You made it clear what you wanted the second you were through the door, and I'm tempted to give it to you. But we have plenty of time for quickies. We're going to relax and welcome 2024 in style."

I don't know what that means, but he's giving me no choice other than to wait.

CHAPTER EIGHT

"Did you enjoy dinner?"

"Yes, it was delicious. Thank you," I say.

"Want to head outside for pudding?"

Please let that be a euphemism. Watching every flex of his muscles and wishing it was from the effort of fucking me, is driving me crazy.

"Yes, sounds good."

He slides open the doors to the terrace.

We step outside.

The night is freezing, but the heaters mounted on the wall warm the surrounding air.

Steam rises off an enormous hot tub. The water bubbles gently up from the bottom. A bottle of sparkling water and one of white wine sit in a bucket of ice. Around the outside of the tub are water and wine glasses.

Morty follows us out, carrying a plate piled high with large, decadent squares of chocolate. The brownies' cut sides reveal chunks of milk and white chocolate. Walnuts are intermixed in the rich, soft chocolate. Along with the brownies are rocky roads. Pink and white marshmallows with cranberry jewels, embedded in chewy chocolate, jut out at delicious angles.

"Hope you like chocolate," Trevor says.

"I can't tell you how much I love chocolate," I say, with a bit too much enthusiasm.

He laughs. "Why does that not surprise me?"

William Mortimer gives Trevor a wave. "See you later, mate. Come by next week, and we can have a proper catch-up."

"Will do, Billy. That was great. Have a good night and give my love to Trisha and the boys."

The door clicks shut.

My eyes fix on Trevor's mouth, and my lips open. He's kept away from me. And it's getting harder to quash my impatience and stop the urgency overwhelming me. I want to jump on him.

"Want to get in the tub? It's good for relaxing muscles."

With indecent haste, I pull my dress over my head, unclip my black lace bra and pull the matching knickers off. I'm naked in under twenty seconds. My clothes lie in a heap beside me. I stare at him, trying to gauge his response to my naked body.

He cocks his head to one side and looks at my face, like he's working something out. "That was quick," he says.

His words sound slow in my head. ADHD does this to me sometimes, if I'm impatient. I perceive words and actions as slowed down, a bit like slow motion but not distorted.

"No time like the present."

"You might want to take your shoes off. They don't look

waterproof."

I look down. I'm still in my black high heels.

He keeps his gaze steady. "On second thoughts, you can keep them on."

In a few steps, I reach the hot tub and lean forward, arching my back. My shoe flips off.

He's still looking at me. But the usual brand of aggressive lust isn't there or he's got it under control. He's cold and in control, like the time we played slutty secretaries in his office.

My skin shivers and I stretch my leg back, so my other shoe hits the deck.

The hot bubbling water moves up around my skin as I step in, "Ahhhh that feels good."

I sit on the seat with my arms stretched out, either side of me, looking at him.

His eyes stay fixed on mine, his smile just about there.

"Are you coming in?"

He unbuttons his shirt like there's no hurry.

For a second, I'm tempted to get out and rip it off his shoulders.

He shrugs it off his back and onto the deck with my dress.

The width of his shoulders is a solid silhouette against the night sky.

I need to take a deep breath but try not to show it.

His belt clinks as he slips the thick black leather out of the loops on his jeans.

The memory is visceral. He's holding me down over his desk, his hand like a vice spread out over my back. The searing pain came in hard, crashing waves, smashing me down onto the desk.

Between my legs gets wetter. My body is hot in the water.

Why him beating me with his belt turned me on so much, still mystifies me. I'm not even into kink.

The top of his jeans lays flat against his hard lower abs.

He undoes the button and pulls the loose dark denim down and off.

His white boxer shorts cling to his thighs.

It takes conscious effort to slow my breathing back to a normal pace, and I try to take in the view without reacting. Panting like a bitch in heat is not a good look.

His expression is unreadable.

Desperation must be emanating from me. No doubt he can smell it.

He walks over to the hot tub and pulls his boxer shorts down and off. They get scrunched into a ball and thrown at our pile of clothes. They land on top.

"Good shot." My voice sounds low and not my own.

"Tell that to the football coach." He laughs and steps in,

settling opposite me.

My foot runs over the top of his.

The air is freezing, in contrast to the hot, bubbling water, but feels good on my shoulders. Lights shine up from the bottom of the tub and down from the walls. The water is a light, clear blue, matching Trevor's eyes exactly. Again, I get the urge to ask if he's wearing coloured contact lenses. Nobody's eyes are naturally that vivid and light. But he isn't, and they are.

The hot tub is big and acts like an infinity pool. We merge into the London skyline of soft lights in different window shapes. Attached to cranes higher than us are strings of lights, warning helicopters. Clouds gather overhead, changing the dark, indigo sky to a deep steely grey.

He reaches for a chocolate brownie and holds it up to my mouth. "These are the best brownies in London."

I take a bite, and the rich chocolate mixture spreads out over my tongue. "I have to agree with you."

He takes a sip of water. "You want some wine?"

Despite all the alcohol on offer, I've had very little to drink. If I was pregnant, a small amount might not do any harm. But I've been careful. And I don't feel like alcohol.

Thinking about pregnancy again is ridiculous.

"Yes," I say, in an attempt to prove to myself I'm not

pregnant.

Tonight is killing me. I want him so much now. And he's taking it slow. Too slow.

"What's your favourite song?" he asks.

"Guess," I say.

He picks up another sleek remote control and scrolls down.

"You don't have a favourite, you like lots of songs."

"True. Why limit yourself?"

"I agree. You're going to love this."

He presses a few more buttons, and on the side of the wall, a screen begins to unfold.

"Wow, you can watch movies out here?"

"Yes, it's an outdoor projector," he says.

"You've really set this place up for home entertainment."

He laughs. "You have no idea."

The unfolding screen stops with a click.

At first, the screen is black, like the night sky. Falling snow or stars follow. The word 'Xanadu' appears in retro red letters. A very young, blonde and bouncy Olivia Newton-John starts singing.

"I haven't heard this for years – great track."

He smiles.

This has gone on long enough, and I need him to do his stuff. I slide over, stretch my thighs on either side of his, and put my hands on his cock.

Immediately it complies and grows bigger.

I'd forgotten how big he is. "Oh, baby," I whisper, close to his mouth. "You're killing me with how much I want you to fuck me." Swept up by the moment, love courses through me. Please don't let those three words slip out of my mouth, again.

Up my back and over my neck, his fingers move through my hair.

Energy runs down my spine.

He grips my hair hard and pulls my head back, holding it still, at an uncomfortable angle.

For a second, I stop moving my hand up and down his cock, remembering how sexually aggressive he can be.

"You like being touched like that? Hard, I mean?"

His lips graze my neck.

I strain against his hand in my hair.

The protest on my lips doesn't make it out of my mouth.

He lets go.

"Don't you ever answer questions?"

My face is close to his.

Still, I say nothing.

We stay looking at each other.

"Your eyes are beautiful," he says.

"Thank you." He must be lying. My eyes are the colour of

muddy green ditch water.

"You know they change colour, don't you?" he continues.

Now that is true. "Yes, hazel eyes do that."

"They look light green and gold in this light."

"It's not the colour making them beautiful." Why did I say that? I'm not even sure what I mean. Looking at him, they are full of something pure and certain.

"What is, then?"

"Do you always have to be so direct?" I can't answer his question. Or rather, tempering my feelings into something that doesn't make me sound as crazy as he is, is beyond me. We don't know each other. It's not that I need to play games with him and hide how I feel. The feeling is indescribable. Romantic isn't the right word. All we seem to have done is fuck. But there's a deep knowing that defies logic. Like my mind isn't able to process how we feel together.

Our faces stay close together.

His eyes shine brighter.

"It's okay, I know," he says, and he frowns for a second. "The feeling is hard to describe."

"You talk too much. Kiss me."

He moves his face towards me.

Warm, soft lips touch mine.

We are the perfect fit.

His other hand slides between my legs and his fingers slip on me, despite the surrounding water.

The chocolate left in his mouth merges with mine.

The desire for more – more of everything – consumes me. I kiss him back, hard.

His hand moves lightly between my legs.

My hips connect and move backwards and forwards to ensure he touches me harder.

"*Let's get physical*," blares out, and I laugh, almost in his mouth.

He laughs back and continues kissing and rubbing me.

Inside my body goes into spasm.

I need him, and now.

"Not yet, baby," he says.

"Why?"

"Because I'm going to eat you into the New Year."

He puts his hands on my waist and lifts me out of the water so I'm sitting on the side.

My hands run over the top of the metal railing. It's a long way down.

The music stops.

Water bubbles over his back.

He lowers his head between my legs.

I put my hands in his thick, spiky hair. It's hard to get my hands around his head.

His tongue makes slow movements up and down my body.

"I'm going to last ten seconds if you keep doing that."

He puts one hand under my thigh and grips half my ass. The other is up on my waist. The odd angle spreads my legs to give him complete access.

He holds me still while he licks in small, light circles.

"I'm going to come."

Stopping, he looks up. "No, you're not. If you come without me saying you can, I'm going to punish you."

"What?" I struggle to stop it and look down. "Are you joking?"

"Try me."

He's not blinking again.

There's no question in my mind. I do not want to 'try him,' as he puts it.

He moves his head back between my legs.

"Trevor, you're going to have to stop."

"Are you plateauing, baby?" he whispers, looking up at me.

Oh. My. God.

He blows on me.

My body comes down a notch.

"Talk to me, baby," he says.

"Yes," I say, meaning, *I think so*. I don't know what plateauing is, but I agree. Right now, I'd agree with anything he says.

He leans down and blows on me again.

Standing up, he towers over me.

My hands go on his hips. I go to move down to suck him.

"Not tonight, baby. We're going to focus on you."

He leans down, his lips on mine, tongue moving in my mouth like it did on my body.

I want to over-breathe but can't. I can't do anything. I'm frozen.

My body shifts forward without conscious movement, so I can rub against his stomach.

He moves away. His head goes back down between my legs.

The thick, wet spikes of his hair come up between my fingers.

This time he avoids my clit and licks all around.

My breath catches in my throat. This feels too good. I've never experienced such a prolonged period of pleasure, ever. How is this possible?

He moves his tongue in and out of my body. The slippery muscles of his tongue flex inside me.

My hips buck up towards him. I try to slide his tongue back up and over my clit.

"You've got to fuck me," I say. "And now. Trevor, please. This isn't funny anymore."

He stops and looks up.

His eyes are full of lust, but controlled.

"It's not meant to be funny. I say when and if I fuck you."

What? No. I take my hands off the rail and run them through my wet hair. This is worse than his sexual aggression.

He stands up, and his hard cock lies up his stomach.

My eyes fix on it.

He reaches for the remote control and presses a few more buttons.

The screen in front of me springs into life.

We are on it, in real time.

With the flick of another button, the camera zones in on my face. My lips are engorged with blood, swollen and red. Love has misted over my eyes, and I look like I'm dreaming.

He turns back to me.

I keep looking up, past him, mouth open.

His broad shoulders flex on the screen.

"If you come without me saying, I will get you out of the hot tub and beat you so hard you'll come again. Then I will get you on your knees and slam your head into the carpet and do you from behind until you beg for mercy."

The words alone make me want to come, and scramble my head. He must be bluffing, but I'm not going to chance it. Please, don't let me come… Or do let me come. I don't know what I want anymore. Why did I come here? He fooled me with his normal-guy act. Dinner and talking…

"You get that?"

I can't speak.

"Answer me. Do you get that?"

"Yes, yes, I get it."

He lowers his head again, with his face angled to the side.

On the screen, his tongue licks my clit, up and down in smooth, slow strokes. The movement is so light it could be a feather.

I close my eyes so I can't see what he's doing, and try to block out the pleasure that has dominated and trapped me.

He puts one hand on my other thigh. And pushes my legs open further. A conspiratorial smile lights up his face. Like this is all one big game.

Three seconds of much-needed reprieve.

I look down at him. I'm in so much pleasure, I can barely see.

This time he slides one finger into me as far as it will go.

The penetration shifts the pleasure to another level.

My body clenches around his finger.

He gives me a hard look. "You didn't come, did you?" His voice is low and serious.

"No, I didn't. Trevor, honestly, I didn't." The pleading tone is real. "My body did that involuntarily."

Does he believe me?

He moves his finger in and out again, standing up, so he can kiss me.

Please don't graze my clit with your hand, please don't touch it. I can't stand it anymore.

I'm going to come, and he's not even touching me.

Big Ben strikes one.

"Trevor, you've got to fuck me, baby."

Strike two.

"Why should I?"

"Please, Trevor, please."

"That's not an answer," he replies.

"I'm yours, completely yours."

Strike three.

"I don't believe you."

Strike four.

He continues moving his fingers in and out of me.

Each time he does it, the skin around my clit moves, still stimulating me. I hold my breath like that will stop time itself.

Strike five.

"Please, Trevor, I'm going to come any second. I can't stop it."

Strike six.

"If you beg me, baby, I'll do it."

He puts another finger inside me.

Strike seven.

"I am begging you."

Strike eight.

"That's not begging, baby."

"I'm yours. I'll do anything for you. Please, Trevor, please. I can't take this."

He stands up. "Not good enough."

"You're the only man for me, and I'm yours."

"That's better. You come when I say you do."

Strike nine.

He grips my hips and angles my body up.

"You ready?"

"Yes."

In one hard thrust, he pushes his body as deep into mine as it will go.

Pain flashes through me. My breath catches in my throat.

His hips move back.

I grab his waist and pull him back towards me.

Another thrust, and he's deep inside me again. He stops and holds me hard up against him.

The pressure of his body against mine tips me past the point of no return.

My legs wrap around his waist on the large screen.

Strike ten.

"Baby, baby, baby." I grip his shoulders and cling to his body. My fingers tingle with how much I want to sink my nails into his skin. They flex instead.

He moves his body back and thrusts into me again.

The pleasure recedes and then soars back up to the top.

I can't stop watching him fuck me on the large screen.

"I'm going to come. I can't stop it."

Whatever the consequences, it's happening now. I cling tightly to his body.

Strike eleven.

"You can come now, baby," he whispers.

He slams his body hard in and out of mine.

Strike twelve.

"Oh my god, I love you," I say.

Relief and release flood every part of me.

He thrusts inside me for the last time. His head rests on my shoulder.

"Happy New Year, baby, I thought we'd never get there. I love you too."

Fireworks shoot up into the dark sky over London. Long red streaks form a pattern, like claws. The whistle hangs in the air. A big burst of blue explodes into a huge electric dandelion. Two orange flares go off next to each other and merge into one.

I collapse in his arms.

CHAPTER NINE

Trevor's bed is the most comfortable place I've ever slept. The sheets are thick and soft, and the mattress feels like clouds, look. I guess he's had it custom-built, as it's bigger than a super king. Everything in this flat looks bespoke. The work surfaces are higher than usual too.

I'm cuddled up to his back with one hand around his hard cock. I don't know what time it is or if he's asleep.

He turns over and runs his hand the length of my body.

A low, contented sigh comes out of my mouth.

My hand moves up and down his cock a couple of times.

His eyes stay closed, but he rolls up, so he's on top of me.

I'm completely in his arms and surrounded by his body.

The sense of safety is overwhelming and makes me want to hold on to him and never let go.

In one slow movement, he pushes into me.

I don't make a sound.

With soft, gentle thrusts, his body moves in and out of mine.

His head is bent down, so the side of his face is resting on the top of my head.

Under his body, my hips move up and down with his slow rhythm.

The covers crinkle around us.

Clinging to his body, the pleasure spreads everywhere.

Our bodies and energy merge into one.

His movements intensify for a few moments, and he moves further up.

My head lays against his chest. His heartbeat gets faster.

We hold on tight and stop moving, staying for a few moments as one body.

He shifts behind me. Both arms wrap around me completely.

Full of him, I back up and put my hands over his arms. This feels like love. Before I got married, this is exactly how I imagined married sex to feel.

We drift back to sleep.

* * *

My head rests under his chin and his arms hold me tight.

Gently, I slide out, trying not to wake him.

His face is completely relaxed.

By the bed, his pink herringbone shirt lies on the floor. I pick it up and head to the door. The heavy pink cotton slips over my shoulders. The smell of him clings to the fabric, and I breathe deeply.

The door makes a soft click, closing behind me.

Sunlight streams through the floor-to-ceiling glass

windows and warms the room. The snow didn't settle. London spreads out below. From this height, the first day of the new year looks peaceful. And for the first time, I'm full of hope that this year will be better.

Anything is possible.

I stretch my arms high over my head, and with my fingers linked together, push up. Then I bend over and lay my hands on the floor, stretching my back. My body feels so good. The feeling of him making love to me is high and light energy. Mellow thoughts stream through my mind, like a soft breeze through trees. I'm connected to everything in the world, and perfect harmony is my natural state. It's easy to forget anything that went before, after a night like that. Wellbeing abounds.

Treading on the cream rug reminds me of walking on soft, thick grass. The floor changes from the rug to wood and then a smooth, hard surface surrounding the kitchen area. The whole flat is spotless. A user-friendly coffee machine sits on the white marble work surface. Lots of different-coloured pods are stacked next to it in a purpose-built black holder. Once loaded, at the press of a button, the water filters through, producing an espresso.

"That smells good. What's the time?" Trevor has one arm up over his head, his hand down into the back of his hair. He walks into the kitchen naked.

I freeze, mouth open.

His light blue eyes squint in the sunlight as they focus on me.

"Who cares what time it is," I say.

In a few steps, he reaches me and puts his hands in my hair. His fingers slip through the long silky strands falling down my back.

My hands rest on his waist.

Our naked bodies push together in a cuddle.

He lifts me off my feet so I'm sitting on the work surface.

I look up to meet his eyes.

He pulls me forward, so I'm held against his chest, and strokes my hair. "You hungry?"

Cue a joke that, full of whatever this dreamy feeling is, I can't formulate. "Yes, you?"

"I'm always hungry."

"So am I."

"That's because you and I are twin flames."

"Not that again. What does that even mean?"

"We're the same soul in two different bodies."

"That's crazy; I'm not even sure humans have a soul. I thought we were fuck buddies."

"Yes, that too," he laughs. "We are everything to each other.

I'm taking you for a special brunch this morning."

I look at him, trying to figure it out. He throws out these comments like he's telling me what we need from the supermarket. As if they are ordinary, and not a grand declaration of love. He shows no emotional fear, like he doesn't know we are strangers, and I'm married to someone else.

* * *

The working man's caff where we met for the first time last year looks different. The decoration is the same. The walls are still thick with decades-old nicotine stains. And everything comes with fried bread. The acrid smell of synthetic tomato sauce and lard imbues the stuffy air.

Who was the stuck-up bitch here last year, judging the people and decor like she was better than them? I'm another person this time around. The ambience of the place is warm and familiar. And represents a working-class cultural heritage I'm proud of and appreciate being a part of.

"What do you want, love?" The old lady from last year asks me.

"Full-works and a coffee, please."

"What about you, Trev? You want your usual?"

"You got me, babe." He smiles at her.

She grins back at him. She must be over eighty. What a

woman, to still be working. And with a smile on her face and a spring in her step. Now that is true beauty.

We find a seat close to the counter.

"Last night was amazing," I say.

"I thought you'd like that."

"Not sure what it was about, but it was fun."

"It's called edging, but it was mixed with a bit of BDSM."

"I did say no kink."

"I didn't believe you."

"Would you really have beaten me if I'd come?" I'm sure the answer is no.

"Like you wouldn't have believed possible, and you'd have come again and again."

Why am I becoming aroused? I've never been into S&M. He's bluffing. "Really?" I'm incredulous.

"Yes, really," he states like the conversation is over.

"Lucky I didn't come then." I try to make a joke, but I'm unsettled. He's borderline psychopathic.

"Or unlucky, depending on how you see it."

"Did you record everything on the big screen?" Please no more revenge porn.

"Yes, but don't panic. I'm not going to do anything with it. We've moved past that. We can watch it later if you like."

He might be able to move past it… The atmosphere changes.

He put me through hell by threatening me with that video. He sent it to my children's school. We can't sail past something so serious.

"How can we move past it, Trevor?"

"Easy. We forgive, forget, and never mention the situation again."

"It's not that easy."

"Yes, it is. You choose to move on. We talked it through after ice skating before Christmas."

"We did, but—"

"No buts, baby. I made the video as a present for you. And yes, I totally agree, using it as leverage to get you to see me was stupid. I was bluffing. And I'm taking responsibility for the error of judgment."

"You make it sound simple. You gave me the clap for goodness sake. Nobody would be happy about that. And you didn't need to start revenge-porning me too. What was wrong with waiting for me to calm down?"

"I didn't know I had the clap, or I wouldn't have had sex with you. And yes, I can see why you'd be pissed about that. I wouldn't say I 'revenge-porned' you. The situation got out of control."

He characterises his behaviour as every day and commonplace. I can't accept what he did and sit glaring at him.

"Look, Alex, we can move past this."

"How?"

"You've done stupid things too. You went to the police to report me for rape. At the police station, they kept asking me if I raped you and they wouldn't believe I didn't. Being accused of rape ruins men's lives."

"Yes, initially I did call them to report you for rape. And that has got to be the worst decision of my life. But I didn't go through with it. At the interview, I told the police the truth." The very fact, doing that, crossed my mind, makes me flush with shame. How was that ever a good idea? "I can see how that would be disastrous for your life."

"I'll say being accused of rape is the kind of shit that sticks. There's going to be repercussions at work. But like you, I didn't think it through. It was a bit of fun in the beginning."

"Fun? What bit of it was fun? You threatened to ruin my life and expose me in the worst possible way. I trusted you, Trevor. My actions were in desperation, trying to protect myself. Yet you did it for a bit of fun."

"I'm sorry, baby, I get where you're coming from. Fun is the wrong way to put it. You didn't want to see me again; I thought threatening to use the video might change your mind. But what's done is done. We can't change the past. But we can move on. It's over. We are right together, aren't we?"

"It's not over, Trevor. You might be charged with revenge porn."

"We have to let the legal situation play out. I meant us. We're good, right? That's what's important to me."

"And what if the press keep investigating?"

"I told you I'd sort the press situation, and I have. There won't be anything more."

We sit looking at each other. My brain freezes in confusion. He's believable, but how can we get from sordid sex in a derelict loo within an hour of meeting, to this? Whatever this is. We barely know each other. Yet the feeling of familiarity and of certainty is total. Last night I told him I loved him. None of it makes sense.

Full plates of baked beans, bacon, sausages, mushrooms, hash browns, fried eggs and bread arrive in front of us, breaking the tension.

We eat in silence, glancing at each other from time to time.

The food is wolfed down before he speaks again.

"Now, baby, do you want to come with me for a walk in the park?" His unnerving, unblinking stare is back.

"You mean for a repeat of the performance in the loo?" I ask.

"You've been giving me *come fuck me* eyes all morning."

"Not sure I've got time, but—"

"For fuck's sake, I should have known." A six-foot blonde

slams her hand down on the table between us and shouts in Trevor's face. "And there was me thinking you were depressed on your own."

She glares at me.

Shit, she looks underage. A model…

"Depressed? And on my own? What? I've never been depressed in my life, or on my own."

"So you think this is a joke, do you?"

"Okay, calm down. I was going to call you later," Trevor says.

"You didn't think to call me back last night? I left you like a hundred messages," she shouts.

"Darling, this is Alexandra. Why don't you sit down and join us?"

"Are you kidding me? You can't eat this food and stay alive. Mum is waiting for me in the car. I was so worried about you after you didn't pick up; she's been running me around looking for you. I should have listened. She said you'd be balls deep in some cheap tart."

Bloody hell, I do not want to be in the middle of whatever shit-storm this is.

He ignores her anger. "Alex, this is my daughter, Chelsea—"

"I don't give a fuck who flavour of the week is. Why did I bother? You never change."

She looks close to tears.

I stand up. “I was just leaving. I’m meeting someone for lunch.”

“Who are you meeting for lunch?” Trevor becomes more alert.

“None of your business,” I say to Trevor. “Sorry, Chelsea, he’s all yours.”

“Don’t talk to me,” she shouts.

Trevor gets up.

“What’s that supposed to mean? None of my business? You can’t do all that and leave. We’re an item baby, 111 and all that.”

“Watch me.” I head for the door.

Chelsea rolls her eyes. “Oh, that old chestnut.”

“This is the real deal, honey,” Trevor says to Chelsea.

“Pull the other one.”

“What about our walk in the park? Don’t go, baby, or let me come with you.”

“Bye, Trevor.”

CHAPTER TEN

Parked outside the café is a smart, black four-by-four with the number plate KRYSTAL. At the wheel sits a peroxide blonde with hair so long, it can only be extensions. Bright pink lipstick is slicked over her pumped-up lips. Her false eyelashes look like they belong on the stage. And a white denim jacket stretches over a visible hot-pink bra. Glittery gold talons tap the black leather steering wheel.

Krystal, I'm guessing, glares at me despite our never having met. She must be Trevor's ex-wife.

Scanning the road for a black taxi allows me to pretend I can't see her scowling.

It isn't long before an orange light indicates one is available. The driver sees me leaning off the curb with my hand out, and stops.

"Can you take me to Charlotte Street?"

"Yes, no problem, Luv. Jump in."

Resting back on the large leather seat, phone clutched in my hand, London goes by outside the window. New Year's Day is quieter than usual. As we move through the streets, nothing in particular catches my eye. Tourists are milling around Trafalgar Square, heading into the National Gallery. The statue of Eros stands high over the Shaftesbury Memorial Fountain.

He's bare-chested, with his bow and arrow, poised to shoot. Shoppers swarm around the endless shops on Oxford Street. Glimpses of the BT Tower come into view as we get closer to Charlotte Street.

What was last night about? The edging, and threatening to beat me, again. I've never experienced a period of prolonged pleasure like that. How did he do it? Watching what he was doing on the big screen was beyond sexy. The night started out normally. Well, not exactly normal. Having a famous chef and three-figure bottles of Champagne wasn't going on up and down the country. But I didn't see where all that was going.

Trevor makes me happy, but there's always a but with him. The problem is squaring the happiness with what he did last year. We can't get anywhere good from where we've started. His explanations are plausible. I'm sure he made the video as he thought I'd like it. But to then threaten me with it. What else would he be capable of? He could be charged with revenge porn and have to go to court. I've withdrawn my complaint, but it's out of my hands. The Crown Prosecution Service will decide if they want to take it forward.

My watch slides up my wrist, and I jangle the gold links back down. I'm going to be late. I'd better tell him.

On my way. Looking forward. See you soon.

No, problem, I'm here he replies.

There's enough time to try Rachel, again. Her husband, Michael, must be back by now. It's been weeks. She never answers my calls. Same as before, the phone rings and rings. I'm going to keep trying. I had no idea Michael was married when we had a ten-minute stand in the changing rooms of Badwell House gym. And I had no idea when I took Rachel on as a client that she knew I'd slept with her husband. After working with Rachel for a year, the sense of responsibility is hard to shake off. Once I know she's okay, I will let it go.

* * *

We pull up outside the door. The metre reads £15:55. "Take twenty," I say to the taxi driver and hand over my card.

"Thanks, Luv."

The interior is dark, although it's just before noon. Ousia is a smart, family-run Greek taverna. It's a bit early for the main lunch run, so the place is quiet.

He sits staring off into the middle distance. His features are familiar but nothing like Marina's. Even with dark blonde hair, you wouldn't mistake him for anything other than Greek. Today he looks much younger.

"Demetrois, hello."

He stands up and kisses both my cheeks.

"Alexandra, I'm so pleased you agreed to meet me. I wanted

to talk to you over Christmas but didn't get the chance. Conty was so angry at the party."

This meeting is odd. We've barely seen each other over the years and never met up alone. Last year on the sailing holiday was the first time I'd seen him in ten years. He was the only person who was civil to me. Marina's twin daughters – his sisters – Vanessa and Sophia, ignored me. I hope he doesn't want to talk about what happened in Greece. There's no need on my account. And I'm guessing he doesn't know about Conty and his mother having a one-night stand. So it can't be that.

"No problem, it's always good to see you," I say, and mean.

"I tried to talk to you on the sailing holiday last year. But things with Conty were bad. And you left partway through, after..." He trails off and stops talking for a moment.

What's going on here?

"I didn't get a chance to say goodbye," he continues, before I have a chance to speak.

Shit, he *does* want to talk about the holiday. Nothing happened between us. Conty and I rowed. And the trip ended with me catching a flight home.

"You didn't do anything wrong, Demetrius. I was in a bad place, and yes, things with Conty were tense. That's why I left. It was nothing to do with you." Hopefully, this will set his mind at rest.

"Let's get a drink," he says.

"Good idea," I agree. He looks like he needs one.

The waiter comes over, and there is a fast flow of Greek between them.

"I've ordered some food, but you're not going to be hungry."

"I'm always hungry," I reassure him, "and I love Greek food."

I'm full from brunch, but I'll squeeze some in.

We sit in silence for a moment.

He sighs heavily and looks like he's about to cry.

"I'm so sorry, Alexandra."

"Honestly, Demetrius, there's nothing to be sorry about. Let's have a nice lunch." I try to lighten the situation – because that is what this meeting is beginning to feel like, a situation. There's no need for this sombre, heavy mood.

The waiter puts a carafe of red wine on the table.

I pour us a glass each, but don't intend to sip more than a few mouthfuls. It's easy to forget I could be pregnant. I'm beginning to think I'm crazy to keep thinking about pregnancy and babies. I'll do the pregnancy test later, to put my mind at rest.

"I don't know if I've done the right thing, meeting you secretly."

Bloody hell, what is it with the youth of today? First, Trevor's daughter has a hissy fit over him not answering his phone on New Year's Eve. Now Demetrius is carrying on like he's committed a heinous crime by meeting me for lunch. Shouldn't they be in bed nursing a hangover and wondering who the hell is lying next to them?

"I don't believe in regrets, Demetrios. Let's move on – New Year and all that." I try again to shift the gloom.

"Conty is my father."

He puts his head in his hands like he's ducking for cover, and doesn't look up.

The words are out of his mouth, but the sentence doesn't equate to meaning in my mind.

His thick black hair spreads out through his fingers, which grip his head.

"What?"

"Conty is my father," he repeats, looking up and shaking his head, eyes sad and hopeless.

"My husband is your father?" I say, like I've only just grasped that Conty is my husband.

"Yes, I'm sorry."

"But he can't be. There's no way. I'd know that."

"He is, Alex. And Vanessa and Sophia are his daughters."

He puts his head back in his hands.

My mouth gapes open for a second before I remember to close it. It takes effort not to put my head in my hands too. He's made a mistake.

"Are you telling me my husband is you and your sibling's father?"

He has made it crystal clear, but it's so unbelievable, I can't help asking again. There's no way that Conty is their father. He's had a one-night stand with their mother, not a long-term affair.

"Yes. I didn't know what to do."

"What about your real father, Marina's husband?"

"I'm afraid Conty is our real father."

"But how? They're cousins. Isn't that illegal?"

"No, they're not, Alex. My mother and Conty aren't related at all. They cultivated that idea with everyone to explain their constant closeness."

"But Conty has always been clear that Marina is his family."

"She's not – not technically his family, anyway. I can assure you, Alex. They were teenage sweethearts. He was her first boyfriend, and she was his first girlfriend. They've known each other since they were toddlers and grew up playing together as young children."

"What? That can't be right. They would have stayed together."

"Conty's family wouldn't let him marry her, as her father was a fisherman, and her family are poor."

"But Marina was married. How could she manage to have three children with someone else?"

This doesn't make any sense at all; he's got it wrong.

"Conty's family sent him to England to boarding school, but he never let go of Marina. He kept coming to Greece, and they ended up producing three children. She passed us off as her husband's."

"That's not possible. You've made a mistake. Conty is not your father."

This is too far-fetched. He might be right about them being teenage sweethearts, but hiding three children? I don't think so.

"I'm afraid he is, Alex. Marina's husband was infertile. That's how I found out. He died when we were young."

"Yes, I recall. He must have known he couldn't have children?"

There will be a reasonable explanation for these outlandish claims.

"I'm not sure he did know, but he died young, so we'll never find out."

"How do you know?"

I'm sympathetic to his pain, but he's got this wrong.

"His mother, who is an old lady now, told me it was a miracle he had babies. The doctors told her he would never be able to father children. He had mumps as a child and lost a testicle. The other one was severely damaged and unable to produce sperm."

"That isn't enough evidence, Demetrius. People defy medical predictions all the time, especially in reproduction. Women can have miracle pregnancies. I'm sure you're mistaken, and he was your real father."

"No, Alex, I'm not mistaken. As I grew up, I realised my mother and your husband were sleeping in the same bed. In Greece, he treated us like his children. I went to the same boarding school as Conty. Who do you think paid for our private education?"

"But he married me."

"My mother told me they stopped sleeping together for a few months around the time he married you, but never for long."

"It can't be the case, Demetrius. Perhaps Conty has been sleeping with Marina long-term. And your father did have some kind of childhood illness that affected his fertility. But that doesn't mean Conty is your father."

It's too ridiculous to take seriously. I can understand he's upset about Marina and Conty having a long-term affair, but it's a big jump to Conty being their father.

"I'm sorry, Alex. I wouldn't be here if I wasn't sure. I

confronted Conty a couple of years ago. He denied it, so I had paternity tests done without his knowledge."

He reaches into his jacket and produces three white slips of paper.

My hand shakes, holding them.

The results are conclusive. Conty is Demetrios, Vanessa and Sophia's father.

"I see. I—"

"I'm sorry to tell you this, Alex, but I thought you'd want to know. You can keep the results. I have copies."

Acceptance is all that's left. Grim acknowledgement that he's right. A large gulp of wine slides down my throat but feels like water.

"Does Conty know about the tests?"

"Yes, and so do the girls. But as you saw on holiday, they are as devoted to him as my mother is. I was angry, and I'm still angry about the lies, the double life and what he's done to you."

Of all the things Conty is, this was not something I anticipated.

"What does your mother think about all this?"

"She's unhinged, Alex. Look at what she's done already, deceiving us and living a double life. She's devoted to him and will stop at nothing to protect him and their relationship."

"There was an incident after the Christmas party. I walked

in on the two of them ... And she sent me a text message Christmas morning, blaming me for Conty's behaviour and warning me to lay off him."

"That doesn't surprise me. Where he's concerned, her loyalty knows no bounds. The Christmas party was the final straw. Watching them deceive you in your own home. And Conty abuse you while she watched. I was sick to the stomach. I left."

He puts his head back in his hands.

I reach over and pull his head up. Putting my hands in his.

He grips both my hands like a child.

"None of this is your fault, Demetrius. You've done the right thing by telling me. I saw the tension between you and Conty last year, but we were in such a bad place I didn't follow it up. I'm sorry you've had to go through this alone. It must have been a huge shock. I'm always here for you."

Tears well in his eyes. "Thank you. You must feel like your whole marriage has been a lie."

"It's okay. I'm glad you told me. You did the right thing, and must focus on your life and finding a way to deal with this."

CHAPTER ELEVEN

The three white sheets confirming Conty is the father of Marina's three children flutter in the freezing wind. Gripped in my frozen fingers, there's no chance I'll drop them.

It's usually easy to get a taxi, standing on the corner of Charlotte Street. Another scan of the road; still nothing. My stomach feels like it's gripped in a squeezing fist. Doubling over in the street isn't an option. Walking might help ease the raw anxiety.

How could Conty do this to us? It's not just me he's deceived, but our children too. Conty told me Marina was his distant cousin. He was always vague about how many times removed. She was at our wedding. They have been inseparable. At first, I thought it was about her mothering him. She does a lot of fussing around him. She calls him her rock. But he's a different person when he's with her. There's no criticism or vitriol. All those trips to Greece were to be with Marina and his other family. The truth is stark.

Still, no taxi.

I text Trevor. *Can you pick me up? I'm on Charlotte Street towards the BT Tower.*

So you went off for a sneaky Greek. Yes, no problem, stay where you are. I'm on my way.

The wind whips me to the bone, and the below-zero temperature stiffens my limbs. Even if I did cry, the tears would freeze on my cheeks. I can't remember London being this cold. I stuff the white sheets into my handbag. The zip cuts into my fingers. My vision blurs. I stare at nothing and shift from foot to foot, in an attempt to keep warm. Time is distorted while my mind alternates between disbelief and numbness. I can't tell how long I've been standing on the street corner, but sleet falls onto my shoulders.

"How much, darling? I'll give ya a tenner," Trevor shouts in his best Cockney accent, from his bright red sports car, pulling up beside me. His window is all the way down.

Not that old gag again. His predictability makes me smile. I try to laugh, but the sound is hollow.

He leans over and flicks the door open.

Getting into the car is a respite from the incessant attempts my mind makes to accept the news and process the implications. Trevor's killer smile and familiar smell help. I know everything is going to be all right when he looks at me like that.

"You okay?" He pulls away from the curb. "Cold, isn't it?"

"No, and yes. Freezing," I reply.

He glances at me again, but the gravity of my mood doesn't leave much doubt. So he doesn't say another word.

He flicks the heating up to max and puts his hand on my knee.

We drive through the streets of London in silence.

* * *

"Jump in the bath to warm up," Trevor shouts from the bathroom.

My leather jacket is hard to shrug off with stiff limbs. It lands on the end of the bed.

Steam comes out of the en suite bathroom.

I stand at the door.

Trevor is bent over the huge standalone bath, chucking a load of expensive oil under the hot, steaming tap. He looks back over his shoulder and swirls the water with his hand.

I've lost the ability to do anything without external motivation.

He grabs a towel to dry his hands. "Here, I'll help you."

I lift up my arms, so he can get my jumper over my head.

"After you've got that cold, it's the only way to get warm."

"Thank you."

"You don't want me to help you out of your jeans. You know where that will lead."

My face feels like it's set in stone, but finally, a smile cracks the numbness.

He moves away. "What take-away do you want? Sushi, Thai, Pizza..."

"I don't mind."

He leaves, shutting the door behind him.

Conty is the father of Marina's children. The stark statement repeats in my head, over and over. He has seven children, our four and three with her. Our having more children is a tiny but useless victory.

The bath is ready.

Standing with my hands on the sink, I try to do the maths. Demetrius is around twenty-five. He was born before Conty married me. Why did he marry me after having a child with someone else? Marina's husband was still alive, I think, but he must have been ill. Conty deliberately kept the details hazy. The twins, Sophia and Vanessa, are at least five years younger. They were born around the time we got married, as I remember Marina had a full-time nanny looking after them. All those visits to Greece, everywhere we went, she was there. And their smart private school educations. All paid for by Conty. It didn't occur to me that they... That he would...

The hot water feels good and brings relief. The distinctive smell of lime and mandarin wafts up around me. My head rests on the edge of the huge white bath. I stretch my legs out.

I'm shocked, but the hurt that should be there doesn't

follow. I'm numb. This scenario is unbelievable. My thoughts can't go past the revelation. I'm going to have to get my head straight before I go home.

* * *

Trevor's laugh carries through the apartment. He's lying on the huge, oversized sofa; his dark blue jeans stretch over his thighs.

He pats the space next to him.

I have to climb on and crawl to get to him.

Some Like it Hot is on the big screen.

His arms go around me.

He smells of shower gel and deodorant. With my head resting against his dark blue camouflage t-shirt, I can hear his heartbeat. The strong and steady thump fills my head. My arm rests over his tummy, and I hold on to him tighter.

He pulls me closer to his body, so we are as tight as we can get.

"Now, Marilyn Monroe, there's a real woman, killer curves and a naughty smile," he says.

No response is required, so I'm able to stay silent.

It's hard to settle in one physical place, let alone find coherence. The film rolls on, but I can't focus or follow the story. My mind splinters in all directions. There's no going back from this revelation.

Trevor's laughing makes me feel better. Whatever experience he's having, he's always totally in the moment.

The closing credits finish, and the screen goes black.

We don't move.

He picks up my chin and pulls my face up to look at him. "Now, are you going to tell me what all that was about this afternoon? Or am I going to have to beat it out of you?"

"What?" I'm alarmed.

"I'm joking, baby. Do you take everything I say seriously?"

How can he be so emotionally intelligent and psychopathic at the same time? I'm not sure I want to tell him. This is beginning to feel like a relationship.

"Who did you have lunch with?"

"Conty's eldest son, Demetrius." The tone is flat and robotic in my head.

"You met your son, and that upset you?"

"No, Demetrius isn't my son, that's the problem."

Trevor shakes his head and raises his eyebrows. "You mean, Conty—"

"Yes, Conty has a son and two daughters with Marina. He passed her off as his cousin and I—"

"Marina? Did you say Marina?"

"Yes, why?"

"I've met her. She came to the Porter Vision Security conference. I thought she and Conty looked tight. He introduced her as his cousin. I thought their closeness was a European thing. Wasn't she with him at the Christmas party?"

"Yes, she went to him after you pushed him over, and he was on the floor. I keep forgetting you know Conty."

"I should have told you before. He sat on the board at Porter Vision; I chair it. Before his first board meeting, around this time last year, he showed me a photo of him and Marina on a skiing trip. I recognised you from that party, and he said you were his wife. That was the day I messaged you, and we arranged to meet for brunch in the caff."

I know the photo he means. I cut a headshot of Hayes from it. "So you knew I was married but still asked if I was divorced."

"Yes, I wanted to fuck you, and when you lied about being married, I knew I had a chance," he says. No hint of shame.

"Why play games, Trevor?"

"This isn't about me. It's your husband who has another family with his cousin."

"She's not his cousin," I snap.

"You know what I mean."

"You know what? I do know what you mean. I'm crazy being here with you after what you did to me."

"Come on, baby, don't be like that. I've explained, isn't that enough?"

"No, it's not enough. And now I find out you completely deceived me when we first met. Why not tell the truth? There's nowhere to go from where we've started."

Before he can touch me, I jump up and go to the bathroom.

He follows me and stands in the doorway.

"I'm sorry. You're right. I should have told you immediately."

"Do you realise how psychopathic you are? I'm going."

"Yes, of course, I do. I've always been self-aware. You're not thinking straight, beautiful. Relax, let's get some downtime, and I'll make love to you. No kinks this time."

"Self-aware? You are to be believed. And don't call me beautiful. In fact, don't call me anything at all. Just don't call me."

I throw the white bathrobe on the floor and start picking up my clothes.

He looks my naked body up and down.

"And don't even think about it," I say.

"Oh, I'm thinking about it all right. And you are too. Come on, honey, don't go. You've had a shock. I'll make you feel better and forget about it for a while. Thinking is overrated."

For a second I freeze, unable to comprehend he's said something I tell myself all the time. Getting out of here, and now, is the only option. I pull on my jeans and jumper.

"No, I don't need you or your sick sex games to feel better."

He watches me get dressed.

With one hand on the bed, I struggle to maintain balance as I zip up my boot.

"Going home in this state isn't a good idea. You need to get your head straight, baby."

Bundling my stuff up, I throw the pile in my bag. I'm not sure if he's going to let me out of the bathroom. And I'm not sure if I'm going to be able to walk past him. So I act as if he isn't there and march to the door.

"You need to do your other boot up," he says. Amusement flickers over his face, and he lifts his arm up so I can go underneath.

"You think this is funny? Why can't you take anything seriously? My life is being destroyed."

"I'm not laughing about that. And your life was destroyed before you found out about his other family. Baby, it's late. How are you going to get home without wheels?"

He's right. At least about my life being destroyed long before. But there's no way I'm staying here. "I'm going to get a black taxi."

"All the way to Northamptonshire?"

"Yes."

If I can get to the street door first, there's a chance I'll get out without fucking him.

He gets there first and bars me from going through.

"Stay, and I'll drive you in the morning."

"Don't tell me what to do."

"If you insist on getting a black cab, at least let me help you find one."

"I don't need your help, Trevor. I never want to see you or your toxic cock or play your fucking warped sex games, ever again. What the fuck was last night?"

"You enjoyed last night. Come on, you don't mean that."

"Get out of my way." I choke the tears back in my throat.

Looking back is dangerous, and the lift will take too long to come. I push through the heavy swing doors to the stairwell, tears blurring my vision. The steps disappear two at a time.

It's a long way down. I'm out of breath but feeling better at the bottom.

Trevor is waiting in the reception foyer. He hasn't put shoes on. Who does that?

I glare at him and make for the exit.

He puts both hands in the air, like he's surrendering. "Relax, I'm going to help you find a taxi. I don't want you wandering around the streets late at night. It's not safe around here."

Fuck off nearly makes it out of my mouth, but I clench my teeth and throw my head in the air.

The glass doors open to the cold night.

Before I've seen an orange light, Trevor is off the curb and whistling for it.

For a second, I'm tempted to walk in the opposite direction and find my own cab, but it's freezing. And I don't want to walk the streets, due more to the risk of frostbite than getting attacked. He doesn't know I grew up around here and went to primary school with half the gangs.

The cab pulls up. Trevor talks to the driver through the window and hands him something.

It's not possible to check he hasn't paid for the trip without talking to him. And I'm not saying another word.

He opens the taxi door and waves his hand.

It's childish to avoid looking at him, but I'm beyond reason now. "Can you take me to Northamptonshire, please?"

"Yes, no problem. You sit back and relax."

Relax? I'm heading home to confront my husband about his other family.

Trevor pokes his head through the door. "Can I have a kiss?"

I'm not gracing that with an answer.

"I'll take that as a no. I've got your back, baby," he says for the second time in twenty-four hours.

He slams the door and bangs the back of the taxi as we pull away.

Through the side mirror, I watch him make a love heart sign with his hands and point towards me.

The memory of when we nearly got caught by the police, fucking in the derelict loo, floods back. When he came out to find me talking to the young Police officer, he pretended I was his wife and we'd met for lunch. As I walked off, he gave me that love heart sign with his hands. And said something like, I love you, and see you at home later. When I got back to my car, I couldn't stop laughing.

He disappears into the tall glass building, his broad shoulders and the width of his hips in silhouette. We should have had sex before I left. He's right. It would have made me feel better.

CHAPTER TWELVE

Conty and the children are due back from Asia any moment.

My heels click on the floor as I pace up and down the entrance hall.

"At what point were you going to tell me about your other family? We need to talk about Marina and your three illegitimate children," I say out loud to the empty space.

No, that's all wrong and designed to hurt him. He'll be very sensitive to the fact they were born out of wedlock. Even if it's as a result of a lifelong affair. Nothing sounds right. And I'm going crazy talking to myself. You can't resolve your husband having three adult children with someone else, no matter how much you talk. The future depends on how willing I am to accept the situation and forgive him. Am I ending our marriage by even talking about it? What do I want him to say? My head spins with questions.

Gravel crunches under the wheels of the car.

They are here.

Breathe. My stomach turns over, again and again. I can't think properly.

The door opens while I'm working out what to do.

"Mummy, Mummy, Mummy," two voices scream. The girls drop piles of luggage on the floor and rush to hug me.

I wrap my arms around them, clinging on for dear life.

The boys follow and join the group hug.

"Did you have a nice New Year's Eve?" Nicholas asks.

"Yes, thank you, darling. How was your trip?"

"Lots of dinners and parties. Dad runs a tight ship. We haven't had a spare moment."

The children disappear upstairs to their rooms.

"The luggage is in the back; the driver is unloading," Conty says, giving me a kiss on the cheek.

I can't remember the last time he did that. I'm taken aback. He looks shattered. They all do. Singapore can be a fourteen-hour flight, and they are jet-lagged.

I've misjudged the situation. Now isn't the time to talk.

"I'll take the cases up," I say.

"I'm going to bed. See you in the morning. Oh, I almost forgot – you didn't accept my event invite." Conty persists with our joint calendar, despite my never using it.

"Sorry, I haven't checked. What event?"

"Lunch with Lucinda and Charles tomorrow. Presumably, you're happy to do that. And I hope you've changed your mind about coming skiing on Monday?"

"Yes, lunch is fine, but no, I haven't changed my mind. I'm not going skiing."

He shakes his head and tuts.

I stare at him. How can he live a normal life, hiding a secret like that, keeping up the pretence? All the time knowing he has another family.

With slow steps, he heads up the stairs.

The weight of all that is yet to be said fixes me to the spot.

His bedroom door clicks shut.

I breathe out. My limbs relax. The tension dissipates and relief floods me. The next opportunity to talk will be Monday, before they go skiing. I'll confront him then.

I'd better get the cases upstairs and head to bed myself. I've got to get some sleep and clear my head.

* * *

My back is hot on the mattress from tossing and turning. The night churns my thoughts over and over. I breathe out hard, gaze fixed on the ceiling. What am I going to do? Mess doesn't quite cover this situation. I'm glad I didn't confront him at the door. Will Conty and I survive this? Perhaps saying nothing is the best option. And carrying on as we were. That's what the rest of the upper classes do. But we can never be the same again. I'm deceiving myself. Pretending not to know isn't an option. Demetrius will tell him I know at some point. This has to be sorted out. Can I accept what he's done? Perhaps if I accept his extramarital children, he'll have to accept mine.

I'm forty-seven years old and could be having a baby. How is that possible? No matter how many times I go through the dates, I can't gain a handle on whose baby it would be. I go in circles. Knowing when I ovulated is the key, but my periods had become sketchy, so estimating when it happened is pure guesswork. Without knowing for sure, there's no way I can hazard a guess at conception. Hayes and Trevor were both in the same week. Was there someone else around that time? The Internet sex was earlier than Christmas. I'd be more pregnant if it was him. Now I think about it, he was paranoid about pregnancy and used a condom. Definitely not Internet man, whatever his name was; don't think I ever found out. Think... was there anyone else? No, it must be Hayes or Trevor.

My hands move to my tummy and my fingers spread out over my lower abdomen. Is there another heartbeat in my body? That has to be my priority. It doesn't matter whose baby it is, it's my baby. I'll do the test in the morning to check.

Another glance at the clock, three a.m. I've been awake now since midnight. I'm so tired, but sleep isn't happening. Maybe I should get up? If I don't get some sleep, I'm never going to get through lunch.

I slip my hand between my legs and think of Trevor.

* * *

A hard rapping on the door jolts me out of sleep.

Sunlight streams through the window. Even with the curtains closed, it's bright. The clock on my phone illuminates 11:33. It can't be that late. I've never overslept for so long. I'm exhausted all the time at the moment.

The knocking continues.

"Are you ever going to get out of bed?" Conty says from outside the door.

"Sorry, I didn't sleep well. I'm getting up now," I call back.

"We are going to be late, again. Alexandra, how many times —"

"I'm up. I'll be down soon, sorry."

The shower feels good on my back. Getting some sleep has cleared my mind. Last year was an anomaly, and I was pathetic. Meeting Hayes took me by surprise. Deep in misery and learned helplessness, he woke me up and kick-started my emotions. I'll never understand how he could make love to me by our pool and then leave me for dead for weeks. He made me question myself, but I know there was something between us, and I wouldn't get that wrong.

I stand naked and survey my body. There's no way I'm pregnant. My body looks exactly the same as it usually does.

Mind at rest, I get dressed.

The red cashmere jumper the girls gave me for Christmas

goes well over my tight, dark blue skinny jeans. A navy blazer and black high-heeled boots complete my outfit.

"How much longer? We need to go." Conty appears, red-faced and scowling.

"We've got an hour. We don't need to be there until twelve-thirty."

"Do you think the rules of time don't apply to you, Alexandra?"

"I'll be down soon."

My make-up takes another five minutes.

I'm ready to go.

My phone springs into life as I'm going down the stairs. I glance down, but Trevor hasn't messaged me.

Happy New Year, Alex. I'm sorry we won't see each other skiing.

There's no time to reply to Hayes.

Conty's eyes are blazing.

A familiar routine starts to play out, the basis of which is his disapproval of me. He complains about how late I am or what I'm wearing every time we go out. This started on day one of our marriage. My wedding dress was over the top. At black tie balls, I often look like 'a woman of the night.' At least we are past me changing two or three times to appease him. Why did I put up with it for so long? He made my life a living hell. Anger courses through me.

We lock eyes.

His irritation doesn't translate into an attack.

The five-minute drive to the Richardsons' is silent. Conty doesn't try to undermine me like he usually does. From the passenger seat, I scrutinise his face. The likeness between him and Demetrius is only obvious now I know they are genetically related. Demetrius is taller and bigger, more like Marina. But his hair is lighter, and his eyes are hazel, exactly the same colour as Conty's. He looks nothing like our sons – both are tall and blond, like me. Sophia and Vanessa have a slight resemblance to Athena, who is most like Conty. The fact I'm examining the likeness between my children and Marina's shocks me.

Was guilt driving his abusive behaviour?

We pull up at the same time as Hayes and Annabel.

Oh great, this is the last thing I need. My newfound indifference to Hayes being challenged, so soon.

Hayes can't have known I'd be at the lunch when he messaged me earlier.

Conty and Annabel greet each other like long-lost lovers. Maybe he's banging her too. Then again, she looks like she'd snap if you lent on her. They head under the stone arch of the porch and through the green-painted wooden door.

Hayes presses the lock button on their car. He looks back at the side mirrors pulling in. The mechanical click is loud in the deserted driveway.

My stomach clenches and heart races, seeing him in person. His hand goes up through his floppy blond hair. He's nervous. On the skiing holiday last year, his every move got seared into my memory. He's wearing an almost identical outfit to me, dark blue jeans with a red cashmere jumper and a navy blazer. He must live in the gym to look like that. His eyes lock on mine.

My best bet is to get into the house without talking to him. I've never been good at in-between. I pretend I haven't seen him and walk towards the door.

"Alex."

He's not going to let me.

"I've just sent you a message. We need to talk."

"Yes, I saw."

"Why didn't you reply?"

"There's nothing to talk about."

I'm not going back to the pain of wanting him but not being able to have him. His casual indifference drove me crazy and I became unable to function. More critically, it exposed a nerve and meant I was incapable of protecting myself from Conty's constant abuse.

"So our relationship was nothing to you?" he persists.

"So it was a relationship now?"

"You know it was. Why are you angry and not replying to my messages?"

"Let me think. Oh, that's right, you have another girlfriend as well as me and your wife. You fuck me then disappear for weeks without a word. Nothing about that screams relationship."

"You dumped me, Alex. And my other relationship is finally over. I'm free now."

"All of that happened before I dumped you. It took you a year to end an affair, really? And you have a funny definition of free. You're married, remember."

"We're both married, Alex. The situation was complicated, and yes, extracting myself took a year. If you give me a chance, I'll—"

"You've had your chance."

"Conty says you're not going skiing. Please come; I'll make sure we get some time together. I understand my behaviour confused you, but life is easier now."

"Easier?" It all has to be easy for him. Forget how he's affected my life, as long as the situation is easy for him.

"Yes, it will be easier for us to see each other regularly."

"Well, as long as it's easy for you, Hayes."

"Don't be like that," he says.

"Like what? I don't know what you want from me. I'm not

going skiing."

I set off for the house again.

"You have every right to be angry. I should have handled our relationship differently. You were having a hard time and needed me, but—"

"But what? It didn't suit you? Wasn't easy enough?"

He looks sad. His dark blue eyes search my face. "No, of course not, you don't understand the situation I was in."

"No, Hayes, *you* don't understand the situation *I* was in."

Or the situation we could be in. His baby's heart could be beating in my body. What would it matter? He's still married. And as he pointed out, so am I. Well, in name, anyway. Conty is clearly committed to another woman and their family. And I don't even know what to think about Trevor. Only that he's on my mind 24/7. I can't believe I didn't notice that before. I think about Trevor literally every second of every day.

This is all too much.

In a few steps, he reaches me.

One cuddle won't hurt.

I rest my head on his chest.

He strokes my hair. "I missed you, Alex. I can't stop thinking about you."

I've spent weeks suppressing how I feel about him. What can I say now? It never lasts. Getting away from him is the only way. His confusing care and non-care is a head fuck. And I've got enough to fuck with my head. At least Trevor is clear and I know him. This is crazy – Trevor and I can't be together either.

I pull away. "We need to go inside or our absence will be noted."

"I'm sorry life is still hard but you are looking well, Alex, and stronger."

"What – because I haven't dissolved into tears in your arms within two minutes of seeing you?"

"No, that's not what I meant."

"I'm sorry. This isn't a good time for me. And I want to get lunch over as quickly as possible."

"Why? What's going on?"

"Not now, Hayes."

CHAPTER THIRTEEN

A big crowd of the usual suspects mills around. As well as Hayes and Annabel, James Woodly and his wife are here. I'm surprised to see Edmund and Henrietta Mulgrave, otherwise known as the Duke and Duchess of Klimpke. Ed and I know each other in the biblical sense, as we seduced each other at a black-tie ball last year. And Henrietta is a close friend of Lucinda's, I now recall.

Ed comes rushing over and squeezes my bottom. "Well, if it isn't the sexy Dr Alex."

I laugh. "The last time you called me that, I was coming on your stairs."

"So you were. And I'm still trying to organise a repeat performance. You are a slippery one, darling."

Henrietta is close behind. She gives me a warm hug and passes me a glass of champagne. "Hello, darling, how was Christmas?"

It takes me a few seconds longer than acceptable to formulate my thoughts into a sensible soundbite.

"That bad? Come stay with us next time and bring Conty, if you must. Ed will find someone important to distract him, and we can get to know each other properly," she continues, giving me a big smile.

"Thank you, I'd like that."

We have an easy relationship with no tension. I'm still not sure whether she watched Ed fucking me on the stairs in their stately pile. Getting to know her 'properly' sounds like it would involve sex. If my life wasn't in crisis I'd be open to some fun. I'm becoming a real bore.

James Woodly moves away from the closed clique he was chatting in and comes over. He clinks his glass against mine. "Happy New Year."

His wife, Camilla, ignores me. Being tight with Annabel and Conty is incompatible with being friends with me. Men can get away with so much more, socially.

"Happy New Year," I reply

I glance over at Hayes, who hasn't taken his eyes off me since we walked through the door.

* * *

The empty bottles of red wine pile up in the corner.

We devour roast beef and Yorkshire pudding.

Sunday lunch with Lucinda and Charles is a treat. They are by far the best hosts in the county, and the food is always top quality.

Hayes is drinking alcohol for once and looks ruffled. His hand goes up to his neck again and again, like he's trying to relieve pain.

He knows I'm looking at him.

I don't care about his emotional state. When he chose the chair beside mine, I insisted someone swap seats. A bit rude, but I can't bear sitting next to him all lunch. I'm next to Lucinda.

"Yes, the boat is booked and sleeps twelve. Plenty of room for everyone," Charles says, loud enough for the entire table to hear.

Charles must know about Conty's other family. My stomach sinks. *Everyone* must know. It's an open secret. And they think I'm gullible and stupid not to realise. He's made a complete fool out of me.

Heat rushes from my head down my body.

I don't follow the various comments around the room, expressing thanks and looking forward to the summer holiday.

"No one bothers with villas anymore. Boats give you more flexibility to travel around," Charles continues.

Our last time on a boat was the sailing holiday, with Marina and their children. All those holidays with Marina, the two of them knowing what they had done to me.

My brain freezes with anger. My jaw clenches.

A sip of water makes me relax.

I'm going to have to leave. This is too much. I'm over taking shit. My tolerance level is depleted to a dangerous low. I'll tell everyone I have a headache and have to go home.

"I'm sorry, Lucie, I've got a terrible head—"

"You can forget plenty of room with Alexandra on board," Conty crows.

The whole table quietens.

Conty throws half a glass of red wine down his throat, his red face hot and swollen.

"The kitchen sink and the entire bathroom get packed," he continues.

"That's not fair, Conty, I—" He cuts me off.

"You'd think with all those products not even she could look that cheap."

How dare he say that.

"Come on, old chap," says James, sitting next to Conty. "There's no need for that."

The room tenses for a second as the exchange between Conty and James sinks in.

Camilla looks horrified at the chance James has taken by publicly defending me.

"You're a lucky man, Conty," Henrietta says, smiling at me. "You need to hire a crane to get my suitcases on board," she continues with a laugh, backing James up and smoothing over the situation.

"You think she's joking…" Edmund adds, giving her a broad smile, approving of his wife's intervention. He gives Conty a challenging stare, designed to put an end to the matter.

Conty would never attack Ed or Henrietta.

Hayes gives me a sympathetic smile.

I refuse to acknowledge him.

The situation should be over, but Conty pours himself another glass of wine and takes a large gulp. "Joking? The ghastly truth is, she—"

"What would you know about the truth, Conty?" I say, louder than I intended.

"A damn sight more than you. Please don't bore the table with your ridiculous protests. No one wants to hear it."

I stand up.

"Perhaps everyone would be interested in hearing about your three illegitimate children with Marina? You know, the ones you've kept a secret our whole marriage? Or maybe everyone already knows. You are the liar, Conty."

He scoffs, and quaffs the rest of his wine. "What, so you're a fantasist now? For a supposedly educated woman, you are as thick as two short planks. Must be those cheap blonde highlights, gone to your head." He roars with laughter, clearly not up to speed with how events are unfolding.

James lowers his head.

"How about I circulate the paternity tests, so everyone can see for themselves?"

His drunk brain processes what I've said.

I am completely sober.

He's stunned into silence, mouth gaping open.

Edmund gives me a twinkly look and a thumbs up, not caring who sees. He's never liked Conty and only befriended him because he wanted to fuck me. Everything amuses Ed.

Annabel puts her hand on Conty's arm in a display of solidarity, as if I've mortally wounded him.

Henrietta gives me a big smile and just stops short from shrugging her shoulders, like it's a minor issue.

No amount of social engineering will smooth this over.

James shakes his head; it's as good as saying, *I can't believe you just said that.*

Camilla glares at me like I've put James in social danger.

The table of open but silent mouths blurs in front of me.

"Thank you for lunch. Delicious as always."

I gently push my chair into the table and walk out.

* * *

My back is warm from leaning on the hot metal of the Aga.

The kettle whistles on the top.

I turn to pour the boiling water over my chamomile tea.

I'm going to wait up until Conty comes home. I expect James will drop him off, as I took the car.

My phone sits next to me. I've had at least four messages from people at the lunch, checking I'm okay. Hayes is not one of them. He saw what happened, but is not following up. Makes me wonder if he realises what he's doing. We embrace in the driveway, he talks about us being in a relationship and him wanting to see me regularly. The shit hits the fan, so what does he do? Precisely nothing. No offer of help or comfort. A simple, *are you okay* would do, but no, yet again he doesn't bother. None of it makes sense. And I'm sick and tired of being the one figuring it out.

Hours have passed, and the shock of what happened at lunch is wearing off. Sitting at the kitchen table, my mind makes another loop of dysfunctional thoughts. I need to get some space from the drama. My packed bags sit by the door. The children are ready for skiing and in their bedrooms. I've already said goodbye. They think I'm going to stay with a friend in London for work. Then they'll be back at boarding school, and I'll visit them there

After what feels like forever, the front door opens.

I walk out to the hallway so he sees me before heading upstairs.

He's sobered up and has his head down.

"How did you find out?"

"Demetrius told me. He gave me the paternity test results."

There's no anger left; unbearable sadness remains. I didn't want to tell him like that or humiliate him in front of our friends.

He's silent. Can he really have nothing to say to me?

"That's why you've abused me our whole marriage, isn't it?"

With hindsight, the situation makes sense. I thought it was his personality, who he was; judgmental and critical. But most damaging of all, is that I thought it was because of who I was. That I was never good enough and always in the wrong. Wrong for simply being me. The truth is, I was not wrong for being me, I was wrong for not being her. He hated me for being in the position he wanted her to have.

He looks in pain, an expression I've never seen.

"I'm not her, and you resented your life with me. So you punished me for the two of you not being together."

Every person who liked me, he must have seen it as a slight against her. He's spent our whole marriage protecting his relationship with her by destroying me.

"It wasn't like that, Alexandra. I fell in love with you and wanted to marry you."

"You're lying. You never loved me."

He goes silent, again.

I'm right.

"I was always meant to be cover, wasn't I? You wanted a face for your marriage. Except I wasn't faceless enough. I drew too much attention."

"No, of course I didn't. And I was going to tell you. The right time didn't come up."

"There is no right time to tell your wife you have a secret family. How could there be?"

I pick up my suitcases.

He doesn't say sorry or ask me to stay.

"Goodbye, Conty."

The lights come on, detecting my footsteps towards the car.

I'm not distressed or confused. I'm solid and silent. This doesn't feel how I expected it to. I'm rewarded with a sense of self-efficacy and security. I've done the right thing. There's no point in looking back. He won't be there. And he never has been. Our marriage has been nothing. I've been a hindrance, wanting the love and attention he wanted to give to her.

I press the ignition button, and the engine starts up.

The headlights only illuminate a short distance in front of me, but it's enough, and I navigate away.

CHAPTER FOURTEEN

"You're kidding me?" Gerry stretches out on the long purple sofa.

Not much shocks Gerry. She's a barrister who specialises in criminal law, so has seen the worst of human nature. The look on her face scares me.

"No, I'm not. That's what he did."

"He edged you to Big Ben chiming in the New Year on his penthouse roof in a hot tub, with the scene projected on a large screen. After playing 'Xanadu,' only one of the best songs of all time."

"Pretty much, yes."

"And he has a big cock and looks like a member of a boy band, but he's around six-foot-eight and built like a mountain. Not to mention being worth a ton of cash. For fuck's sake, Alex. How do you do it? That blonde innocence you peddle is catnip to men. I need a new husband. Can you introduce me?"

She's joking about the husband bit. Michael is a top banker, and they are blissfully happy. She's into all sorts of kinky shit, so Trevor is on her wavelength.

"It's not all moonlight and edging. He choked me with his cock last year. And he tried a bit of autoerotic asphyxiation as I was coming."

"Wow, what was it like? I've heard autoerotic asphyxiation is phenomenal, a real high."

"It was absolutely mind-blowing, but I'm not keen on repeating the experience. The real problems started after I didn't want to see him again."

"Are you crazy? He's a keeper."

"He gave me the clap, remember?"

"Not ideal, but that's easily sorted out. And didn't he tell you he didn't know he had it?"

"Yes, I guess so. But he tried to use the video he made of us as leverage to get me to see him. That looked and felt a lot like revenge porn."

"What was the video like?"

"Every time I watched it, I wanted to wank. Which, under the circumstances, pissed me off. At one point he was slapping me, and I told him I loved him. There's something wrong with me."

"Don't be ridiculous, there's nothing wrong with you. On second thoughts, the fact that you're not definitely leaving your toxic husband for kinky dream boy does make me question your sanity."

"What bit of that didn't you understand, Gerry? He's a brutal psychopath. And recorded us having sex without my knowing."

"I thought you said he made the video for you as a surprise present? And explained the situation got out of hand. You of all people understand how that can happen? Everything with you is out of hand."

"Haha, true. I can't believe I almost had sex with Conty's son."

"Thank goodness you didn't go there. All I'm saying is, it sounds like Trevor's heart is in the right place."

"That's a bit of stretch, especially in this day and age. But yes, fundamentally, he's… I don't know how to describe him. The scene in his office freaked me out. He beat me so hard with his belt, the medics at the STD clinic thought I was a victim of domestic violence. I took photos of the bruises."

"It was consensual though, right?"

"Yes, of course it was consensual, and I was freaked out after the event. At the time, I enjoyed it. Well, the beating was a shock to the system. And really hurt. But I went there to play slutty secretary gets punished. I've never been into kink, so wasn't sure what to expect. And I got more than I bargained for."

"He sounds perfect. Didn't he take care of you on New Year's Day, after the Conty bombshell?"

"Yes, he did, but… there's always a but with him. I found out he lied about knowing I was married at our first meeting. I told him I didn't want to see him again. My head was all over the place. How can I ever trust him? And now he could be charged with revenge porn? I've withdrawn my complaint, but there's no guarantee the Crown Prosecution Service will drop the case against him."

For the first time during our conversation, she frowns. "Yes, I agree, there's a strong chance he'll be prosecuted. That's a sticky situation. Revenge porn is a hot potato. They might make an example of him as a high-profile person and give him a custodial sentence."

"I know, right? He could easily do time for it. And I'm worried the story will get into the public domain."

"Not necessarily. He'll have to consult his barrister about privacy. But yes, jail time is a very real danger. I'd un-end the relationship and concentrate on having a good time with him now."

"There is no relationship with Trevor. He's got some crazy ideas about love, but it's all about sex. Did you miss the bit about Conty and his other family?"

"Yes, sorry I'm not helping. Too busy falling in love with Trevor. You've got to bring him to my fiftieth birthday party."

"I'll think about it. Conty won't want to go."

"I can't believe you just said that. Don't get me started on Conty. You don't want to know what I think about him and your toxic marriage. You never have."

"I already know."

"I'm sorry, babe. You don't need a lecture. Let Trevor make you feel better. See where it goes."

"How can there be anywhere for it to go from where we've started?"

"It's an unusual start, but I've seen a lot worse. And the good outweighs the bad, right?"

"I suppose so. The bad boy bar is set high with your clients. But you have to admit, pretending to post us on a porn site that turned out not to be a real porn site, and sending photos to the children's school, is extreme."

"Yes, but you went to the police to report him for rape, didn't you? I would have advised you against doing that, by the way. I don't want to end up representing you. All I'm saying is, good people can make bad judgements from time to time."

"Yes, I did go to report him for rape, but only to get leverage. At that point, I thought he was going to destroy my life with that video."

The bolt on the industrial cargo lift door slides open, and Michael, wearing a grey pinstripe suit, walks in.

"We're over here, babe," Gerry shouts.

Michael comes over and gives her a kiss.

"Hey, gorgeous," he says to me.

"You're never going to believe this," Gerry says.

"Please don't start with the edging again," I say. "Conty has another family, *that* is the news." I don't add, *I could be pregnant and don't know whose it is*. Putting the prospect out there will make it real, and I'm not ready to deal with that.

"Another family? What the fuck – seriously? Tell me about the edging first. I need a drink before we start on that prick," he says.

* * *

Gerry clears up the dinner plates.

The steak salad was just what I needed. I'm exhausted all the time. We didn't have alcohol, thank goodness. They do drink and take drugs, but during the week, it's clean living.

"Why are you here and not falling onto Trevor's cock for support?" Michael asks.

"Not you too. Does nobody care Conty has another family? He has three children with Marina."

I'm beginning to feel exasperated by their avoidance of the subject.

"Don't, Michael," Gerry warns, narrowing her eyes at him.

"I'm sorry, Alex, but Marina has done you a favour. Remember the early days of your marriage? Conty destroyed your confidence and isolated you from all your old friends.

You became a recluse. He made you frightened of your own shadow."

"Yes, but it wasn't because of him. I was having a hard time adjusting to life in the country, and we either had toddlers or I was pregnant. Not an easy stage of life for anyone. A lot was going on."

"No, Alex, his behaviour is called coercive control and emotional abuse."

"Our marriage has been hard. All marriages are, but those are strong words."

"No, Alex, they're not. What you experienced was abuse. You're still too close to it. You'll see his behaviour for what it was the further away you get. At best, he's a bully. And at worst —"

"I wasn't perfect. It must be hard having a relationship with someone like me. I'm not exactly normal."

"You're not a monster, Alex. Being neuro-diverse has nothing to do with how he treated you. Even now, you're loyal to him," Michael says.

"Loyal? Are you kidding? I've slept with countless men behind his back."

"Yes, but you lasted ten years before you started fucking other people. What I meant was, you'd never have left him. You've always kept your head down and got on with life. How you survived so many years with him is beyond me."

"He's my husband. I meant those vows."

"You can't keep using that as an excuse. Honestly, Alex, you can't be held to vows you said in good faith decades ago. He has three children with someone else and has deceived you your entire marriage. What are you going to do?"

"I... I'm—"

"You don't have any real intention of leaving him, do you?" Michael sounds cross.

"We can't carry on as we have been."

"As I said, Marina has done you a favour. The children have their own lives now. This is your ejector seat. You need to think about your future."

"Please tell me you are going to leave him, babe," Gerry adds.

"I'm here aren't I?"

"Well, yes. But I know where I'd be if I were you..."

* * *

I lie in the dark with my phone on the side table.

The terror of leaving Conty grips my stomach. How can I be on my own? If there is one thing Conty has been right about, it's that I'm not designed to be alone. All the feminist theories in the world won't change my personality. Yes, standing on my own two feet is possible. Could I develop life skills and be on my own? Of course, yes. But do I want to? No, I need and want to be with a man.

Finally, I give in and grab my phone.

I'm sorry, I type.

I'm going to make you sorry, baby, he replies.

You have a one-track mind.

He makes me laugh.

Just like you. Where are you? I'll come and pick you up.

Not now, I'm staying with friends in the City.

Why not now? You know I don't have any patience.

Like me. It's called ADHD.

We're twins, baby.

Not that again… I settle down into the soft purple haven and put my phone down.

Gerry and Michael are right, but I'm not sure I can leave Conty. He's a good father, and if I'm pregnant, the baby needs a father. No one would believe Conty is the father. I'm tall and blonde, though, so it could take after me. Now, with the leverage of his other family, he might swallow a pregnancy for the sake of peace. He will know the baby isn't his.

I have to do a pregnancy test.

I'll stay at Trevor's for a while until I figure out what to do.

CHAPTER FIFTEEN

The front door bangs against the wall.

Trevor holds me up against the hard metal with his body.

My hands go around his waist, and I pull him into me.

Cold air clings to us.

He moves back to undo my jeans.

I let go of his waist to shrug them down a bit.

His hands slide down into my knickers, and he pushes two fingers up, deep inside me.

"God, that feels so good," I whisper.

My hips move against his hand.

His other hand is on my shoulder, pushing down.

I angle my head up to him.

Light blue eyes meet mine, but he doesn't move to kiss me. I'm tempted to tell him I could look into his eyes forever, but don't.

He moves his hand off my shoulder and up into the back of my hair, holding my head.

"Kiss me," I say.

His face moves down to mine, so we are eye to eye.

His breath is close to my mouth.

The desire to bite him morphs into me pulling against my own hair to kiss him. The fear of igniting his sexual aggression stops me.

Finally, his lips push down on mine.

"I missed you," he says.

"You only saw me a few days ago."

"I still missed you."

"I missed you too."

"Welcome home, baby."

* * *

January has flown by in a haze of domestic bliss, and this morning the flat is flooded with early morning sun.

"I've got to get to work early. My head is already in car-fixing mode. I'll get onto it later," he says, kissing me hard on the lips.

I grab his belt buckle and pull him back.

"Baby, baby, baby, don't do this to me. I've got to go. Later," he says.

I laugh and let go, but I'm upset.

"Your stuff will be here by lunchtime," he calls, heading out of the door.

"What do you mean, my stuff?"

"Can't remember the name of the removal company. I got someone from the office to organise it. I'll work on your divorce later."

"My divorce? We're not at that stage."

"Why do you think that ponce sent you his solicitor's details?" he calls.

The door clicks shut ten seconds later.

Not sure, but I'm going to find out. I pick up my phone and press Conty's number. He'll be sitting in his office surrounded by estate paperwork.

Without so much as a hello, he barks, "Didn't you read my email? My solicitor's details are there?"

"Yes, but I don't understand, Conty. Don't you want to talk this through?"

"After the stunt you've just pulled, my lawyer has instructed me not to talk to you at all."

"What are you talking about?"

"Don't play games with me, Alexandra. Who knows what you're capable of after that."

"What stunt? I called to talk about us."

"Talk to my lawyer."

The phone goes dead.

I have no idea what he's talking about. He can't know about Hayes or Trevor, or he'd have said something. It will be some minor infraction, no doubt. In his world, using the wrong cup is akin to a heinous crime.

Settling down to do anything constructive is beyond me. I'm getting a steady stream of interested clients, but after what happened with Rachel, I need to reset. All over the place isn't an ideal headspace for a therapist. I fucked her husband. I didn't even know his name, let alone his marital status. I met him walking off the gym floor. After we got caught, the manager called him Mikey. It didn't occur to me that Mikey would be her Michael. The incident slipped from my memory completely. I'd have struggled to remember it at all, had Conty not gone on and on about me leaving the gym to spite him. I could hardly tell him I had to leave because I'd got caught fucking another member in the women's changing room.

Rachel and I didn't have regular sessions over the eleven months I was treating her, and there were no signs she knew I'd fucked her husband. By her own admission, the therapy sessions helped. Mikey's sex addiction had been going on long before our brief encounter. The wheels came off our sessions after he disappeared, and she blamed me.

I'm not sure what to do with myself.

I pick up my phone again.

"I've spoken to Conty, and he says I've pulled some stunt."

"I'll sort it out later, baby, I can't talk now. I'm under a car. Go to the local gym and relax. I've signed you up. You can pick up the card at reception."

He's right. I need to focus on something else. I stare out of the window.

My phone beeps.

Annabel told me what happened with Conty. You don't have to do this. There's another way. Can we meet?

I reply, hoping to be let in on the insider intelligence. *Do what? I have no idea what you're talking about*

Can we talk in person? Today?

I spent months and months wanting Hayes to contact me, desperate for the tiniest scrap of attention. Now he wants to meet today.

Now isn't a good time

I throw my phone down on the sofa and walk over to the window.

London spreads out below me. It's been a long time since I lived in the city. I was born here, but you get used to the countryside. Conty and I started our relationship in London, marrying at St Andrew's in Chelsea. The top of the spire might be visible from this high up. I've never understood how knowledge in the present can rewrite the past. Now I can. Demitrious was right. Our whole relationship has been based on a lie.

Our wedding took place over twenty years ago, but I can still picture Marina's face as I walked past her down the aisle to meet Conty. In contrast to everyone else's smiles, she looked shell-shocked. I wondered what was wrong with her. Conty wasn't watching me approach the altar. He was staring off into the pews, and I couldn't turn to follow his gaze. At the time I thought he was searching for his mother, or checking on an elderly relative. Now I'd guess he was trying to comfort Marina. We stood face to face, but he was unmoved, more like he was doing his duty than marrying the woman he loved. He avoided eye contact throughout the service and didn't even look at me as we said our vows. He could have been completing a business deal. I assumed this was his way of dealing with stress.

I waited for him to notice me. Every word of my vows was sincere, and the service moved me. I didn't expect to enjoy the service, but saying those vows was the best part of our wedding day. After the Anglican priest pronounced us man and wife, I kissed him a bit too passionately. He froze and said, 'Steady on, time and place,' or something to that effect. Public displays of affection are frowned upon in his world. Or rather, public displays of affection with me.

Walking out of the church, he didn't take my hand. As we passed Marina, she was wiping tears from her eyes. It's not out of place to cry at a wedding, so no alarm bells rang.

I barely saw Conty during the wedding breakfast. He refused to have an evening reception, calling it vulgar and common. So we had a formal sit-down lunch at a local exclusive tennis club.

Later we had dinner with our close family at a small Italian restaurant. Marina was there, and being his cousin, she sat next to him all night. I tended to my guests. Conty told me he wasn't 'in the market for new friends'. He thought he was too different from them to form any real relationships.

Looking back, his feelings were obvious. He didn't love me in the way he should have. But there was no one for me to compare him against. He was my first real relationship. I was blinded by love. How could I have got choosing a husband so wrong? My brain doesn't experience or read emotions like other people's. But the red flags were unmissable. His attitude to my family, and his judgemental nature, so different to mine, should have ended the relationship before it got serious. Thinking back, it's a miracle we met and stayed together. What did we like about each other?

Our marriage was a blur for ten years while we had babies and got on with life. His hatred of me was there, but in the early days, it was smothered by a baby needing feeding, a toddler needing dressing or an older child needing organising. Funny how Marina had full-time nannies, yet I was left to do pretty much everything alone. Now it makes sense. This suited Conty, as motherhood put me in the background. So Marina was free and did everything with him socially.

Eventually, I came out of the haze of having young children

and rejoined society. And he became more obviously abusive, and I took refuge in other men. Marina was established as a fixture in his life by this point. And I bet they stayed together at his flat in London. I was an inconvenience to them.

How could I have not seen what was coming? They were inseparable.

The door clicks, and someone walks in, probably the cleaner. Trevor has daily help.

"You, again. That's a record, more than a week. It must be serious," Trevor's daughter says with a sneer. "I'm joking about the serious bit, by the way."

"Chelsea, hello. I'm sorry, I didn't know you were coming here."

"Must be his idea of a joke, letting me work here, with you around. Mum has the film crew at home. It's too noisy and busy to concentrate. He's deluded if he thinks I'll ever like you."

"You don't have to be hostile. We can be friends. I have a daughter around your age. What are you studying?"

She walks over and puts her face close to mine.

"You are the deluded one. I will never be your friend. Keep away from me and my father, you gold-digging bitch, or you'll regret crossing me."

The level of hostility floors me.

I back away. "No problem, I'm going."

"Good," she snarls.

CHAPTER SIXTEEN

The gym is close, but I walk slowly, trying to clear my head. The wind whips the hair around my face. A complex of high-end properties overlook the River Thames and stretch back to form a concrete village. Clean grey lines rise up to the sky, and endless glass reflects the bright winter day. A helicopter takes off from the nearby heliport. Most of the residents live here part-time and commute from country mansions.

I stop and lean over the solid grey stone wall, looking down at the freezing, grey expanse of water flowing past. Left and right, bridges connect South London to more affluent parts of the city.

Trevor and I both grew up in Battersea, the wrong side of the tracks, but we never crossed paths. He fully embraces the vibrant and raw energy of being a South Londoner, using it to his advantage in every way; to be cool, to be real and to have come from somewhere. After his father made money and plunged him into one of England's most famous public schools, his strong sense of pride in coming from the hood, and total security in his identity, ironically afforded him complete acceptance. I too drifted into the English public school system but never achieved a seamless merging of the two worlds. Trevor and I mirror each other in many ways.

Chelsea's hostility is understandable, and based on fear. I'm threatening her relationship with her father. Trevor demands an intense level of intimacy, which might account for the strength of her anger and hatred. Good to know the therapist part of my brain is still working. After what happened with Rachel, never working again is a possibility, either because she has reported me, or I can't get back into that headspace.

Rachel still won't answer my messages. I've emailed a couple of times. I pick up my phone, press her name and start walking. I'm going to try one last time. She's giving me no option but to drop it. Her name flashes up on my screen, but it rings and rings. Voicemail clicks in.

"Rachel, I hope you're getting my messages. I wanted to check you are all right, and Michael has been found. Please call me back."

She never does.

Up ahead is a big black sign. *Rampage* is written in jagged sliver graffiti over the entrance to the gym.

The doors open automatically, and I'm hit with a smell like deodorant.

A lady manning the reception smiles at me like she knows me.

My phone rings in my hands, and I back out of the door to answer it. Thank goodness.

"Rachel, I'm so relieved you called back. I've been worried about you."

I move the receiver away from my ear. The torrent of shouting isn't decipherable.

"Rachel, please calm down. Has Michael been found?"

"Yes, you fucking bitch. You destroyed our lives. While I was sitting in your office talking to you, he was forming a relationship with someone else. Stop calling me and keep the fuck away from me."

"Let me help you. Can we meet up? I'm living in London now. We can have coffee."

"Go to hell."

The phone clicks off. In my mind, one of those old red telephones has been smashed down.

My rational brain knows the events in her life are not my fault. But I feel responsible. Michael has left her? That's odd, as there was nothing in his behaviour indicating he'd leave her. Fortunately, she hasn't reported me for misconduct. Not that I did anything wrong by treating her. She deceived me, or I'd never have agreed to see her. I have to let this go.

The gym is predictably slick and ultra-modern. It's part of many facilities attached to the concrete village: a small supermarket, hairdressers, restaurants and a few bars. I dread to think how much membership costs.

The receptionist greets me by name. “Mrs Clarke-Lawrence, welcome. We’ve got your membership card ready.”

“Thank you,” I say.

“If you can sign here.” The receptionist slides a card across the desk. “Mr Porter has taken care of the rest. Enjoy your workout.”

I sign the card. “Thank you.”

“Would you like a tour and personal trainer today?”

“No, I’m good.”

One gym is like the next. And I’ve been to so many. My workouts are automatic now.

I’m already in gym gear, so bypass the changing rooms and head for the gym floor.

Super-fit, glossy clientele in expensive activewear fill the space.

The next forty minutes disappear in a haze of cardio and weight training.

The encounter with Chelsea has faded by the time I’m finished, and I mull over what to do about Rachel. Perhaps I should go to her house.

I head to the drinking fountain to fill up my water bottle.

Parts of the gym are like Badwell House. The shame of what happened there with Rachel’s husband hits me again. I don’t understand why I had sex with a man I’d literally just met. We didn't even know each other's names. There was no thought of anything other than I liked the look of him.

"He's going to chew you up and spit you out like all the others," a voice says. I look up to see a blonde, her head cocked to one side, her long ponytail falling on her tanned shoulder. Her big smile is in contrast to her hostile, blue eyes.

"What?"

"You can drop the dumb bitch act with me. I know what you're about."

It must be Kira or Victoria. They look remarkably similar.

"I don't think so."

My heart compresses in my chest.

She laughs. "You think you're something special with your high society life and title. But once he's played with you, he'll drop you like the piece of shit you are."

A raw nerve is exposed, and I don't have an answer.

"That's enough, ladies." The woman who was manning the reception approaches us.

"I'm going anyway." I head off towards the restaurant.

My legs shake as I stand in the queue. She looked like the woman he was with at the Cedars Christmas party, but I'm not sure. Recognising faces isn't a strong point. Trevor evidently specialises in a certain type of identikit blonde – around five feet ten, with long blonde hair and even, symmetrical features.

This woman can't be more than thirty. I'm a lot older. Unease settles in my stomach. After what Trevor did last year, perhaps she's right. Am I a game to him? And once the reality of a real relationship hits, he'll be off.

No, she's wrong. He's been married and had children. He knows what long-term relationships are about. He's not a thirty-something playboy with no life experience.

The woman from reception arrives beside me. "Sorry about that, Mrs Clarke-Lawrence. I was concerned something like this would happen when Mr Porter signed you up."

"Call me Alex."

"I'm Gabrielle, but everyone calls me Gab. I'm the guest relations manager."

The barista puts my coffee on the counter.

"Here, let me help you." Gab takes my coffee.

I follow her to a small table looking out onto the frozen, deserted outdoor tennis courts.

"Have you just moved to the area?" Gab asks, putting the hot mug down.

"I was born in London, but yes, I'm staying here for the moment."

"London is great. We love it."

"Have you been working here long?" I ask.

"No, not really; we moved to London a few months ago, also

from the country."

"What brought you to London?"

"My fiancé is a freelance personal trainer, and there's more work in London," she explains, "and with my hospitality management experience we found work together."

"Thank you for intervening."

"At this level of service, we get to know and look after our clients. Are you sure you're okay? I think Kira's bark is worse than her bite."

"Yes, I'm absolutely fine."

So it *was* Kira, the woman from the party.

"I guessed it wouldn't be long before she saw you and Trevor together and caused a scene."

"Why?"

"Trevor and Kira trained here together a lot. I think they met on the gym floor. They were an item. Kira is here most days. I couldn't imagine a female friend of Trevor's going down well."

"Sounds like a safe assumption."

"I wasn't expecting her to know who you were, though, so it took me a while to realise what was going on. Do you two know each other?" Gab asks.

"No, we don't. My husband and I have an annual Christmas party, and she was there with Trevor. She must know me that way."

"Husband? You're married?"

"Yes, but we're taking a break. It's complicated."

"I'm sorry, I didn't mean to pry."

"It's okay. I guess you don't get two women arguing over a man on the gym floor very often."

"Oh, you'd be surprised what goes on."

Except I wouldn't be surprised. I can imagine. But she's trying to make me feel better and I appreciate that.

"Thank you again for stepping in."

"No problem. We're here to help. Sorry, I'd better get back to work. Enjoy the rest of your coffee."

Gab heads off towards reception.

I'm surprised Trevor thought it was a good idea to sign me up for this gym, as he has history with a woman here. I should change gyms.

My phone pings. *Can you come to my office this afternoon?*

I'm not playing slutty secretary gets punished again, I reply.

Haha, not that office. I was only at the garage this morning. I'm at Porter Vision now. The head office is on the Strand. We can play slutty secretaries after if you like. See you at 2?

Done, I confirm, before adding, *No slutty secretary.*

CHAPTER SEVENTEEN

The tall glass building dominates the Strand. Porter Vision Security is written in big metallic-grey letters. A neon blue infinity symbol surrounds the words. It must be the company logo. It's slick and striking. I wasn't expecting anything as grand as this. Porter Motor Repairs is a small garage in a rough part of South London. I can still remember Trevor putting on a mock Cockney accent to tell me his heart was in 'mota' cars. He was keen to show me his garage, and we were walking there, through the park, and found ourselves in the derelict toilet. He did tell me about his IT company, and that it was successful. But not quite as stratospherically successful as it is.

The traffic is heavy, and it will take too long for the taxi to turn around.

"Stop here. I can walk across the road."

I jump out and hand the cabbie my card through the window.

"Thanks, Luv."

The cab pulls away.

He can't be summoning me to his office for sex. I'm staying at his flat, so the tap is never turned off. He said we could play slutty secretaries after. After what?

Dodging buses and black cabs, I narrowly avoid bumping into pedestrians as I cross the road. What does he want?

Imposing double doors fit seamlessly together in a wall of glass. The doors slide open automatically so I can walk through. A steady stream of people move around the vast foyer. I head across the white stone floor towards a long grey counter, manned by a small army of men and women wearing black. They all have handheld devices. It's hard to believe Trevor created all this.

It's not clear who you report to on arrival. A woman with short, spiky black hair approaches me. She's tiny, around five foot three, but radiates cocky confidence. Her tight, dark jeans and even tighter black t-shirt cling to her body. A faded leather biker jacket sits over her shoulders.

"Are you here to see Mr Porter?" she asks.

"Yes, he's expecting me at two."

"Mrs Clarke-Lawrence?" A security guard approaches us.

"Yes," I confirm.

"Follow me. I'll take you to the board room."

"How unoriginal, he's usually more creative than that," the woman says.

"What?" I ask her.

"Enjoy your meeting." She walks off, black biker boots

stomping on the floor.

I follow the man to the bank of lifts, and he gets in with me.

"Who was that?" I ask.

Please don't tell me she's another of Trevor's ex-girlfriends.

"Not sure, we get a lot of foot traffic."

With a low mechanical hum, the lift propels us up.

"Does she work here?"

"Not in the building, but I've seen her before. She's likely a client or contractor. There must be over five hundred people working in this building. Hard to remember everyone."

Questioning him further will look odd, so I stop. The lift mirrors are way too clear. I'm hot and sweaty, with my hair still tied up in a ponytail from the gym. Going home to change wasn't an option, not with Chelsea working there.

We must be going to the top. Up and up we go.

The doors open and the security guard ushers me along a sleek modern corridor. Off to the sides are banks of desks. People look up as we go past.

I keep my head down. At the end is another lift.

The security guard presses the up button, and we wait.

It's unlikely she's an ex-girlfriend. She's not remotely Trevor's type. And he has a type, if Kira and I are anything to go by. He's probably right, and she is a contractor of some kind, but she didn't give that impression. Her attitude was hard to place.

The lift pings open, and we emerge into another large foyer with a reception.

The lady at the desk looks up.

"They're in boardroom one."

There's more than one boardroom?

The security guard walks me a short distance to a tall, dark-wood double door.

I shift my weight from foot to foot again and again. Whatever he has in mind must involve sex of some kind.

The security guard knocks.

Trevor opens it.

"Mrs Clarke-Lawrence, Trev."

"Thanks, Rob."

My breath catches, and I stare at his blue eyes, contrasting with the soft charcoal of his smart pinstripe suit. I try not to let my gaze sweep from his black leather brogues up to the spikes of his thick brown hair, pushed over to the side. My eyes rest on his belt, and I don't want to think what I'm thinking.

"You want me to punish you, baby."

"What? No, of course not."

"You just thought about it though."

"Well, maybe… Yes, I did. I – I wasn't expecting to see you in a suit."

"You weren't expecting to see me in a suit?" he repeats, amused.

"Yes, that's not how you left for work this morning." I should shut up, and now.

"You're blushing."

His smile is a lethal weapon all on its own. It's obscene how good he looks in a suit.

"I've just never seen you in a suit," I say, not adding, that I'm tempted to drop to my knees in the doorway.

"We don't have time now, baby."

"For what? I didn't say anything."

"You don't need to. I know what's going on inside your head."

"How?"

"I'm not sure, it's a bit odd. Anyway, we need to get down to business. Now, don't let this freak you out. It's just a meeting."

He opens the doors to an expansive suite of rooms.

Papers are spread out over a section of the large glass tabletop, and a few people in grey suits sit with their heads down. A blank whiteboard covers half the wall. An open door on the other side of the room reveals a kitchen.

A woman with short, heavily layered blonde hair gets up and moves past Trevor. She offers me her hand. "Lady Clarke Lawrence, hello."

I take it. Firm grip.

“I’m Cressida Archibald-Bronlow, from Pilkington Baron.”

Her cut-glass tones could shatter the windows.

Pilkington what? This sounds serious. And Lady; she’s done her homework. Is he still pissed at me for going to accuse him of rape? And going to get me back with some legal summons? This feels like a trap.

Two women and a man introduce themselves next, but my mind is racing so fast, their names blur into a haze.

Everyone ignores that I’m dressed for a workout.

“Let’s all take a seat,” Trevor says.

“What’s going on?” I ask.

“This is going to be a difficult time for you, Lady Clarke-Lawrence. But we are here to take the pain away,” Cressida begins.

Not Lady again. I wish she’d stop calling me that.

“What do you mean? Call me Alex.”

“There are two separate processes. The divorce from Lord Constantine can be completed quickly. You will be a free woman in about sixteen weeks, if not sooner. However, the financial settlement could take more time and that will need to be agreed upon before we can legally divorce you. And we can disregard the spurious complaint about harassment. They have no proof.”

I'm stunned.

"Divorce? No, hold on a minute—"

Trevor cuts in and presses an intercom. "This is going to be a long meeting. Can someone send up coffee and those chocolate brownies? Oh, and call Morty, tell him to send over dinner."

"What spurious complaint? I spoke to Conty this morning."

"You spoke to Lord Constantine today?" Cressida presses me for clarification.

"Yes, and he accused me of pulling some stunt."

"Lady Clarke-Lawrence, as your legal representative, I strongly advise you not to enter into independent discussions with Lord Constantine. From now on, please communicate via your legal team. In the first instance, that will be me."

"My legal team? Stop, this is all going too fast. I don't want any of this. What is he accusing me of?"

"He has requested a restraining order after a slaughtered lamb was nailed to the door of Cedars Estate, your marital home. The word 'crow' was painted in blood."

"Oh my goodness, really?"

"I'm afraid so. A restraining order is heavy-handed. They have absolutely no evidence you were the perpetrator."

I'm aghast, and sit down. The poor lamb. I run my hands down the sides of my face.

"Come on, baby, you can't let his lies get to you. He probably did it himself. I wouldn't put it past the sick fuck," Trevor says.

"I would never… Our children could have seen it. Who would do something like that? Hurt a lamb…"

"Lady Clarke-Lawrence, I'm sorry this is so distressing for you, but we need to go through your financial position in some depth. The divorce will be straightforward, as Lord Constantine's legal team has indicated he won't contest grounds of infidelity."

"He has admitted infidelity?"

Alarm rises fast. This isn't like Conty.

Cressida looks confused for a second.

Trevor answers, "He can hardly deny he's got another family. And you've just caught him in bed with the mother of his other children. At least he's giving you that, baby. You didn't do anything wrong."

"He's agreed to a divorce? There must be some mistake. He doesn't believe in divorce. He'd never agree," I say.

"Yes, we've settled on how to proceed. I've worked with his legal team before, and the divorce will be a smooth process. We will serve him immediately and start proceedings. This is a paperwork exercise," Cressida says.

"What did you think was going to happen, baby?" Trevor says gently.

"I don't know, but not this. I'm not getting divorced, and I'm hardly the innocent one. We've been fu—" I stop short. "We've been seeing each other for a year. You attacked Conty. And you're currently being investigated for revenge porn… against me. No, I can't do it."

I get up and head to the door.

Mild concern registers on Cressida's face. "You attacked Lord Constantine?"

Trevor stands up. "Don't worry, Cress. I didn't hit him. He won't press charges."

"I'm pleased to hear it," she replies.

"We need to talk about the revenge porn misunderstanding, but let's focus on the divorce first," Trevor says.

"Agreed. I'm going to have to pass you on to my colleague. The charges have serious implications. You're going to need an experienced criminal barrister. We have the best, and she'll be in touch."

"Criminal charges? Don't tell me you've been charged with revenge porn?" I say, and sit back down.

"Okay, I won't," Trevor says.

"We need to wait for the courier before we can go through the disclosure documents. I'll give you two a moment," Cressida says to us.

"My office is opposite, Cress. Go and have a coffee."

Cressida and her team leave us alone.

"You could go to prison." Tears form behind my eyes, and I choke them back.

Trevor puts his hands on my shoulders and moves down, so we are eye to eye.

"Don't worry. I'll deal with the consequences."

"But I am worried." I want to say, *you can't leave me*, but my throat constricts and no words come out.

The grief and fear that getting divorced prompts, is overwhelming. Tears fall down my face.

"Getting divorced isn't a walk in the park, baby."

"Yes, but I thought he'd at least fight for me. Why does he want to get shot of me so quickly that he'd agree to grounds of adultery?"

"He's a prick and doesn't deserve you."

I put my arms around Trevor's waist, and my head on his chest.

His heartbeat, loud, strong and slow, is comforting.

He strokes my hair.

There's no going back, anyway.

* * *

I slump over the desk and put my head on my arms. It must be past eight. My head whirls with words I've never heard before and never want to hear again: decree nisi, decree absolute, consent order, discovery, deposition, dissolution. On and on the meeting went, making my head thick with confusion and pain. I wish the situation would go away. The finality is jarring.

I walk over to the window. The reflection in the glass is sobering.

My lifeless, limp hair is plastered to my ashen face. Pain is etched into the muscles, and I look harsh, jaded and old.

The theatre district below hums with life. People, going about their business.

Trevor has gone to his office to finish some work.

I thought Gerry was scary, but this lawyer was on a whole new level. This reminds me to message Gerry and ask if she's heard of Cressida.

Do you know Cressida Archibald-Bronlow from Pilkington Baron? Trevor has hired her as my divorce lawyer.

Wow. I didn't think she was taking on new clients. Apex Predator, that one. Wouldn't like to come up against her. You're in safe hands. And she's a safe pair of hands too.

Haha. I'd hardly call Trevor a safe pair of hands. He actually told her at one point, he was going to take me home and spank me hard later. She didn't bat an eyelid. He scares me.

Let's hope he means it. Lucky you. Sorry, got to go am pulling an all-nighter. Court tomorrow.

I don't reply.

An older blonde woman arrives, carrying a white tablecloth and cutlery.

"Hi, I'm Kitty, Trevor's secretary. Can I get you anything?"

Judging by her soft tone, she can sense how shell-shocked I feel.

"Time machine. Sorry, no, I'm okay, thank you for asking."

"We could all do with one of those, but as you get older, quite honestly, you wonder why you made it all so hard," she replies. "It will be all right, love."

"Thank you."

I don't know why I said that. There's no question I'd have done anything differently. I've never regretted marrying Conty. How could I? Our marriage produced our beautiful children. Acceptance is the key. This isn't how I wanted it all to turn out. But fighting against the tide is only going to exhaust and kill me. I have to make peace with whatever happens going forward. Like most things in life, easier said than done.

Kitty transforms the boardroom into a dining room in record time. She's evidently done this before.

Trevor appears a few minutes later with a chilled bottle of Sauvignon Blanc and an ice bucket.

He's ordered half the menu. A selection of seafood dishes with potato three ways and sautéed greens are set out in front of us.

"Take as much as you want, Kit," Trevor says.

"I'm good thanks, Trev. Going for a curry. Not sure what time I'll be in tomorrow. So see ya when I see ya," she replies, giving him a wave as she shuts the board room door.

He gives her a thumbs-up and turns his attention to me.

"Hungry?"

"Not really," I say.

"You will be when you start eating this."

He's right. One mouthful and I'm ravenous.

We sit in silence. It's not awkward. More a companionable quiet. Conty and I sat in silence a lot, but his was a cold, disapproving silence. Like he couldn't bring himself to talk to me after my last heinous mishap. Being me was enough to warrant his disgust.

I glance at Trevor. The contrast between his pretty-boy face and huge size hits me every time I look at him. He's a combination that shouldn't be possible.

I'm subdued by the seriousness of dissolving so many years of my life, but appreciate him sorting it out. People talk about getting divorced all the time. It's an everyday event. But it is different when you are the one involved in it. And I'm scared by the lamb incident. Who would hurt a poor lamb and write the word *Crow*?

"Why write the word Crow?" I ask Trevor.

"You're not still thinking about that, are you?"

"How could I not? Don't you think killing a lamb is serious?"

"No, not really, and I don't give a fuck that someone has got it in for that slimy cunt. We've all got our enemies. But I do care he's trying to pin it on you."

"But why a bird name?"

"How should I know? Because they are evil and eat each other's eggs, babies, or whatever. Ask a bird watcher or twitcher or whatever you call those people. I think we should forget about him and concentrate on us."

"It's an ornithologist," I say.

"One of those too. I'll set up a meeting with a world expert asap," he jokes.

"You're so funny."

"Are you laughing at me?"

He pushes his chair back and pulls me over, so I'm sitting on his lap.

For a second, I think he's going to make good on his promise to spank me, and I tense up. But he pulls me closer and cuddles me.

"It will be okay, baby," he whispers in my ear. "This shit show will pass, and happily ever after will be left."

He's not much bigger than Hayes, but he feels more solid.

Being held by Hayes feels completely safe, like he'd never hurt me. With Trevor, there's an edge, like I'm never quite sure what he's going to do next. Why am I thinking of Hayes? We never go anywhere. And the irony is, he's never around. Trevor is here for me.

I put my arms around Trevor's neck and rest my head on his shoulder. How can I be scared and comforted by him at the same time?

He strokes my hair and holds me tight.

CHAPTER EIGHTEEN

I stretch out in bed and prop the pillow under my head. The bed is warm, and my body sinks into the mattress. The soft duvet moulds around my naked body. My lower stomach glows where Trevor put his hand as he reached over to kiss me goodbye. He went out early. The contentment and sense of love is soothing, and for a moment I'm tempted to go back to sleep. Usually, I can't wait for first light, so I can spring out of bed and take sanctuary in the gym. But since I've been staying with Trevor, all I want to do is sleep, listening to his heartbeat, strong and steady with mine.

I can't explain what's happening between Trevor and me. Or the connection between us, which is as inexplicable and indescribable, as it has proven indestructible. Just one of the events we've been through should have been enough to stop a relationship from developing. Yet we are like magnets pulling together. Trevor has some crazy ideas about twin flames and the red thread of fate, but I've never believed in concepts like that. In my therapy practice, I've found romantic theories that tie you to another person are delusions that cause pain. And are used as justification for staying in toxic situations.

That's what I did with Hayes; stayed in a situation that was detrimental to me for much longer than I should have done.

Meeting him was like being hit by a thunderbolt. At the time, I didn't identify the feeling as love, but in his arms, for the first time in forever, I felt something. I carried on like a love-struck teenager for months. Hayes changed everything. Whatever was between us is technically over, yet I have no sense of closure. Perhaps Hayes is right and we do need to talk.

I'd better jump out of bed soon. I flick my laptop open to run through my morning routine of weather, news and emails. I'm going to look up crows, to gain insight into why the person who killed the lamb at Cedars would write *crow* in blood.

The news loads.

The headline reads, *LATE NIGHT LIASON AT PORTER'S STRAND OFFICE.* I click on the link so I can read the text. *Trevor Porter was spotted leaving his office hand in hand with a new blonde. Porter, who only weeks ago was marched to a waiting police car for questioning over an undisclosed sex crime, wasn't letting his legal woes stop him from business as usual, as he put on an amorous display with married Lady Alexandra Clarke-Lawrence. The loved-up pair couldn't take their eyes off each other as they made their way hand in hand to a waiting car.*

I can't read any more and close my laptop. What's Conty going to say?

.I type Trevor a message: *Where are you? You need to come back now.*

I'll be back soon. What's the matter?

We're in the news again. And this time I'm named. I thought you sorted this out?

Oh, that. Yes, I sorted it.

Well, you clearly didn't. You've seen the article and didn't say anything?

They can't prove anything, baby. So what if we were seen together? My lawyer will take a look, but there is not much they can do legally. I do have a sexy new blonde. And we are loved up.

FFS. This has to stop. You might not care what people think, but I do. My children might read it.

Calm down. I'll be back soon to talk. Or I can just fuck you until you can't think of anything else.

I type, *I was wrong, Sex isn't the answer to everything.*

It's not?

I laugh.

My phone vibrates, and I pick up the call.

"Hysterical, right?" Gerry laughs. She has couriered me over an outfit to wear to her party tonight.

"Sorry, the parcel hasn't arrived yet. Someone is knocking now. I'll call you back."

I grab Trevor's t-shirt off the floor and throw it over my naked body. The white cotton hangs down to the middle of my thighs.

The doorman hands me a square cardboard box.

I dread to think what Gerry has sent. The box is small for an outfit. Her fiftieth birthday party is fancy dress and has a uniform theme. Trevor should be getting his outfit now. But what he's doing is anybody's guess. He's been gone a while.

The box tips to the side under my arm. Something slides inside. Sounds like an object. I kick the door closed with my foot.

I put the box on the kitchen work surface.

The silky red ribbon comes undone immediately. The box is sealed with packing tape, so I angle the kitchen knife down and over the seams underneath. Shiny brown tape splits beneath the sharp blade. I pull open the flaps and peer in. Must be a leather bikini or something that will barely cover me.

My body tenses. I force my breathing to start again.

I back away from the box.

What is that?

The low edge of the glass coffee table hits the side of my leg.

I topple over one side, and my palm hits the table to right myself.

My brain won't compute what's in the box.

The floor drops away; I feel like I'm treading on thin air. Everything around me is untethered.

With the tips of my fingers, I pull open the flaps again.

The air stays held in my lungs.

Tiny muscular tubes are spilt in a deep red pile, strewn outside the matted brown fur. Its little mouth gasps again. The creature is alive but disembowelled. Around the dying rodent lie three little mice with their heads cut off. The heads aren't in the box.

Trevor walks up behind me.

"Hey, what's the matter? The doorman gave me this for you." He's holding a long, white cardboard box, with a pink ribbon.

My hand clamps over my mouth. I bend over for a second, to stop the vomit.

"What is that?" he asks.

I can't speak.

He takes the box and looks in. He doesn't flinch or register any emotion.

Fear makes my eyes water, but there are no tears.

Without a word, he closes the lid and strides out of the door.

The box is gone.

I flick the switch on the kettle and stare at its chrome surface. My face stretches, distorted in the reflective metal.

The rush of electricity through the elements makes a harsh whooshing noise.

I rub my eyes. The image of those poor creatures is illumined in the black of my mind.

The tea burns my lips and throat. I wince, trying to swallow.

Gerry's parcel sits on the kitchen top. The last thing I want to do is go to a party.

The door slams, and Trevor is back. "I'm sorry you had to see that."

"Where did the box come from? That animal was still breathing. The doorman must have seen something. He handed it to me."

"The doorman doesn't speak English. He said, a woman."

"What woman?"

"He doesn't know her. I asked what she looked like and he pointed to his head. Whatever that means."

"The universal sign for crazy?"

"I don't think so. He picked up his hair."

"He must mean she looks like him? Short, dark hair? Is he Spanish?"

"Not sure, possibly. I have a lot of enemies, Alex. Let's forget about it."

"How can you say that? Didn't you see what someone had done to those poor animals? It's sick." The words barely make it out of my mouth. "And it must have been done minutes before, as the animal was still alive." I narrowly avoid retching at the thought. "I can't just forget about it."

"No point in getting wound up."

"It must be the same person who slaughtered the lamb at Cedars." Panic now courses through my body. "Somebody is out to get me."

"It's not you, honey. This is a coincidence. That's all."

"I don't buy it. Someone is targeting me. Harming animals is a truly awful sign, and every piece of research points to escalation. They will try to harm a person."

"Put the mug down. You're going to shake tea everywhere."

He takes the hot drink off me and puts his arms over my shoulders.

"We have to go to the police," I say.

"I don't think the police will be able to do much. But we can report it if that will make you feel better. Why don't you go to the gym or for a walk, clear your head?"

* * *

I make my way to the gym. The Saturday morning streets are busy, but everything around me is a blur. My head swarms with half-formed thoughts I can't make whole. It must be Marina, but why? What could she gain from hurting an animal so horribly? An act like that is for hate's sake as opposed to instrumental. Although, Conty did blame me for what happened at Cedars. That might have pushed him over the line with getting divorced.

Rachel could be behind a stunt like this. Her hostility continues to be staggering. And she did say I'd ruined her babies' lives. But how would she know where I live? Surely reporting me for misconduct would be better revenge.

No, it must be Marina. Demetrios was right; she is unhinged and will stop at nothing where Conty is concerned. But how would she know I'm staying at Trevor's? They think I'm staying with Gerry and Michael.

The three-minute walk flashes by like seconds.

I push through into the gym. Gabby waves from reception as I go past.

The gym floor is unusually quiet for a Saturday. No sign of Kira, thank goodness. Maybe she did it. Sounds like she was invested in her relationship with Trevor and thinks she knows him, but a stunt like that is beyond jealousy. The killing of animals makes me think a man is responsible. Women don't tend to harm little animals; a bit of hostile stalking, maybe, but what someone did to those poor animals is sick. Maybe Trevor is right, and it's to do with him. Anyone could be the culprit. We might not know them.

The dashboard on the cross trainer starts counting down from twenty minutes.

My muscles won't work properly, and my legs are shaky. Each step is an effort. Going to the gym has been a mistake.

What's wrong with me? I can't work out. I press the stop button. It's too hard with no energy.

Kira appears and leans against the machine.

Oh great.

"Something wrong?" she snarls.

A rush of nausea makes the world shift around me. I'm dizzy. Her face blurs in front of me.

I use my last bit of energy to rush to the loo. The cubicle door stays open behind me. The vomit forces up from my stomach and out of my mouth. My stomach clenches with each involuntary retch.

"You okay?" Gabby puts her hand on my back.

"Yes, sorry."

She hands me a tissue.

"Bad morning?"

"You could say that."

I head over to the sink and wash my hands.

"Is Kira bothering you again? I saw her follow you in."

"No, it's not her. She did speak to me but—" I stop. "She followed me into the gym?"

"Yes, you didn't see her?"

"No, I—"

"I've spoken to the manager, and we're going to give her a warning. And ban her from approaching you again."

"I've got to go home."

CHAPTER NINETEEN

"How are you feeling?" Trevor shouts from the TV room.

I close the door. "Kira did it."

"Did what?"

"Kira is behind the slaughtered animals. The receptionist told me she walked in behind me. And then Kira asked me if something was wrong. I thought I was going to faint on the cross-trainer. And she—"

"You nearly fainted on the cross-trainer?"

"Yes, sort of. I was dizzy and then vomited."

"Vomited? You're not pregnant, are you?"

I freeze for a second.

"Sorry, I shouldn't be joking," he continues. "I'll talk to her."

"No, I don't want you going anywhere near her."

"Are you jealous, baby?"

"No, I. Just. No." He's right, I'm jealous. I don't want him interacting with her. "The manager of the gym is going to give her a warning about approaching me. So you don't need to."

"Has she been hassling you?"

"No, not really, just a few comments."

"I'm pretty sure killing animals isn't her bag. Unless it's for the latest handbag. Anything is possible then."

"You think this is a joke? The image of those poor animals

is branded in my memory. I can't stop thinking about how horrific it must have been for them. How can anyone hurt little creatures?"

"I know it was a shock, baby. I'm sorry. Let's watch a movie and then get ready for the party."

He comes over and leans down, cuddling me.

My arms go up his back, and I put my head on his chest.

"You're right, there's nothing we can do today," I say.

He takes my hand, and we head over to the sofa.

"Jump on."

I crawl over the sofa and settle down.

He grabs a blanket and lays it over me.

"Want popcorn?"

"No thanks."

"No popcorn? Now we are in a crisis."

He sits next to me and puts his arm up.

I fit underneath and snuggle in close to him.

"You'll have seen this, but you can never get enough of how funny this movie is."

The big screen springs into life, and Trevor scrolls through until he finds *The Wedding Crashers.*

"No, I haven't seen it."

"What? You're in for a treat. It's got the best marriage proposal I've ever seen."

Conty tends to frown on popular culture. I've seen just about every opera and ballet, but movies, not so many.

I watch the movie through a thick veil of dread, sadness and fear. I can see the jokes are clever and funny, but I'm not experiencing the emotions I know they should generate.

Trevor laughs and laughs.

His carefree laughter and physical proximity are helping. He makes me feel safe.

Finally, the closing credits roll.

I go to the kitchen for a glass of water, saying, "I'm heading for a bath. If it wasn't my closest friend, I'd cancel."

The champagne cork pops in Trevor's hand. He pours me a glass. "Take this with you and relax. I'm going to take your mind off everything when you get out. And we're going to have fun tonight."

* * *

Finally, I open the parcel Gerry sent. A short, black-and-white-striped dress with a matching cap lays on red tissue paper. She's included a black leather dog collar which has a long chain with a ball on the end. I'm meant to carry the ball around. I'm a convict. This is her idea of a joke.

I stare at the steaming water as it rushes out of the tap. Turning it off is an effort. Every movement is laboured from the heavy emotion settled on me.

My gym gear is tighter than usual, and peeling it off hurts.

The glass of champagne sits on the table next to me. I've taken a sip or two. I can barely touch alcohol at the moment.

Trevor is playing an 80s compilation, and Human League's 'Fascination' comes from the speakers in the ceiling.

He's forgotten the sick scene in the box and is carrying on like nothing happened. How can he be so blasé about someone killing animals? The movie helped a bit, but every time I'm left with myself, the terror-stricken face of the little animal taking what could only be its last breath, fills my head. Who in their right mind would slaughter a mouse and her babies? I assume it was female, and they were her babies, but the truth is, I'm not even sure they were mice. Could have been a rat or some other kind of rodent.

The still water separates when I step in and sink down low. My neck hurts so I rest it back on the rim of the bath. Lights from the ceiling blur my vision. Tears form but don't fall. My life is unrecognisable, and I'm scared. Scared of my marriage ending. How can I cope without Conty? I don't know who I am. I haven't felt the urge to sleep with other men since I've been living with Trevor, but it's only been a few months, and that's been my modus operandi for so long I'm scared I will fall back into it. And I'm scared of Trevor, and the way I feel when I look into his eyes. He says *I love you*, but that's not the issue. I feel romantic love for him too. What scares me isn't love. Love is the tip of the iceberg. There's something deeper between us that I don't understand. The trauma of seeing those animals is making me crazy. I need to stop thinking nonsense and get ready for the party.

I grab a towel and step onto the fluffy white mat.

Trevor shocked me, joking I was pregnant. I survey my body in the full-length mirror, turning to the side to look at my stomach. I'm reassured there are no signs of pregnancy. But... that line of thought isn't helping as it would be too early to be showing, anyway. I've always stayed slim during pregnancy. Even at six months pregnant, my bumps were barely noticeable in my clothes. I'd have to be naked for people to notice. I'm clearly not pregnant. Still no period, though. I could be menopausal. The average age is fifty-two, but it varies. After the party, I will do the test so I can tick this worry off my list.

I slip on black lace knickers but don't bother with a bra. The dress skims my thighs but isn't indecent. I give my hair a quick blast with the dryer. Long, thick blonde strands hang down my back in waves. My hair is amazing at the moment.

Even in the stripy cap, I look indecent. Adding skyscraper red stiletto heels tips the outfit over the edge. I don't bother with tights. It will be freezing, but we are going from the car to Gerry's flat. I won't be outside for long. I wonder if I can get away with not wearing the dog collar. Second thoughts – I might as well. Adds to the convict, prisoner look. I make my eyes a little darker and add some red lipstick.

Goodness knows what Trevor is wearing. He's been in and out all afternoon; the caff, his brothers and his beloved motor shop.

I step out of the bedroom, and Trevor is in silhouette against the London skyline. He's in uniform.

CHAPTER TWENTY

My heels click on the floor, and Trevor turns around.

Neither of us moves. We stare at each other.

In front of me is a police officer. A truncheon and handcuffs hang off his belt. He's clean-shaven. The uniform is authentic, but on him, totally indecent, like a stripper.

I smile at him.

He doesn't smile back. His light blue eyes move from my fuck-me shoes up to the stripy cap.

There's no discernible sign of appreciation. His head tilts to one side.

The last time I was on the receiving end of the brutal expression on his pretty-boy face, I ended up in an STD clinic covered in so many bruises, that even the doctor was alarmed. Fast forward a year, and here we are.

A flash of fear momentarily freezes me. "Okay, let's go," I say, keen to get some people between us.

We both walk to the door.

He gets there first and puts his hand high, on the cold metal door, barring my way.

His aftershave, deodorant, or soap reaches me. Not sure how he always smells so good.

I breathe deeply.

"Are you telling me what to do?"

"No, would I do that?" I joke.

"You think ordering me around is funny?"

"Come on, Trevor. I don't want to be late. I'm not in the mood for your kinky shit."

"What did you just say?" His voice is low.

"I'm not playing games. Today has been awful. I can't forget about that parcel and—"

"And, what? I'm not playing games either."

He flicks the handcuffs around my wrist in one quick moment.

If I was going to object, it's too late.

"Nice bracelet," he says.

I'm wearing the diamond bracelet from the Tiffany advent calendar.

"Haha, now let's leave. We don't have time for this."

"I say what we have time for," he says.

He's serious. Here we go… I'm not in the mood.

He grabs my other wrist and pulls my arm behind me, putting it in the other handcuff. He leans over me and kisses my shoulder.

I shiver and lift my head up to kiss him.

He doesn't kiss me.

"You want me to kiss you?"

"Is that a trick question? Yes, of course, I want you to kiss me."

Okay, now he's getting my attention. My body is overriding me and saying yes. I suppose we could have a quickie before we leave for the party. Be fashionably late.

"Don't talk to me like that."

He walks me over to the kitchen table. My hands are cuffed behind my back. They must be made of real metal as they are heavy and cut into my wrists.

"So what are you going to do about it," I say, warming to the game.

Exciting; he's going to fuck me over the kitchen table. I can dig that.

A chain hangs off the collar around my neck. And he picks up the link of metal and pulls my face up towards him.

His lips meet mine, and his tongue pushes into my mouth.

He's so good at kissing, I'm lost. Every time he touches me I'm gripped with a lust that knows no bounds.

"Get on your knees," he says.

I salivate at the thought of running my tongue over his cock. I bend my knees and sink down. My face moves towards his crotch, and I bite the rough material and smile up at him.

"What are you doing? Did I say you could go near my cock?"

He pulls a chair out and sits down.

"No," I say, now unsure what's going on. "But—"

"Get over my knees."

"No. Are you crazy? Absolutely not, no. Just no," I say.

There is no way I'm getting over his knees. I close my eyes, not wanting to accept what he has in mind. At least he's still got his belt on. It could be worse.

I'm unnerved. I'm not sure what he'll do if I object. Perhaps a bit of spanking might be fun, especially if he'll fuck me after.

Still, I don't move.

"When are you going to learn to do what I tell you?"

His hand goes across my cheek, hard enough to sting. I take a sharp intake of breath, shocked he's slapped me without warning.

He grabs my hair and drags me up, forcing me over his knees.

"That hurt; I was going to do it." Wetness spreads between my legs.

"Not fast enough, baby. Don't pretend you don't like me putting my hand across your face and pulling your hair. I bet you just got really wet."

How does he know that?

"No, I'm not," I protest.

Not satisfied with my position, he moves me further up over his knees.

I'm still in my dress, but the position is exposing and maximises vulnerability.

He presses his finger to the back of my knickers.

"You just lied to me."

My breathing gets heavier. "Come on, baby, touch me harder, put your fingers inside me." I attempt to shift my body back onto his fingers.

"You're embarrassingly wet already, and I've barely touched you. You've fucked just about any man you've taken a second look at, yet in my hands, you act like an amateur who can't please me."

He tips me over the edge.

"You've got to fuck me." I start squirming over his lap, out of control and so desperate to feel his cock inside me, I'd do just about anything. "Come on, Trevor, give me your best shot."

He moves his fingers out and leans over me.

"This is not exciting me at all."

"I'm going to suck your cock so good, and you're going to pump your hot cum down my throat. And I'm going to swallow every bit of you while you shudder deep down my throat. Getting excited now?"

"Not even close."

I'm nearly panting, he's got me so wound up. "Let me suck your cock."

He doesn't say anything.

I squeeze my legs together and try to rub myself on his lap.

He slides his hand up my dress and moves his palm over my back.

His knees are wide, so the position isn't uncomfortable, and I stretch my back. "That feels so good. Come on, baby, let me make you cum."

He doesn't reply. His hand slides into my knickers again and over the contours of my ass.

"I love the way you run your hands over me," I say.

"You're on the verge of an orgasm, aren't you?"

"Just keep going, baby, keep going." He's right, I'm going to have an orgasm any second.

He pulls the stretchy material of my knickers back. His fingers move lower.

"When we met the lawyers at my office, you wanted me to hit you with my belt, didn't you?"

I push my body up, ignoring how it forces the metal into my wrists.

"No."

"Yes, you did. You wanted me to take you into the board room, and in front of those lawyers, pull your pants down, put you over my knee and spank your ass until you were so sore you couldn't sit still during the meeting."

"I can't believe you just said that. That would be so humiliating. You wouldn't really do that, would you?"

"Yes, I would and you would have enjoyed it."

"No, I wouldn't. I'd hate that."

"Are you lying to me, again?"

He stops touching me.

"Well, it did cross my mind." I change tack in the hope he will start touching me again.

"You're seriously wet already, baby. I'm not going to touch you anymore."

"Please, just one more time."

I lift my hips up, and my ass closer to his face.

He rubs me from behind in one soft stroke, and his finger slips from my clit back down again.

The pleasure it generates is blinding.

"Have you been fantasising about playing slutty secretaries in my office?"

"No."

"Stop lying to me. I can read your mind."

He pushes one of his fingers a little way inside me.

I can't take it anymore. "I'm going to come. You've got to fuck me, baby."

He doesn't reply.

I need him to fuck me now. The intensity is unbearable.

He pulls his finger out and runs his hand over my ass again.

His hand is so big it covers my whole ass.

"Tell me the truth."

The pleasure is at a peak but doesn't tip over the edge into a full-blown orgasm, despite me writhing around over his lap.

"If you don't stay still, I'm going to stop doing anything to you."

I stop moving and try to stabilise my breathing.

"Yes, I think a lot about what you did in your office. Now, please fuck me."

He pulls my dress up until it is bunched in the middle of my back. My cuffed hands rest high on the material, and the metal digs in further.

I push my hips up, desperate for him to touch me again.

He pulls my knickers down until they are stretched on my thighs.

I'm beyond caring about the humiliation. Every nerve ending in my body is fired up to exploding point.

He runs his hand over my ass again, so softly I can barely feel it.

I arch my back as far as I can, to push my ass up towards him.

Again, his hand makes a slow circle over the contours of my body.

The urge for him to touch me harder is sudden. “Spank me, baby,” I say, desperate, worried he’s going to change his mind and do what he’s threatened and stop.

There’s silence for a second.

“I need you to hurt me, baby.” Where is this coming from?

“Why?” He moves his fingers between my legs and applies soft pressure.

“Keep going, that feels good.”

I flex my body against his hand. The sexual pleasure builds again, trapping energy between my legs. The desire for him to rub me is intense. I frantically move my body.

“I said keep still. I asked you a question.”

“What?” I say, unable to engage my brain.

He takes his hand out. “Why should I spank you?”

What is the right answer? Please don’t let him stop. Does he want me to say I’ve been bad, is it for his pleasure? I don’t know. “Because I need it.”

“Good answer.”

His hand hits my ass hard.

The slap rings in my ears. I take a sharp intake of breath from the shock and relief.

He brings his hand down again, harder.

“Fuck that hurts.” How can his hand hurt this much? He’s hit me so hard it doesn’t sting for a second. I wasn’t expecting a spanking to hurt this much.

"That's the point."

Again and again, he slaps me.

My ass feels like it's on fire. I screw my eyes tight shut. "Oww."

"You're going to learn the hard way I'm in charge."

Don't panic, don't panic. "I'm sorry," comes out of my mouth on autopilot.

He's going to stop soon. I hold my breath for a second as my body is shifted forward into his knees by the hard slaps.

The burning on my skin intensifies. "I'm sorry," I say again.

He stops for a second and rubs the hot skin.

My body adjusts. This isn't so bad.

His fingers reach the back of my neck, and he grips my hair, holding my head down and keeping me still at the same time.

"I'm going to make you sorry." His voice is cold.

He brings the palm of his hand down so hard across my ass, the sound is deafening.

The pain explodes in a flash of white.

My body automatically pushes up.

He holds me still with one hand. The other moulds into my flesh as he follows the slap through.

The adrenaline rush allows me to force my head to the side, so I can talk. "Ow," I scream.

He ignores me and keeps putting the palm of his hand over my ass, again and again.

That was clearly the warm-up act, and this is the main event.

He tightens his grip on my head and pushes my face down, so I can't scream.

Fast, hard slaps come again and again.

The pleasure between my legs builds, and I clench my thighs together.

"I'm going to come."

"No, you're not."

He stops for a second.

My breath is hard and fast.

"Oh baby, I love you," I say.

He hits me again, harder.

The pain is blinding. My mind empties to nothing.

He loosens his grip.

I manage to say, "That really hurts."

He keeps going.

The pain is almost unbearable, with his heavy hand hitting me again and again. The skin burns red and hot.

The tears start. For a second, the spanking stops feeling sexual. And something has been unlocked.

"I'm sorry," I cry.

"It's okay, let it out," he says.

I try to stop crying but can't. The release washes everything away.

He spanks me again and again.

Snot is forced out of my nose, I'm crying so hard. I go limp and can't take any more.

Finally, he stops and pulls me up.

I stand in front of him, shocked. Tears stream down my face.

He is calm and in control. I can't detect sexual satisfaction.

Is this feeling humiliation? I've never felt sexual humiliation before. My mind is clear, and I'm relieved. Relieved?

"Now go and clean yourself up," he says, turning me around.

He unlocks the handcuffs.

I rub my wrists.

"You've got to fuck me now, baby?" I say. Sexual pleasure floods back through the punished flesh.

"No, I don't."

"You can't do that and not fuck me?"

"Yes, I can. Now go and sort yourself out, or we're going to be even later for the party."

He doesn't help me pull up my knickers, which have fallen

to my ankles, or pull down my dress, stretched over my tummy.

I walk towards the bathroom.

"And one more thing, baby. If I think you've wanked yourself off in that bathroom, there will be no party, and I'll spend the night spanking your beautiful ass until you understand that *I* say when you come."

I'm dumbstruck and say nothing.

He's read my mind. That is what I would have done, wanked myself off. I don't want to take the chance of him thinking I've done it. He's very believable, issuing threats like that.

Gerry will laugh her ass off if I have to admit we didn't make her fiftieth birthday because…

He's smiling when I come out of the bathroom.

I'm clear-minded and relaxed, but I need to come.

There isn't time. We have to leave.

I suppose it makes a change from the sick, abusive shit Conty used to pull every time we were about to leave for an event.

"I love you too, honey. And you look beyond beautiful, by the way," he says as we walk out of the door.

CHAPTER TWENTY-ONE

We stand waiting for the lift to take us down to the car. A police officer and convict are reflected in the polished chrome. He's almost exactly a foot taller than me.

He picks up my hand and looks deep into my eyes.

The coldness is gone, and the blue is lit from behind by warm light.

I smile and link my fingers through his. The monumental release of suppressed negative energy makes me light and free. An overwhelming contentment floods every cell in my body.

The lift door pings open.

We walk in together.

A round red sign illuminates *Down*.

The door swooshes shut, and he moves towards me.

My arms go around him, and my head rests on his chest.

In his arms, holding me tight, reality fades away.

We merge into one. There's no separation, not between us or anything in the Universe. Our consciousness expands to complete peace, utter joy and pure love. There's nothing else. And it's simple.

The moment could be forever as time distorts around us.

Ding, and the door slides open with a low, mechanical whoosh. Our focus returns to the world and our physical bodies.

We pull back from each other.

He's smiling at me.

Did he spike me with some kind of mind-altering drug? I try to cling to the moment we've just experienced. It's like an altered state of consciousness. I want to explain the feeling, but it defies logic.

"Your car is waiting, Mr Porter."

The doorman pulls me further back to reality and going to the party.

"Thanks. You can call me Trev, mate."

"Mr Trev—"

"Just Trev, but whatever you want is fine." He takes the keys from the doorman and pats him on the back.

Trevor grips my hand and we walk across the lobby.

His red sports car comes to life as we approach.

He opens the door for me.

Inside, I try to settle into the seat. My ass is burning and bruised. Using my hands I lift myself to relieve the pressure on my skin. Slowly I ease myself lower until the pain settles.

"You didn't need to hit me so hard."

We pull away from the kerb.

"Yes, I did. And what do you mean, hard? I was going easy on you."

He makes out he's joking, but I'm not sure he is.

"Does it hurt now?"

"What do you think?"

"You can't sit there and honestly tell me you're not squirming wet in your seat. I bet every bump in the road is torturous."

How does he do that? Are my thoughts so easy to read? I'm so wet I want to wipe myself, but don't to avoid the pleasure of my hand. I keep wanting to squeeze my thighs together to relieve the built-up sexual energy. And I can barely sit still with my ass on fire.

"What's wrong with you? Why are you so… So, dominant?"

"There's nothing wrong with me. It's in my nature, baby. Kink is in my DNA. I love it."

"Hurting people is in your nature?"

"It was only a little spanking. Spanking hardly counts as a kink these days. That ponce of a husband of yours, he's the real deal, hurting people. Look at the way he treated you at the Christmas party. I should have punched that fucker after the way he spoke to you."

I'd forgotten he was at the Cedars Christmas party.

"Don't remind me about that. Pushing him over was

enough. I'm glad you didn't hit him. He'd have pressed charges," I say. But I can grasp what he's getting at. Every time we left the house he'd make it clear how awful I looked, and I'd end up changing outfits sometimes two or three times.

"I'm dressed as a policeman. Thought I'd get in the mood. I think uniforms suit me?"

"But you have hurt me." I don't confirm that he looks insanely sexy as a police officer.

"I know, baby. It was meant to hurt. For a woman with sex addiction, you're surprisingly naive. Haven't you heard of BDSM?"

"Yes, but that's between consenting adults, and I don't have sex addiction," I say.

"We are consenting adults. I wouldn't do that to just anyone. You were enjoying what I did like I knew you would. I can give you a safe word if that will make you more comfortable?"

"How did you know I was enjoying it? You slapped me around the face, and I was crying." I'm glad he's dropped the sex addiction line.

"You're the therapist, not me. I was reading you. You know I'd never hit you in anger. It wasn't very hard, and it was part of the scene. I had to stop as you were about to come at one point. You were crying because you were letting go of the negative emotion. It's okay to cry. I'm not afraid of tears. I love to cry. We'd had a bad afternoon, and I thought a bit of light BDSM might take your mind off the parcel. I wanted you to have a good time tonight without the incident hanging over you." He perseveres with his theory.

"And you weren't enjoying it?" I say.

"I was getting off, baby, trust me. Especially when you started talking about sucking my cock. I was tempted to stop there and then and let you go for it."

"Were you not affected by seeing those poor slaughtered animals?" I ask.

"No, not particularly. I'm sorry, but honestly, no, I wasn't. But I could see you were. And you feel better now, don't you? And you'll feel even better after you see what I've got in store for you at the party."

He gives me a megawatt smile.

How can I be so lucky? I glance in the wing mirror. My black eye-make-up is smudged a bit too far down my face, and my hair looks like I've just been pulled through a hedge. But I'm truly lit up from within; glowing doesn't quite cover it.

Please don't let whatever he has in mind involve public humiliation and please don't let me enjoy it.

* * *

We walk through the industrial, sliding metal lift doors of Gerry and Michael's warehouse apartment.

The party is in full swing. Large groups of people stand around drinking. The uniform theme is a hit. A bar has been set up on the other side of the huge, open-plan space. The dance floor is packed. Loud music blares out of the speakers. Nothing I recognise. Sounds way too hip for me.

"I love this track," Trevor says.

"You've heard it before?"

"Of course."

Now I feel old.

I take Trevor's hand and lead him through the crowds to find Gerry and Michael.

As we walk, the novelty hits me; I'm holding his hand and leading him somewhere. Aside from the fact that I'm not with my husband, we never held hands, not even in the early days. Trevor is unfamiliar and completely known at the same time.

People look past me at Trevor as we make our way through the crowd.

I'm used to all eyes being on me. It's not that I'm wildly attractive, but being tall and blonde attracts attention. Every move Trevor makes, people turn to watch him. I guess being very tall attracts attention, and that's before you add his pretty boy looks and crazy charisma.

Some of the women glance at me next. The envy on their faces is unmistakable. And not something I've ever experienced. Nobody would sexually covet Conty, but Trevor... I can't identify the emotion it provokes, but it's not jealousy. Trevor has always made me completely sure of his feelings. Now I think about it, he's never expressed any doubt about me or held back in any way. That in itself is odd.

We find Gerry. "So this is the gorgeous Trevor," she almost purrs.

"Hello," Trevor says, extending his hand.

Gerry shakes it. "I had no idea just how..." She trails off, shaking her head.

He looks shockingly attractive in his police officer uniform. Lucky Michael isn't the jealous type.

Trevor smiles. "Happy Birthday. I've got a present being delivered to you tomorrow."

First I've heard of a present.

"Wow, can't wait to see what it is," she coos, eyes fixed on Trevor's mouth.

"Neither can I," I add, imagining it will be something sexual.

Michael isn't far behind. "All right, mate." He shakes Trevor's hand.

"Great party," Trevor replies.

The opening bars of Depeche Mode's 'Just Can't Get Enough,' blare out. "I love this song," Gerry says.

"Me too," Trevor says, adding, "This is the remix version, isn't it?"

"Yes, it is. Wow, quick recognition," Michael says, taking Gerry's hand before she can proposition Trevor on the spot.

"I'm geeky about music and lyrics."

"Geeky is not a word I would use to describe you," I say.

"How *would* you describe me?" Trevor says, giving me a challenging look.

I'm unable to answer his question, so focus on the music. "Dance with me."

Without a word, Trevor picks up the chain around my neck and leads me to the dance floor.

Thank goodness he can't dance. He has perfect rhythm, though, and somehow manages to make what might be a bit like Dad-dancing cool. I suppose looking that good, nobody cares if you can dance.

He laughs, pulling me into him.

I turn and twerk my bruised ass in his crotch.

He puts his hands on my hips, moving with me.

"We're way too old for this," I call back at him.

"You're never too old for dancing, baby."

His enthusiasm is infectious. I love the way he throws

himself into whatever he is doing, like joy is his natural state.

* * *

The night wears on, and we work the room. Trevor doesn't need hand-holding. I've noticed how well he gets on with everyone. He has an easy charm with people, even other men. He's gravitated to some IT people and is talking code. Software development gets him more animated than usual. His next big thing is developing online video games.

Gerry slides her hand around my waist. "You lucky bitch. Look at him. Fuck me, he's spectacular. Look at the size of him."

"Honestly, you have no idea how good he is at just about any sexual act."

"Trust me, I'm imagining."

I laugh and give her a big hug.

Gerry is one of the few friends who stuck around and withstood Conty's years of isolating me. She never gave up calling, and even stood up to him a couple of times. Conty realised she was on to him and barred her from any events he and I attended together.

"What do you think? Seriously, Gerry, I know he's like a Chippendale, but forget about how he looks. There's something psychotic about him."

"I think you are truly happy, Alex. And calm and contented,

for once. Instead of the nervy wreck, Conty turned you into. And that's all I care about. Now can we get back to how he looks?"

"That might have something to do with him spanking me so hard before we left that I couldn't sit down in the car."

"That will help. BDSM done well is better than any drug on the planet. So you're on a kink high."

"A what? You know kink has never interested me. Yet he had me begging him to spank me at one point."

Her eyes open wider. "He's the perfect man. You know that, right?"

"What about the revenge porn last year? I'm not sure."

"We've been through this. Open your eyes, Alex. You're glowing. The two of you are radiating some serious love energy. If I was into auras, I'd see the two of you surrounded by a rainbow of the brightest colours, and sparks like dandelion kisses blowing wishes to the wind."

The opening bars of 'Xanadu' ring out.

"What the—" I start to say.

Gerry screeches with laughter. "That's what I came over to tell you. I requested 'Xanadu'. The DJ thought I'd gone bonkers, but it's my party and I'll play what I want. Come and dance."

Gerry picks up my hand and leads me to the dance floor, singing along.

We start dancing, and she spins me around.

She's right – I'm happy and contented. And severely punished. Hard to believe the two are connected.

Trevor turns up mid-way through. "Ello, ello, ello – you're under arrest for public indecency with that dancing." He slaps the handcuff on my wrist.

Gerry raises her eyebrows and gracefully backs off, giving me the thumbs up as she goes.

Trevor leads me off the dance floor and up the only stairs in the place, along a wooden corridor. "This is our song, baby."

I laugh. "So we have a song now?"

"We're going to have lots of songs, not just one."

"No, just no." I realise where we are heading.

"Remember that police officer who nearly caught us fucking in the toilet when we got together in the park?" he continues.

Got together? He thinks we got together then.

"Yes, he looked very young and shocked."

We reach the loo.

"I laughed my arse off all day after that." He closes and locks the door.

He undoes the handcuffs.

"You called me a slag after, remember?"

"Do you take everything I say seriously?"

"No. Yes. I'm not sure." I can't think with his eyes fixed on me like that.

He laughs. "Well, you are an old slag, aren't you?"

"Trevor," I say in mock horror, "enough of the old."

"I'm going to fuck you like the dirty whore you are."

At least he's not planning on making me lick his boots or something.

He walks towards me.

I'm pushed back.

He picks up my hand and pushes it down on the front of his black trousers.

I start rubbing his already hard cock laying up his stomach.

Using the chain attached to my neck, he pulls my face towards him.

His soft lips touch mine, and his tongue slips into my mouth.

We kiss slowly.

"I'm never going to *hurt you,* hurt you — if you know what I mean," he says.

"I know what you mean."

He lifts me up onto the sink. Even through my dress, the cold metal soothes my ass, still burning, red hot.

He lifts up my dress and slides both his hands up my thighs. He moves one hand into my knickers from the side and rubs my clit.

"Oh my god, that feels amazing."

I've been on the verge of an orgasm all night. My hips rock backwards and forwards on his hand.

His finger edges inside me, and he pushes up as far as it will go.

The relief is like a reflex, and I let out a long breath.

I undo his belt and fumble around with the button, clip and zip.

He helps me undo it and pulls his trousers down.

Moving back, he lifts my hips up so he can slide my knickers down and off.

The cold metal against my bare skin makes me gasp. My whole body is super sensitive, much more so than usual. Must be the spanking.

He kisses me again whilst using his cock to rub me up and down.

My tongue is frantic, moving with his, and I put my hands in his hair and through the thick spikes.

He drops to his knees and spreads my thighs, licking me hard.

I can't take it and want to come with him inside me.

"I'm going to come, fuck me now."

In one smooth movement, he moves up and pushes himself

inside me as far as he can go. The base of his hard cock, pushes against my clit. His hands grip my ass, and he pulls me into him.

I wince; "Ow," slips out of my mouth.

"Fuck me, baby, your ass is burning. I did a good job of spanking you."

I can't speak; the cold metal basin against my skin, his hands on my hips, his cock inside me, his body pushed against mine.

He moves in and out of me in hard fast moments, each time pulling me down, so the thickness of his cock hits my clit.

Losing control, he thrusts harder.

My hands grip his shoulders.

He pushes in as far as he can go.

I explode all over him, biting down on the rough material of the police jacket.

"Shit, don't bite it, this is my brother's uniform, and he has to wear it tomorrow."

I shudder in his arms. My orgasm calms down.

"What? Your brother is a police officer?"

"Yes, and before you ask, the handcuffs are real. I did promise him I wouldn't use the truncheon, though."

"Thank goodness for that."

"Now get on your knees, like a good girl."

CHAPTER TWENTY-TWO

The doorman looks at me like I'm a madwoman.

"I said, who. The person, who gave you the parcel to deliver?"

"No person, Mr Porter had a parcel," he says.

"No, not the white parcel, a woman with a box," I say, making a box shape with my hands.

"Oh your papers, you want papers, yes?"

He heads out to the back of his office and brings the morning papers.

"Yes, thank you, but the parcel – what did the person look like?"

"No person, I don't understand."

"No problem," I say.

I'm going to have to let it go. Perhaps we'll never know who delivered the parcel of mutilated animals.

I head back up to the flat.

Trevor eats in the caff a lot, but today we are having breakfast at home.

He's in his boxer shorts, no top, cooking. The muscles flex in his back as he whisks the hollandaise sauce.

"Eggs Benedict, okay?"

"Yes, sounds great," I say.

I walk up behind him and slide my arms around his waist. With my head against his back, I breathe deeply. Gerry was right. I'm happy and everything about him is right.

He doesn't turn around. His hands go over mine and squeeze.

The moment doesn't need words. This is real domestic happiness.

A vibrating on the marble worktop startles me.

Trevor reaches over and picks up his phone.

"Hang on a second." He presses mute. "Can you watch the rest of this stuff? Needs a few minutes. I've got to take this."

"Yes, of course, you go."

Trevor's voice, talking from the bedroom, is muffled. The shower starts up thirty seconds later.

I lay out two plates and add the toasted muffins, hash browns, bacon, poached eggs and wilted spinach. The hollandaise sauce spreads out on top of the pile. I add chopped parsley and salt and pepper. Freshly squeezed orange juice sits in a jug.

A hot cup of coffee warms my hands as I wait for him to come back.

Trevor appears in faded light blue jeans and a grey camo t-shirt. He changes personality. There's Trevor who started the wildly successful IT company, and Trevor who wants to fix cars and owns a local repair shop. Today he's going to play mechanic. He's more mellow, if you could ever call him mellow, with his head focused on cars.

"Who was that?" I ask.

"You should have started without me." He picks up his knife and fork.

One mouthful in, and his phone rings again. He picks it up. "I'm thinking. I'll call you back."

Too late for him to lie. I saw the name flash up on his screen. "Is that someone from Pilkington Baron?"

"Yes, it's my barrister."

"About the criminal charges?"

"Yes, but I don't want you to worry. You need to sign those divorce papers."

The pile of papers sits ominously on the vast kitchen work surface. If they were glowing radioactive, that would match how I feel about them. The lawyer had a courier drop the bundle over last night. All I have to do is sign.

"Signing them is hard."

"So you want to go back to him?"

"No, but I don't want to be divorced."

"I've been there and done that. It never works. You can't go back, ever. No matter how much you want to. You have to cut your losses and move on."

"Done what? Tried to go back?" I clarify.

"Yes, after I found out about Krystal and the tennis coach."

"Tennis coach – really?"

"Yes. What can I say? The woman is a walking cliché. I tried to make our marriage work after, but couldn't. The betrayal was too deep."

"I have to confess, I thought—"

"You thought I'd been unfaithful to her?"

"Well, yes, I assumed—"

"The tennis coach wasn't the first man she slept with behind my back. She said she'd never do it again. And I believed her. But once someone has crossed the line of fucking someone else, there's no going back. I've been on the other side of the fence too. And it's only a matter of time before you or they find another partner in crime."

"I'm sorry. Must have been hard."

"It's getting hard right now, watching you stuff food into your mouth."

For a second he gets the look on his face that precedes something sexual, but he doesn't follow through.

"I mean it, baby. Going back never works. I learnt the hard way. You have to move on. Don't view signing the papers as pulling the trigger. At the very least, pressing ahead shows that fucker you're serious about not putting up with what he did."

He's right. Conty will see I'm not the person I was.

"But the lawyer says she can get us divorced quickly, and he won't contest it."

"Trust me, baby, divorces take time."

"What do you mean, divorces? You've had more than one?"

"I've been through two."

"Two? You've had two marriages?" I hadn't suspected another one.

"What can I say? I'm a hopeless romantic. Now let me stick my cock in you before I go to my cave."

* * *

The workout helped, but the endorphins are wearing off. The warning must have worked, as although Kira shot me hostile glances the whole time I was on the gym floor, she didn't come near me. I'm doubting she was responsible for the animal stunt now. The parcel incident is fading, thankfully. Getting any information out of the doorman was near impossible.

Gabby waves as I walk past reception and leave the gym.

The memory of my old life is like the lingering feeling of a dream I can't quite remember. There's no way back, even if I wanted to. I have to let go of this marriage. Whatever Trevor says about divorces taking time is not the case with us. There are no fiery arguments or angst about losing each other. Our marriage was a business arrangement, and the divorce is an administrative exercise. And now I've signed, the whole thing will be done and dusted in record time.

I walk past the caff, where Trevor and I met for the first time, over a year ago. My relationship with Conty at that point had reached an all-time low. Hayes had tipped my world upside down; I'd been hit with love that I'd thought was impossible and couldn't process. But Hayes's erratic and inconsistent behaviour messed with my head. I wonder what he's doing; I haven't heard anything from him. No surprises there. Maybe I should send him a message? Or maybe I shouldn't. Nothing good can come of it. But we don't feel over.

The park looks the same. It was on this path that Trevor gripped my hand and pushed my palm down on his hard-on. Outside the loos, I can almost see Trevor eclipsing the door frame, his face squinting in the sunlight at the police officer who'd almost caught us in the act. The rush of lust I felt looking at his arrogant, satisfied expression, floods me again.

Perhaps I'll swing past the motor shop and give him a quick blow job. Better use of my time than worrying about Conty and our divorce, or what Hayes is doing.

With each step, I get more excited. He looks seriously sexy

in his dirty overalls.

* * *

I freeze.

The woman who accosted me at Trevor's Strand office walks out of the yard. Her short, dark, spiky hair is slicked back. She's doing the buttons up on her tight blue shirt. Her jeans sit low on her hips, and she's wearing cowboy boots. Whatever's just happened has her ruffled.

I step back so I'm out of view.

She's already on her phone and distracted before she reaches the road.

He wouldn't, would he?

She pulls a black leather jacket over her slender shoulders. Someone on the phone is on the receiving end of a torrent of her shouting. I can't hear what she's saying.

We fucked in his office, or rather, played a sex game, so she must… What else would she be doing there, coming out half-dressed?

The roar of the motorbike resonates in my head as she rides away.

How could I have been so naïve, trusting him?

I rush into the yard.

Trevor is coming out of the loo.

"What's up?"

"What the fuck were you doing with that woman?"

"What woman?"

The yard is deserted, like when…

"How dare you lie to me. The woman I saw leaving."

"Oh her; she's barely a woman." He laughs.

"You think this is funny?"

"No, of course not, I was just saying—"

"You were fucking her. She was getting dressed. You must think I'm stupid, Trevor."

He holds me in his gaze.

His eyes are hard to read.

My body fizzes with unbearable energy.

I reach up and try to slap him.

He grabs my wrist to stop me from hitting him, then steps back with his hands up. "Hey, calm down. You've got it wrong."

"I trusted you. And you've—" The words choke in my throat; the anger isn't enough to quash the sudden fear of the power he has to emotionally hurt me.

"Not guilty. Her name is Maxine. She's a freelance journalist, and the one behind the newspaper articles."

"Don't lie to me. You were coming out of the loo. And where is everyone?" I spit.

"At the chippy, probably, it's lunchtime. I invited her over to warn her off, and she tried it on, but I didn't do anything, I swear. I love you and only you."

"Love; this is what you call love." My voice is breaking.

"We are the real deal, baby."

"You call targeting me with revenge porn and putting me through hell, love?"

"Let's not go there again. I'm sorry for what I did to you. If I could change it, I would. Why don't you come and suck my cock, and you'll calm down?" He puts his hand on his crotch.

I'm floored. How can he? He's on another level of ...

"No... you... I–"

My head is all over the place. I actually went to hit him. That's not who I am. How could I have resorted to violence? I'm scared. Of him, of how he makes me feel, of being without Conty... I'm scared of everything.

I turn around and run out of the garage.

CHAPTER TWENTY-THREE

The door to the flat is open when I arrive home. Everything is sparkling clean. The chemicals from cleaning products hang in the air.

Walking has dampened the adrenaline, and I feel better.

The door slams behind me.

I press the coffee machine and breathe deeply.

I text Trevor. *I'm sorry. I can't believe I went to hit you.*

Nice right hook, haha. It's okay, baby. I get that you're stressed.

Is he telling the truth? I want to believe him, but she was doing up her top. He wanted me to give him a blow job. He'd hardly do that if he'd been fucking her. But he was coming out of the loo so having had a wash isn't beyond the realms of possibility.

I pick up my phone again.

I miss you.

Not sure why I typed that. He probably won't reply.

I miss you too.

An instant response from Hayes is a novelty. Usually, a reply takes anywhere from days to weeks and could be months.

Are you okay? Annabel told me that Conty is pushing forwards with a divorce.

What do you think?

Can we meet up? I need to talk to you.

Where, when? I ask.

This is a bad idea. If Trevor finds out, I don't want to think about the consequences. But he's hardly keeping it pure, he did admit he invited Maxine over to talk. Why would he do that? Surely going over to 'talk' is a euphemism for sex? Well, it is in my world.

I'm in London tomorrow. I've got a meeting close to One Five One Thames Reach. Do you know it?

Yes. That works for me.

Hayes must have a project nearby. There is a lot of building work going on, both residential and commercial. I think I remember him saying he owns a property company now. He has no idea I live here. The official line is I'm staying with Gerry and Michael in the City.

Helico Bistro around 11?

Done.

Meeting close to home is risky, but Trevor would never go into Helico. He prefers local places that have been here for decades. Plus he tends to associate with old locals, so we will be safe. And I've got a feeling he's working at his Strand office tomorrow. Besides, I'm allowed to meet one of my friends.

Who knows what else he's been up to, after what just happened with Maxine.

Coffee in hand, I head to the bathroom. I need to wash this day away.

My coffee mug hits the floor, and I back away.

CHEATING BITCH has been scrawled across the mirror in a love heart. The thick, dark liquid drips off the sink, and into a pool on the floor.

It looks like blood.

I grab my phone and run out of the apartment.

My finger is on Trevor's number as I wait for the lift.

He answers on the first ring. "You feeling better, baby?"

"No, you've got to come home now."

He hangs up.

The lift door slides open.

What if whoever did it is still in the flat?

The lift door closes behind me.

Relief follows.

I stand outside the building. My heart is racing, but the danger has passed.

A car I've never seen before pulls up. Trevor jumps out. His dirty navy overalls have been pulled to his waist, and his grey t-shirt stretches over his chest.

"Someone broke into the flat and left a message in the

bathroom," I say.

He puts his arms around me and holds me.

My arms can barely reach around his body, but I cling to him.

"Stay here. I'll go up and check."

I wait in the lobby, too stunned to use my phone or sit down, pacing up and down.

Trevor reappears in what must be less than five minutes.

"The cleaner is on her way back. No one is up there. I'm going to speak to the doorman."

Judging by his slowed speech, he's having about as much luck trying to communicate with the doorman as I did.

He gives up and comes back over to me. "He didn't see anything out of the ordinary. Let's go up."

We walk back to the lift, my hand held tight in his.

I'm anxious, walking back through the door.

"It's going to be okay," he says.

I walk over to the window. London is spread out below. The grey sky is low and threatening.

Trevor heads towards the kitchen. "You want a cup of tea?"

"Yes, please."

"Builders, coming up."

"Is it blood?"

"I don't think so."

"We need to call the police. Someone has broken into the flat."

"We can report it to the police. But they didn't break in. I think they had a key. There's no sign of breaking and entering. It's pretty difficult to get through one of those doors, and there'd be visible damage."

"How can some random person walk into the building? You need to talk to the doorman again. And you think they had a key?"

Trevor hesitates for a fraction of a second.

There's something he's not telling me.

"I'll have the locks changed today," he says, finally.

"Who could it be?" I ask.

"I'm not sure."

"You must know who has keys to your flat?"

I can't believe I'm having to ask him a question like that. Most people know who has the keys to their home.

"There are several women, including my daughter and ex-wife. And Kira refused to give me the key back. Turns out she was cut up about our breaking up. And is being vocal about it."

"What? Like sending you messages? Are you still seeing her?"

"Yes, messages mainly, and she did turn up to my office once. But no, baby, I'm not still seeing her. I'm sorry you had to ask that question. Kira and I were all about fun. She told me she wasn't over her ex and was using me to make him jealous. She knew how I felt about you and said she was okay with it. She changed her tune when we got together. I had no idea—"

"I bet she's behind the dead animals as well."

"Honestly, that's not who she is, she's all about getting rich and famous for nothing, super quick. Getting a key cut isn't hard. I don't guard my keys at work. Max claimed she had a tip-off from someone at Porter Vision the night we got photographed leaving. It could easily be a pissed-off employee."

"You know she accosted me in the reception before I went up to see you for our first meeting with the lawyers."

"Who, Max?"

"Yes, and said something about you usually being more original or creative than that. Have you slept with her?" I ask, but I'm not sure I want to know the answer to that question.

"Yes, but it wasn't a relationship or even a fling. We had an arrangement."

"An arrangement? What does that mean?"

"We met up to play out pre-discussed scenarios."

"Seriously? Like what?"

"You can be surprisingly naive, Alex. I don't think details will help."

"I've never heard of anything like that."

"Let's just leave it at our kink needs were well matched. So we had a transactional arrangement."

He's right, I don't want to know the details.

He hands me the tea.

"Thank you."

Thoughts rushing through my mind blur into each other. Kira has been to his office and she still has a key. She was around at the time the parcel of slaughtered animals arrived; Gabby told me she followed me into the gym.

Why didn't he say something before? I don't know what to think about his 'arrangement' with Maxine.

"Someone must have seen something," I say.

"I'll check the security camera in the lobby. I'm sorry you came home to that. And I'm sorry about lunchtime. You have to believe me. I didn't do anything with Max today. She was pissed off but she'll calm down."

"You think she could be responsible? Writing, 'cheating bitch' is not random. It must be someone who knows us."

"I doubt it. Max tends to approach life head-on. There's no sneaking around with that one. She'd track you down and tell you to your face."

"Well, who then?"

"I don't have the answers, baby. I've got to go back to work, but I'm taking you out for dinner tonight, and we are going to forget about all this."

He picks me up off my feet to kiss me.

I sink onto the sofa. The hot tea is comforting in my hands. Perhaps I should cancel seeing Hayes tomorrow. Why chance getting caught?

* * *

"You're kidding me," I say.

We pull into the car park of a fast-food chain.

"Don't pretend you don't like burgers and fries." Trevor holds the door open for me.

The harsh yellow lighting does nothing to dampen his youthful features, but I'm pretty sure it won't be doing me any favours. Self-consciousness is a novelty.

"Grab a table, and I'll bring the food over," Trevor says, joining the queue.

I sit down and watch him. If I didn't know him, I'd assume he was some flash boy racer, young and exuberant. He's wearing dark blue jeans and a pink t-shirt with a black leather, racing-type jacket.

We sit opposite each other in a plastic booth with the food in front of us.

Trevor tears into a huge burger like a child. He can't stuff the fries down his throat fast enough. He's displaying zero signs of concern about the break-in – or rather, non-break-in. All I can think about is that someone was in our home. What if I'd been at home at the time? My stomach sinks. They must have known I wouldn't be there.

"Do you think they're watching us? It must be someone who knows my movements. They knew I wasn't home."

"You still thinking about that?"

"Yes. You're not?"

"No, totally off my radar. But in answer to your question, no, I don't think anyone is watching you or us. Don't get paranoid, baby."

"Have you checked the security cameras yet?" I ask.

"Yes, but she's wearing a scarf, so no shots of her face. She has dark hair and could be older, but you can't identify her. It could be a man in disguise. Who knows?"

Marina springs to mind, but her being the culprit is logistically improbable. She'd have to be in London a lot. Conty owns a flat here, so that might not be too much of a stretch. But how would she know where I live? I guess she could have asked the delivery company where they dropped my stuff. How would she know what company? I'm clutching at straws.

"Who do you think is doing it?" I ask.

"Not sure. And I don't care. Let's move on. We could

speculate all night and get nowhere."

"Marina has dark hair and is older." I voice my concerns out loud.

"You haven't done anything to her. She's the one who fucked you over. Why would she go to all that trouble? And how would she have got a key? Doesn't make sense."

"It's hardly the actions of someone rational. Who knows what's going through her mind."

"It might be a he. I'd guess I've pissed someone off and don't remember it. And they got a key from an old workman. I've had a lot of work done, and it wouldn't be hard to get a key."

Maybe he's right, and someone is targeting him, but 'cheating bitch' was aimed at me. Rachel could be behind it. I did cheat with her husband. But again, how would she get a key? She doesn't even know where I live. He's right – speculating isn't helping. I'm going around in circles.

"They're pretty serious incidents."

"It's minor. I think we should move on." He continues with his line of thinking.

"Really, you think slaughtering a lamb and then what they did to those animals is minor? And now going into the flat?"

His face is blank. "Could be different nut jobs, and the incidents aren't related. But, yes, minor, in the general scheme."

"Talking of the general scheme, going to prison for revenge porn against me wouldn't be minor."

"I'm a big boy, I can deal with the consequences."

"What's going on with the lawyer? You don't have to hide what's happening from me."

"Nothing much, I'll deal with all that."

"You've been charged though, right?"

"Yes, I got charged because the headmistress at the school is giving evidence against me. I only sent them the photo of your outfit, but in the email, I threatened to send a video, to the entire school. And you'd already emailed the police a file of my text messages, bluffing I'd do it. Then there are the photos of the bruising on your body, and the evidence of the doctor saying you presented as traumatised."

I put my head in my hands, and try to suppress the rising anger – at him, at me and at everything. "This is a mess. And for the record, I was traumatised when I was at the STD clinic, but it was over Conty's sustained abuse. I'd forgotten about the bruising until they pointed it out. Honestly, Trevor, it beggars belief that you thought bluffing about the prospect of revenge porn was a good idea. And that it would persuade me to see you."

"It's not all bad. We're together now. I got bail, and I'm pleading guilty, so there won't be a trial."

"Bail ... Oh no."

"What? You'd prefer me behind bars?" He laughs.

"Don't plead guilty." I put my head in my hands again.

"The whole thing will be easier and over more quickly if I do. A trial will be a circus. All sorts of shit will be thrown around in the media. And in court. And we don't want all that out in public."

"You mean about me and what we were doing behind Conty's back?"

"Yes, and I'm assuming you were distracting yourself with more men before me. Once the press start digging they won't stop, and your past will be dragged out publicly. They'll have a field day. Sex addiction is proper media fodder. If I plead guilty you won't be named. And it will all be over quickly."

"How did it come to this?" I shake my head.

"Baby, we found each other. I'd go through anything for you. Don't lose sight of the bigger picture. We're going to get through this. Let me deal with the criminal side. You concentrate on getting over your divorce and eating your burger. When I get you home, I'm going to make you forget about all this."

I start stuffing fries in my mouth quicker.

He watches me, not with the obvious sexual intent sometimes on his face, but with a combination of love and amusement. Above all else there's never any doubt; he's certain about me and us.

The night is cold and wet as we head outside to the car. Sleet falls around us, disappearing into the dark, wet puddles on the ground.

Trevor hugs me tight against him as we walk towards the car.

"So much for spring being in the air," I say.

The headlights flash as we approach.

Trevor opens the door for me.

He gets in.

I put my hand on his knee. I'm feeling better. His lack of concern about killing animals and someone going into the flat is rubbing off on me. Although the therapist part of my brain works in the background, adding his lack of emotion as more evidence he's on the psychopathy scale.

The ignition starts, and he pulls away. A red warning light flashes.

He's forced to stop the car. "Hold on a sec, flat tyre, I think. Sit tight while I check."

I can tell by the look on his face something is wrong.

Within seconds, I'm out of the car next to him.

Sticking out of the tyre is the handle of a knife.

My mouth drops open, and my hand goes up to my face.

"Now, don't overact, baby. This is a rough area of London, and we are in a two-hundred-K sports car. It's not the first time someone has damaged the car while it's sitting in a car park."

"But a knife is pushed up to the hilt."

He pulls me over to him and cuddles me tight.

"Trevor, this is serious."

"It will be serious if I don't get you home in the next five minutes. Grab your stuff."

I reach into the back seat for my handbag.

A loud whistle comes out of his mouth, and a taxi pulls over a second later.

"You're going to leave the car here?" I ask.

"Yes. Eddie, the manager at Porter Motors, will sort the car out later, don't worry about that. You need to start worrying about what I'm going to do to you when I get you home."

His strategy is working, and I start relaxing, or rather tensing up. The prospect of sex combined with what he's capable of wipes away the worry.

* * *

"I promise it won't hurt."

"Are you crazy? I've been on the receiving end of one of your spankings before. Of course, it's going to hurt."

"Come and lay across my lap."

Trevor is sitting on the side of the bed in his white boxer shorts.

"I'm feeling fragile, baby."

"I know. This is going to be soothing and pleasurable at the same time."

"How can a spanking be soothing?" I'm not convinced. He spanked me so hard before Gerry's party, my ass was bruised for weeks.

"I don't know how it works, it just does." He gives me a gentle smile.

"Really?"

"Trust me, honey."

I walk over to the side of the bed, naked, and bend over his lap.

He pulls my body up and into him so I'm completely over his lap.

My body tenses.

"Relax, this is all about comfort and pleasure. Nothing to do with punishment. Concentrate on the sensation."

With one hand he strokes my hair. The other is resting over the back of my thighs.

"Mmmm." His hand feels good stroking my hair.

"Are you comfortable?"

He pulls my legs up so I'm completely on the bed, stretched

over his lap. No part of my body is uncomfortable.

"Yes."

"Relax your head," he instructs.

I move my head to the side and sink into the soft duvet.

The strands of my hair fall down.

He smooths them back.

The position makes me feel completely secure and relaxed, like I could go to sleep.

He runs one hand over my back. The other hand caresses my ass. His fingers barely touch my skin.

"That feels good, baby."

With his hands massaging my body, I forget he talked about spanking. The position itself seems to induce comfort.

The moment his hand turns from running over my ass to a light patting isn't discernible.

His hand pats my ass again and again.

The rhythmic patting makes me relax further into soft, warm comfort.

With his other hand, he kneads the muscles in my neck.

"Are you are okay? Stretch your neck forward."

"Yes, this is amazing," I say, letting out a long sigh.

The patting turns into a firm tap, but again, it's not possible to notice when it changes.

I want to move my body up and down with his hand.

He continues, putting his whole hand over my ass.

The sense of security is overwhelming.

The taps turn into light smacks but continue at an even pace.

"Wow, that feels so relaxing," I say.

My ass feels warm, like it's glowing.

"I told you it would feel good. Forget about everything and focus on the feeling."

His hand barely makes a noise each time it lightly smacks my skin.

"Mmmmmm." I never want this to stop; it feels so good.

The rhythm of his hand hitting my ass is reliable and reassuring.

Each time, the smacks become firmer.

I feel sleepy and mesmerised by the repetitive motion of his hand.

My ass becomes warm like the soft morning sun, but it doesn't hurt.

"Don't fall asleep, baby. Slide up the bed and turn over."

I move up the bed and roll over on my back, contented. "Thank you, darling. Feel so much better."

He slides up the bed after me, and his hands go under my warm ass.

My fingers automatically move down to this hair. The thick

spikes move through my fingers.

His head moves between my legs, forcing my thighs open.

"Oh, baby, you don't need to do that. I could literally fall asleep this second."

He doesn't listen. His tongue moves up and down my body in soft, gentle strokes. Slowly he licks me and moves his mouth in to suck me.

"I love you," I say, drowsy and not wanting to wake up from the sensual dream.

He stops and moves up on top of me.

My eyes stay closed; I put my hands on his hips, pulling him towards me.

His hard body pushes gently into mine.

"I love you too. Always, baby."

I move my body up to meet his.

His lips come down on mine.

My hands move up his back.

Strong arms are completely around me.

I can't tell where he ends and I begin.

Every gentle movement of his hips washes pure pleasure through every fibre of my being.

We move up to the pinnacle and hold each other tighter.

"We are one," he whispers in my ear.

"One soul, always," are the last words out of my mouth from

the edge of consciousness. I don't even understand what it means, but know it's true.

He rolls over behind me and pulls me back into him.

I lift my hand up so we can link fingers.

* * *

We sit in the early morning sun, drinking coffee and eating pain au chocolate.

"Thank you," I say into my phone.

"What did she say?" Trevor asks, putting his mug down.

The phone is dead, but I hold the receiver to my ear anyway. Cressida's cut-glass tones reverberate around my head.

My stomach sinks.

"We will be officially divorced by early summer." I'm unable to comprehend the words. "Conty signed the papers and returned them pronto. He's giving us everything we asked for."

"That's good news, honey. The rest of your life awaits."

"This feels like defeat."

I'm emptied. Just over twenty years of marriage, and he's not even going to put up the pretence of fighting for me? Can I retract my consent? What would be the point? He obviously doesn't want me. And never has. So much has changed, I don't even recognise the person I was before.

"You just need time to recalibrate."

I pick up my phone but don't know who to contact. I'm tempted to leave a message for one of our older children, but they are settled back in boarding school, and I don't want to worry them.

A message pings through before I have a chance to contact anyone.

Looking forward to seeing you later.

Oh shit. I'm meant to be meeting Hayes today. He's not worth risking what I've found with Trevor. I'm going to cancel.

I don't think our meeting is a good idea.

I've got to see you, Alex. We both need closure if nothing else.

He's right about that.

Okay. See you at 11ish.

I should have said something has come up, and I can't make it. Now I've got to see him.

"Have a good day, honey," Trevor says, bending down to kiss me. "I'm at the Strand office today, so can't get back as quickly, but if anything happens, give me a ring immediately."

"Thanks."

He picks up his laptop and a pile of papers. The door clicks shut softly behind him.

CHAPTER TWENTY-FOUR

On the way out I stop by the doorman's office.

"Can you describe the woman who came into the flat yesterday?"

"The cleaner, yes?"

"No, the other woman?"

"No, other woman. I tell Mr Porter, only Mr Porter."

"Yes, I know you spoke to Mr Porter about it, but what did the other woman look like?"

"Only Mr Porter, nothing more," he says.

"You will only talk to Mr Porter?"

"No, yes, only Mr Porter came in. I tell him this."

I try a different approach.

"Can you show me the security camera footage?"

"Yes, is possible."

He turns to the monitor in front of him and puts in the dates.

I lean over the counter so I can see the screen.

He presses a few buttons but nothing comes up.

"Where is it?" I ask.

"Yes, yes, gone. Mr Porter took, now I remember."

"Mr Porter took the footage from the computer?"

"Only Mr Porter is not a problem for me."

This is hopeless. He can't understand a word I'm saying.

* * *

Every time the door of the coffee shop opens, I fail to ignore it. I don't know why I agreed to meet Hayes. There's no point. It never translates into anything concrete. One minute I think it's happening, but then he goes silent, again, like he can't sustain the connection continuously. I'm involved with Trevor now. Seeing Hayes isn't worth it.

The internal fixtures of the coffee shop are bland and uninspired. The cream walls are covered with a selection of flower prints that look like they belong on a hospital wing. The high-backed chairs are hard and uncomfortable. There's no ambience, like in the caff.

My phone rings. Don't tell me, He's not coming.

It's Conty. The warnings from my legal team not to talk to him directly aren't strong enough to stop me from pressing the pick-up icon. What if he's seen the newspaper...

"Alexandra? Is that you?"

"Yes." I'm not sure who else he thinks could be answering my phone.

"If you don't stop harassing me, I'm going to file a

restraining order against you, and that may affect your financial settlement."

The pompous tone sounds riled, unlike him.

Dread fills me.

"I have no idea what you're talking about, Conty, I haven't been near you or Cedars. And don't threaten me. I don't care about the settlement."

"You've been warned." The phone goes dead.

My phone is gripped in my hand. What's going on? Harass him? I don't think so. I take a deep breath and push the air out of my lungs. I will have to call Cressida, or whatever her name is, later.

I'm on edge, and the call from Conty hasn't helped. I'd been aiming for cool, calm and collected. Not scared, sad and all over the place.

Hearing Conty's voice reminds me of when Hayes and I first met. I was in a terrible headspace, starved of love and care. He saved my life on the ski slope, and straight after kissed me so gently.

A message from Trevor comes through. *You okay?*

Yes. I'm meeting a friend for coffee.

No need to add the friend is male and someone I've been involved with; someone who could be the father of my phantom baby.

A photo loads.

Trevor has sent a photo of his cock. It looks like he took it during a work meeting, as several pairs of feet are also visible under the desk. Let's hope they were absorbed in some boring spreadsheet or piece of code.

I laugh and send him a photo I took this morning in the shower.

Unease churns my stomach over and over. What if I really am pregnant? With everything going on, I'd forgotten about that prospect. I'm going to have to do a pregnancy test to make sure I'm not. Still no period, and I don't feel right. I slept with Hayes and Trevor days apart. I run through the circumstances again. The day I found out about Hayes's other girlfriend, I went to Trevor's flat. A few days after, I rowed with Hayes, and he fucked me on my bedroom floor. I honestly thought I was fast-tracking to menopause. I didn't think I'd be ovulating. I can't be pregnant, but it wouldn't hurt to check.

Hayes walks through the door.

The warm coffee shop becomes like a sauna. My face must be flushed and covered in a film of sweat. Not a good look.

He hasn't used an umbrella and rain drips off his floppy blond hair and onto his navy blazer. He runs his hand through it, dark blue eyes scanning the restaurant, looking for me. His other hand grips his black phone.

I pretend I haven't noticed him arrive.

He's not much shorter than Trevor, but he looks as tall as he's slim. His dark blue shirt lays flat against his torso.

So far, so good. I'm not feeling anything like I used to feel every time I saw him. He's ground my feelings down to nothing with his lack of contact. No matter how much you try – and I tried for a year – eventually, sporadic contact dampens it down to nothing. Still, I don't trust it, not yet.

"Alex, it's good to see you," he says.

"You too," I say, but I'm not sure it is good to see him.

"Where have you come from?" he asks.

"I'm staying with my friends Gerry and Michael in the City." Why did I say that and not tell him about Trevor?

"I know you don't trust me after everything that's happened, but I want to be there for you. I tried to talk to you at the Sunday lunch but you didn't seem keen."

Didn't seem keen? Well, that's one way to describe it. What did he expect after blowing hot and cold for months? That I'd be desperate for him to throw me some crumbs of attention? And he's right; I don't trust him. It felt like he strung me along last year. I'm in a different place now, not starved of love and being pounded into the ground by a bullying husband.

"It's all water under the bridge," I say.

"But it doesn't have to be, Alex. You know how I feel about

you. I wasn't free last year to pursue us, but I am now."

"What do you mean, Hayes? You're not free?"

"I mean, my other relationship has ended. It took a while, as we'd been seeing each other for close to ten years. That doesn't go away overnight," he says, in a tone that implies a ten-year affair is not important.

"You were having a relationship with someone else for ten years of your marriage?" I say, unable to hide the shock.

"Yes. On and off. I'm going to get a coffee. Do you want another one?"

"No, thanks."

He walks to the counter, still looking like he's stepped out of a romance novel. He's almost untouchable with his boy-next-door looks. I remember struggling to translate him into base sexual desire. Trevor is pretty too, but he has sexual brutality written all over his face. Within an hour of meeting up with Trevor, he'd nearly dislocated my arm fucking me from behind in a filthy, abandoned loo.

He was sensational, but all I could think about was Hayes.

I glance over at Hayes's back, as he stands at the counter. The young woman serving is smiling at him. I can nearly see her pupils dilate. I know how that feels.

He comes back, looking serious.

"I'm going to leave Annabel," he announces.

"What? Why?" I say, trying not to sound as alarmed as I feel. Leave his wife – really?

"Don't give me why, Alex. We both know we are meant to be together. I love you."

"What?"

"You heard what I said. I mean it."

He talks a big game. Is that how he managed to stay with someone for ten years whilst married? Saying he was going to leave his wife? Annabel must have been pregnant and had their two children during that time. And this woman stuck around for ten years.

"I'm not going back there," I say.

"Last year was difficult. I had to keep away from you. I barely stopped Claire from telling Annabel about us. And there was a strong chance she'd have told Conty if she'd found out about you. I couldn't take that chance."

"You didn't need to behave the way you did. Not answering my messages or initiating any contact, then every time I saw you acting like you cared. It was confusing."

Anger flashes through me at everything he put me through with his hot and cold behaviour. He turned me into a crazy woman. Always attached to my phone, constantly checking for messages, and in tears, on and off.

"I do care. You know it wasn't like that, or at least not

deliberately. I was dealing with a lot. We lost a baby late on, and that was hard."

Shit, I feel bad now, worrying about a few messages.

"But Annabel didn't—"

"No, not with Annabel. Claire and I lost our baby. It happened at the beginning of the year. I found out on the last day of our skiing holiday. Unfortunately, it wasn't the first time. The fallout was... Well, it wasn't pretty. So I didn't contact you."

"I can imagine," I say, not wanting to imagine how horrible a situation like that must have been. Alone and grieving for a baby you were having with a man who belongs to someone else. Tears spring up. I could be having his baby. What if something happens?

"Don't cry. I'm ready to take things forward now."

Ironic how, now I'm with someone else, he finally says all the things I've longed to hear.

He picks up my hand and kisses it.

"I'm not, I can't, it's... you don't understand. I'm in—" The words choke me. I can't bring myself to tell him about Trevor.

No, it has to stop. The familiar network of emotion fires up.

The image of Trevor's cock is on my phone. He's the real deal. But how can he be? I'm deluded. He's currently being charged with a sex crime against me. Why am I staying with him after that? I'm crazy to think our relationship can work out. And who knows what else he's been up to, with Kira. He admitted they'd been in contact but he didn't say in what way. And then there's Maxine and their sick arrangement. It looked like he'd been fucking her in his garage. I've been to his motor repair shop for a 'meeting.' The kink with him scares me. I have no idea what he's capable of. Trevor is dangerous, and I'm being sucked into believing his romantic shit about love and twin flames. And he's... Trevor could be the one behind the slaughtered animals. He's not keen on reporting what's happening to the police and every time — oh god.

Tears fall down my cheeks.

"Please give me a chance. We can make it work."

Calm down. All I'm doing is investigating if Hayes and I could have a future. I'm not doing anything wrong. And I'm not obligated to Trevor. Just because I'm staying at his flat while I get divorced, that doesn't mean I can't see anyone else. That was all it was meant to be. A place to stay.

"We need real-time together," I say, squeezing his hand.

"Maybe we could spend the night together. I haven't figured out how I'm going to leave Annabel yet, but I'll work on making it happen." He keeps hold of my hand and leans over towards me.

I lean forward and kiss him.

He kisses me back.

Shit. I jump back and drop his hand, but it's too late.

"Hi, Alex, we missed seeing you today," Gabby says.

"I, er—"

"Sorry, I didn't mean to disturb you." Gabby looks uncomfortable.

She definitely saw us kissing and holding hands.

"No, it's fine. I was. We were just—"

Hayes gets up. "I was just leaving, actually." He picks his phone up off the table.

"Hang on, I—"

There's nothing I can say to him with Gabby standing there.

"Goodbye, Alexandra," he says like he's ending our relationship.

Hayes heads away from the table and is out the door and gone before I can object further.

"I sneak here a couple of times a week for lunch. I'm addicted to the real milk lattes and doorstop sandwiches. You can't live on the juices and lettuce leaves they serve at the gym." Gabby's jokey tone aims to smooth the situation over.

Should I explain that it wasn't what it looked like? Two people having a clandestine affair. Hard to interpret it any other way. We were kissing and holding hands.

"I know what you mean. It's the first time I've been in here, and I'm definitely coming back." I follow her lead and allow the situation to be forgotten. If there's one thing I've learnt from Conty's set, it's that moving swiftly on is best. The least said and all that.

"Sorry, I scared your friend off. I'd better order and get back before I'm missed," she says.

"Yes, no problem." I stand up. "I've got to get home."

"See you tomorrow." She walks over to the counter.

The cold air is sobering.

Will she tell Trevor? Perhaps I should ask her to keep it to herself. Or the best option might be to not mention it at all. Surely she will work out that mentioning I was kissing and holding hands with another man isn't a good idea. Being discreet is baked into management at that level, isn't it?

I should never have come here. Meeting Hayes close to home was too risky.

I text Hayes, to reassure him. *Sorry about that. It was only a manager at the gym I go to.*

Nothing.

The minutes tick by.

I reach into my bag again and goad my phone into life.

No response.

CHAPTER TWENTY-FIVE

The knife-in-the-car-tyre incident was weeks ago now. I think Trevor is right about the dead mice and the break-in not being connected to that. The police were no help, as Trevor predicted. They told us to call if anything else happened. And nothing else has happened.

Only the telephone calls. When I called Cressida to find out what Conty was talking about, it turned out he too is getting a lot of calls where someone hangs up. He blames me. Why I would bother calling him and hanging up? My not having a motive hasn't occurred to him. His narrative will be I'm cut up about the marriage ending, and this is yet more evidence of how much he's had to put up with and how he had no choice but to divorce me.

I glance at the printout sitting on the kitchen worktop – confirmation of our flight times from the travel concierge company. Trevor has scheduled a private jet to take us to New York. He's hosting a table at an annual ball and we are going to celebrate my divorce coming through.

Trevor bounds through the door, home from work, and thrusts a package into my hand. I open the box. A state-of-the-art smartphone gleams back at me.

"Time for a change of number. Should stop those prank calls you keep getting."

"Good idea," I lie. I'm not ready to let go of my old phone, but I'm beginning to learn that agreeing with Trevor is the best option. It's not that he demands my agreement, just that he's usually proved right.

"Thank you, darling." I put my arms around his neck.

His cock grows against my stomach.

* * *

"You want a glass of water?" I ask, getting out of bed.

No answer.

Trevor is asleep. He could sleep for England. Nothing stops him from sleeping.

I pick up my old phone and take it over to the window. I love seeing the world outside. In the darkness, when I'm mellow after sex, the city is in soft focus. Our sex drive is out of control. We have sex most days, sometimes morning and night. No wonder I'm not thinking about other men. Well, that is not strictly true. After Hayes didn't reply to my message when we got caught kissing in the coffee shop, I've been thinking about him, a lot. One minute he was telling me he loved me and was going to leave his wife, that we should spend the night together; the next, nothing. He's true to form, at least.

London below is bright and still very much awake. The night is alive. Sending him a message is like a reflex. There's no reason, and I'm not sure I want to hear from him. Yet I still do it.

I send a one-word. *Hayes?*

The silvery moonlight combines with the warning lights on the top of the cranes to brighten the room. I don't recognise my life or me in it.

My phone stays silent. There are no messages from anyone. I wasn't expecting him to reply immediately but hoped he would. His phone may be off this late, so he won't read the message until the morning. How can he say those things? Tell me we are meant to be together and that he's leaving his wife. Yet silence, like everything he said, means nothing. He would have been freaked out by the coffee shop incident, but he could have shared his distress with me.

I catch my reflection in the glass and turn around slowly. My body looks different. My stomach is rounder. I must be imagining it. I'm sure it's imperceptible to others, but I can notice the change. After four children, I know what to expect. I'm going to have to do a pregnancy test in the morning. Women have babies all the time after not realising they are pregnant, don't they?

A movement behind me is reflected in the floor-length glass.

"Trevor?"

An envelope has been slipped under the entrance door.

I pick up the formal-looking letter; it's addressed to me. Must be Cressida with yet more divorce information, probably the decree absolute. I rip the white paper open. A razor blade drops out and hits the floor with a ting.

Please don't tell me it's more shit. I pull the letter out.

Watch your back, Cunt, is all it says. Each letter has been cut from a magazine or newspaper.

"Trevor, wake up, wake up."

"What? Not again. Get your mouth on my cock, and I'll think about it."

"No, it's not that. Someone has put a letter under the door. Go and see if they're still around."

He jumps up naked, pulls on his boxer shorts and a t-shirt.

I pass him the letter, then stand at the door, waiting.

He comes back, laughing. "How retro is this? I love the concept. Genius to go for the eighties horror genre. Now we know how old they are. It must have taken forever to cut each letter from a newspaper. Remember that movie—"

"Was anyone out there?" I'm not amused.

"No, the doorman said someone dropped it off this

morning, and he only just remembered. So he slipped it under the door."

"The woman with the dark hair?"

"No, a man, apparently."

"This is ridiculous. A man?"

Without warning, Trevor picks me up and throws me over his shoulder.

I scream.

"I'm taking you to my cave. You can't wake me up, stand there naked and not fuck me."

***

I step off the cross trainer. I'm going to have to abandon weight training. I can't function today. I've got no energy and need some food.

The gym café is packed, as usual. I stare around the room at familiar faces. When you go to the gym a lot, you get to see the same people, but often they don't become real friends. More context-dependent friends you only interact with at the gym.

Smoked salmon and scrambled eggs are plonked in front of me. "Let me know if you need anything else," the waiter says.

"Thank you."

One whiff of the rich fish, and I can't eat a mouthful.

I push the plate away and stare at my new phone.

My old one pings from the bottom of my gym bag. I'm pretty sure Trevor won't go through my gym stuff. In fact, I don't think he'd bother snooping at all.

I rummage around the bottom of my bag. Please let Hayes message me back.

I'm sorry I haven't been in contact. Can we spend that night together? I can escape next week.

I think for a moment. I'm not sure what Trevor is doing from one day to the next, but I could say I'm going to do something at one of the children's schools. Theo has his annual musical theatre picnic next Thursday. The children know about Trevor, but they haven't met him yet. I think we'll get away with it.

Wednesday night is best for me. What do you have in mind?

"What are you up to then?"

I jump.

Gabby sits down opposite me.

"Nothing, I just—"

"I'm joking. You didn't do your usual weights today? I wondered if you were all right," Gabby continues.

"Sorry, I was lost in thought. Not much energy today," I try by way of explanation.

"Are you sick?"

“No, I couldn’t stomach the fish,” I confess.

“Oh, you’re pregnant, aren’t you, babe?” Gabby says.

“What?” I say, alarmed.

“I’m sorry – I shouldn’t have said that.”

If she can notice, anyone can. But then again, she sees me at the gym most days, so will be used to checking out my body.

“Well, I’m not… er, yes, I’m not sure. I think so,” I admit. She’s the first person I’ve told. “Do I look pregnant?” I can’t stop myself from asking.

“No, not really. Well, maybe a bit, if you’re looking. But guess what? I’ll let you into a little secret. So am I. And I can’t work out as hard, and fish makes me feel sick.” She throws her arms around my neck, and our blonde hair merges together.

I look her up and down. “Wow, you’re like me, not showing yet.”

“I’ve read first babies don’t show as easily,” she says.

“Yes, I remember the reading everything stage. You can spend hours and hours researching every aspect of pregnancy.”

Gabriella looks quite a bit younger than me and is in the honeymoon period of marriage. It feels surprisingly good to have someone else on the planet know. And someone not connected to my life.

“We’re so excited,” Gab continues.

“Congratulations. The first baby is a wonderful experience.

You can't ever get that time back. So make sure you enjoy it."

"Shit, sorry, that was insensitive. You're going through a divorce, right? And still living with Mr Porter?"

I didn't mean to sound sad, but my situation is very different to hers. Not sure how she knows I'm going through a divorce.

"It's complicated, but yes, Trevor and I are together. The divorce is over."

I'm not going to add that by complicated, I mean I don't know who the father of the baby would be. The man I'm currently living with or the man I'm about to start another affair with.

Silence hangs in the air.

"Is Kira still hassling you?"

Thankfully Gabby changes the subject. After our encounter on the gym floor, the management followed through and officially warned her to keep away from me.

"No, I haven't seen her. The warning must have worked."

"She's been here a lot, but I'm glad she's keeping away from you."

Gabby works at the reception desk, so she sees everyone's comings and goings.

"I'd prefer it if you didn't say anything to anyone about the pregnancy for the moment. Absolutely nobody knows. In fact,

I'm not a hundred per cent sure if I'm pregnant myself."

"Haven't you got four children already?"

"Wow, you've done your homework."

"People talk. Well, Kira actually, to anyone who will listen, and a few who won't. Mum's the word, but maybe we could meet up, the two of us, and talk babies?" She picks up her phone. "I hope I'm not overstepping the mark, but we've seen so much of each other, and I don't know many people in London, so feel very isolated. Could I possibly have your number?"

"Of course, I understand. I felt like that; alone and pregnant for the first time in the countryside."

I give her my new number and put my phone away. It would be easy to mix up the phones, and I don't want to let Trevor know I'm still using the old one.

Gabby disappears back to the reception.

I pick up my old phone. Hayes has replied.

Wednesday works. Can you book the White Horse in Oxford? It's a restaurant and hotel. We can have dinner first. I can get there 7ish. I've called to check they have rooms, but I can't put a night away on any of my cards for obvious reasons.

Yes, will do, I confirm.

I have to know for sure if what Hayes and I had is still there.

Within seconds my new phone rings in my bag.

"Hey, baby," I say, thinking the undisplayed number is Trevor, from his office.

The phone goes dead.

I wouldn't put it past Marina to be behind these calls. It would be easy enough for her to get my new number from Conty, and what better way to make sure that my relationship with Conty is well and truly over by making out I'm crazy.

Trevor's daughter continues to be a problem, and his son won't meet me. They don't have my new number, though.

I've had no more contact with Rachel. I doubt she's behind it, though I did leave her my new number, in case she has a change of heart.

* * *

Each step home is a struggle, weighed down by seriousness. The pavement is grey, and the clean-cut buildings jut out at sharp angles.

The doorman doesn't look up as I pass. He's engrossed in some kind of video game. Trevor is probably using him as a test subject. No wonder he doesn't notice anything.

My heart pounds in the lift, thumping hard against my chest. Why am I putting myself through this? Of course, I'm not pregnant, its just paranoia. I'll go back and put Gabby straight later.

The lift pings open.

I take a deep breath. I'll do the test as a precaution. Just to be sure.

Today the flat is like entering an alternate reality. Through the lens of anxiety, everything looks unfamiliar. Trevor won't be home for another hour or so. Once I've confirmed I'm not pregnant, I can have a shower and put the prospect behind me.

The test is easy to find, zipped into the lining of my suitcase. The wrapper is gone from when I opened it at Christmas. The flimsy, white plastic stick shakes in my hand. *Don't think, do it.* I've put off knowing for too long.

I sit on the loo. My body won't pee. *Come on.* What's wrong with me? A little stream starts. With concentration, the stream becomes faster. I hold the white absorbent tip in the stream of pee.

The tension breaks. This is ridiculous. There's no way I could be pregnant. I'm forty-eight this year, and menopausal. That's why I haven't had a period. I laugh at myself and smile. All this worry. Doing the test at Christmas would have been the best option. I put the test on the floor to keep it flat and pull my gym gear up. The pee is travelling in a dark line over the two windows.

I'll make a cup of tea, then get rid of the evidence. And with it the niggling worry – or rather, fantasy – I've indulged. I feel silly now, thinking I'm pregnant, pathetic to be thinking I could still conceive at my age.

The test sits on the marble kitchen surface while I boil the kettle. I'm feeling slightly disappointed now. Perhaps this is what I've wanted all along, another baby. Would being pregnant be so bad? Shit, the test might still have some pee on it. I grab the spray bottle from under the sink.

The door slams. "Hi honey, I'm home," Trevor shouts. He's early.

"I'm just running to the bathroom," I call back. "Been at the gym and need a shower."

I close the door hard in an attempt to deter him from joining me.

Two lines are bright red in the test window.

"I'm coming in," Trevor shouts.

"Okay." It comes out as a croak.

I'm pregnant.

I shove the positive pregnancy test to the bottom of my gym bag, alongside my old phone, and strip off as quickly as I can.

Trevor appears and kicks off his trainers. He begins getting out of his blue grease-stained overalls.

"You all right?"

"No, a bit shell-shocked by the divorce moving so fast."

"Divorce is a shit show by all accounts. The only people that win out of it are the lawyers." He turns the water on full blast.

I jump in first and put my head back. The hot water cascades off me.

He gets in with me.

This is a custom-made walk-in shower, but he fills up the space.

I put my arms around his waist and my head on his body.

He cuddles me, and his big hand runs over my smooth wet hair.

"You're not okay, are you?"

I look up at his shining blue eyes. He's so beautiful.

"Yes, I will be, just need some quiet time."

You might know something is possible in theory, and be expecting it. But when it actually happens, it's a shock.

* * *

The hotel is booked. Hayes and I are going to spend the night together. It's more important, now I'm pregnant, to know once and for all if anything is still there. I need to feel him once more. Then I'll choose who the father is.

"I've got to go to a school event next week. Theo is in an outdoor production of *The Lion King*. I'll stay up there the night before," I announce as casually as I can to Trevor. He's engrossed in testing a prototype of his new car game, so I'm not expecting much of an answer.

"You want me to come with you?" he shouts over.

"No, I'll be fine. I'm not ready to explain you to the children or other mothers."

Trevor accepts my explanation, and I relax. The children are a great cover as he can't contact them to check.

CHAPTER TWENTY-SIX

The flames lick higher and higher. I sip my hot chocolate in front of the roaring fire. The drawing room of the hotel is designed to mimic a country house. Over the mantelpiece hangs an oil painting of a man surrounded by dogs. The stuffy atmosphere and being in the country remind me of Cedars. And my old life… I will always have the children, but Hayes is the last link to the person I was.

I've checked in. Hayes is late, and I'm nervous about seeing him. Why are we spending the night together? What I have with Trevor is more than enough for any woman. I know the answer isn't running into Hayes's arms, but I owe it to myself and the baby to at least explore what was between us. That's a narrative I can run with.

Next to me, on the blue and cream wide-striped sofa, my new phone lies unusable, completing an update. Something is wrong, and I'm getting blank messages three times a day. Looks like I'm receiving photos, too big to download. Trevor thinks the problem is a software bug and will resolve itself if I turn my phone on and off. The first line of attack for any IT support; recycle the power.

I pick up my old phone. My hands shake, scrolling through the news. But the only news I can concentrate on is that I'm pregnant. I can't remember sleeping with anyone other than Hayes and Trevor, but I can't be sure. Getting a scan will clarify the timings. As soon as we're back from New York, I'll organise one.

My new phone pings. The download is complete and the power turns off. Trevor thinks I've got rid of my old phone and will be suspicious if I go silent. I've taken a few porn shots to send him later, as he'll ask for them. I'll have to pretend I'm tired if he wants phone sex. Finally, it powers up again and the screen lights up. The emails are loading.

Photo after photo of extreme porn, mainly rape scenes interspersed with eviscerated small animals, flashes up on my screen.

A video clip starts playing. A huge man covered head to toe in black rubber is walking towards a woman with a hunting knife in his hand. They are in what could be a warehouse basement. She is secured in a stress position, suspended horizontally from two hooks in the ceiling, like cattle. Her hands are tied behind her back, and her feet stretch up. Around her wrists and ankles are rings of blood and bruising. Her spine contorts as she flexes her body in panic. Her wide eyes are red and swollen, and look like they might pop from her head as the man walks towards her. She has a ball gag deep in her mouth and hooks in her nostrils. Her head shakes violently against the black leather straps, blood drips from her nose. The man gets within feet of her face, and urine drips from the groin of her naked body.

Oh god. The scene looks real. I fumble with my phone, looking for the stop button, but drop it on the floor. I get it back in my hands to see the screen glitch.

A close-up of a knife cutting through soft pink flesh is in high definition. The high-pitched squealing is loud. The camera pans out to show a piglet being disembowelled.

The video glitches again, back to the woman.

Fuck, the video is still playing. How do I stop it?

The sound changes to a woman having an orgasm.

People at the surrounding tables give me quizzical glances.

I fumble around, trying to turn the sound off or press stop. Finally, I work out to swipe up and stop the sick scene playing out.

The phone vibrates again, but this time a call comes through. Is this his idea of a joke? He's into BDSM, but that was too much. Way too much by a long shot.

"Hey baby, you want photos of my cock yet?"

"Don't ever send me shit like that again." It must be him. He called immediately after I got those messages; a read receipt must be on.

"What?"

"Hardcore porn of women being raped and mutilated, dead animals. And that video is sick."

A few people close by tut.

"You've never complained about me sending you porn before. Except when you were the star." He laughs.

I lower my voice. "It's not funny, Trevor."

"You're kidding me, right? I like porn like the next man. And yes, I'm a kinky fucker, but rape isn't my thing, at least not the real deal. I consider myself a feminist. And you know I love animals."

"You, a feminist?"

Is he gaslighting me? He sent me sick email after sick email last year, threatening me with that video of us.

"Yes, I've already told you that. I'm still at work."

A video request appears on the screen.

I accept.

Within seconds Trevor is smiling, sitting at his desk.

"I haven't had a second today. I'll send you something kinky later if you like. Missing you already, baby."

"I don't believe you, Trevor." I hang up.

My old phone bleeps in my bag. A message from Hayes comes through.

I'm sorry, Alex, something has come up. Can't get away tonight. I will make it up to you, I promise.

Why did I agree to this? I was crazy to think spending the night with Hayes was possible. And crazy to think he has changed and this time things would be different.

I grab my bag and head up the stairs to what would have been our room.

I'm tempted to go back to London, but I've committed to the school picnic now. What's the point? Perhaps a night away from Trevor will do me good, and I'm not happy after he sent those messages.

The prospect of Trevor being responsible for all the things that have been happening moves from the back of my mind to the forefront. He could easily have done every single one of those acts. The doorman didn't seem to think a woman had been in the building the day of the alleged break-in, and Trevor appeared seconds after I opened the box of mutilated animals. He could easily have put a knife in his car tyre before we went into the restaurant. And, and, and … There is no evidence for him or anyone else being responsible.

I'm angry.

Maybe a bath will help. I turn the tap on and put my hand underneath. The hot water floods out. I find a mini-bottle of bubble bath and tip the whole lot in.

Stripped off, I examine my body in the mirror. Hard to believe another heart is beating in there. Even though I know I'm pregnant it doesn't seem real. I've spent so long convincing myself I'm menopausal, I'd rather run with that, but time is running out. What am I going to do?

The water surrounds me and relaxes my whole body.

Should I tell Trevor immediately? He's always been totally sure of us. But will he understand if I tell him I don't know who the father is? Our holiday to New York is coming up. May as well tell him after. A few more weeks won't make any difference.

Perhaps I overreacted. The porn video must be fake, nobody records somebody being murdered. The email *From* line was blank on that one, but some were from different addresses. Trevor is the only person I know with the technical expertise to pull that off. I want to believe he sent them, but in truth, porn like that isn't his thing. He's obsessed with us being twin flames and meant for each other. Ultimately he's a pleasure seeker, and the kink is about pain being pleasurable.

Who else could it be? Not many people have my new number. Trevor could have sent the messages by accident; perhaps they were meant for his friends. Can't imagine he'd be keen on admitting to that. I'll call the mobile phone network in the morning and ask if they can trace the sender.

Thick white towels are everywhere, and I reach over and place one on the floor to step out of the bath. I've got to take a break from thinking about the state of my life. Comfort food and a movie coming up.

I shrug the thick towelling robe around my naked body and call room service.

Pizza and chips arrive twenty minutes later.

I'm watching a romantic comedy and feeling a lot better. I love the power of movies to transport you somewhere else and change your mood.

I drift off to sleep with happy endings coursing through me.

* * *

I can't scream with the rough hand over my mouth. The faint smell of engine oil under my nose.

My body jolts up off the bed.

His hands pull open the white towelling robe and move between my legs.

A forearm is across my chest, pinning me to the bed.

My eyes are wide. But I can't see anything, only the moonlight edging along the side of the curtain.

Two fingers push inside my body.

The covers are gone.

He's leaning over me.

His hand lifts off my mouth slowly.

I scream.

"Shhhhhh, it's only me. We'll have the police at the door if you scream. We're not in a Hitchcock movie," he laughs.

I'm livid. "Seriously, you scared the life out of me."

He gets up. "Well, I thought it was funny."

"How did you know where I was; how did you get in?"

"I've got you on-location services, and I pretended I was your husband late from London, so they gave me a key. You seemed stressed, so I thought I'd come and surprise you."

He's wearing a navy suit and is very believable. Plus it was a woman at reception. I've seen how his smile affects people.

"What, you can tell where I am from my phone?"

"Yes, and you can see where I am."

Gosh, that was close. Hayes could have been here.

I'm not sure what's shaken me up more. The fact that Trevor pretended he was a rapist, or that he could have caught me in bed with Hayes. Thank goodness Hayes cancelled at the last minute. I dread to think what would have happened if he hadn't.

"I wanted to say sorry for earlier. Now let me make it up to you," he says, pulling me down the bed and opening my legs.

Make what up to me? So he did do it?

He lowers his head.

My fingers spread out in his hair, and I forget about everything.

* * *

"Don't you love hotel breakfasts?"

Trevor has ordered a full English, and his plate is piled high with just about every pastry available from the breakfast bar. He ploughs his way through the food with abandon.

I watch him. "Yes. I do." I take a gulp of my latte.

Why was I planning to meet Hayes, when I have Trevor? I'm absolutely crazy to have contemplated betraying Trevor for him. I'm over sneaking around, now I've experienced a healthy relationship. Affairs are cold comfort all around, whatever side of the fence you're on, and I've been on both sides now.

"Are you still pissed about last night?"

"Someone sends me sick porn, interspersed with animal torture, and then you pretend to break into my room and... What do you think?"

"Fair point. I'll look at the phone later and see if I can find out where it came from. The number was withheld?"

"Yes, must have been. Odd, as some messages came through as an email, but there was no address."

"We had something similar going around the office every time the computers powered up."

"Really?"

"Yes, we had it for a week or so. I got your phone through Porter Vision."

I relax. That sounds probable.

"You scared me last night."

"I'm sorry, but I did make it up to you."

My cheeks flush at the thought. It's obscene how good he is at oral sex.

"Hmmm."

"You weren't saying hmmm last night. Something along the lines of, 'Oh my god, Trevor, I love you. Baby, baby, baby, you have no idea how much I love you. Don't stop, don't stop.'"

The couple at the next table look over.

I laugh at him. "Would you like to say that a bit louder? The couple in the corner didn't hear."

"Don't tempt me. I'm better than Meg Ryan. We should watch that movie."

"That I can believe."

"We may as well get me meeting the children over," he says.

"I'm not sure that's a good idea."

"I'm all in, baby. Let me come with you."

Thank goodness, I based this trip partly on reality, and there is a real school event to go to.

"A public outing at Theo's school wasn't what I had in mind

when I thought about you meeting the children."

"There's no good time. Come on, we'll have fun. I've ordered a hamper. It will be here in an hour. Gives us enough time for me to better last night's performance."

"Is that even possible? Okay. You've convinced me."

"Yes, it's possible. And you're going to love these hampers."

"I'm going to love your magic tongue more."

CHAPTER TWENTY-SEVEN

We pull up outside the school. Trevor's bright red sports car stands out against the fleet of black four-by-fours arriving.

All eyes are on us, and we aren't even out of the car.

It wasn't long ago I stood outside these school gates and threw my phone at the wall. The headmistress had requested a meeting, and I was messaging Trevor before I went in. How improbable that we are now here as a couple, with me introducing him to one of my children?

Trevor opens the car door, and I jump out.

My misgivings turn into full-blown fears. This is a mistake. It's not fair on Theo. I turn up at his school with my new boyfriend, a man he's never met. He will likely tell his father I was there with some man. Conty sits on the board of governors, so if he doesn't, one of the teachers or another parent is bound to call him by the end of the day. Hard to switch off caring what Conty thinks. The habit of thinking I'm married is hard to break. The new circumstances haven't sunk in yet.

"Okay?" Trevor opens the boot and gets the picnic basket out. He hands me a rug.

"No, I'm not. We shouldn't have come here. It's too public, and not fair on Theo."

"Boys his age are more interested in their friends and the performance. If he sees you're having a good time, he'll be happy."

"I guess so."

The alternative was me here alone. I would have set up a tiny picnic as far away from people as possible and kept my head down until the event was over. No adult would have talked to me or openly acknowledged me. Instead, they would have given me pitying glances, glad they weren't an outcast.

Trevor takes my hand, and we walk over the lawn.

"Over here?" Trevor chooses the most prominent spot.

Everyone will see us from here. "Let's move towards the corner."

"No, I'm dumping the stuff here. Me caveman, need food," Trevor jokes.

"What? We've only just had breakfast. You can't be hungry."

"I can and I am."

Trevor lays the red tartan rug on the lush grass, groomed to within an inch of its life, and puts the large wicker basket next to it.

We both sit down.

"Please, behave—"

He pushes me back and almost gets on top of me.

"Is this acceptable behaviour?"

"No." I push him off.

"Can I have six of the best?" he laughs.

"What? No, just no."

"I'll give you six of the best. Or rather six inches of the best," he laughs.

"Your cock is a lot bigger than six inches."

"Who's counting?"

"I can't believe we are discussing the size of your cock. How did we get to that?"

"I can't help it if you're always thinking about my cock."

"Okay, you're right. But seriously, Trevor, ease up. This is my child's school. We should be throwing sly glances around, checking out the other parents, while pretending not to notice, and attempting to present a relaxed front."

"Both my children have been through schools much worse than this one. Try the London private school system. This is benign in comparison. I know what this place is about."

"Do you? And what's that? Actually, on second thoughts, don't tell me. It's too depressing. Open the champagne."

I start unpacking the hamper.

The champagne cork pops into the air and Trevor misses catching it in his mouth by a hair.

He laughs. “Eyesight isn’t what it used to be.”

“You’re getting old.”

“Just a number, baby.”

I search for the tall, glass flutes.

He takes a swig from the bottle.

The families who have set up picnics nearby steal surreptitious glances at us. They are familiar but not friendly faces. Most of the women pointedly ignore me. But to be fair, some of them are ignoring each other too. They subtly show their disgust that I’m here on a rug with Trevor. It doesn’t help that his loose dark jeans and a blue camo t-shirt look like they belong on a twenty-five-year-old, while their husbands are in the uniform of beige chinos and white, blue or pink shirts, brown boat shoes or loafers. The women carefully unpack picnic food from the same high-end supermarket. The idea is to present a down-to-earth but upmarket facade.

Trevor continues swigging champagne from the bottle and has another go at getting on top of me.

I narrowly avoid dropping the glasses, but laugh.

We are having way more fun than is acceptable for a school picnic.

He lies on his back and starts doing something on his phone.

Theo runs over in an animal headdress. The theme is *Lion King*.

Trevor jumps up. "All right, mate." He extends his hand. "Nice set up here."

Theo shakes his hand. "Yes, I love it."

"Mummy." He turns to me and throws his arms around my neck. "I'm so glad you're here. You look so well."

"Thank you, darling. This is Trevor, my friend."

"Okay." He elongates the word and looks at Trevor before adding, "Mum, you do know Dad is going to be here, don't you?"

"Of course," I say, brightly. Oh fuck. *Fuck.* No, of course I didn't. He probably told me, but I was more concerned about my subterfuge with Hayes.

"Great hat." Trevor pats Theo on the back. "Looking forward to the show, mate. Love *The Lion King*."

Theo smiles. "Thanks, better go." He disappears.

"What should we do?" I say, panic building.

"Watch the show, drink champers, feed each other strawberries then make out behind the bike sheds."

"I think we should leave now, quickly." I pick things up.

"Relax, it's hardly a big deal. We're going to cross paths sooner or later."

It's sooner; I hear Conty's booming voice before I see him.

Five seconds later, he appears walking with a few other families. Nobody I know. These aren't people who were in our inner circle. They survey the lawn for a clear space. He hasn't spotted us.

I lower my head as far as I can.

Trevor goes back to playing with his phone.

Conty stops, and they put their picnic baskets and rugs down.

They are in our eye line. If we are not leaving, maybe we should move further out and away from them.

My hands shake, unloading the food, pretending to be busy. This can't be happening.

The twittering going around the small field sounds like birds in a tree. We are the subject of the chatter, no question.

"Trevor, we have to go. Us being here with Conty isn't going to work. This is his domain."

Keeping calm is impossible. I chance a glance to see if they've seen us and come eye-to-eye with Marina.

Her eyes widen, and she opens her mouth.

Looking down quickly, I pretend I haven't seen her. In my peripheral vision, I see her whisper to Conty and point us out.

He jerks his head up in our direction. Disgust spreads over his face.

"Let's get this over with," Trevor says. "I want you to enjoy the afternoon and not worry about that prick."

Trevor gets up.

"What are you going to do?"

"Punch him, obviously."

"What?" I jump up too.

"Don't panic. You're so gullible." He laughs. "As if I would hit him in a field full of people. I'm going to clear the air and say hello."

Trevor turns and takes my hand, removing any doubt we are here as platonic friends.

We walk over to Conty and his cronies.

"Conty, hello." Trevor extends his hand. "No hard feelings?"

Conty takes his hand and shakes it. His face is tight and flushed. It's clear he doesn't want to touch Trevor, but has no choice.

Trevor adds, "Hello, Marina."

She's speechless for once, and looks to Conty for a lead.

"Hope the weather holds for the performance," Trevor continues, like this isn't awkward at all.

All eyes are on us.

Trevor moves back and puts his arm over my shoulder, as if our appearing hand-in-hand wasn't clear enough.

Conty would never make a scene in front of a field full of other parents. And he isn't used to Trevor's confrontational approach.

"Alexandra, I thought—"

He thinks I'm staying with Gerry and Michael.

"Now, we're all grown-ups, so let's make the day about the children. It's not about us," Trevor says.

I say nothing.

Trevor smiles at Conty and Marina.

Conty blusters away, spitting out half-formed words I can't hear, something about the Christmas party and not having a repeat performance.

Marina gets behind Conty. Her mouth stays open.

Trevor laughs in response, but I'm sure he can't hear what Conty is saying either.

"Enjoy the show," Trevor says as a parting gesture of goodwill.

He puts his arm over my back and guides me away from them, back to our picnic.

"See, wasn't that bad, was it?"

I put one hand upon my face, my fingers half-covering my eyes.

His eyes sparkle, and he gives me a wide smile.

"I love you," I say, not sure where it came from, but a rush of love is what I feel. Thank goodness Hayes didn't turn up. One of his children goes to this school, I think. I hope he's not going to be here later.

"So pleased you've got with the programme, baby."

He picks me up off my feet to his level and kisses me.

How did I get so lucky?

CHAPTER TWENTY-EIGHT

The hotel is in the centre of Holborn. Dotted around the vast bar are groups of people, the majority having business meetings. The booths are secluded and designed for privacy. Elaborate glass chandeliers hang from the ceiling. The glass front of the building is half-frosted in dove grey, protecting the people inside from passers-by looking in.

Gerry's chambers are around the corner. I've surprised her with my unexpected visit, and she's dressed for court. I'm not used to seeing her in formal court robes. We've been friends since our teenage years. To me she will always be that beautiful and quirky girl who had an instinctive understanding of me, so I didn't need to pretend to be normal.

"What brings you out here, babe?"

"I was in law land, as I've just been to Cressida to pick up the decree absolute. The finality is sobering. This was never what I wanted." The sadness has turned to resignation. Our relationship is completely over.

"Nobody wants marriage to end in divorce. You had no choice."

"I'm still in shock. I had no idea a marriage could be dissolved so fast. Conty instructed his solicitor to do the paperwork as quickly as possible." I sip my virgin cocktail.

"How are you feeling?" She gulps down half her glass of water. "Sorry, silly question, I can see you're upset."

"Pregnant."

She laughs, "Oh, you think he's going to propose?"

"You mean Trevor?"

"Er, yes. Who else would be proposing?"

"Sorry, no one, I don't think so. He's been there and done that, twice as I've now found out."

"Alex, what's going on?"

"I meant physically pregnant. Not pregnant as in waiting for something to happen."

"As in having a baby, pregnant?"

I nod.

Gerry's expression scares me. Aghast is the only word to describe her face. She knows better than to ask if I'm sure.

"I thought at forty-seven women were past having babies?"

Gerry has never wanted children and hasn't, publicly at least, ever mentioned regretting her choice.

"So did I. I thought I was menopausal. But evidently, old women can conceive babies. You need to watch out." I attempt to lighten the mood.

If she wants to ask if I'm thinking about an abortion, she

doesn't voice the prospect out loud.

"Ha. We've both made sure that isn't going to happen. Please tell me you know who the father is?"

"Trust you to cut to the chase."

"Fuck, Alex, really? How can you not know who knocked you up?"

"I honestly don't."

"You must have some idea?"

"My best guess is Trevor or Hayes."

"Yes, but you must know which one?"

"How can I? They were within days of each other. I don't have a sperm tracker."

"My money would be on Trevor," she says.

"I'm running with that," I confess.

"Have you told anyone else?"

"No, I've been in denial. Still am. I hardly dare admit to myself a baby is growing in my body. I keep forgetting, and then shock hits me."

"Only you could keep forgetting you're pregnant."

"Forgetting is the wrong word. I'm always aware, but I keep putting the thought to one side until I work out what to do. But yes, who knew how easy it is to bury your head in the sand."

"You've had twenty-plus years to perfect that skill, babe. Nobody else would have lasted that long with Conty. You're lucky the pregnancy isn't showing. But soon you won't be able to hide a bump."

"It's already becoming visible."

"You're on borrowed time. What are you going to do?"

"I don't know."

"You've got to come clean and tell Trevor the truth. I'd say that's the only viable option. He will understand that shit happens. Does he know about Hayes?"

"No, of course not. I'm going to have to tell Hayes too."

"Fuck Hayes, he's not important, and you're not in a relationship with him — are you?"

"Well—"

"Alex, please don't tell me you're seeing Hayes behind Trevor's back."

"I'm not seeing him, exactly."

"You don't sound very definite."

"We've been in contact, and I did try to spend the night with him, but Trevor turned up at the hotel."

"Shit. You almost got caught?"

"Yes, lucky Hayes cancelled."

"Why, Alex? Isn't Trevor more than enough man for any woman to handle?"

"Yes, of course he is. You've seen him. He's overwhelming. Even though we are living together, he's like a dream. I never get used to seeing him. And I've never experienced the kind of connection we have, ever. I didn't even realise love of this depth was possible. In fact—"

"You're not giving me an explanation. Why, just why, would you jeopardise what you have with Trevor for some crush you had over a year ago? Wasn't it unrequited, and he drove you crazy"

"I'm not sure. And yes, sort of unrequited. There's something between Hayes and me. He's unfinished business."

"Sort of? Are you crazy? There is nothing between you and Hayes. He ignored you most of the year, right?"

"We have a real connection. And I need to see whatever we have through."

"Through to where, exactly? You need to finish whatever you think is between you. That's all you need to do. And I don't mean by seeing him and fucking it out of your system. You've done that a lot with men. The way you think about Hayes needs to change."

"I'm trying, but it's hard."

"No, it's not hard at all. You look into Trevor's blue eyes, and you never look away. Let him give you what you've always wanted. True love. He's never let you down, Alex."

"It's not so easy. Don't forget everything he did last year, threatening me with the video of us having sex. He's psychopathic."

"You go on and on about what he did with the video, like you've never done something that seemed like a good idea at the time. Your ex-husband systematically destroyed you as a person. You've experienced real abuse. What Trevor did was foolhardy and reckless, but he came clean and tried to make it right."

"How can you stand up for him? He put me through hell. He sent a photo to my children's school."

"I agree his behaviour was unacceptable, to put it mildly. But he's owning his shit, Alex. And he's likely going to get a custodial sentence. You're using what he did as an excuse. I think you're frightened, of genuine intimacy, after what Conty did to you. So you are being drawn back to an unobtainable fantasy, namely Hayes. With him, you don't need to face a real relationship and be emotionally vulnerable."

"What, so you're the therapist now?"

"No, of course not. I'd be a hopeless therapist. You know how blunt I am. But I'm good at finding solutions and telling people what to do. Seeing Hayes is dangerous, whatever the reasons you're telling yourself. Don't see him again. And go all in with Trevor. Tell him everything."

"But I need to get Hayes out of my system. And that involves seeing him."

Gerry throws her hands in the air. "What bit of this situation aren't you getting? I'm sorry for being cross, but this is serious. You're having a baby and don't know who the father is. If you tell Trevor now he'll understand. But he doesn't come across as a man who'd put up with being lied to."

"I'm not so sure, Gerry. What if he leaves me?"

"I'm right, Alex. He loves you beyond reason. He told me you were twin flames at my party, which made me laugh. Where does he get this New Age shit from?"

"The way he goes on is so funny. He told me we were 111 not long after we met, and I had to search it up. He's romantic and throws himself into love like he does everything else."

"Before I forget, can you tell him the sculpture looks phenomenal in the flat?"

"Sculpture, what sculpture?"

"The 'woman in her prime' he sent for my birthday. It's about as tall as he is and cast in a swirl of bronze which pans out into a beautiful older woman. Truly magnificent and everyone comments on how wonderful it is. A new artist sponsored by Porter Vision made it."

"Wow, I had no idea."

"Alex, I love you, but you better drop the vague blonde act and get up to speed. You need to sort your life out. At least you're officially divorced and independently wealthy. That's a win, but the pregnancy situation isn't going to go away."

"I love you too. And you're right as always. I'm figuring out what to do."

CHAPTER TWENTY-NINE

"Welcome on board, Mr and Mrs Porter," the pilot says.

Neither of us corrects him. It feels natural to hear us referred to as married.

"We're expecting smooth flying conditions and an arrival time of eight-thirty a.m. local time at JFK International Airport. Teresa will be looking after you. Rest and enjoy the flight."

"Thanks, mate." Trevor acts like he's known the man his whole life.

The pilot disappears into the cockpit.

I sit back and buckle my seat belt.

The grey tarmac rushes by at a frightening pace. I've never enjoyed flying so do my best not to think about the mechanics of planes.

Gerry's reaction to my pregnancy unsettled me. She's right, I have to tell Trevor, but I can't do anything until after this trip.

As usual, Trevor has been thinking about his stomach and ordered tons of food. It's a night flight. So we'll have dinner and then aim to get some sleep.

I stretch my legs out.

Trevor puts his hand on my knee.

My hand goes on top of his.

We link fingers.

"So, how does it feel to be free?"

I turn to face him.

He's staring at me intently, waiting for an answer.

The plane speeds up. The power rushes through our ears, and we are pushed back into our seats. The nose of the plane lifts into the sky.

The question I couldn't answer drifts further away, and I keep looking at him.

His ice-blue eyes stay fixed on me.

When we look at each other like this, there's what feels like a merging of energy, sort of how I imagine inner peace.

He smiles and leans over, pushing his warm lips softly on mine.

"How about an easier question? What would you like to eat?"

"Don't you ever stop thinking about food?" I say.

"Don't you ever stop thinking about sex?" he replies.

I laugh." Both are essential for survival."

* * *

Supper over, the stewardess discreetly joins the captain in the cockpit.

Our heads are together, and I'm drifting off to sleep. A huge, impossibly soft and warm cashmere blanket spreads around the two of us.

"This is what it will be like when we're old. We can sit together holding hands under a blanket," he says.

"How can you be so sure?" I ask.

"How can you not be sure?"

I change the subject. "Thought you weren't getting old."

"I'll do anything as long as I'm with you," he says.

My sleepiness recedes. "Anything?"

"Aren't you already a member of the mile-high club?" he asks.

"What? You mean sex on a plane?" I act like that's not what I meant.

"Isn't that what you meant by anything?"

"Yes," I admit. "And no, I've never had sex on a plane. Have you?" I ask, sure the answer will be yes.

"No."

"Seriously? I'm not that gullible."

"It's sort of true. Not with someone I love."

"You're so funny."

"You're not going to be laughing in a minute." He gives me a mock threatening look.

"Won't the pilot know? Isn't that a bit cliché?"

"Yes, probably, but pretty much par for the course on a private jet."

I shrug the blanket off and unclip my seat belt.

We stand together.

The door is narrow, and Trevor squeezes in first. I slip in behind him.

Trevor bolts the door closed.

We both reach for our jeans at the same time.

I manage to get one leg out of the tight cream denim and my light pink lace knickers; I slip my boot back on so I'm taller.

His boxer shorts go down around his thighs.

He bends to kiss me.

I stand on tiptoe.

"How shall we do it?" I ask.

"Usually, I put my cock in you."

I giggle and can't stop.

He starts laughing too.

"We're never going to get through this," I say.

My hands snake around his neck.

Our lips meet in soft kisses.

He lifts me up and holds me against the wall with his hands under my ass.

I brace my feet on the loo.

My hands move up and down his warm, hard body.

“We can get through anything, baby,” he breathes in my ear.

His thrust pushes me up the wall and takes me by surprise.

I’m not laughing anymore and stifle a cry.

He puts his hand over my mouth.

“Shhh.”

The pleasure follows and spreads out into my abdomen.

Slower this time, he thrusts into me.

My head falls on his shoulders, and I cling to him.

Moving his hips backwards and forwards, he picks up pace.

I try not to cry out again as he makes sure he’s hitting the right spot.

“I’m close to coming. Are you nearly there?” he asks.

“Yes, keep going, baby.”

“Sorry, I’m going to come any second. Not sure what’s wrong with me tonight,” he whispers in my ear.

The feeling of him breathing close to me pushes me over the edge and I let go, concentrating on the pleasure he’s driving through me with each thrust. And boom, the explosion between my legs radiates out around my whole body.

He shudders to a halt inside me, his arms tight around me, and his body deep in mine.

The connection between us is clear and strong; love pulses through me.

“I love you,” comes out of my mouth before my brain can kick into protection mode.

"I love you too, baby."

His sperm drips out of me, and where he's been inside me aches for the rest of the journey. I'm sure the stewardess and pilot know what we've been up to, so I keep my head down for the rest of the trip.

Trevor and I keep looking at each other and smiling.

* * *

"Can we get a yellow taxi?"

"I've ordered a car, but yes, of course, no problem."

Trevor has a house in Manhattan and at one point lived here for two years. But he's booked us into his favourite spa hotel for a couple of nights before we head to his house. We're going out tonight, to a society ball.

I've only been to New York a few times. Having grown up in London, I'm used to city life, but New York is on a whole new level of overwhelming. The culture is raw, diverse and vibrant. So much to take in.

The taxi speeds past walls of graffiti. There are neighbourhoods with real discernible character, and people that look like they've stepped out of a movie walk along the streets.

We pull up outside a tall, anonymous glass building. There

are no signs to indicate we are at a spa.

"I've booked us both massages on arrival, good to get over long-haul, and they have these beds that are like sleeping on a cloud. They do the best brunch. Eggs Benedict like you've never tasted. And they have a hairdresser and make-up bar if you want to use them before the ball. Kitty booked you slots, but you can cancel."

"Sounds good."

The ball is an annual event and attracts anybody who is anybody. And there's a lot of pressure to look good and wear the right outfit. Every year there is a different theme but I haven't paid much attention. Something about red and fire. We're hosting a table of top executives from Porter Vision Security's New York office, and investors in Trevor's new gaming company. Who knew there was so much money in developing video games?

* * *

Not buying a new dress was an error of judgment. I've completely underestimated how dramatically the body can change in a short space of time during pregnancy. I can barely squeeze into the red silk sheath. My bust spills over the top. And I can't reach the back.

I shuffle into the drawing room of the suite, where Trevor is waiting.

"Can you help me zip my dress up?"

Trevor pulls the heavy material together and somehow manages to zip it up.

"There you go."

Thank goodness the dress is so well made it doesn't rip. Breathing in and out is near impossible. I should have tried it on before, but I assumed the dress would fit as it's always been a little roomy. My body feels like it's doubled in size over the last week alone, and holding my tummy in is touch and go.

Trevor is going to notice soon. Perhaps I should tell him immediately. Not tonight. I'll do it over breakfast tomorrow.

"Thank you."

"You look absolutely radiant, baby. My own 'Lady in Red,' only one of the best songs of all time."

"Really? You say that about all the songs you like."

"What do you mean? That song is an all-time classic. Are you questioning my taste in music?"

"Would I do that? No, I'm not saying another word."

"Because I'd need to punish you if you were." His blue eyes fix on me.

I try to read his face, but can't. I hope he's joking.

My breathing speeds up, and we stand looking at each other in silence.

"There's nothing more beautiful in the world than you," he says, changing tack.

I stay speechless, staring at him. He looks lethal in black-tie. My mind can't comprehend the feeling of us. I don't think he can, either. There is no separation between us. No sense of where he ends and I begin.

"Did I really just come out with something so cheesy? Perhaps you're right. My questionable taste in soppy music has gone to my head. Fortunately, my taste in jewellery is sound."

There are two boxes on the glass table. He picks up the larger one and opens it.

Draped over the royal blue silk lies the most beautiful necklace I've ever seen. It has large platinum links, rounded like infinity symbols which seamlessly merge into many vibrant red gems, surrounded by pavé diamonds that sparkle as you move your eyes around. The abstract design makes the gems look like burning flames along either side of the necklace. They connect to a large, heart-cut diamond in the middle. The parts are seamless. The overall effect is delicate but bold, elegant but edgy. The piece is simply breathtaking.

"Wow." I'm stunned.

"Do you like it? There's every kind of ruby you can get." He looks at me, watching my face intently, like he's reading reactions others aren't able to see.

"I love it."

"Do you? Really? It's a bespoke piece, I had it made."

I put my arms around his neck and kiss him hard, like I've never kissed anyone before, pushing my body against his. My fingers run up into his hair. And for the first time, I give myself completely.

He puts his arms around me and holds me tight.

"I never knew love could be like this," I say.

"Believe it, baby, it's real."

"Thank you. Perfect is an understatement."

"I got matching earrings, too. Here, I almost forgot."

In the smaller box are matching drop earrings like the flames with vibrant red gems and diamonds.

He helps me put the jewellery on.

"All set?" I say.

"We'd better leave before we start tearing each other's clothes off," he says.

"Or you can give me a good spanking. I'm really getting off on that now. It seems to make me more sensitive and the sensations stronger."

"As if that's possible with you – but don't tempt me."

* * *

I keep running my hands over my forehead to clear the

sweat. May is not exactly warm in New York City, but the heat comes in waves and washes over me.

Trevor puts his hand on the small of my back and ushers me out of the door.

I keep trying to take deep breaths to steady my nerves.

My tummy feels like it is protruding at an odd angle.

I sit in the car and close my eyes.

Breathing in and out easily is impossible.

Panic rushes through me.

I have to control this. As soon as we arrive, I'll go straight to the loo and undo the dress. I'll have to find someone to lend me a pashmina or send someone to find one. I'll tell Trevor the dress has ripped. The world keeps shifting around me, blurring in and out. I need to breathe.

"Are you okay? You seem vague."

"Yes, just tired. All that relaxing has relaxed me a bit too much."

"We'll spend another day at the spa tomorrow. You're going to love aromatherapy. Then we can head home, as in home in Manhattan."

"Good plan." Are you allowed to have aromatherapy if you're pregnant?

Buildings and people go in and out of focus outside the car window, even though we are crawling along the packed street.

"It shouldn't be too long. We are in a queue of cars waiting to drop off," the driver says.

The wait is agonisingly slow. I try to get control of the panic. Heat hits me in waves. My body is fizzy. I'm going to have to ask Trevor to undo the dress now. I can't wait. I have to take a deep breath.

"You are good to go," the driver calls from the front.

Too late, we're here. If I can make it to the loo, I can undo the dress and get some water.

The driver holds the door open for me. I can't do this. The ground looks unreal below me. I step out carefully, making sure my whole body moves together.

Trevor follows me out.

Camera lights flash in our faces.

We make our way to the high arch of roses marking the entrance to the ball.

Along the red carpet, Trevor has his hand on my back.

I look up at his megawatt smile and easy manner.

"Trev, Trevor, over here," a reporter calls. "Tell us about your new video game."

"I'll be back in a moment." Trevor moves away towards the reporter.

I want to shield my eyes. The flashes make me dizzy...

* * *

A light shines in my eyes.

I'm dazed.

The pain across the back of my head is deep in my skull.

Many voices swirl around above me.

"How long has she been out?"

"It's okay, baby, I'm here."

"Trevor?"

I try to open my eyes and lift my head up, but I can't and fall back down.

Consciousness fades out again.

CHAPTER THIRTY

Sunlight streams through the window.

I reach out for Trevor and squint up around the room.

The decor begins to form around me.

Why are we in a different hotel? We were staying at the spa and then going to Trevor's house.

I lift my head off the pillow a fraction, and pain shoots through my skull.

Whoa, that can't be good. I must have drunk too much. I remember vomiting in a car. No, it wasn't a car. I can't remember, and my head hurts.

My hand hits bars on the side of the bed, and Trevor isn't there. I sit up fast and open my eyes.

Where is he?

My head spins. Panic grips me. Fear deep in my psyche jolts me up.

A few seconds later, my focus sharpens.

Trevor is sprawled on the floor.

I calm down.

He's asleep. The black-tie around his neck is undone, but he's still in his suit, cummerbund around his waist. In one hand, his fingers are loosely curled around a bottle of vodka.

A woman dressed as a nurse walks in.

"You're awake. I'll call Dr Barnes."

Shit, I'm in hospital. Of course I am. This is America. This hospital bears no resemblance to the NHS hospitals where I had my babies. Conty doesn't believe in private health care, at least when it comes to me. The room has wall-to-wall carpets. And she's not dressed as a nurse; she's a real nurse.

Trevor stirs, lying next to the bed. The nurse won't be able to get near me until he moves.

The nurse stares at Trevor.

"Why am I here?"

"You don't have any memory of last night?" the nurse says.

"Yes, we went to the ball. And I drank too much?"

Trevor struggles up. "Morning, baby, how are you feeling?" He stands up, clearly not awake or paying attention.

Dr Barnes arrives. "Alexandra, is it? Do you know where you are?"

"Yes, call me Alex. I'm in a hospital in New York."

"What's the date and year?"

"I never know the date, that's not a good cognitive assessment. I'm compos mentis."

Dr Barnes gives me a hard stare, clearly not impressed.

"The eighth of May, and the year is twenty-twenty-three."

"Close enough. Can you remember how you got here?"

"I'm guessing I fainted at the ball. And someone called an

ambulance."

"Yes, but you don't remember that?"

"No. I remember vomiting in a car, though."

"It was the ambulance, but yes, you're right. What about before?"

"I remember the flight to New York, and we... We had an amazing meal on the plane. And..." I stop, unable to finish the sentence.

"You've got a big appetite, baby," Trevor adds, laughing.

"What about after the plane?"

"We were at the spa having massages, and we spent the afternoon... napping."

"Napping?" Trevor laughs again.

His jokes go over the doctor's head, or she chooses to ignore the subtext. Her only interest is in establishing medical facts.

"And the necklace." I put my hands up to my neck.

"Don't panic, it's in my pocket," Trevor says.

"You fainted and banged your head. It's not uncommon for the memory immediately before an accident to be patchy. Once we've done a CAT scan, we'll be able to give you more of an idea of what to expect, but the fact you vomited does indicate head trauma," she says. "However, you haven't vomited again and are cognizant. Both are good signs. Still, we'll need to make sure there isn't any damage."

"A CAT scan?"

"Yes, the procedure is scheduled in an hour. The nurse will complete the consent forms, and we'll send a team to collect you around nine a.m."

"I'm going to find some Alka Seltzer or whatever the fuck it is they take here for hangovers, and some breakfast. You want anything?" Trevor asks.

"We'll leave you to relax until then."

"Thank you, doctor." I try not to let the panic show in my voice.

CAT scan... I reach for my phone, which someone has put on the side table next to me.

Can you have a CAT scan pregnant? I type into a search engine.

Shit; CAT scans are not recommended for pregnant women unless the benefits outweigh the risks.

Think. I need to convince the doctor I don't need it. I could simply refuse. On the grounds of... Of what? Objection to radiation? Yes, that's it. I'll say I'm concerned about radiation levels. They will think I'm odd, but I need to stop this and buy more time.

The nurse comes in, holding the paperwork, "We need to run through a few forms." She sits down next to me, pen and clipboard in hand.

Down the list, I can see the question, *Are you pregnant?* I must be around five months pregnant.

"I'm sorry, but can you give me a minute?"

I can see my tummy pushing up under the covers. Every week the bump gets bigger. I'm going to have to tell Trevor. I'm not sure I will get away with it for the rest of the holiday. What if I faint again? What if there is something wrong with the baby? What if...

Trevor comes back with a bubbling white liquid.

"I persuaded the nurse on the desk to give me something, and I've ordered breakfast. It's like a bloody restaurant in this place. There's even a paper menu."

Persuaded will be a bit of an overstatement. He probably just smiled at her, and she agreed to give him whatever drugs he wanted.

"Okay, what's the matter? You look like you're going to pass out again." He sits on the bed next to me.

He might leave me. Being pregnant was never part of the deal. Whatever this deal is, it doesn't include a baby. Who wants to go back there when you've got grown-up children?

"Trevor, I'm, er, there's something I need to tell you." I start but stop.

He drinks his bubbling painkiller in one gulp and puts the glass on the side table.

"I'm all ears and cock, baby."

It's funny, but I don't laugh. I stare at him. Is this the last time he will want me?

"Do you want me to jump into bed with you?"

Maybe I should take him up on that offer first. No, what am I thinking? I have to tell him now.

"I'm pregnant."

His face freezes for a second.

I close my eyes. Is this the end?

CHAPTER THIRTY-ONE

"I'm going to marry you today. I assumed we'd get married at some point, but today is as good a day as any. I don't want to spend another day without you being my wife."

That was not the reaction I was expecting.

He jumps up and lifts me out of bed. I put my legs around his waist. The hospital gown flaps out around my bare ass.

"Is that even possible?"

"Anything is possible. This is New York, and we're having a baby."

He rams his tongue down my throat.

My fingers go through his hair.

The doctor walks back in. "I'm sorry, I didn't mean to disturb you. The nurse said you didn't complete the consent forms, and I wanted to know if there's a problem?"

We both turn to face her.

"There's no problem. We are getting married and having a baby." Trevor directs his full-beam smile at her.

"Congratulations." The doctor's words are in complete contrast to her concerned expression.

"Get dressed. We're going to file the paperwork now." Trevor puts me down.

"I strongly advise you to stay in the hospital. The signs are good, and given you are pregnant, a wait-and-see approach can be taken. I doubt there will be any danger to the baby."

"I'm fine, but we'll let you know if there are any problems. Thank you, doctor." I reach for my dress, hanging on the back of the door.

* * *

We walk out of the City Clerk's Office onto Worth Street. Grey brick buildings rise high above us. Pedestrians walk by, and the traffic speeds past like this is a normal morning. Trevor is still in his black tie and has the marriage licence in his inside pocket. You have to wait twenty-four hours after filing the paperwork before turning up at New York City Hall for the ceremony, but Trevor has secured a judicial waiver, courtesy of the fact that he is a resident of Manhattan. Who knew? Well, that and Cressida Archibald-Bronlow's international clout. She had to get involved and send my divorce paperwork. The plan is to head to the marriage bureau this afternoon.

"Do you think we need to go back to the hospital? The doctor wasn't keen on us leaving so soon."

"Do you feel okay?"

"Yes, I feel back to normal, but—"

"You're fine, but we can go back to the hospital if you're worried."

"No, I'm worried about the baby."

Not having any scans feels reckless now. I should have at least paid for a private scan before we left. Having four babies successfully will make you blasé.

"We can get a scan, but first…" He starts singing.

"What are you doing?" I giggle.

People look at him singing on the street in his black tie.

"You'll see."

He hails a yellow taxi. "First, we are going for breakfast, baby."

Settled on the black leather seat he phones Kitty, his secretary in London, yet again. She must be in bed. It's the middle of the night in the UK. He's already tasked her with sorting out the details of our shotgun wedding and organising a private jet for his brother, who will have been airborne for a while by now. He asks her to find an ultrasound specialist.

Trevor looks beyond handsome, sitting there in his black tie. But his exuberance bowls everything and everyone over. How can he be so sure? He acts like an impulsive child most of the time. A bit like toddlers who are so excited they've learned to walk, they are a danger to themselves as their brains haven't caught up with their motor skills.

I want to throw my arms around his neck and tell him, I love you. But I just watch him.

He gets off the phone, and I ask, "Do you think we can do that? Find someone for a scan so quickly."

"Yes, of course. Kitty will find the best.

"Fifth Avenue, please," he says to the cab driver.

People start a new day as we go past. Every moment is a chance for a new start. Life is everywhere and bursting with love.

Trevor pays the taxi driver and helps me out of the car. His eyes are a similar colour to the light blue sign above the door. He starts singing again.

"Oh, that's what you were singing earlier. 'Breakfast at Tiffany's.' I love that song."

A uniformed doorman ushers us through the heavy brass ornate double doors as we step off Fifth Avenue.

We walk around the counters until we find the ring section. As we walk, people look at us. I'm still in my floor-length red silk gown. The material stretches open across my back; the zip's only done up halfway so I can breathe. I'm not chancing fainting again. And I've got my necklace back on.

"Now, we just need a cup of coffee and cat masks."

"I'm getting you, baby. Love that movie, almost as good as *Some Like It Hot*," he replies.

A sales assistant approaches Trevor. "Good morning, sir. What can we help you with today?"

"We're getting married this afternoon and want to buy two wedding rings. They have to be ready by lunchtime."

The sales assistant acts as if we're an everyday occurrence. A couple turns up, hand in hand, dressed in black tie and asking for wedding rings at short notice. Perhaps we are.

"Of course, sir."

We are ushered to a private room with armchairs and a low glass table. Everything smells expensive in here, like new leather and blackberries.

"Now, what did you have in mind?"

"I'm thinking rose gold with pavé diamonds." Trevor smiles at me.

"Sounds perfect." He has no idea that rose gold is my favourite precious metal.

"I'll call our diamond expert. Can we offer you a glass of Champagne?"

"No, we'll have coffee, pains au chocolate and cat masks, please," Trevor says.

"Sorry, sir?" The sales assistant is confused for a second before adding, "Of course, leave it with me." He backs out of the room.

Trevor leans over, takes my hands and kisses me.

It looks like the morning sun is blaring in his light blue eyes, the ring of black around the colour making them unnaturally bright. Like in a fantasy movie where a superhero is drawing the power of the Universe towards them to cast a spell.

We stay staring at each other.

"You and I, we were always inevitable, always. You can't escape yourself. We are two halves of the same soul. And the heart beating in your body between us is a miracle."

I freeze in fear. He can't ever know.

"Don't be frightened, baby. Let go of doubt and believe in us."

"Do you think we have time for a blow job before he comes back?"

He roars with laughter, "Baby, you're so funny. But I like the way you're thinking."

* * *

The ultrasound clinic waiting room resembles a sleek, comfortable home. A plush grey carpet stretches from wall to wall. Diffusers are dotted around, giving off a light scent. There is a coffee machine and a biscuit basket. We sit on the two-seater sofa, our hands pressed together a little too tightly.

We can't have been waiting more than five minutes, but time elongates painfully. I try to stabilise my breathing.

"What if something is wrong with the baby? I should have

gone earlier."

"When did you find out?" he asks.

"A week or so ago, but I haven't had a period since Christmas. I thought it was the menopause."

"Relax. The baby will be fine, I know it."

A woman appears. "Mr and Mrs Porter, you can go through now."

The memory of pretending to be Teresa Porter at the STD clinic when Trevor gave me gonorrhoea breaks the tension, and I laugh. At the time, I wasn't laughing.

"What's so funny?"

"Nothing, I'll tell you later."

"Hello, I'm Amanda Dixon, head sonographer, and I'm going to be scanning you today. Alex, is it?"

"Yes, and this is Trevor."

"Lie down and relax."

I hop up onto the examination table. I've had to take my dress off, so I'm in my knickers.

Trevor sits on the other side of Amanda, holding my hand. The sonographer dims the lights. I close my eyes tight, willing everything to be okay, visualising us walking out of here, content and happy.

Amanda squeezes a dollop of thick, sticky gel onto my tummy. The machine clicks into life.

The real-world fades.

Attached to the machine, the hard pad slides over the gel and around my tummy.

The silence is deafening.

Trevor and I both stare at the monitor.

I remind myself to keep breathing. Please, God, let the baby be okay.

She points out the baby's heartbeat. It flashes; a rhythmic light.

"Thank goodness," I say.

Trevor squeezes my hand and kisses me.

"Would you like to hear it?"

"Yes," we say at the same time.

The most reassuring sound in the world is your baby's heart beating in your body.

The sound comes through.

Thump, thump, thump fills the room.

I stop looking at the screen and close my eyes.

Trevor's lips come down hard on mine again.

"Everything is okay, see?" Trevor says, leaning over so he can embrace me.

The pent-up tension of months drains from my body. I take a deep breath and let it out. Everything really is going to be okay.

The lady points out the parts of the baby. She's checking the brain, the heart chambers and the limbs.

Trevor is transfixed by what he's seeing. I don't exist for a moment. He stares intently at the small monitor. The alien images project what's going on in my body.

I'm so relieved the baby is alive and well, I'm euphoric.

I can't make out what she's pointing at.

Trevor claims he can follow what she's showing him.

We squeeze our hands together.

This is the first time I've had a scan with a man present. Conty refused to attend a single scan for any of our four children. He only attended the birth of our first baby from the other side of the room, and even then made it clear he didn't want to be there. I gave birth to our other three children on my own.

"I'd estimate you are around twenty-five weeks pregnant." She taps the number into the computer.

Could that mean there's no doubt, and Trevor is the father?

"We must have conceived just before Christmas? When you came over to say sorry," Trevor says.

"Yes, I didn't think I was ovulating so had no idea."

The baby is moving around a lot on the screen, but I can't feel it properly. Sometimes there is a little tapping if I stay really still.

"Do you want to know the sex?"

"No," we say at the same time.

In a flash, the lights are on, and that is probably the last time we will see the baby until he or she is born.

"Could you do us a favour?" Trevor asks the sonographer.

"Yes, sure."

"We're getting married this afternoon at City Hall. Can you be our witness?"

"Congratulations!" She beams at us. "Of course. I'd be honoured."

She turns the screen off.

My gut wrenches. The magic mechanical link to our baby is severed.

Trevor is going to be my husband and the father of this baby. That's the end of it.

All that's left is the photos to remind us. Trevor takes every photo we are offered.

"This is the best thing that has ever happened to me. You are the best thing that has ever happened to me."

He snaps a photo of the scan and uploads it as his screen saver.

CHAPTER THIRTY-TWO

On the side of the busy street, Trevor hails a yellow taxi.

"This isn't quite how I imagined us getting to our wedding venue," he laughs. He holds the door open. "City Hall, please. But I've organised a surprise for getting home."

"Shouldn't we spend some time apart and arrive separately?" I say. "At least follow some traditions?"

"No. I'm never letting go of your hand, baby. And there isn't anything traditional about us or our relationship."

"True."

Trevor follows me into the taxi.

"You've thought about this before?" I say

"Yes. I knew from the second I saw you, we were going to get married."

"Really?"

We sit holding hands.

"No question about it. Are you ready?"

The world around me is dreamlike. Reality has shifted to the best version of my life. Magic is in the air, and in the late afternoon sun, the city exudes vibrancy and love.

"I'm ready."

We reach Lower Manhattan. City Hall is a grand white building.

My legs shake stepping out of the car, but it's not weakness; I'm full of fast-moving energy. My body is high and light, like I'm not really here in the real world.

Trevor's brother and Amanda meet us at the entrance.

"Thank you for coming, mate." Trevor hugs his brother, Callum, who has arrived straight from the airport.

"You can't do this without your wingman. I was in the middle of a shift. You owe my sergeant."

"Ha, hope you told old Gaz I'd make it worth his while."

"He knows you're good for it," Callum replies.

Trevor introduces me. "This is Alexandra."

Callum turns to me. "Lovely to finally meet you. We've heard a lot about you. Congratulations." He gives me a warm smile and a big hug.

This is the first time we've met. The resemblance to Trevor is striking. They are both around six foot eight, with blue eyes and dark, spiky hair. But Trevor is solid, while Callum is slimmer and average-looking.

"Thank you," I reply. Two words are all I can manage this high on love.

"Thank you for agreeing to do this," Trevor says to Amanda.

"I'm honoured to be a part of your big day. So much love.

Truly, I'm in awe."

Trevor takes my hand. "This is it, baby." He pats my stomach. "Mummy and Daddy are getting married."

The marriage bureau is quiet, which I gather is a rarity. Two other couples are in the queue.

We sit holding hands on the long green seats in the waiting room. Trevor keeps looking deep into my eyes and holding my gaze.

111 flashes up on the screen.

"Our lucky number," Trevor says and we all jump up and head over to the administrator to complete the paperwork.

Callum and Amanda make small talk, as if what we are doing is completely normal.

"Take a seat, there shouldn't be a long wait," we are instructed.

We head back and sit down, still holding hands.

"I can't wait to be married to you," Trevor says.

Pure joy powers my smile back at him. I'm speechless.

An officiant calls our names. "Trevor and Alexandra? Follow me," he instructs. "We are off to the West Chapel."

"I'm going to love you forever and beyond. Everything in our lives has led to this moment," Trevor tells me as we walk.

I grip his hand tighter, my eyes wide and filling with tears.

The room is small and bright, with blue abstract artwork

covering most of the pale-pink-painted wall. The official conducting the ceremony stands behind a dark wooden podium.

We stand facing each other.

"I'm scared," I say. "How can it be this good?"

Trevor takes my hands and holds them out in front of us.

"How can it not be this good? We were made for each other, and I love you, baby." He holds my gaze.

I burst into tears.

He wipes my face. "Please tell me those are tears of happiness?"

"They are. I just never thought it would be possible to feel like this. How do you know I'm the one?"

Amanda wipes tears from her eyes and takes Callum's arm.

Callum puts his hand over her arm; tears well in his eyes too.

"The question isn't, how do I know, baby, but how could I not know? From the second I saw you, Alex, I knew."

Trevor's eyes look glassy, and we are both in danger of dissolving into tears.

We move in for a cuddle and cling to each other tightly.

I don't want to let him go, not even to move back so we can start the ceremony.

"If I could stay like this, at this very moment, forever, I would," I whisper to him.

Trevor wipes the tears now falling down his cheeks. "Oh baby, we are eternal. We've never been apart. We are one. And we were always meant to be."

He's right. Everything in my life has led to this point. It all makes sense now. We are predestined and every step has led me to Trevor.

"One and always," I say through tears.

The marriage officiant stands with a benevolent smile on his face.

"Now, let's get you two officially married, before we all end up in tears."

"Trevor and Alexandra," he gestures to us, "if there is anybody present, who knows of any legal reason why this couple should not be married, speak now or forever hold your peace."

The atmosphere changes from excitement to sober in a split second, the gravity of what we are doing grounding us.

"Do you, Trevor, solemnly declare to take Alexandra as your lawful wedded wife?"

"I do," he says, eyes fixed intently on mine.

"Do you promise to love, honour, cherish and keep her for as long as you both shall live?"

"I do."

"As a symbol of your promise, please place the ring on

Alexandra's finger."

Trevor pulls the ring out of his pocket and takes my hand. He pushes the ring along my finger and smiles at me.

I'm in awe of him. The innocence with which he gives all of himself to me, as if he's never loved before or knows marriage can fail, is the real miracle. And he makes me feel as if I've never loved before, and he is my first and only love. What passed as love up until this point was nothing but a passing liking.

"Do you, Alexandra, solemnly declare to take Trevor as your lawful wedded husband?"

"I do."

"Do you promise to love, honour, cherish and keep him for as long as you both shall live?"

"I do."

"As a symbol of your promise, please place the ring on Trevor's finger."

Callum gives me the other ring.

My hands no longer shake. I take Trevor's hand in mine and slide the ring on his finger.

His joyous smile could power the whole of New York.

The emotional tears of joy and happiness are replaced by intense optimism and excitement. Strength fills me to the brim. This is everything I've always wanted. This is coming home.

"By the power vested in me, by the laws of the great State of New York, I now pronounce you husband and wife. You may now kiss the bride."

Trevor lifts me off my feet and kisses me hard.

I kiss him back.

And we are legally one.

"Mr and Mrs Porter, congratulations," the officiant says, coming around the table and giving Trevor the paperwork.

"Thanks." Trevor shakes his hand.

The service took barely two minutes.

Trevor punches the air as we walk out of the room. "Yes!"

An official tries to usher us to another room for photos. Trevor ignores him and picks me up like he's carrying me over the threshold. Somehow he manages to manoeuvre us through the revolving door without banging me on anything.

We emerge into the late afternoon sunshine, and lights start flashing in our faces.

The photographer Kitty has hired runs around us, snapping away.

A red Ferrari is parked on the street with a huge white ribbon placed over the bonnet.

"Nice touch," I say.

"Kitty is a gem. The next best thing to La Peche. More like her twin."

"La Peche? What's that?"

"The name of my first car."

"I can't believe I've just married a man who names his car. I had no idea. Please don't tell me you have a name for your cock too."

He laughs. "Baby, this is the tip of the iceberg and only the beginning. But no, I don't have a name for my cock. We can make one up if you like?"

He carries me to the passenger side and opens the door, putting me in the seat.

I watch him walk around the car.

"No, I don't think that will be necessary," I laugh.

"We're going home to celebrate." He pulls away.

People beep their horns; Trevor and I laugh. Love is palpable in the air.

We pull up outside his townhouse. He walks to my side of the car, opens the door, reaches in and picks me up.

We go up the steps; my arms are around his neck.

Somehow he gets the key in the lock and carries me across the threshold. He slams the door shut behind us with his foot.

He puts me down in front of him.

"What now?" My hands go up onto his shoulders.

"We fuck on the floor, order pizza and watch a movie."

I laugh. "That's it?"

"What else is there? We live our happily ever after."

He pushes me back against the door. "I've been waiting to do this all day. It did occur to me to take you to the loos and consummate the marriage there and then. But I was worried we might get arrested."

I laugh like he's joking, but he's serious.

"You won't be laughing in a minute, baby," he continues.

"That I can believe."

"You can believe in us."

"Always?"

"One and always, baby."

He pulls the zip on my dress the rest of the way down, and runs his hand over my breasts, which are spilling out.

His other hand is between my legs moving up and down.

I put my hand on the front of his trousers.

His cock strains against the thick material.

He undoes the silk cummerbund, and his zip goes down.

I kick off my shoes and sink to my knees.

His cock comes out.

"And I've been waiting to do this all day."

He puts his hands on the door above me.

I lick his cock up and down, and my fingers caress under his balls. My mouth goes over the head, and I suck lightly.

He takes his jacket off and slings it on the floor.

I keep running my mouth up and down his cock while he undoes his buttons and throws his white dress shirt off.

He drops down on his knees and twists so he can flip his shoes and socks off, followed by his trousers.

He pushes me back on the floor.

I slide my dress off from under me, and throw my knickers in the direction of his clothes.

He holds my arms above my head.

Naked in his arms is where I always want to be.

In one swift movement, he pushes his body deep inside mine.

And I'm there, the pregnancy hormones raging through my body, making everything extra sensitive and responsive.

He lets go of my hands and shifts his body further up, above me.

I put my hands on his shoulders and hold onto him.

He fucks me hard on the floor by the door until I'm coming all over him.

"I love you. Oh god, I love you so much," I say.

He lifts his face out of my hair. "I love you too, Mrs Porter and our growing family."

"I never knew life could be so good," I say, breathless from the intensity of the orgasm.

"Welcome to forever, baby."

CHAPTER THIRTY-THREE

"The entertainment company are meeting us at Porter Vision around midday. I think her name is Petra."

"Do we really need to have a big party?" I ask.

"Yes, we're going to celebrate our wedding. This is the last one either of us is going to have, so let's make it a big one."

"If that's what you want."

"Are you worried about tonight?"

"Yes, it's hard not to be," I reply.

We're having dinner with Chelsea and Rowan, Trevor's children. Trevor thought it best we go to a public place, as that might create less of a scene. According to him, Chelsea loves a bit of drama, like her mother. He wants to tell them face to face we are married, and about the baby.

"They will see how happy we are and come around," he says.

"I think it might be better to tell them over the phone, before they turn up. So they can get over the initial shock."

"We can if you want. I'll think about it. I've got to go, busy morning."

"You look smart."

"Are you trying to make me late?"

"No, but I can try."

"Knock yourself out, baby."

* * *

"Do you have any idea what theme you'd like, Mrs Porter?" Petra's extremely straight, long black hair falls over her eyes as she lowers her head, frowning.

"Do we need to make it themed? A party is a party."

"Right," she says, elongating the word, her frown turning into a full-blown look of concern. Her long, blue, glittery nails go up to her mouth as she's thinking. "Well, no, but themes provide a framework for us to work with."

"Sorry about that." Trevor appears from the next room and puts his phone on the table next to us. "Where were we?"

"Are we having a theme?" I ask.

Petra looks at Trevor expectantly.

"I'm thinking red, and twin flames."

I laugh. "You would be. I have no idea where you get this stuff from."

"Twin flames are a real thing, baby. We are spiritually one soul."

Petra looks relieved. "Loving the spiritual bent. Red and fire, we can run with that."

Trevor's phone rings. "Sorry, my barrister, again. I have to take it."

He heads out the door for the third time.

"So I'm thinking..." Her voice trails off.

His barrister is calling a lot. He won't tell me what's going on, as he doesn't want me to be upset. There isn't going to be a trial if he pleads guilty. Gerry thinks he'll be given a custodial sentence, whatever he pleads. So I'd prefer him to plead not guilty. If we go to court, we can explain what happened. Yes, he did use our sex tape as leverage, so technically committed the crime, but he didn't mean to hurt me and... We are never going to get away with that. The argument sounds weak, even in my head.

"... at the entrance, guests can walk through flames, going up over an arch, and—"

My brain catches the last sentence. "An arch of real flames? Seriously?"

"Well, we want to go all out, don't we?"

This is out of control already.

* * *

"Wow, six months is a record." Chelsea approaches the table.

I stand up and offer her my hand. "I'm sorry you feel this way. We can be friends."

Her model-beautiful face contorts into a sneer.

I step back and sit down.

"Why didn't you tell me she was going to be here?"

"We wanted to share our news with you together," Trevor says.

Rowan is hot on her heels. At fourteen, he must already be approaching six foot five, so looks a lot older. Seeing him is like a time warp. I imagine this is exactly what Trevor looked like as a teenager. Judging by the sullen expression, he feels the same way as Chelsea. Or if he doesn't, he's not interested in wading in to support his father.

"Hello, Rowan. I'm Alex." I don't bother offering him my hand.

"What news?" Chelsea looks down on us. She is an imposing figure at six foot, and makes it clear this is a scene.

People at the tables around us stop talking and eating for a second, and glance over.

"Sit down, and I'll explain." Trevor tries to ease the tension.

This has been a mistake. There's no question of them accepting me in any way at all.

Chelsea pulls out a seat.

Rowan follows and sits next to her.

"We can spend time together, and you can get to know Alex."

"What the fuck?" Chelsea jumps up from the table.

She picks up Trevor's left hand, her fingers pinching his

wedding ring. She throws his hand back at him.

"Since when have you worn a wedding ring?" she snaps.

He stands up and goes to embrace her.

She steps back.

"We wanted to tell you—" Trevor somehow stays relaxed within the unfolding scene.

Chelsea turns her attention to me. "You fucking bitch."

I don't think he gets the gravity of the situation. He thinks they will come around, but I'm not sure.

"Calm down, darling. Alexandra didn't do anything. I wanted to marry her. And we're having a baby."

* * *

"She did what?" Gabby's eyes widen and her mouth opens.

We are sitting in the gym café for our now near-daily coffee. Pregnancy has bonded us. She looks much more pregnant than me, although we are around the same distance along, about 26 weeks. Amazing how women's bodies are different.

"Yes, she threw the nearest glass of champagne all over me." I shock myself again at the memory. "She stormed out of the restaurant straight after. All in all, it must have lasted three minutes. Rowan followed without saying a word."

"Sheesh, that's rough. What did Trevor do?"

I laugh. "He offered to go with me to the loo and help me sort out my wet clothes."

"He's so nice," she says, the subtext going over her head. "What are you going to do?"

"Nothing. Ignore it. I've never been happier, and we're going shopping this afternoon for baby things."

"So that's it?"

"What more is there to say? They hate me, and we need to accept their feelings."

She changes the subject. "Baby yoga is starting next week. Do you fancy it?"

"I've always been hopeless at yoga, but at least I'll have the bump to blame."

* * *

Outside the gym, I lean against the wall waiting for Trevor to pick me up. He's running late. My hand automatically runs over my round stomach. I'm obviously pregnant now. I've never been one of those women who revel in being pregnant and make a real deal of it, but this time around is the last time, and the experience is different.

"Congratu-fucking-lations," Kira sneers, coming out of the gym behind me.

I turn to face her. "What have I ever done to you, Kira?"

"Nothing, other than stealing my man. He's going to drop

you when he gets bored. That's how he operates."

"You don't know him at all."

"Wanna bet? I'm guessing he's spun you his twin flames story and you're so arrogant and stupid, you've believed him. Just talk to his ex-wives, he says that to everyone. He plays mind games, and you have no idea how kinky he actually is. Just talk to Max about the sick shit he got up to with her."

Anger takes over the rising fear. "We're married now." I lift my finger at her.

"You're more naive than I thought if you think that ring and baby trap will protect you. It's probably not even his. From what I hear, you're happy to spread the love—"

"Just fuck off and keep away from me."

"I will. You deserve what's coming to you, bitch."

She half-laughs, half-smiles and walks off in the direction of the car park.

A wave of heat rips through my body. I want to run after her and slap her smug face.

Does she know? I'm being paranoid. There is no way she could know. The only person I've told I'm not sure who the father is, is Gerry. And there's no way she knows Kira, or would say anything to anyone. I guess people talk, and she's taking shots in the dark.

CHAPTER THIRTY-FOUR

Trevor pulls up.

Kira is wrong. Trevor and I are the real deal.

I jump in and put my hand on Trevor's knee, bent to the side so he can fit in.

"Ready for some serious shopping?" he says. "I'm thinking we should buy one of those Moses baskets. We can move the baby around the flat with us. And a city stroller, that you can close with one hand."

The temptation to question Trevor about Kira dissipates. He looks magnificent in his smart pinstripe suit. The light grey highlights the iridescent blue of his eyes. I'm going to get swept up in love and lust for my new husband and his enthusiasm for baby shopping, not ruin our special time over some ex-girlfriend's toxic comments. The more I think about it, the more Kira seems the likely animal killer. She's unstable, delusional and scorned; a bad combination.

"Yes, definitely. Moses baskets are very useful. Did you have one the first time around?"

"Not sure. The nanny – well, one of them – did everything. Krystal was too busy with her reality TV career to be involved in real child care."

"You had more than one nanny?"

"Yes, we had morning and night covered. To be fair to Krystal though, I was empire building, so I wasn't around for her as much as she needed. So I threw money at it. And now I'm reaping the rewards, with Chelsea anyway. I need to find a way to reconnect with her."

"I sometimes think having children later in life, after you've already had the experience and made your mistakes, is better. You can enjoy the pregnancy and the baby in a way you couldn't before." I smile at Trevor.

"This is our second chance, baby. We are going to have our happy ending."

* * *

We stand on the escalators; he's two steps below me,

My arms rest on his shoulders, and our faces are on the same level.

He kisses me.

I close my eyes and rest my cheek on his.

He pulls me in closer to him.

Shoppers and the bustle of the department store fade away for a few moments.

The baby floor is buzzing with people. Couples like us

walk around hand in hand, smiling and enjoying this rite of passage; shopping together for your first baby. As well as loved-up couples, there are women alone or in small groups. Sleek city strollers in bright colours glide in and out of the aisles. Those pushing them have been the couples shopping together, nervous and stroking their baby bumps. But now they're on the other side, blissfully happy, marvelling at the miracle gurgling back at them.

This situation is novel. Conty kept away from me for most of my pregnancies, so I ordered everything online. I may as well have been a single mother, that's how alone I felt. My conversation with Hayes in the coffee shop drifts back into focus. It must have been hell for his girlfriend to lose a baby late on, and not have him for support. How can you legitimately gain support for losing a pregnancy you shouldn't have had, with someone else's husband? A loss is a loss, but I'm betting most people make value judgements.

Hayes's behaviour that year makes sense now. All the long gaps between messages and on and off contact. Hardly surprising he couldn't pursue or maintain a relationship with me. I shouldn't have slept with him after he ignored my first message. I should have dropped contact and not pursued him.

The unwelcome thoughts trigger unease in my head. I don't want to think about Hayes, or anything about his life or the time we shared. We were nothing, and I have to believe the baby is Trevor's. Trevor is my husband now, and he wants to spend every second with me. He loves running his hand over my expanding tummy, and he is in awe of the miracle occurring in my body. At every hospital appointment, he's by my side, holding my hand and smiling at me. I love the fact that he has no anxiety about the pregnancy. Like me, he assumes everything will go well, and we will have a healthy baby. He's right about this being our second chance. He makes happily ever after real.

"Sir, Madam, can I help you?" A shop floor assistant approaches Trevor, eyes gleaming.

"Yes, let's start with buggies."

"Of course, sir, follow me."

We follow him across the shop floor. Trevor grips my hand.

"What did you have in mind?" the sales assistant asks.

"We need one for the city," I say.

"This is the most versatile buggy on the market and can be folded up with one hand," he explains, eyeing up Trevor's shoulders.

Trevor slides the stroller over to me.

I push it in and out of the other buggies.

I've never tried anything like this. With the others, I had an off-road buggy, as we were in the country. Pushing the small, sleek frame around is a revelation, so easy to navigate around small spaces.

"Wow, so light and easy to push."

"What colours does it come in?" Trevor asks.

"You can order the hood in these colours." He hands Trevor a swatch with an array of colours.

"We'll take blue," he says to the shop assistant. "You like that shade?" he says, remembering to check with me.

"Yes, but what if the baby is a girl?"

"It's a boy, I have a feeling. But nothing wrong with blue for a girl."

"How can you have a feeling?"

"You must be able to tap into the baby's energy?"

The sales assistant outright swoons at Trevor. I can't tell the baby's sex, but I can tell that he'd like to have a baby with Trevor himself.

"No. I… well, I can feel the baby, but not tell the sex."

"Another thing I love about you. You're uncomplicated."

"I'm not sure that's a compliment," I say, laughing.

"Are we going with the blue?" the shop assistants asks.

"Yes, blue sounds good," I say.

"Can I help you with anything else?"

"Yes, we need everything," Trevor says.

"Always hard the first time around," he sympathises. "You

have to buy everything."

"Oh, no, we're old hands," Trevor says. "We've got six children between us."

The shop assistant's mouth drops open.

* * *

Trevor leans over and kisses me. "That was fun, wasn't it? The whole experience feels like the first time with you."

"Yes," I agree. "Somehow, it does."

"You go up. I've promised to look at Callum's car. He's dropping into Porter Motors in the next half an hour."

I open the door and jump out of the car.

Trevor waves. "Enjoy the rest of the afternoon."

"Thank you, darling." I wave back.

The lift is waiting. I press the up button. The woman reflected in the wall-to-wall mirrors as the lift propels me upwards is unrecognisable from the jittery, gaunt mess of a year ago.

I sit on the bed and slip my trainers off.

Trevor is doing all the things I dreamed about before I had children. The way I thought having a first baby would be, in my best dreams. Those wishes never became a reality. I was alone – always alone, with my hopes and dreams for the baby and with the practicalities of having a baby. I thought non-involvement was a class thing, that people of Conty's class didn't make a fuss about pregnancy or birth. The truth is, he just didn't want to be involved with me. I'd guess he supported Marina through her pregnancies.

Hayes drifts into my mind for the second time today. He must have tried to support his girlfriend when she lost the baby. He must be wondering why I've been silent for weeks. There's no harm in looking at my old phone. I'm not doing anything wrong.

The phone is nestled in a zipped pocket in my small carry-on suitcase sitting at the top of my large, walk-in wardrobe. This will be the first time I've checked for messages since we got married. Trevor still doesn't know I kept it.

Alex, where are you? I'm worried about you

Please reply to my messages.

I need to talk to you

Where are you?

I've got to see you

You've got to answer my messages

Just tell me you're okay

I type him a quick reply: *There's nothing between us, Hayes. I've moved on*

This is the end, and I have to shut him down completely.

He replies: *I don't believe you.*

So it *is* possible for him to reply immediately.

I got married.

Since when has that been a problem?

I don't answer him. I'm not that person anymore. I don't dare sleep with anyone behind Trevor's back. I don't even want to.

* * *

"Hi, honey, I'm home," Trevor calls from the door.

He says this all the time. It's become a joke now. I laugh. Most of the time I end up on my knees giving him a blow job.

"I'll be out in a sec." I throw my old phone back in the suitcase. I hoist it back up onto the top shelf.

I go out to greet him.

He grabs me around the waist. "I missed you."

I laugh. "You saw me less than ninety minutes ago."

"Felt like forever." He kisses me on the lips.

I pull away and take the bag of takeaway he's brought.

He grabs some plates and cutlery. We sit on the bar stools.

"Everything okay?" I ask.

"I don't want you to get stressed. Try not to read the papers. A lot of sensationalist crap about my conviction will likely be in the evening news."

"*Conviction?* What?"

"The court hearing was this morning, and I pleaded guilty.

But you aren't going to be named. They have nothing to link you to the offence. Plus I've got my lawyers working on a gagging order for the press."

"All that time shopping and you didn't tell me?"

"I'm not spoiling our special time over this."

"So what next?"

"A date later this year has been set for the sentencing, but don't put it in your diary yet. My lawyer thinks it will be shifted."

My phone beeps beside me.

The text message says one word: *Cunt*.

I put my phone down and say nothing.

Trevor moves on to tell me about the past hour of his life, like he hasn't just been convicted of a sexual offence, against me. He smells of engine oil, and his hands are dirty. His thick hair has got slightly longer and sticks up. The wax he put in this morning is still there, and the spikes are clumped together. He looks dirty.

I look at his animated blue eyes as he relays fixing Callum's old blue Ford Cortina. He follows the trajectory of my eyes down to the crotch of his jeans.

"At least let me eat my dinner. Then I'll get my dirty hands on you."

* * *

I turn my phone to silent and type, *Trevor Porter's conviction* into a search engine.

TECH BILLIONAIRE TREVOR PORTER PLEADED GUILTY

PORTER FACING PRISON TERM FOR SEX CRIME

BILLIONAIRE PORTER CAN'T BUY HIS WAY OUT OF JAIL TIME

Under one headline is a photo of Trevor leaving the court with a female barrister. He's not smiling, but he's not in distress either. How can he be relaxed? He might go to jail. Is this really going to happen?

I don't click on any of the links.

What's the point in reading the full articles? I need to think of the baby and keep calm.

More messages come through. I turn over and press my face into the pillow. Eventually, I pick my phone up again.

Bitch

Bitch

Bitch

Bitch

Bitch

Bitch

I don't scroll to the bottom of the messages; there are too many to read. And they are identical. The word *bitch* repeated.

Trevor is naked and near unconscious.

I put my arm over his side and rest on his stomach. He turns over in his sleep and puts both arms around me.

Folded into his body with my head resting on him, I press my ear against his chest so I can hear his strong, steady heartbeat.

Only then can I go to sleep.

* * *

"That's all it said?" Trevor says over breakfast.

"Yes, just the word bitch," I say.

"There's no doubt those messages are meant for me. I'm betting the dead mice and break-in were about me too." Trevor picks up my phone.

I pour more coffee but splash a mini tidal wave over the side of the mug.

Trevor says nothing. He never does. I keep expecting him to express irritation, but it's like he doesn't see my clumsiness.

"Odd – the number isn't withheld. There's nothing," he says, holding the phone out in front of him.

"Whoever is doing this is sick and needs professional help," I say.

"They've got too much time on their hands, that's for sure."

"We need to involve the police."

"Honestly, baby, forget about it. It's only a few texts. We've got Callum's birthday party this weekend at the football club. He's hired a karaoke machine, and I love singing."

"Of course, you do," I laugh. "Can't wait."

Hard to imagine Trevor not being good at karaoke.

He gets up and heads to the kitchen.

"Rachel must be responsible. She's one of the only people who has my new phone number. I've called her a couple of times to check she is okay."

"Rachel?" he asks, getting his stuff together for work.

"She was a client and... Never mind, it's not important. I'll call her again."

"Bye, honey," he calls, and the door slams hard behind him.

I dial Rachel's number, again. She was reasonable at the end of our last session, and I'm hopeful I can sort things out. Feels like a lifetime ago now.

"Rachel?"

"Not you again."

"You have to stop sending me messages. It's not fair. I had no idea he was your husband. I tried to help you."

"Help me? You're deluded. You destroyed my life. And you never do, do you, Alex? You never know. You do whatever you want and expect to get away with it. This time you won't. Karma will get you, bitch."

"What you're doing is dangerous. I've already reported your mouse stunt to the police, and I will go back if you don't stop."

"I have no idea what you're talking about. Stop calling me."

The phone goes dead.

CHAPTER THIRTY-FIVE

Trevor pulls up on the field at the football club. There are a lot of cars parked already. Usually, the vast green space is bustling with families coming to watch a game or cars picking someone up from practice. This evening we're here for his brother's birthday.

"You ready to party?"

I ignore him.

Neither of us attempts to open the car doors.

"You know, you look sexy in your football kit." I lean over and put my hand on his knee.

He moves my hand up, over his cock.

I rub my hand up and down.

His cock strains against the rough cotton of his dark blue jeans.

"Do I?"

"Yes, with that blue and white t-shirt stretched across your shoulders, and your thighs in those blue shorts."

"Should've worn my football kit then," he laughs.

"Not sure about partying, but I am ready for you coming down my throat." This is odd, as I've never been into sperm. In fact, I'd go so far as to say it has always slightly repulsed me. But with him, there's no pulling back.

"I'm not going to argue with a pregnant lady."

He undoes his belt and shrugs his jeans down.

His hard cock lies up his stomach and on the crinkled material of his light pink shirt.

I lean over and put my mouth down.

Licking him up and down is like heaven.

Trevor pushes a button on the side of his seat, and it shifts back. He flexes his hips up towards my mouth.

My lips touch the head, and I slowly open my mouth. I suck gently, moving my tongue in circles underneath.

His cock flexes, and he sighs.

I take my mouth off and move my head further down, so I can lick from the base of his cock up to the tip.

He runs his hand through my hair, and pushes a few strands back so he can see my mouth.

My tongue on his cock, I smile up.

"How did I get so lucky?" he says, smiling down at me.

I go back to licking him up and down. I love everything about his body. One hand moves over his thigh, pushed against the car door.

With light flicking movements, I make my way up to the top of his cock, enjoying the stretched skin under my tongue.

"I can't get enough of you," I say.

My mouth goes back over the head, and I suck gently, moving down slowly until he is as far down my throat as he will go.

He sighs harder.

I make a conscious effort to disengage my gag reflex and move down further. I still can't get him all the way down my throat, like I want to.

Back at the top, he lifts my head off and bends down to kiss me.

Our tongues move slowly together.

I move back down to this cock. My tongue moves in light swirls around the head.

He runs his hand through my hair again.

With my mouth completely over him, I begin moving up and down again and again.

"Mmmmm. Feels good, baby."

I can't do it for long as he's so big.

He moves his hand down and wanks the bottom.

Sucking the head, I move up and down in time with his movements.

His breathing becomes heavier, and his hand faster.

My mouth goes down further.

He lets go of his cock.

My hand goes where his was, and I wank him in time with

my mouth going up and down.

The movement of his hips up towards my mouth causes the soft black leather car seat to give and creak.

I step up a gear.

"You're making me come, baby."

The hot sperm goes down my throat, and I swallow.

He hardly makes any noise but lets out a low sigh.

"That was sensational. Thank you."

His head rests on the back of the seat.

A bang on the back of the car startles us – well more me – and I jump back over to my seat.

Trevor puts his cock back in his jeans and does his belt up.

His door is opened seconds later.

"Ello, 'ello, 'ello, what's going on in here then? You two should be arrested for public indecency or having an insanely hot car. It must cost a fortune in petrol to have your heater on so high."

"You fucker, pervert. Have you been standing there long?"

"Haha, no. I've just come out to find my phone. Emma's battery has gone dead, and we need to contact the babysitter. You were up to something, right?"

"What do you think, you're the copper?"

"Not a place I want to go." Trevor's brother moves back from the car so we can jump out.

"Happy Birthday, mate."

* * *

I sit at a table with Emma, my new sister-in-law, and listen to people having fun with karaoke.

"Next up is Trev and 'Forever in Blue Jeans,' where are you, Trev?"

On the other side of the table, Trevor is dissecting the premier league results and which football team he'd like to buy.

His companion nudges him. "You're up."

Trevor smiles and heads to the stage. The organiser gives him the microphone.

"This is for Alex, my very hot new wife. I love you, baby. And can't wait for our new arrival."

The remote possibility the baby isn't his get pushed to the back of my mind. I've convinced myself it's his, and I'm not dwelling on it anymore. We're married now and going to become a family. Thinking any other way isn't an option.

The opening bars of 'Forever in Blue Jeans' rings out around the hall.

Despite the fact I've married him, he still wants to show off in front of me, and checks I'm noticing him. How can anyone not notice him? I don't take my eyes off him for a second.

He moves his hips and stares at me suggestively. He's so focused on me, I'm sure he's going to miss the opening line.

How is it possible he looks that good up there? His light pink shirt lies down on his hard stomach. No matter how much he works out, or how much weight he loses, he looks slightly fat. The proportions of his body mean he'll never be slim. He fills me with an astronomical level of lust that never goes away. Hard to focus on love when all I can think about is the taste of him in my mouth, his cock, and what he does with it.

He doesn't miss a beat and starts singing, not looking at the autocue. He clearly knows the lyrics.

His eyes are electric and filled with love. He belts out the words. He's not a great singer, but his insane charisma makes up for his lack of singing ability.

Emma squeezes my arm. "How lucky are you? Look at him up there."

"Yes, very lucky; he's a force of nature."

Trevor continues singing, emphasising the more romantic parts of the song, banging his heart at points and aiming the words at me.

"Think he's watched too many live Neil Diamond clips," she adds.

"Definitely," I agree.

"Everything he does, he gives it his all," she concludes.

He finishes, steps down off the stage and walks over to me.

I stand up and walk towards him.

We kiss.

"You like that? I'm going to sing 'Cracklin Rosie,' next."

"You're the spit of a young Neil Diamond."

"Haha, thanks for lying, baby. I need a slash. You want a drink?"

"I'm not into water sports," I joke.

"Do you ever stop thinking about sex?"

"No," I answer truthfully.

His eyes meet mine, and he stops blinking. His face changes to a combination of brutal intent and amusement. I've seen him look at me like that before. The other side of him chills me, as I suspect I don't know half of it.

"Baby, I'll beat and edge you until you can't tell what's pain and what's pleasure, and when you end up on the floor, crying and begging me to finish you off one way or another, I'll piss all over you, and you'll be grateful. Want to go there?"

For a second, I'm stunned and can't talk. "I'll have sparkling water," finally makes its way out of my mouth.

His face softens, and he laughs. "I'll take that as a no water sports then. No problem, sparkling coming up."

I sit down and catch my breath. He scares me. As he heads off to the loo, my eyes move down to his thick black belt. I can almost feel the pain that took over my body when he held me down on his desk. And the loss of self I experienced. The inability to find a way out of the pain to tell him to stop. He's right. It became impossible to work out what was pain and what was pleasure. After beating me, he put his hand between my legs; my ass and back were on fire, but I was so aroused, his hand slipped on me. And it was like I was already coming.

He's gone, and I'm left staring off into the middle distance. I shudder.

"He's definitely met his perfect match with you," says Emma.

"You think?"

"Absolutely. I've never seen him so happy. He mentioned you last year, and it was clear you were the one. The look in his eyes."

"He mentioned me last year?" I ask, surprised he would say anything about what was clearly a casual hook-up.

"Yes. Callum was ribbing him about becoming un-marriageable, and he told us he'd met his twin flame and was going to marry you as soon as he'd won you over."

"Did he say how he planned to win me over?" I ask, curious to know if they are aware of his revenge porn conviction.

"Not at that point, but we do now. The press are going wild with it. Callum thinks he's going to prison for what he did to you. He's always been unconventional, but that was a bit much, even for him."

"I don't think he realised how serious it was at the time. It started out as a game, a bit of fun, but he was too convincing and I believed him."

Trevor is at the bar now. He's finishing a conversation with the man next to him and shaking his hand.

"He doesn't seem worried about it," Emma says, looking confused.

"Yes, that's unusual; his lack of anxiety is psychopathic, and all the talk about twin flames and spiritual connection is a crazy contrast."

"You're the therapist. We've always thought he'd fit into Silicone Valley with his wacky ideas and obsession with creating the perfect video game."

I laugh. "You're right. I could see him loving all that. I'm not moving to America, though."

"And then there's his questionable taste in music. Do you know 'Xanadu' is one of his favourite songs?"

"Er, yes."

Him edging me in his hot tub on New Year's Eve was months ago, but feels like another lifetime. It seems impossible so much could have changed in such a short space of time.

"Well, you certainly satisfy his teenage Olivia Newton-John fantasies. And then there's Buck Fizz and 'The Land of Make Believe.'"

"What? Bucks Fizz? No, surely not. He wouldn't go that far."

"Seriously, he hasn't played you 'The Land of Make Believe' yet? He loves that song. We had to listen to it hundreds of times one skiing trip. He kept playing different versions. At least The Carpenters are mellow. I don't mind their music so much."

I laugh. "He's a real child of the eighties though."

"We've always thought he was a bit autistic. He gets obsessed with things and doesn't realise how intense he is."

"I'm not sure, he—"

"What are you two talking about?" Callum cuts in.

"Nothing you and your crazy brother need to worry about," Emma says. "In fact, we're going to dance."

Emma grabs my hands and pulls me away.

I've never been good at dancing, and with my centre of balance shifting as the pregnancy progresses, I'm more hopeless than usual. But I go along.

Frankie Valli and The Four Seasons' 'Oh, What a Night' has started. Emma swirls around in front of me. She's got wonderful rhythm.

I shift from foot to foot in an attempt at dancing, content with watching her.

Trevor comes up behind me and puts his arms over my shoulders. It's like being enveloped in a warm, strong blanket. He smells intoxicating as always, and I take a deep breath. A lot is going on with him, but for better or worse, till death do us part, I meant it. I'm his wife now, and I never want to let go. This is forever.

I take his hands and sway with him, my body automatically bending and pushing back into him.

"Now we're going to slow things down with the 'Lady in Red,' so grab that special someone, or just grab anyone and smooch," the DJ calls out, making a meal of the word smooch.

The mellow opening bars of Chris de Burgh's classic hit fill the hall. A sound that can only be from the 80s.

The atmosphere changes.

Relieved at not having to try and dance anymore, I turn around, into Trevor's arms.

I'm still in skyscraper heels. Flat shoes don't suit my gait, pregnant or not, and this makes it easier for us to dance face to face.

I smile at him. He takes me in his arms. My hands move up to his shoulders.

He looks down at me. "I'll never forget how beautiful you looked in your half-done-up red dress the day we got married."

"It's a miracle I didn't vomit on it when I collapsed."

"Someone snapped a photo of me picking you up and carrying you to the ambulance. You were unconscious, and your hair fell down in waves past my arm. You looked sensational. People were moving out of my way, and the photographer caught other photographers papping us. Unique shot, and a phenomenal photo. I'm getting it blown up."

"Really? Amazing someone would snap a photo of someone having a medical emergency."

"Yes, but it doesn't look like a real medical emergency, it looks staged. You're going to love it."

"Can't wait to see it."

"You must be tired?"

"Yes, a bit, but I'm okay."

"I'm going to take you home soon and make love to you all night."

"Sounds like heaven."

I hold on tighter and rest my head on his chest.

He strokes my hair, and I feel him kiss the top of my head.

The beat of his heart is strong in my ear. How is it possible that in his arms, nothing can hurt me? But he has just told me he wants to beat and piss on me?

We sway together, not really dancing.

Nothing else exists. Holding each other is the realisation of everything I've ever wanted or thought or valued or needed. No line of thought leads to us being apart. No question is left unanswered. There's nothing to fuel uncertainty. The pain is gone. It's not possible to feel pain, filled with pure love.

Nothing is holding us back, no reluctance, no petty gripes. But most of all, fear has dissipated. The fear we'll say or do the wrong things; that's not a possibility open to us at this point.

This is unconditional love, and it's indestructible.

CHAPTER THIRTY-SIX

The screaming down the phone hits the pit of my stomach.

"Mummy, Mummy, Mummy."

"It's okay, everything is okay," I repeat over and over.

The crying is intermixed with incomprehensible words.

"Dead."

"Slow down. I can't understand what you're saying."

"Mummy. Mummy. Is it really you?"

"Yes, I'm here, darling."

"Woman."

"What woman?"

"I was so scared," she chokes out.

"Keep going."

"Dead."

"Just get it all out," I say.

I sit down at the kitchen table. My legs are shaky. I lean forwards and cradle my bump with my other hand. The phone vibrates, and I pull my face away from the screen to see what the problem is. Conty is trying to call.

"I can't believe you are okay."

"Yes, darling, it's really me, and nothing is wrong."

"Thank god," Athena wails. "I thought you were dead. A lady from the police called and told me you had been killed."

Or at least, I think that's what she says through the sobs.

"What?"

"It was the police. They said you'd been killed, and that Daddy was picking me up to take me to the hospital to say goodbye." She's becoming calmer.

"I'm fine, sweetheart. Someone must have made a mistake."

"But Mummy, it was the police," she says, not quite believing I'm on the other end of the phone.

"I'm going to drive to the school so we can have a hug."

"Okay," she says. "Drive carefully, Mummy."

"I will, sweetheart. I'll see you soon."

Conty is ringing again.

I pick up.

"Is this your idea of a joke?" he says.

It obviously hasn't occurred to him that I have been killed.

"Of course not. Don't be ridiculous."

"Well, someone called our daughter and told her you'd been killed."

"Yes, so I gather. I'm driving down to her now."

"I don't think that will be necessary."

"You didn't speak to her. Trust me, I need to go. She thought I'd died."

"I did speak to her. You don't need to be so melodramatic. I'm going to call the school. This is totally unacceptable."

* * *

I stare out of the window at the motorway rushing past. I'm not sure I can stand any more drama. I can still hear Athena's harrowing screams when she thought I'd died. Trevor thinks we should take the bull by the horns and get on with it. A Sunday lunch has been organised at a country pub with my children. We're picking up the two youngest, Theo and Athena. Nicholas, who now has his driving licence, is taking Elizabeth.

Trevor always drives fast, but this time I'm too distracted to care. I've put off telling the children about getting married and the baby. I wanted to let the dust settle after the I'd-been-killed stunt. They probably suspect something, as it was reported that Trevor was newly married in one of the news articles, and Theo has already met him, at the school picnic.

"Are you worried about how they will react?"

"No, not exactly, but I'm obviously concerned someone is targeting us. And the incidents are escalating."

"Yes, that prank call was nasty."

Theo and Athena stand by the gates of their smart private school. We pull up beside them.

"Cool car," Theo says, squeezing into the back seat.

Fast cars impress fifteen-year-old boys.

"You can have a drive if you like," Trevor says.

"I'd love that."

"Trevor, he's fifteen."

"So, he can have a drive."

"Hello, Mummy," Athena says.

"Hello, sweetheart. This is Trevor."

Trevor turns around and shakes Athena's hand. "Hey," he says.

"Hello," she replies, her voice barely audible.

Athena is subdued, but can't take her eyes off Trevor. He couldn't be more different to Conty and most of the men she's known. At least he's distracting her from the trauma of thinking her mother had died. She's been withdrawn and sullen since. The school keep calling Conty and me to discuss either her work, which has deteriorated from a consistent grade A, or her mood, which is apparently low. Conty holds me responsible, of course, like I in some way caused the whole thing.

The police said there was nothing they could do. The number was withheld so there was nothing to trace. Whoever called had Athena's mobile number. The police think they possibly got it from Conty or me. Neither of us has, willingly at least, given our mobile phones to anyone. The truth is she's a teenager, and I'm guessing with social media, getting hold of someone's mobile number isn't hard.

The pub is a ten-minute drive from their school. The country lanes blur outside the car window.

"Wow, you can feel the power," Theo says.

"You're going to love getting behind the wheel." Trevor gives me a sideways smile.

The rebuke forming in my mind dissolves and I smile back.

* * *

The pub is bustling and warm. We walk towards the small, cosy booth where Nicholas and Elizabeth sit chatting.

My oversize jumper can't hide the growing bump, but they aren't looking. The children are too interested in Trevor and the novelty of the situation.

I can't stand the tension any longer. "Before we sit down, I wanted to tell you that we got married in New York."

The news is out, and I hold my breath.

"Congratulations," Nicholas says, not missing a beat. He stands up to shake Trevor's hand.

Trevor takes his hand and goes in for man hug.

"Thank you, mate, appreciate your good wishes. I'm always going to look after your mother, and you guys are very much part of that package. I always wanted a big family."

Is he for real? This is the first time I've heard him say anything about my children. We spend so much time naked or in a bubble of love, blended families haven't come up. And his children have been hostile or absent.

"We're so happy for you," Athena says, sounding genuinely more upbeat. She still can't tear her eyes away from Trevor.

"We're going to have a blessing and a party," Trevor adds.

"You're not angry we didn't include you?" I say. "It was a spur of the moment thing, in New York."

"No, of course not, Mum. We're not babies, and just want you to be happy," says Elizabeth.

The warmth is real, and there's no undercurrent of disapproval or hurt. I'm sensitive to the children's feelings and would know if they were unhappy in any way.

"Our marriage isn't a secret, but I'm not sure how your father is going to take it."

Silence goes around the table.

Theo looks at Nick for guidance; he's never been able to keep secrets.

Elizabeth looks down.

Athena takes a gulp of water.

Trevor is oblivious. "I'm starving – hope the food arrives quickly."

"What?" I say. Something is going on that they aren't telling me.

Again, I'm met with silence.

"What is it?"

"Dealing with Dad is a bit tricky, isn't it?" Nick says, carefully.

"It's not your responsibility. I can tell him. I called him last week about summer holiday arrangements, and he was civil. The lines of communication are open," I say.

"No, Mum, you don't need to talk to him," Elizabeth adds quickly.

Again everyone sits in silence.

"For goodness sake, why do you all look so worried? Conty is just going to have to deal with the fact I've re-married."

"It's not that," Nick says.

"Well, what is it?"

Trevor is paying attention now, and realises something is wrong.

"I'm sure this won't be news to you, but Marina moved into Cedars a few months ago."

"Oh." My stomach contorts like I've been punched to the floor. "Of course she has. That makes sense. I think your father mentioned it," I lie.

Trevor fixes me with a quizzical stare.

"And, he, erm, Daddy has proposed, and they are getting married over the summer." Elizabeth gets the words out of her mouth fast, like she might not tell me otherwise.

Everyone holds on tight, looking at me.

I freeze.

Trevor shrugs his shoulders and gives me his *who gives a fuck* look.

This is serious news, and it's totally normal to have some feelings about your ex-husband remarrying, I reassure myself.

"Well, I'm very happy for them," I say.

How can he replace me so quickly? Oh, that's right, it's not quick. He replaced me twenty years ago.

Getting through the rest of lunch is a struggle, and I can barely string words into a sentence. I concentrate on eating as quickly as possible. The pregnancy hormones must be making me more emotional than I would usually be.

The children and Trevor chat incessantly amongst themselves. He understands teenagers in a way most forty-something men don't.

I'm not following the conversation so stare out of the window.

Nobody mentions the bump, but I'm sure they can all see I'm pregnant. The news of our wedding, and the bombshell about Conty and Marina getting married, is enough for everyone to take in. I appreciate their not mentioning it, and we'll tackle the pregnancy another day.

* * *

"See you soon, Mummy. Love you so much. Thanks for lunch, Trev." Athena is transformed and sparkling with happiness.

"I love you too, darling." I pull away.

"You've got my number now. Any problems, give me a call," Trevor adds.

"I will, but I'm feeling better now, thanks."

He's probably hit her with his new-age, spiritual bullshit about well-being.

"Bye, darling," I say.

We watch her back disappear through the high, wrought-iron gates. She waves. Athena is gone. I hope Nick gets Theo back to school before dark. He's taken him off to Cedars for a dog walk.

I'm glad we didn't openly talk about the pregnancy. I don't want Conty to know yet.

Trevor shuts the car door behind me.

I stare out of the windscreen, still reeling in shock. When was he going to tell me Marina had moved in, and that they're getting married? What they do is none of my business, but surely informing me is common courtesy. I suppose the same common courtesy I showed him by getting married and not telling him.

Trevor ducks into the driver's seat. The car door rings loud in my ears. His hands grip the steering wheel and he spreads out his knees. His hips flex upwards slightly.

A wave of pleasure moves through my pelvis and my mind goes blank.

"What the fuck was that about? You spent the whole lunch checked out," he says.

I don't know what to say, so continue staring out of the window.

"Why should you care?" he continues.

Feeling shocked and upset is irrational. I can't explain why, so don't try.

"Suit yourself." He presses the ignition and we set off.

"Slow down, you don't need to drive so fast."

He glares at me.

"Look at the road, Trevor."

He slams his foot hard on the brakes, and we skid to a halt on the hard shoulder.

"You can only stop on the hard shoulder in an emergency," I say.

"This is an emergency."

For a moment he's like a stranger. We've never had a row. We've had talks, but not a hot domestic dispute, like how this situation is going down.

He leans over.

I freeze, unsure what he's going to do.

"You are my wife now, and this is my baby. That ponce is history. Is that clear?"

"You don't have to be so threatening."

His light blue eyes flash with cold anger and fix on me.

"I said, is that clear?"

"Are you jealous?" I say, trying to lighten the situation.

He ignores the question. "Don't fuck with me, Alex. I'm not Conty and you're not going to sleep around behind my back."

"Is that it? You don't trust me? You think I'd do that?"

"At best chronic infidelity is a habit, and you've got a lot of form. I've been burned before. Don't forget, Alex – I've seen you in action, with me."

"I only behaved like that because I was unhappy. It was a decade before I slept with anyone behind Conty's back. And it was lucky I did, or we would never have happened."

I put my hand on the back of his neck and run my fingers up, massaging him.

He moves his head back on my hand.

My fingers go through his hair.

His hand stretches up and over mine.

The energy changes and he relaxes.

"I trust you, baby. Without trust we have nothing. I've

learned the hard way. There are always consequences of fucking other people, even if your partner doesn't find out. You know what you've done, and that will always put distance between you."

"Do you believe in complete honesty, even if it would hurt the person?" I have to tell him the truth about the baby.

"With what I know now, yes, I believe in complete honesty," he says.

He might think I trapped him into marriage. I should have told him before we got married. I can't do it now. The time for honesty has passed. Tears spring up. I'm frightened. How could I have ignored something so critical? I could be pregnant with someone else's baby. The secret will always hang over us.

"Don't be upset. I'm sorry for being angry. We're both grown-ups, and this is not our first rodeo," he says, to reassure me.

I can't do this. How did I get myself into this situation? What should I do? If I tell him now, he might leave me, but If I don't tell him and he finds out…

Calm down, calm down. There's no way he'll ever find out. Hayes has no idea there's a baby, let alone that he could be the father. And Trevor has no idea about Hayes. Besides, we weren't in an exclusive relationship at the time. So if he did find out I'd slept with someone else, that wouldn't be a deal-breaker. Technically there is nothing to tell. I have to forget about this.

"I'm okay. It's hard to have no feelings about the person you were married to for so many years getting married again."

"I understand. I've been there and done that too."

Our fingers intertwine.

I lean over and kiss him. "I'm sorry, baby."

He seems satisfied and starts the car.

Would I have had sex with Hayes if he'd turned up at the hotel? Perhaps I would have stopped. We'd have got caught, if he'd been there. But Trevor and I were not married at the time. Who am I now, after everything I've done to Conty? Thinking is overrated, and I need to stop now. This is tearing me to pieces. I have to forget all of this for my own sanity. The problem is, how? As Gerry says, I need to look into Trevor's blue eyes and never look away.

CHAPTER THIRTY-SEVEN

We stand in the lift up to our apartment. The rest of the journey home after lunch was subdued. Trevor has gone into work mode and is on the phone.

The mechanical power behind the lift makes a low hum, propelling us upwards. The yeasty, coppery air trapped inside with us, repulses me. Pregnancy sends my already strong sense of smell into overdrive. I make a conscious effort to relax the muscles in my face and breathe slowly. This usually holds off the wave of nausea so I don't end up vomiting. I've been feeling more sick as the pregnancy continues. With the other pregnancies, I was sick every day, multiple times a day, for the whole nine months. At least the early stages of this pregnancy were relatively nausea-and vomit-free.

Trevor grips my hand. With his other, he holds his phone up to his ear.

"Go with the results and alter the dashboard."

I rest my other hand under my bump.

"Yes, I agree. The earlier version was more engaging, but that might be a bad thing, too much going on is a distraction from the driving."

The heat in the lift is stifling. I let go of Trevor's hand and bend over, clutching the rail.

"You okay?" Trevor says to me.

"Yes, I just need to sit down. I feel sick again."

"Sorry, not you, I was talking to my wife."

Trevor rubs my bent-over back as if I'm in labour. He was not only in the antenatal classes, but paying attention.

"Get the A-team to trial both versions again."

The lift is taking forever today. I hold my breath for a second to block the fetid air going up my nose. My head spins. I breathe out, and the ground becomes more solid.

I replay his words in my head: With what I know now, yes, I believe in complete honesty. I'm going to have to tell him. As soon as we're in the flat, I'll explain the situation. But... Now isn't the right time. Talking when emotions are running high rarely has a good outcome. Once I've had some sleep, my mind will be clearer, and then I'll talk to him. Letting the children know about our marriage, and learning about Conty's wedding plans is enough for one day. Is there ever going to be a good time to say, I don't know if the baby is technically yours? I have to tell him tonight.

The ping indicates we've arrived.

Thank goodness.

I head out of the lift.

Trevor hangs back, still talking.

The smell gets stronger. What *is* that?

Up ahead, it looks like our entrance door has been splattered with eggs.

A broken shell crunches under my foot.

Closer to the door, the scene comes into ultra-high definition, a bit like our sex tape, and I see them.

The small, non-seeing eyes are bulging and black, with the sheen of jelly. Tiny claws protrude at the end of their half-formed feet. Fine white hairs sprout from their tiny rounded bodies. The texture of their skins is like they've never been out of water. Multiple chicks are strewn around the hall. Some are more developed and look like they were ready to hatch before... Others are alien-like and surreal. Blood-splattered impact marks cover the metal of the door to the flat. All are dead, but the mess is still warm. The copper and yeast smell has settled in the heavy air.

Vomit rises up and spills out into the mess. I brace my stomach muscles and bend over, clutching my abdomen.

Trevor pulls my hair back, out of the stream of vomit.

My stomach retches, over and over, with a force that makes me pray the baby won't be harmed. Please, don't let me go into premature labour. The baby is my priority, and I have to block this horror from my mind.

"This has gone too far," Trevor says.

The retching won't stop. The vomit continues to pump up out of my stomach. I close my eyes so I can't see it, mixed with the carnage strewn in front of me.

"I'm here, baby. Relax and let everything out."

Nothing is left, but my body shudders as my stomach tries to rid itself of bile.

I stand up, wiping my face with the back of my hand.

"Oh, god," I say.

He puts his arms around me. "Everything will be okay."

I lay my head against his chest.

My eyes are wide but not seeing, and my head is light with the relief of vomiting.

We edge our way around the mess and into the flat.

"You get cleaned up. I'll deal with this."

* * *

I sit on the bed with one hand over my face and the other cradling my bump. Bile runs down my jumper in dark yellow streaks. My bump was too big to avoid the vomit.

I'm shaking under the numbness.

Lifting my jumper over my head, the vile liquid catches in my hair.

My bowels loosen, and I limp through to the en-suite

bathroom and pull my jeans down, only making the loo seat with seconds to spare. Now for the other end.

My body is intent on purging all fluids.

Please let the baby be okay.

When I wipe, the pure white tissue comes up with blood smears.

I burst into tears.

The blood could be from my bowel. If I don't calm down, this situation is going to get worse.

Peeling the jeans off my feet, I stand up and unclip my bra.

Being naked feels better. This is a bad sign, as I get the desire to be naked when I'm about to give birth. And I should know, having given birth four times.

I'm need a bath. The vomit has gone everywhere. And the stench makes me retch.

I wipe again.

The smear turns to an alarming red, soaking the tissue.

Fuck. Should we call an ambulance?

"Trevor," I call.

"I'll be there in a sec. The police are arriving."

"Can you come now?"

His head appears around the door seconds later. "You okay?"

"I'm not sure. I'm bleeding."

"Stay right there." He leaves the door open.

A radio hisses. "Go ahead".

"This is Officer Smith. Can we have an ambulance to One Five One Thames Reach, Penthouse? We have a pregnant woman at the scene, bleeding."

The radio hisses again. "Roger."

Trevor comes back through the bathroom door. "An ambulance is coming. Sit down. I'll find some clothes."

Disbelief that this is really happening stops the tears. Shock stuns me into silence.

Trevor comes back with a dress and some knickers. He bends down and picks up each of my feet, putting them in the underwear. He helps me to stand. I'm not in pain, but my legs are weak. He pulls them up.

"Well, this is a novelty. I'm usually pulling your knickers down."

A little laugh escapes my dry mouth.

"You haven't lost your sense of humour, then. And we're not losing our baby. He's a fighter, like his old man. Going to the hospital is just a precaution."

I'm calm, but fear and helplessness course through me.

"I've read somewhere that shock can bring on premature labour."

He slips the floral dress over my head and pulls the light cotton down over my ass.

I sit back down on the loo.

"You're not having the baby now. Have you got any pads in case there's more blood?"

"I don't think so." Only a man who has had children would ask a question like that.

"I'll pack more clothes so you can change at the hospital."

He reaches up to the top of the wardrobe for my small cabin suitcase.

Shit, my old phone is in it, and I'm not sure I put it back in the lining. He'll know I've kept it.

"No—" I say, the panic rising.

"Mrs Porter, Alex? My name is Susan, and this is Maggie." Two female paramedics enter the room.

Trevor moves his hand back down from my suitcase and comes over to me, gripping my hand.

I let out a long breath. That was close.

"We're going to take you to the hospital, and they can check the baby is okay."

A stretcher chair is wheeled in with them.

Trevor picks me up and lays me on the black plastic.

"I'll just grab you a jumper."

"No, stay with me." I reach out to Trevor.

He comes back. "I'm here, baby."

He pulls off his jumper and puts it over me. The smell is

immediately comforting.

We head out of the bedroom and through the flat.

The door hangs wide open. I brace to pass the mess, holding my breath and burying my face in Trevor's jumper. Another bout of vomiting might finish me off.

The paramedics ignore the splattered avian foetuses as they walk us back to the lift.

"We will follow you to the hospital," the police officer says to Trevor.

CHAPTER THIRTY-EIGHT

The hospital is a ten-minute drive from the flat in an ambulance. In a car, it's not unusual for the journey to take half an hour plus.

Trevor holds my hand.

Susan is driving, and Maggie sits at the end of the stretcher.

Tears fall down my cheeks. "The baby isn't moving."

Trevor wipes my eyes. "Our baby is a fighter. He's going to be okay."

"How can you be so sure?"

"We have to believe he will be okay. What more can we do?"

My head goes back on the blanket, and I close my eyes to block the flashing lights and medical equipment around us. Please, God, let the baby be okay.

The ambulance stops, and Maggie opens the back. Susan comes around and they wheel me out and through double automatic doors. We enter a back area of the accident and emergency department.

"Take her straight up to gynae, they are waiting," a nurse instructs the paramedic.

"Got it," Maggie says.

We head through more automatic double doors. Trevor walks alongside the stretcher. Under the blanket, I clutch my tummy, willing the baby to move.

Endless white corridors filled with people disorientate me. The journey is never ending. Up in another lift, higher. More corridors of white walls, hung with artwork of flowers and blocks of colour.

The agony is prolonged.

Trevor is riled. I can feel his energy tightly coiled. Whatever he's saying, he's frightened.

We are greeted by a young male doctor, who doesn't look older than twenty-five.

"This is Alex, vomiting and diarrhoea. Second trimester, bleeding."

"Hello, Alex, my name is Dr Heath. We'll scan you first, and check how the baby is doing."

"Thank you."

"And this is the father?"

"Yes, Trevor is my husband."

"Scan room two, please," Dr Heath instructs Maggie.

Trevor helps Maggie lift me on to the scanning table.

"Good luck. I hope everything is okay with the little one." Maggie leaves. Her job is done.

A fresh wave of tears fall down my cheeks. "What if the baby isn't okay?" Oh God, please let the baby survive.

Dr Heath switches the machine on. "We'll know more soon."

"He's going to be okay, keep calm," Trevor says.

I lift my dress up and bunch the material out of the way of my tummy.

I'm gripped with fear.

Trevor holds my hand tight, his poker face doesn't let him down.

We both stare at the screen.

Cold, wet slime is smothered over my bump. Time elongates while he gets the pad ready to apply to my skin.

Tension is thick in the air.

I'm too scared to cry and feel frozen.

The pad transmits the live image to the screen.

The baby is visible.

"Why can't we hear the heartbeat?"

"We don't use sound initially."

I force myself into slow, deep breaths.

Dr Heath moves the pad around the swelling skin of my tummy.

His expression is unreadable.

Trevor concentrates on the screen intently, like he wants to tell for himself.

Moving the pad around every angle of my tummy goes on for

an excruciating amount of time.

Silence.

"The baby is fine."

"Are you sure? Why isn't the baby moving?" I can't trust the news is positive.

"I'd guess the baby is sleeping," Dr Heath says.

"Sleeping?" I query.

"Yes. I can't detect any problems."

"Why was I bleeding?"

"You were vomiting and potentially burst a small blood vessel in the vagina or pocket of blood in the cervix, but often we don't find a reason. Bleeding a small amount is never normal, but neither is it uncommon."

"It wasn't a small amount. It soaked a tissue."

"Even a teaspoon of blood can look like a lot," Dr Heath explains. "To make sure everything is fine we'll monitor the baby's heart rate and keep you in for a few hours so we can check there's no more bleeding."

"Thank god." Trevor puts his head to my head. "Oh, baby. Thank god."

Tears start falling again, down my cheeks, and mix with his.

We cling to each other.

I'm wheeled into a maternity triage area, and a heart monitor is stretched around my tummy.

"You can speak to her now," Dr Heath tells the police officers.

The two uniformed officers from the flat come over to my chair.

Trevor starts pacing up and down. "If you don't do something about this, I will."

"Calm down, sir. I can understand why you are angry, but I strongly advise you not to take matters into your own hands and let us handle the investigation."

"This has to stop. My wife is pregnant and I won't let anybody hurt her or the baby."

"Does the building have security footage?" the officer asks.

"Yes, but it didn't capture the sick fuck last time," Trevor says.

"I wanted to look too, but the doorman said you took it?" I say.

"Yes, I gave the clip to our best analyst to see if they could find anything, but they drew a blank," he confirms.

"We're going to need that footage, Mr Porter."

Trevor picks up his phone. "Kit, can you ask Corey to send over the footage from my building. I need to send it to the police. No, I'm at the hospital. The doorman can show them up to the hall, the mess will be evident. Call you back in a bit."

"Do you have any idea who could be targeting you, Mrs Porter?"

"No. Well, yes. A few people spring to mind."

"Can you run through the names?"

"Do we have to do this now? She needs to rest. And what if my wife isn't the target? It could be me, and they're getting at me through her."

"Yes, that's a possibility, we can't rule anything out. But at this stage, these are acts of vandalism. Our options are limited. We can take statements at a later date."

"Are you joking? Someone has been killing animals. The last few months could be described as a sustained campaign of harassment against us. Our children are being targeted too, and our daughter was traumatised by a sick call while she was at school."

This is the first time I've heard him accept how serious the situation is, and I'm touched he called Athena 'our daughter.'

"I'm only aware of one reported incident. Are you saying there are more?" the police offer asks.

"Yes," I confirm. "A lot has happened."

"We're going to need you to write a statement with a timeline of everything that has occurred. And we'll take it from there."

Trevor's phone rings. "Thanks for sorting the cleaning, Kit. We'll be at the hospital for a few hours. Tell them to start so it is done before we get back."

The police officer nearest to me gives me a card. "Make an appointment, and we'll go through the statement with you. I'm glad everything is okay with the baby."

"Thank you."

"We'll be in touch," Trevor adds.

The police officers leave us alone.

I reach out for Trevor's hand. He kneels down and hugs me. I hold on to him.

He tightens his arms around me. His hands run up from my back and into my hair. "Let's get away from all this and have a proper honeymoon. Did I tell you we own a villa in St Tropez?"

CHAPTER THIRTY-NINE

Two days into our belated honeymoon on the French Riviera, and dead animals, antenatal scares and ex-husbands remarrying, have faded to sun, sea, and long hot nights wrapped up in sexual alchemy.

Trevor pulls himself up out of the water and back onto the boat.

I lie on the deck in the late afternoon sunshine.

He lies next to me, the sea clings to his body, cooling my hot skin. And he runs a cold, wet hand over my stomach.

The baby shifts position.

"Did you feel that?"

"Yes." He moves his hand in the direction of the baby and pats my tummy. "Now go to sleep. I need to talk to Mummy."

I raise my eyebrows. "Talk to me?"

"Yes, I want to tell you again how much I love you, both of you. Now turn over."

"Tell me? Don't you mean show me?" I smile at him.

"Am I that predictable?"

The sun beats down on us.

"Yes, and I love that about you, but not here. Let's go inside."

"The crew aren't interested in what we're doing on the deck. These people are paid to be discreet."

He slips his hand down the front of my bikini bottoms. He moves his cold fingers up and down. His mouth comes down, still wet from the water, to kiss my lips.

The salt from the sea merges on both our tongues.

He pulls his fingers out from between my legs and puts his hand on my shoulder, rolling me on my side.

I put my hand behind me on top of his wet board shorts.

His cock is hard and warm, straining against the soaked cotton.

He pulls my bikini bottoms down, and his hand moves between my legs from behind me.

My hips push back towards him.

He pulls his own shorts down and moves in to wrap his body around me. His cock is pressed hard up my back. Strong arms cuddle me tight from behind.

I sigh.

Pushing on the skin, about to enter me, the head of his cock seems too big to fit inside me.

Arching my lower spine to get the right angle, I put one hand back to touch his thigh.

He edges deeper and deeper inside me, and at the same time, pulls my hips towards him.

"That feels amazing," I say.

With a soft, slow push, he's as deep inside me as he can get.

"Ahhh, baby," he whispers in my ear.

He moves his body in and out of mine.

Being pregnant makes me more sensitive than usual, and I'm at orgasm plateau quicker than he is.

He pulls his hand back from rubbing me and runs his fingers the length of my back and up to my neck.

I stretch my body under his hands.

He stops and pulls out.

"Want to get on top?"

"Yes."

We've only recently got into doing it in this position. Trevor told me he prefers to be on top, holding me down. But as my bump has grown, we've had to adapt.

I ease my body down, expecting it to hurt, but the pain doesn't follow. I'm relaxed and open.

He takes the strings of my bikini over my head and pulls the top off.

My enlarged breasts ease up and down, as I move my hips backwards and forwards.

His hands spread out over my thighs and his hips push up off the deck into my movements. He reaches up and pulls my shoulders down harder, so he's deeper inside me.

"Oh baby, there are no words for how good that feels," I whisper.

An intense wave of pleasure floods my body.

"You talk too much."

Sinking forward, our tongues move together, while he pumps my body full of his come.

Finally, I collapse over him.

He shifts position, so we are face to face on our sides.

"You said that when you fucked me on the day we met."

"And I love you today as much as I loved you then."

"You called me an old slag after."

"I can't help being romantic."

"We are perfect for each other," I whisper.

"I know."

Naked in each other's arms, we drift along with the boat into the best dreams either of us has ever had.

We are in heaven, our hearts beating together with our baby.

* * *

Back up on deck, the stars materialise above us in the darkening night sky.

My long, cream, Grecian-style gown skims the light wood, and my hair falls loose over my shoulders.

Trevor's white shirt stretches across his chest; white chinos hang off his broad hips.

We clink glasses.

"Here's to us and our future together," he says.

His eyes are so light; they never go dark, not even in the darkest night.

"Do you still think we're having a boy?" I ask.

"Yes, what do you think?"

"I'm not sure."

"Have you thought of names?" he asks.

"No, have you?"

"Yes, I like unusual names."

"Like what?"

"Thor or Maximus."

"Thor as in the superhero?" I laugh.

"Yes. Do you prefer more traditional names?"

"Yes I do, but I like those names too."

The head of the crew approaches us. "Mr and Mrs Porter, dinner is ready. I've set up dining at the front today, so you can watch the sunset."

The sky is completely clear, with endless blue in all directions. The sun is a mellow red, round glow, moving down towards the horizon. Every minute passing deepens the blue transforming the day to night. Although there's barely any breeze, the air is fresh.

A white tablecloth covers the wooden table. Two fine dining places are set.

Trevor and I sit beside each other facing the sunset.

He puts his arm over my shoulders.

I'm curious about him loving me the day we met. "Did you really know I was the one for you when we first met in the café?"

"Yes, absolutely. From the second I saw you in person and before. After Conty showed me his holiday photos at the first board meeting he attended, I spotted you, and knew. The push from the Universe to see you couldn't be defied. That intuitive drive has been the single most powerful force I've ever experienced. But it started before that. There were so many signs bombarding me. I lost count of the number of times I came across the name Alexandra, not knowing the significance. I could feel your energy with me long before you came onto my radar. I thought I was imagining the feeling. But the moment you walked into the café, it all made sense."

"Really?"

"Sounds crazy, right?"

"Well, yes, it does."

"I knew you were my twin flame from day one."

"I've never believed in soul mates."

"Twins flames aren't soul mates. We're the same soul in

different bodies. You're the divine feminine and I'm the masculine."

"Now that *is* crazy."

"Crazy, but true, baby. How do you think I knew what you wanted the first time I fucked you in the loo? I know what you need all the time. I can feel it."

"You have a gift for reading people, sure, but I'm not the only one. You read every one with scary accuracy."

"True, to an extent I do, but with you, I experience a deeper knowing."

"I have read a bit about twin flames, but the concept of being the same soul in two bodies is far-fetched."

"You'll find out I'm right. It doesn't matter if you believe in the concept or not. We are the same soul."

I can't accept his outlandish claim. But he's right. What I believe doesn't matter. This is the greatest love I've ever experienced, and he's home.

"Whatever belief system you use to explain the connection between us, I agree, we are meant to be," I say.

"Are you scared?" He asks.

"No. Are you? Why should I be?"

"I don't feel fear like normal people, so I'm not scared, but it doesn't usually work like this."

"Like what?"

"We meet, get married and are in union. There's usually a pattern to twin flames. A separation that leads to a spiritual awakening. This has all been too easy."

"A what?" I laugh. "I have no idea what you're talking about."

"You've never heard of ascension?"

"No, never. And you have a funny definition of easy. We met while I was married and not interested in you, and you're likely going to prison for a sexual offence against me, that you actually committed. There's nothing easy about that. Am I missing something?"

"Those are minor, superficial events in the general scheme. And our baby is a miracle. I'm serious, a twin flame journey is not usually this easy."

A wave of energy skims over my skin. What is that? A feeling of dread comes next. *Our baby;* he's right, instantly I know he's right. All of it was predestined. And I can't lose him now. I'm not buying into this crap.

"You need to forget all this New Age bullshit. We're together and going to stay that way," I say.

* * *

I'm glad to be off the boat and sleeping in an actual bed. I say sleep, but I haven't slept properly for weeks now. My tummy makes finding a comfortable position impossible. I'd forgotten about that aspect of pregnancy.

I get out of bed and walk naked through the double doors onto the wooden terrace.

Sunlight bathes every inch of my skin, and the warmth penetrates my soul.

I've secretly always disliked bright light, and left to my own devices I close all the curtains, but today is different. The soft morning light is healing.

Trevor emerges behind me. "Morning, beautiful."

My body and mind are strong. This level of peace in myself and the emotional connection to another person is a miracle. New Age superstition is not me. All this talk of twin flames and running, chasing and cycles of separation, is utter rubbish with no basis in reality. This is it for us.

We embrace in the sunlight.

Our naked bodies pull together like magnets.

"I love you." The words and sentiment are a poor description of what's between us. Being away together on our honeymoon has intensified my feelings.

"I love you too, and our little family." His hand runs over my bump.

The baby kicks.

Our eyes meet.

I laugh. "The baby agrees."

"I can't wait for him to arrive," Trevor says.

My smile goes from ear to ear.

"Want a massage?" I ask.

"Is that a trick question?"

He walks back in and grabs the baby oil.

"Lie here," I instruct.

He lies face down on the yoga mat.

I love massaging him. I'm able to examine every inch of his body. Everything about him is big. As always, it's impossible to take in how good he looks. The oil covers my hands, and I start on his back. My hands run over the hard muscles under his soft skin. I make gentle circles with my palms, around and around.

"Keep going, baby. You have magic hands."

"I could run my hands over your body all day."

No hurry to do anything or be anywhere.

The contours of his shoulders are broad and square under my hands. My fingers snake up his neck and through the bottom of his thick hair.

He flexes his neck.

I work my way down over his back and the contours of his ass. It's obscene how perfect he is, for me, anyway. Not all women like men this size, but to me, he's everything I've ever admired in a man.

My fingers slide down to his ankles.

He turns over.

I start at his ankles and make my way back up his body.

The sun shines down. The heat grows as time ticks on.

He puts his hands up and on my thighs.

Heaven is a place.

He pulls me by my thighs closer to him, lifting one leg up so I straddle him.

I smile down at him, knowing what he has in mind. Generous as a lover doesn't quite cover sex with him.

He reaches over to another towel and rolls it up to place it under his neck.

My eyes stay fixed on his.

He pulls me lower until I'm kneeling over his face.

Gently, he flicks his tongue on me.

I open my mouth and take a deep breath, letting the air out slowly.

He pulls me down a little further. His tongue traces around the entrance to my body.

My hips move towards him so that his tongue moves over me.

He doesn't let me guide him and holds me still.

His tongue makes slow, soft licks up and down.

"Oh baby, you have no idea how good that feels."

He stops and blows a little.

The sun warms my skin. My eyes close against the golden rays of light.

He starts again with soft licking all around.

I strain to move my hips with his mouth.

He makes me slow down and enjoy the moment.

Stopping, he rests his tongue on my body and flexes it again and again.

My breath stops for a few seconds.

He moves back and blows on me again.

I'm suspended in intense pleasure, a never-ending orgasm.

He starts with his tongue again, and his long fingers massage my ass and lower back.

The tension in my spine releases, inducing intense relief.

My tummy half covers his face so I can't quite see him.

The wind moves through my hair.

Every sense is heightened and every nerve ending is fired up to a plateau at peak pleasure.

He's edging me, but not as part of a sex game. He's doing it for pleasure's sake and there's no power at play.

I'm lost in endless wet, soft, waves of pleasure.

"I love you, I love you, I love you," I say.

"I love you too, baby. Turn around."

He pulls my legs back until I'm lowered over his face and his breath touches my skin.

I move forward and put my mouth on the head of his cock, sucking lightly.

His hips move up and down slowly so he's moving in and out of my mouth.

Time is lost and the world slips away.

* * *

A soft knock at the door wakes us from unconsciousness.

We've spent the morning asleep, naked in each other's arms. I don't want to move. We haven't had sex, just him licking me and me sucking him. And I need him to make love to me now.

His body is hard against my leg.

"Mr Porter, the car is here to take you to lunch?" Mr Jones calls through the door.

"Trevor, Trevor, wake up. The car's here. Are we meant to be going out for lunch?"

He stirs and lifts his head. "What's the time?"

"Sir, the table is booked for two p.m. You didn't want lunch here today? Is there some mistake?"

"No, there's no mistake. I booked a table at Le Club 55, sorry I forgot. Yes, we're coming," he replies.

We're both so content we don't move.

He buries his head in my hair. "We don't have to, baby, we can stay here all afternoon, making love."

I think for a second. “Let’s have lunch first, and go for a swim. Doesn’t that restaurant have a private beach?”

“Yes, let’s go.”

Trevor pulls on white boxer shorts and beige chinos. I love him in pink and he puts on a soft linen baby pink shirt.

I slip a tight white dress over my ever-increasing bump, and some white gladiator sandals. My long blonde hair is tussled by his fingers.

Five minutes and we’re out the door.

“After you, Mrs Porter.” Trevor puts his hand on the small of my back and guides me out the door.

CHAPTER FORTY

The car stops at the entrance to the beach restaurant.

Trevor gets out first, and holds the door open for me.

I slide over the black leather seats and out of the cool, air-conditioned car.

The mid-afternoon sun is scorching.

He takes my hand and helps me up.

We stand under the straw veranda. The restaurant is on the beach, penned in by makeshift low straw walls. A bar stands in the middle of the tables. People come here to be seen.

The first lot of diners have exited the restaurant. A later set are settling in for the duration. It's not packed, but busy.

Trevor surprises me by talking to the maître de in fluent French.

He turns to me. "Would you like to sit at the bar and have a drink first?"

"Yes, good idea."

We look out over the beach to the sea.

A number of touring yachts are moored, and rigs ferry passengers to the beach and restaurant.

"Two Kir Royales and a sparkling water, please," Trevor says to the barman.

The last time we had Kir Royale was New Year's Eve at

Trevor's flat. Morty cooked us supper, and Trevor introduced me to edging in the hot tub... My body aches for him to fuck me.

"Maybe we should skip lunch and go back to the villa," I say, looking at Trevor suggestively.

He smiles. "Baby, I never thought I'd meet my match, but you are it."

I freeze. My eyes fix over Trevor's shoulder.

"We should go now," I say.

"What is it?" Trevor follows my eye-line."Oh, that ponce. I'm not leaving because of him. The French Riviera is big enough for both of us."

Conty and Marina are holding hands and in heaven themselves. I've never seen him so happy and relaxed. I zone in on their fingers, locked together. In twenty years of marriage, he never once held my hand.

They haven't seen us and are shown to a large table on the other side of the restaurant.

I glance back at Trevor in alarm. "I want to go."

"I'm not leaving because of him, baby. Ignore them."

I try not to look, but struggle to stop seeing them in my peripheral vision. Marina smooths his auburn hair over his ears. They can't see anyone but each other. I can't bear to see them so happy. What is wrong with me? Why should I care?

I try again. "I need you to fuck me, baby. We can do this tomorrow."

"We can go back after lunch. He's not driving me out of a restaurant. He's nothing to us."

My stomach is in my mouth. I stroke my bump. If I'm stressed, the baby is stressed; I need to stay clam. After the bleed, I'm terrified of doing anything that might jeopardise the pregnancy.

Their table is filling up with people. James Woodly and his wife, Edmund and Henrietta, Charles and Lucinda…

Trevor is talking to a waiter and ordering food.

"Follow me." The waiter indicates we should follow him to our table.

My legs are weak.

Trevor ushers me in front of him to follow the waiter.

I try to maintain tunnel vision.

We are led towards Conty and Marina's table.

They are going to see us.

Anonymity isn't possible in a restaurant this size. Especially in this scene, where people specialise in checking out who is who and who is with who.

I make my feet move. Trevor has his hand on the small of my back.

As we make our way across the restaurant, Conty and I lock

eyes.

He whispers something to the table.

Everyone turns around to stare at us.

I turn back to Trevor, hoping he's willing to leave now.

Trevor waves over to him like they are old friends.

Conty's eyes widen as he clocks I'm pregnant.

Marina puts her hand up to his cheek as if he's been mortally wounded.

As if he cares. He'll use the baby as another thing to justify the abuse he peddled year after year, and why he was forced to end our marriage.

James shakes his head.

Lucinda looks shocked too, but I suspect for different reasons. I should have told her. She's one of my close friends.

They will all know we are married by now, as the children will have told them, but my being pregnant is completely out of the blue.

Hayes ducks under the door frame and walks straight at us.

My heart comes up to my throat, and I can't breathe.

Annabel is in front of him. Her eyes rest on my pregnant tummy.

I think I'm going to drop to the floor.

Annabel turns and says something to Hayes.

Hayes's eyes widen; he pushes past his wife and marches

over to us, Annabel follows.

"Alexandra, you didn't tell me you were pregnant," Hayes says to me.

It could be an innocent comment, but it's too late. The way he said it leaves no doubt…

I'm wide-eyed and silent.

"And what the fuck is it to you?" Trevor cuts in.

"This is your new husband, I take it?" Hayes says.

James Woodly rushes over. "Now, gents, the show is over." He tries to steer Hayes towards their table.

Conty and Marina don't move, their faces fixed.

Edmund is twinkly as ever, watching events unfold.

"You bastard," screams Annabel, catching up with the significance of what Hayes has said. She goes to hit him.

Hayes moves back out of the way, and her hand grazes Hayes's face.

"That's your fucking baby, isn't it?" Annabel screams.

Marina springs into action and runs over to embrace Annabel, who is clutching her chest like she's been shot.

A crack rings out as Hayes's fist connects with Trevor's face.

James tries to get between them, but he only reaches their shoulders and isn't strong enough to pull them apart.

Trevor lands a punch that connects with Hayes's face.

Hayes steps back.

Thank goodness.

"I can't take this again. No, not again, please no," Annabel wails, like an animal caught in a trap.

Seconds later, Hayes runs at Trevor in a rugby tackle.

They fall through the makeshift fence around the restaurant.

A loud thud comes off the sand.

James isn't deterred and heads after them.

People scramble out of the way. A couple of onlookers angle their phones at the fight.

Annabel has sunk to her knees and is screaming, "No, no, no. It can't be true. Please tell me her baby isn't yours."

Marina gets on her knees too, comforting her.

"Fight, fight," shouts Edmund, delighted.

Conty glares at me.

I freeze for a second, unsure whether to try and stop them from fighting. My hand runs over my bump.

Henrietta appears at my side and leads me over to the restaurant entrance.

"Come on, darling, let's have a sip of Champagne while they work it out."

"But—"

"It'll all come out in the wash, as they say. Don't sweat the small stuff. A baby is always a blessing. You're glowing and healthy. Quite honestly, most of London society has no idea whose baby is whose, not that anyone would admit it. Best not to open Pandora's Box. Must be why we all look the same." She hoots with laughter.

"I think I'm going to faint."

"You're going to be fine, darling. And so is the baby."

Through the poleaxed fence, a flurry of fists emerges from the beach.

James can't get his footing on the sand and struggles to separate them.

Trevor and Hayes throw punches at each other.

A few men on the beach come to James's aid. Two grab Trevor and pull him back.

James shouts at Trevor, "Go to your wife. She needs you."

Evidently, James is unconcerned that Annabel is still screaming on the floor and might need Hayes.

Hayes stays on the floor.

"I can't go through this again. I can't. I just can't do it," Annabel continues to wail.

"Anybody would think someone was murdering her," says Henrietta rolling her eyes.

"Alex needs you," James shouts at Trevor again.

His strategy works.

Trevor storms through the restaurant, blood pouring out of his nose and all over his shirt. His eye is already swollen.

Henrietta stares at him with undisguised lust.

"Oh my. You like them big and good-looking, don't you, darling. Lucky you."

The anger on Trevor's face is total.

My eyes widen in fear.

Trevor grabs my arm and drags me out of the restaurant.

"Good luck, love," Henrietta says, lifting her glass and sipping her champagne.

CHAPTER FORTY-ONE

Blood and sand are splattered in streaks down his pink shirt. His eye is swollen and closing after fighting with Hayes in the restaurant and on the beach. He paces up and down the length of the villa's sitting room. Blood drips out of his nose, and he wipes it away, smearing red across his face and into his hair.

The staff made themselves scarce the minute we walked through the door.

My hand goes under my heavily pregnant stomach. After the scare, the hospital said I need to keep calm. A version of the truth has to be my best strategy.

"Who the fuck is that cunt?"

"We had a thing last year, but it's over."

"You were fucking him at the same time you were fucking me?"

I start walking up and down with him.

"No. Not exactly—"

"Not exactly? What does that mean?" He glares at me.

Panicking isn't going to help, but regulating my breathing is hard.

"I was still married to Conty, and..."

"And, what?"

"I wasn't thinking straight."

"More like you weren't thinking at all. You were fucking anything that moved. And he was one of them?"

"No, that's not true."

"Isn't it? Then why did I have to plead guilty to protect you from the press investigating what happened between us."

"I'm sorry."

"Do you even care I'm going to do time?"

Pointing out that if he hadn't pretended to revenge porn me in the first place he wouldn't have been charged isn't an option. The situation is escalating. And he's getting angrier. I need to find a way to calm him down.

"Of course, I care. Baby, I need you. Our baby needs you."

"The only thing you need is cock. I'm not going to ask you again, who the fuck is he?"

"Don't say that. I have changed. You know I have. Since we—"

"Answer the fucking question – who is he?"

"We met on a family holiday. He's the husband of one of Conty's old school friends. We were on a skiing trip, he saved my life on the slopes and we, I… It doesn't matter. Hayes means —"

"Hayes? Is that his name?" He stops pacing and walks towards me.

"Yes, but there's nothing between us."

"The first time I fucked you, in that loo, you said his name, didn't you?"

I say nothing.

The fury on his face is arresting.

I back away.

He grabs both my arms.

"Answer me. You called his name as I was fucking you in the loo, didn't you?"

Hayes is hardly a common name. How can he remember me saying that? I was thinking of Hayes the first time we had sex in that abandoned loo, and at that point I was crazy in love with him. I'd only met Trevor an hour before, how could I have known?

"No," I say. There's no way I'm admitting to that. "No, I didn't."

"Don't lie to me," he says. "I know when you're lying."

It's like he can read my mind. Tears well in my eyes.

"What, so now you're going to get all emotional? Now you've been caught out."

"No, I just want this to stop."

"Is this his baby?"

"No. I don't... It's... Well... Trevor, nothing has changed. I'm your wife now, and this is our baby."

"Don't you ever answer questions? Is this his baby? Yes or no. It's a simple question."

He grips my arms harder.

Tears start falling and I can't talk.

"Let me help you with that; he thinks it is. And judging by the way his wife was screaming on the floor, she does too. Did you hear what she said?"

"No, I—"

How could he have heard what Annabel was saying, when he was fighting with Hayes?

"Of course, you didn't, you never listen to any fucking-thing, and you were probably trying to work out how you could lie your way out of it."

"I wasn't, honestly—"

"She said, 'I can't take this again. No, not again, please no.'"

I keep crying. Please don't let him leave me.

"He's done this before," he shouts in my face.

"No, Annabel was being melodramatic," I manage to get out of my mouth.

"Seriously? You fuck her husband, and she thinks he's got you pregnant, yet you think she's overreacting by crying?"

"She's a real bitch—"

"Are you kidding me? What the fuck, Alex? Now you're calling her a bitch?"

"No, that's not what I meant."

"What did you mean? It was pretty clear to me."

"She's got it wrong."

"So now you're defending him? Thought he was nothing to you?"

I've got to find a way to placate him. Everything coming out of my mouth is making it worse and worse.

"No, I'm not. Please, Trevor, nothing has changed. We've only been married a few months. This is our honeymoon."

"What, so we're back to poor you? Going to run off and fuck the next man who looks at you because you're distressed, are you?"

"Stop shouting. No, of course not. That's unfair. You know how toxic life was with Conty. And I'm not defending Hayes. You are my husband now. He's nothing to me."

"Is this his baby?"

He lets go and moves back from me.

I rub my arms where he's held me and back away. How can I answer that? *Think*. What can I say?

"Alex?"

He walks towards me again.

I back away. We've never had a screaming row. In this state, he's unknown. Keep calm. He won't hit me. But I don't know that for sure. I've never seen him this angry. What does he need to hear? I could just say the baby is his. That won't work; he's not going to believe me.

"Are you even listening to me? Is this his baby? Answer me."

I wring my hands like I can get rid of the situation by squeezing the emotion out.

"I don't know." The truth is out.

"How can you not know? How?"

He grabs my arms again.

My phone beeps in my handbag.

Shit, he's heard it. I should have left my old phone hidden at home. Why did I take it with me?

"No, Trevor, no. Leave it."

He ignores me and grabs my handbag off the floor, pulling out both my phones.

"You kept it as a burner phone? That says it all."

"No. Well, yes, I kept it. I. I still needed stuff off it. I was wiping everything."

I close my eyes.

"Open your phone."

"No, it's nothing."

"If you've got nothing to hide, open it."

He's so tall I can't see who has sent me a message. It might not be Hayes. He's never bothered messaging much before. Surely he's dealing with Annabel and the fall-out of the revelation I'm pregnant.

"This is a bad route to go down."

He laughs. "What? You don't think we've already gone down a bad route?"

"There's no going back from not trusting each other and invasions of privacy."

"You think? Open the fucking phone. Now."

I'm going to have to do it. Please don't let it be Hayes. "The code is 1111. Remember, you said that to me, not long after we met, 'We're 111 you and me'. I had to look it up."

"Do you really think I can ever forget that?" His face softens for a second.

"Baby, it's only ever been you. The rest have been white noise," I say.

He puts the code in to open my old phone and turns around.

I stare at his back and hold my breath for a second. Time stretches out unnaturally, and I can't tell how long we are suspended in this state of tension.

He turns to me, his face frozen in fury.

Terror grips me and I shrink back. Oh fuck. This is going to be bad.

"You went to spend the night with him before the school picnic."

Shit, I didn't delete any of those messages. "No. Yes. I wasn't going to go through with it. I was getting closure."

"You planned to get closure by spending the night with him?"

"Not exactly, but—"

"You would have slept with him?"

"No, I wouldn't have done it."

"That's not true. You only didn't because he cancelled," he screams in my face.

I want to get on the floor and put my hands over my head. The tears fall harder, and I can't stop them to think properly and find a way out of this nightmare.

"You and I spent the night in that hotel," I say through the tears. It's the best I can come up with.

"You know if he'd been there, I'd have caught you in bed together."

I put my head in my hands for a few seconds.

"Do you want to know what he's just messaged you?"

"No, no. I don't care. He's nothing to me."

"You know I love you, Alex. Why didn't you tell me you were pregnant the last time we met? You know I'll look after you and our baby."

Trevor lowers the phone and walks towards me. He struggles to gain control. His heavy breathing forces blood from his nose to drip on the floor.

I shrink further back.

He stops a foot away from me. “You’ve been fucking him all along, haven’t you?”

“No, not since we got together on New Year’s Eve.”

“You fucking liar,” he shouts in my face.

I flinch and put my hands under my bump. This can’t be good for the baby.

He throws my old phone across the room, smashing it on the stone wall.

I brace, eyes wide.

“You don’t know what the truth is do you?” he shouts, close to my face.

“I’m sorry. Trevor, please, you’re scaring me. I need you. Cuddle me and make love to me. I can’t take this,” I plead in panic.

“Make love to you?”

He practically lifts me off my feet and marches me towards the loo.

We’ve done a lot of fucking in loos. Perhaps this is going to be all right, after all. I should have told him before we got married. Gerry was right. He would have understood if I’d told him earlier. Why am I so stupid?

The door smashes back on the wall as we go through it.

He pins me against the wall by my neck and puts his hand up

my dress. Two of his fingers push up hard inside me.

"Ow," I say, but the pain isn't physical. He's not hurting my body. Intense relief he's touching me follows. Thank goodness, he's going to fuck me, and we can put this behind us.

He undoes his trousers and pulls them to his knees.

I put my hands up to cuddle him and wipe the drip of blood coming out of his nose.

"Get your fucking hands off me." His light blue eyes look lighter and bloodshot.

I can't bear the pain on his beautiful face. "None of this matters. I want you and only you."

Standing on tiptoes, I try to kiss him.

He won't bend down, so I can't reach his mouth.

"All I want is you, baby," I continue, encouraging him to keep going.

He pushes me to my knees. "All you want is my cock?"

"No, I love you. What we have is real. You're right. We are twin flames; the same soul in two bodies. I can see that now."

He grips my hair and rams his cock into my mouth.

"It was real to me, but never to you. And now you decide you want to believe in twin flames. I've been deluded. My cock is all you've ever been interested in, isn't it? You have no idea and don't even care who I am as a person. As long as I'm giving you sex."

I'm not ready for his cock to go so far down my throat, and I gag.

He doesn't let me reply, holding my mouth down on the base of his cock.

Bile spills out of my mouth and makes yellow spots down the front of my white dress.

I rock back against the wall, trying not to fall with the pregnancy affecting my centre of balance.

"You've only ever wanted sex. Admit it."

He grabs my hair, so I'm pulled back up towards him. His hips move back so he can thrust hard into my mouth again.

I grip his thighs, my vision blurry from the tears.

When he pulls out, I gasp for air. "No, Trevor, please listen."

"Listen to what? You call his name while I fuck you."

"He's nothing to me and never has been."

"Have you been fucking him since we got married?"

"No, I told you, it was when I was married to Conty, and before we were really together."

As long as he fucks me we are going to be okay.

"Don't lie to me. I saw his face when he saw you were pregnant. And he's just texted you. He thinks the baby is his. And you never stopped seeing him."

"You're wrong. It's you I want, only you."

"Do you think I'm stupid?"

"No, of course not—"

"This is all you want, isn't it?" he says, moving back and taking hold of his semi-hard cock, like a weapon.

"No, I love you," I say.

"All you love is cock, and it doesn't matter whose."

He rams his body down my throat again.

Tears flow down my cheeks. I'm reassured by the sexual contact. There might be a chance.

He pulls back out of my mouth again.

"Don't leave me. I need you." My worst fear spills out of my mouth.

He gets on the floor with me.

Blood drips out of his nose, landing on the white rug and stone floor.

"Please cuddle me."

I need to feel him holding me. The thought of never being in his arms again is paralysing.

He can't see out of one eye at all now, and squints down at me. His face flashes with emotion I can't fully read. Anger and pain, but nothing good. I keep scanning his features for reassurance and the start of him softening. But there's nothing.

He pulls his belt out of the loops of his trousers.

Having been on the receiving end of his belt once before,

I start crying harder. This is sick, but I need him to do something, anything to me, just so long as he doesn't leave.

"Don't look so frightened," he says but doesn't mean. "You do realise that kink is about love, right? I can only do that because I love you and want to please you."

"Yes, I do." Thank god he said he loves me: present tense.

The belt gets thrown across the bathroom floor like he was going to use it but has changed his mind. He looks at me with a coldness that freezes every cell in my body.

"I love you. It doesn't make a difference, I'm your wife now," I plead.

He puts his hand in the back of my hair and pulls my neck back hard.

"What doesn't make a difference? That you fucked him behind my back or that this could be his baby?"

"It wasn't behind your back. We weren't… You were—"

"Not that shit again. You've used what I did, again and again, to avoid being emotionally close to me. I'm going to prison for it. You really do think I'm stupid. I've just read about your affair with him in black and white."

"No. I don't. Trevor, I don't think you're stupid. You've got it wrong."

He moves back and turns me around, so I'm on my hands and knees. This is the only position we can fuck in with me this pregnant.

I start breathing hard. He's going to do it.

He puts his hand on the back of my neck.

I start sobbing harder. "Don't hurt me."

"Is that what you think? I'd hurt you? I'm no fucking wife-beater. I took my belt off so it wouldn't dig into you."

"I didn't mean physically," I say, instinctively more frightened by his emotional coldness than anything he might do to me.

He grabs my hair and pushes my head down on the hard floor.

I move my head to the side. There's no physical pain. Only my heart compressing, but he's not leaving. I stretch my hand back so I can touch his leg.

He lifts the dress over my back, so the material stretches over my bump, staying where he's put it. With his other hand, he pulls my knickers down so they stretch across my thighs.

He spits on his hand, then it goes up and down his semi-hard cock.

Relief spreads out in my body. In seconds we are going to be one again. My breathing becomes slower and more even. I'm calming down. He does still care or he wouldn't fuck me.

His cock doesn't get harder, and he stops.

"Fuck me, baby. I need you to do it," I say.

His hesitation makes me think he's weighing up whether he wants to give me that.

"Please, Trevor, please. Fuck me. Do it now."

He leans over me, so his face is next to mine.

The purple and blue swelling surrounding his eye makes me wince. His breath on my face is slow and heavy.

I try to breathe him in, every particle of him, inside me.

"Baby, I'm all about love. And you, you're not capable."

"I'm sorry. I'm so sorry," I say.

"Sex is all you want, isn't it? And it doesn't matter who it's from. Why can't you admit that?"

He's calming down and back in control.

"No. I love you. Please don't leave me."

"You keep saying you're sorry and that you love me. But you're only sorry because you got caught, and you don't know what love is. You never have," he says.

This isn't about sexual pleasure, but I need him to fuck me, so I know everything is going to be all right.

He lets go and stands up.

The lack of his body inside me is devastating.

I stay on my hands and knees, knickers down, dress halfway up my back. I twist my head to look back and up at him.

"Trevor, we are twin flames. I can see that now." I catch my breath. "Please, baby. It doesn't need to be like this."

Now he looks like he's going to cry, and it's worse than his anger. His anger I deserve and can deal with, but his pain – I can't bear hurting him.

"I was stupid to think you'd change for me. Whatever the fuck you think is love, it isn't."

"You've shown me. I've changed," I say. Tears make him blurry in front of me. "You can't leave me like this."

"Watch me." He pulls his trousers up. "Now you can have all the cock you want. But it won't be mine. Welcome to a new kind of hell. Now get out."

He walks off, leaving me lying on the bathroom floor.

The door swings open behind him.

A scream comes out I'm not expecting and can't stop. The force makes me put my hands over my ears.

Silence follows.

I stay on my hands and knees.

The front door slams.

I've got to stop him going.

I jump up and run to catch him.

Mr Jones, the house manager, stretches out his arms before I reach the kitchen.

Despite my speed, I manage to stop before running into him.

"Please, Mrs Porter. I'm sorry, but Mr Porter has instructed me to escort you off the premises. We can help you pack your things. The car can take you wherever you need to go."

The tears fall harder, and I can't stop them. "I want to go home."

"I will organise the jet to take you back to London immediately, and the car can take you to the airport," he says, ignoring the fact that my knickers are now around my ankles. "I will make you a cup of tea, and Amanda can pack your things."

"No. That's not what I meant."

"I'm sorry, Mrs Porter, I must have misunderstood."

There's no point explaining. Trevor is home, not our flat in London or anywhere. Home isn't a physical place. I don't want to be anywhere without him. Finally, I pull my knickers up and my dress over the squirming baby in my body, flooded with stress hormones, and turn around. But I can't work out where to run; the bedroom, where our bed is still warm from where we lay sleeping naked in each other arms all morning? The patio, where I'd given him a massage and... Everywhere, is him. And us. And I can't escape.

I over-breathe for a few seconds, unable to comprehend the blinding pain.

All I can see is the door. I head out.

CHAPTER FORTY-TWO

How did I get here?

Lush greenery either side of me is dull. The ground below is blurry. Dust clouds, mist around the bottom of my feet, as I'm not picking them up enough. And the sun's relentless rays burn like I'm going to disintegrate into dust on the road myself.

My hand hurts.

I look down.

My fingers are fixed in a claw grip around my mobile phone. I will my brain to let go so I can use it.

It drops to the floor.

I'm slow to stop walking, so it takes a few attempts to pick it up. Dirt is forced under my nails.

The mechanical action of each step helps calm me enough to press the buttons.

He doesn't answer.

I must have repeated this action sixty times.

A car pulls up beside me.

Through the tears, I look back. "Trevor?"

The driver jumps out. "Mrs Porter, please let me take you somewhere."

Without a word, I walk back to the car. No idea where I am.

Trevor's smell clings to the seats and want to scream again. We sat here barely an hour ago to go to the restaurant for lunch, yet the world has shifted into pain.

Tapping on his mobile phone, the driver looks back over his shoulder at me.

"Take me to the airport," I say.

* * *

Tears stream down my face. The sobbing has taken on a life of its own, and is beyond my control. The trauma is acute. My memory has blurred and skewed since the moment I ran out of the house in the South of France. Flashes of the scene in the villa stay with me. Trevor holding me against the wall with his fingers inside me. Hurt emanating from him as he lashed out. My not being able to explain, not because he wouldn't listen. The fact he wouldn't listen is irrelevant. But because there is no explanation for what I've done. He's never judged me for anything and has always provided a safe emotional space for sharing any and every shameful thought. There was no reason to lie to him, but many reasons for withholding the truth.

The pain is overwhelming.

"Would you like anything?" the air steward asks.

I say what I think is no, and bury my face in a bundle of

tissues. My eyes hurt from so many tears, and my face stings from the acid in them.

"How about a cup of camomile tea?"

"Thank you."

I've lost all sense of self-consciousness. How could I have been so stupid? I should have told him earlier I wasn't sure who the father was. The memory of the coldness on his face jars me over again. I've never seen him like that. He hates me. His face turned to pure hatred, and I can't bear the thought of him feeling like that about me.

My heart is in spasm, stomach in a never-ending free fall.

Reality is a haze of disbelief, none of this can be true.

The baby moves in my body. I must keep calm.

Thank god for Gerry organising a flight so quickly.

* * *

Gerry is waiting in the arrivals hall. Kitty, Trevor's secretary, stands with her. The grave expression on their faces sets me off again.

"I'm afraid Trev – Mr Porter – has asked me to escort you to the flat to remove your immediate belongings. I'll organise for the rest of your stuff to be sent on." Kitty is sympathetic but firm.

Gerry is grim-faced.

"No, I'm not leaving." I collapse in Gerry's arms.

"Is this really necessary?" Gerry asks Kitty.

"Mr Porter was clear. I'm to escort Mrs Porter to the flat to collect her immediate belongings and take the key. Her things from St Tropez will be shipped to your address."

Gerry sighs. "Let him calm down, Alex. Come and stay with us."

"I can't go to your house."

"Let us look after you for a bit."

"No, there are too many memories of him at yours."

The tears are so forceful the words struggle to get out of my mouth. Never could I have imagined such pain.

"We'll discuss what to do later. Let's go to the flat first and pick up your stuff."

Gerry and Kitty help me to a waiting car like I'm an invalid.

We stop and start along the M25 in the middle of the evening rush hour.

Each second is painful and stretches out unnaturally.

Silence magnifies my sobs.

* * *

"Don't do this to yourself. What's the point in going up to the flat? I will find what you need."

"You're too upset, Alex," Kitty adds. "We can get what you

need."

I press Trevor's number again.

It rings and rings.

Voicemail kicks in.

Hearing his voice is searing.

We pull up outside our building. Gerry gives me her jumper. "Put this on. It's cold today."

Nothing is registering, but I take her jumper.

The glass building looms over us.

I remember how Trevor picked me up and threw me over his shoulder the night I came for a nightcap after the club. We'd only met a week before. He claimed he didn't want me to step on his bare feet in my skyscraper-heeled boots. So he grabbed me and wouldn't put me down until we got to the sofa.

I press Trevor's number again.

Voicemail kicks in.

Another crying garbled message isn't going to help.

Out of the car, we walk to the lift.

The countless times we've stood in this spot together, my hand in his, my body in anticipation of being alone with him.

The lift pings and the door opens.

Kitty presses the unmarked button that takes the lift up to the penthouse.

We start going up.

I look down.

The memory of Trevor on his knees, tongue working on my body, my hands in his hair.

Tears start falling off my cheeks again.

How could I have jeopardised everything we have for a passing fancy for Hayes?

I press his number.

The ringing starts.

"Stop calling him, Alex. He's not going to answer," Gerry says.

The door to the lift opens.

The day I moved in flashes across my mind. Trevor held me up against the wide-open front door. He had his fingers inside me and said, "Welcome home, baby". I thought he meant to the flat, but it was him. He was home.

"He can't leave me."

"I'm sorry you're having to go through this, Alex," Kitty says.

"You've done this before?" Gerry asks Kitty.

She doesn't answer.

I open the door.

The memory of him on New Year's Eve greets me.

He had a towel around his waist, hot and sweaty from the gym, ready for a shower. His damp hair sticking up in thick spikes. I wanted to get on my knees the second I saw him.

Immediately I see the photograph Trevor told me about. He

must have had it put up as a surprise for when we got back.

I stand below the huge, frameless, blown-up print hanging over the fireplace. The bright colours depict the day before we got married, after I'd fainted on the red carpet on the way into the ball. Trevor is walking with me in his arms under the arch of red roses. He's in black tie, and his blue eyes are lit by camera flashes going off around us. I'm in the strapless dress that became my wedding dress. The necklace and earrings he gave me sparkle like they are powered by electricity. My arms hang down, and my hair falls past his waist, the silky gold waves contrasting with the black of his suit and the deep red of the dress.

He's carrying me to an ambulance that isn't in the picture. Lights are flashing around us, causing a rainbow halo. The colours must have been enhanced by an editor. An army of photographers are scattering as Trevor walks forward, some taking photos of us. The movement within the photo hits you.

Trevor was right. I love it.

Somehow it looks staged, like it's been shot as part of an advertising campaign. For what, I don't know.

"This is masochistic, Alex. Pack what you need so we can leave."

"I can't leave, Gerry, not ever. Don't you understand?"

"You've got to pull yourself together. This is enough already.

Let me take you home. You've got to give him time."

Kitty follows Gerry over to the kitchen. "I can help you pack your things," she says.

Ignoring her, I walk into the nursery.

The Moses basket has been unpacked, but everything else is in boxes. The walls are white, and a half-painted jungle scene runs in a line around the middle. I can almost see us having sex on the floor. Then lying there, his hand on my stomach, telling the baby he's going to love sleeping in the jungle. Will he come home to this room and have the same memories to deal with, or will a team of people come in before he gets back, to clear the flat of any reminders of me and the life we were starting together?

Calling him is like a survival reflex.

His phone rings once and then stops.

He must have pressed reject call.

Kitty appears at the door. "Alex, let me help."

"You can't help."

I head over to Gerry, who is typing on her mobile phone. "The taxi will be here soon. So pack what you need now."

I bend over, cradling my bump with one hand, the other hand gripping the kitchen surface. The pain is physical. My chest is full of pressure. Can you die from emotional distress?

The baby reassures me by moving under my hand.

I press his number again.

This time it doesn't ring.

Gerry puts her arms over my shoulders. "He'll calm down."

"You didn't see the way he looked at me."

His contemptuous stare was devoid of love or even lust. He hated me.

"The situation is rough, but let's take what you need and go home. We can work out what to do later, just focus on one minute at a time."

I head to our bedroom, and over to his chest of drawers. I start going through his t-shirts, looking for the blue camo one. He was wearing it the first time we met in the caff. There's something hard at the bottom of the drawer. I pull out a phone. Did he keep a spare phone? And there's a roll of shiny brown packing tape. I scramble around further and find a Stanley knife; it's got blood on it.

"Alex, we need to go, the car is here," Gerry calls.

No, it can't be. I'm not thinking straight. The box of slaughtered animals was taped up with packing tape. No, there must be some other explanation.

"Now, Alex, the car is here. We have to go." Gerry sounds angry.

I'm running out of time. It must be in the washing basket, I can't leave without that t-shirt. Finally, I see it crumpled at the bottom. "Thank god," I say and clutch it to my face.

"Alex, enough," Gerry calls, poking her head around the door.

"Can I have a pen and paper?" I ask.

Kitty comes back with a notepad and a pen.

111 One and Always. That is all I write.

"Now, let's go." Gerry walks over to the entrance door. "Where's the rest of your stuff?"

"There is no stuff," I say.

"We've come up here, and all you want is a t-shirt?"

"Yes," I say.

"I'm afraid you can't take his t-shirt, Alex. And you have to leave your keys. Trevor has asked me to take your wedding ring too," Kitty says.

I put the note on the kitchen table with my keys.

"You know, I never picked him as a coward." Gerry shakes her head. "Getting you to do his hard emotional labour."

Kitty ignores her. "I'm sorry, Alex, but you have to give me the t-shirt and the ring."

"Tell him he'll have to kill me first. I'm not taking my wedding ring off, ever."

"He's not going to miss a t-shirt," Gerry adds.

Kitty is confused for a second like nobody has ever defied Trevor through her. She has one last try. "Can you give them to me now?"

“I will send them on, Kitty. What’s good for the goose and all that,” Gerry says.

For a second I think Kitty is going to object more forcefully.

Gerry’s face hardens. “As I said, I’ll send it.”

Seeing the empty flat as I walk out is more than I can bear.

The baby kicks again, and I run my hand over my bump.

My body is rapidly releasing natural opioids and I’m going numb. Surviving every moment is an act of faith.

The door clicks behind me.

We wait for the lift in silence.

All I can see in my reflection, distorted by the cold metal lift doors, is his face. And all I can feel is the blue of his eyes. He can’t leave me lost without him, without me. This can’t be how it ends. He’s right. This is a new kind of hell. And the worst thing is, he’s lost in it too. We’re both lost in Blue.

TRUE BLUE

Will Alexandra have her happy ending?

Coming January 2024

ACKNOWLEDGEMENTS

I am thankful for and grateful to the following; my loud and lively (that's an understatement) family, who supported this project in so many ways, both directly and indirectly; all my wonderful friends both in the UK and NZ; Coffee Club with Fun Nights Out for endless fun (usually sexual) banter and not expelling me from the group when I always go too far; Sophie F. (Wifey and Love Bomb), Becs S. (Hubby and Guru) and Amanda D. (the voice of reason and hair to envy) for literally keeping me sane; LB for continuing to unknowingly be my muse (I still know you'd be unwilling too, but you'll never read it so I'll keep getting away with it hahaha); the well-read and astute Alison N who generously offered time and analysis on early drafts, Nigel F, who continues to (frequently) works miracles with all things information technology related, and finally, the exceptionally talented Sue C., who provided technical writing expertise and comprehensive analysis - a dream to work with. Many offered unconditional support. All offered endless enthusiasm and valuable advice. Thank you.

ABOUT THE AUTHOR

Parker Arding

Parker Arding has a PhD in Psychology and a background in policy related academia. Parker grew up in inner city London but now lives between rural England and New Zealand.

Printed in Great Britain
by Amazon

40239474R00274